ALANA BITES BACK

(Book 3)

A Novel By

K. ELLE COLLIER

Thank You For Your Purchase

Great reviews mean everything to a writer. If you enjoyed this eBook in any way, please take a moment and go to Amazon and let me, and other readers, know what you thought. Once again, thank you and enjoy!

Alana Bites Back

© 2013 by K. Elle Collier

Createspace Edition

ISBN: 978-0-9816495-5-9

Cover Design by Tamara Ramsay

More books by K. Elle Collier

My Man's Best Friend (Book 1)

Kai's Aftermath (Book 2)

Intimate Stranger

Are you ready to write your own novel? Pick up...

From Concept to Kindle:

A Step-by-Step to Writing, Publishing and Marketing your Novel on the Amazon Kindle

For more tips and a bunch of great stuff visit:

www.modernwritingworks.com

http://www.kellecollier.com/

Follow me on Twitter @K_ElleCollier

Like Me On Facebook - Author K. Elle Collier

"Writing is a dance with words, you start off slow and build to a beautiful rhythmic flow".

~K. Elle

Contents

"Never confuse a single defeat with a final defeat"

~F. Scott Fitzgerald

Two Years Later...

ONE
ALANA

It had been one year, nine months and three days since I last saw Todd. One thing I knew for sure, it wouldn't be the last.

"Alana Brooks, please step to the counter and claim your belongings." The thirty-something woman announcing my name in a flat, unmotivated tone was dressed in a gray two-toned polyester uniform.

I took one last look at Evelyn Jackson, the heavyset security guard with an overgrown mustache, dyed blond hair, black roots and two tarnished gold-plated front teeth. She was a sight to see, something no one should be mandated to look at for two years straight. Prison was bad enough as it was.

Today was my release day from jail and I couldn't be more pleased. From the day I arrived until this very moment, I was known as inmate 15915-731 at the federal prison camp near Gurney, Illinois. My main home was A camp, a low security facility for women deemed non-violent and sentenced to under five years. I was given a three-year sentence, did my time in under two. I have never been one to play by the rules, never have never will.

I do have to say, Todd really knew how to throw a sister off her game by locking her up. I mean, so what if I broke into Kai's house, waited for them to return home to demand that Todd stop this nonsense and come back to Chicago with me? I AM the woman for him, not Kai and it was frustrating as hell that he didn't see that, but he will. One thing I was taught growing up, was that tenacity always wins in the end...always. I hope Kai was happy spending time with my man because Alana Brooks is back, a free woman and on a mission to claim what was rightfully hers for good this time.

Evelyn Jackson—or as I liked to call her, Evillene, the wicked witch of the north—darted her eyes at me as she stopped to scratch through her two layers of god-awful weave. Evillene wasn't a fan of the nickname I so elegantly bestowed on her the first day I arrived at Camp Gurney. Just the sight of her charging toward me on damn near all fours, breathing like an untamed raging bull, nostrils flared to the size of golf balls and sweat beads running amok along anything not covered in polyester. All I could think of at the moment was that song from *The Wiz*, "Don't Nobody Bring Me No Bad News." I tried to explain to Evillene that her name was a sign of endearment, but I was afraid she didn't see it like I did. It probably didn't help that I snickered under my breath every time I used it.

Evillene reached down and pulled out a large bag that held all of my personal items that I had arrived with when I first checked into prison. I stood patiently, biting my tongue as she chopped, minced and dissected each and every designer name associated with my belongings. English 101 was clearly not required to land this job.

"One Carter watch," she said

"That's Cartier," I corrected

Evillene rolled her eyes as she shifted from side to side, and then slowly proceeded. "One hermay scarf."

"That would be Air-May."

"Uh huh. One pair of Christian..." Evillene's eyes went to a narrow squint as she fought to pronounce the last word in front of her "Lou-bow-tin shoes."

"Ew-we, you almost had that one. Say it with me, Lew-bit-tawn," I said slowly with a satisfying smirk.

Evillene's nostrils flared one last time and she slid a white slip in front of me, "Sign here for your belongings and your release."

I picked up the chain-bound black felt pen to sign my paperwork. "Will I get a copy of this for my lawyer?"

"Sure, I will personally messenger it to you, how does that sound?" Evillene responded with an arched eyebrow and a fuck-you smirk. Her lips were pursed together so tight her mouth morphed into the letter O.

I gave her a broad smile and slid the white slip back to her. "Take care, Evillene."

"You call me that again and I will lock your ass back up, ya hear?"

I chuckled as Evillene snarled at me through her clenched teeth. I leaned in close to her, just to ensure she heard every last syllable about to leave my mouth.

"Let me put this in a way you can understand. As of now, I *is* a free woman, so *I gots* the right to say whatever the *hells* I want. Got it?" I took two steps back, swung my Air-May scarf around my neck and checked my freshly applied lip gloss in her gold- plated front teeth. "Toodles, bitch. Stay fat and greasy."

I swiveled on one foot and strutted out of the Gurnee Illinois Correctional Facility for women as if I had just won my first Oscar.

As I exited, I heard Evillene mutter one last comment, "I'm not greasy."

I watched as all the male security guards smiled at me and the female ones cursed my name. I was use to the attention, both positive and negative.

I pushed through the glass door and out into the fresh air of freedom. I stopped at the bottom of the stairs and basked in the sun that shone on my caramel skin that was in desperate need of a body wrap, massage and an orgasm. I pulled out my BlackBerry that was dead to the world and sighed looking at it. It was time to upgrade to an iPhone. I tossed my phone in the nearby trash and saw a silver and black Escalade pull up beside me. I smiled as my agent and good friend, Emanuel Vaughn III, jumped out. He looked like a kid on Christmas, skipping toward me with all his gayness. I couldn't have been happier to see his round cocoa face.

"Oh, child, you look like re-heated grits on a hot summer day," Emanuel said before placing two air-kisses on each one of my cheeks.

"Don't remind me. Do you have my appointments confirmed?"

"Yes, you have a mani/pedi at noon, mineral body wrap at four and your hair at six."

"Those words are music to my ears." Emanuel opened my passenger side door and I stepped up into his black Escalade and sunk into the soft cream-colored leather seats. *Oh, how I missed luxury.*

Emanuel headed around the car and jumped into the driver's seat, then turned to me. "I have some fabulous news." He was beaming ear to ear.

"Well? What the hell are you waiting for?"

"I, Emanuel Vaughn III, being one of your dearest and biggest fans, as well as your agent, submitted you for a part in a new sitcom co-starring Jennifer Taylor."

"The diva of divas?"

"Yes, child. And the producers want to see you in LA." Emanuel squealed like a tiny Catholic schoolgirl.

I sunk deeper into my seat. I was not happy at all. "LA?"

"Yes, LA auditions are next week. I thought you'd be thrilled."

"Excuse me if I don't join you in your squeal fest. Tell them thanks, but no thanks."

Emanuel did a circular movement with his body along with his head in tow, his way of facing me. Gays are so dramatic.

"Girlfriend, have you lost your ever-loving mind? Did you not hear me? A co-starring role with Jennifer Taylor."

"Yes, I heard you and I'm not interested," I firmly repeated.

"Hmph," Emanuel said as he folded his arms, sitting back in his seat. I turned to look at him and he stared forward, with his top lip damn near curled over his head.

"What is that supposed to mean?"

"If this doesn't have Todd Daniels written all over it, then I don't know what does."

"Well, I won't deny the fact that Todd and I belong together."

Emanuel threw his arms up, palms flat and kept them there while making his next point. "For the love of Sister Shy, leave his ass alone! If you haven't forgotten, he is the one who threw your pretty little ass in jail, replacing your Pradas with Payless shoes."

"It wasn't Todd; it was that bitch, Kai. It was her who put him up to this, I know it. Todd loves me, always has and always will."

"It doesn't matter. He agreed to it, not to mention, the moment he gets wind that you are out, he will file another restraining order."

"Oh, there are ways around that. I didn't spend two years in jail and not pick up on a thing or two."

"Darling, for me, please, just let it go. Look at you. You're beautiful, smart, witty. You will find someone new."

I turned to Emanuel and looked at him dead in his eyes. "Maybe I didn't make myself clear the first time. I am not going to LA. Todd is in New York, so that is where I need to be, are we clear?"

Emanuel turned and sank back into his seat. "Fine. If you go to New York, I might be able to get you an independent film or two, but the pay is crap, and frankly, darling, you're broke and being broke is not a good look, especially for you."

Emanuel was right. I was pretty damn broke.

"Besides, if you get this part in LA, it could launch your career to the next level and with that, doors of opportunities will just fly open faster than Taylor Swift's legs. You could even land that guest-hosting spot on that new show *Good Morning Gossip* in New York, which by the way is my favorite show."

"Why can't you get me that part now?"

"Because no one knows who you are, darlin'. Two years in jail is like ten years in entertainment years. Out of sight, out of mind."

"Well, if no one knows who I am, how did you get me this audition in LA?" I asked.

Emanuel looked away then back at me, his expression turning into a blushing not so bride. "I'm kinda sleeping with one of the producers on the show."

A broad smile spread over my face and I felt like a mama bear to her cub. "Is that right? I was indeed impressed.

"A diva's gotta do, what a diva's gotta do," Emanuel said without shame.

"That she does, look at you using your booty nepotism to get *moi* an audition."

"So will you go?" Emanuel turned back to me, clenched hands, eyes wide.

"If it will eventually get me back to New York and close to Todd, I'm all over it."

Emanuel was about to let out yet another school-girl squeal.

"Save it, Sally," I said, "let's head to the spa. This body is not going to massage itself." I sunk back into the soft leather seats. I didn't want to disappoint Emanuel, but I also didn't want to stray from my number-one priority—Todd. Two years was way too long to be away from my man. It was time to reclaim what was rightfully mine and show Kai that Alana's *bite* was so much fucking worse than her *bark*.

TWO
KAI

I jerked awake to the cry of my son, Kristopher. I headed for his room and saw Todd sitting comfortably in a padded baby-blue rocking chair, attempting to soothe our two-year-old son back to sleep.

Todd looked up when he saw me enter. "I think he just wanted a little company," Todd said as he gently kissed Kris on his forehead. I leaned against the doorway, taking in the moment. It was a loving picture that was almost too precious for words.

"I think he's morphing into a sly negotiator like his father." I shot back my comment to Todd in a whispered tone, making sure I didn't disturb Kris.

"Go back to sleep, I got this," Todd said, and he cradled Kris closer to his chest.

I glanced at the clock, as the red digits flashed 4:45 a.m. I sighed, thinking it would be useless to go back to sleep at this point. Who knew what time I would eventually wake back up?

"No, I'm going to hit the gym. What time do I need to be back before you have to take off for work?"

Todd didn't answer, and continued to rock back and forth in the cushioned, baby- blue rocking chair while Kristopher's eyes grew heavy with each passing second. "Take your time, I'm in no hurry today."

"You sure? I could just do a quick thirty-minute run, no weights?"

"Positive," Todd said as his eyes diverted back downward. Something was definitely not right with him, although at 4:45 a.m. it was probably not the time to discuss it.

"Okay, honey, I will see you when I get back. I won't be long." My last words didn't warrant a response from Todd as his eyes were now shut.

I headed down the hall, back to our bedroom, thinking of all the stuff I had to get through today. After I dropped Kristopher off at daycare, my plan was to finish our unpacking of the last few boxes. It had been two years since Todd had moved to Brooklyn and opened his own practice. The moment he moved in with me, I knew it would be only a matter of time before we would need to find another place to live. Although Toni was open to having us stay as long as we needed, I knew deep down it wasn't the right thing to do, considering Toni and I had a sexual history. I think Todd wanted to move as well, especially after I told him what went down between us. His face was uncaring as he just stared at me and said, "Really, Kai, again? Am I going to have to watch my back all the time now?"

"No, not at all." I pleaded with him. I swore to him as long as we were a couple that would never happen again. I'm sure Todd still questioned my sexuality. I still questioned it myself. It's hard to shake the beliefs you were raised with. My mom was a huge advocate of loving whoever you feel comfortable with, man or woman. She never condoned cheating or infidelity, and that was where I went wrong. Technically, when I was with Toni, Todd had been with Alana, so I didn't technically cheat on him, like when I had slept with Alana behind his back.

Alana's name rarely came up between us. There was a somewhat silent agreement between us not to discuss her, or what went down with her. I still thank God every night for bringing Todd back to me and promised that I would never do that to him again. He hadn't deserved what he had gone through and I had been selfish to keep the affair between me and Alana going on as long as I did. Like I said, Toni was different, unexpected and definitely unplanned.

Even though Toni and Todd were both cordial with each other, it was not a comfortable situation when all three of us found each other in the same space for longer than two minutes. So Todd and I agreed that the moment we could find another brownstone to rent we would jump on it.

It took over a year to find a place since we needed to stay close to the area due to the fact that Kristopher was settled in his daycare and Todd's practice was less than five miles away. Toni and I remained friends after we moved out, we saw each other in passing, a casual text here and there, and of course through Facebook. While I think Todd moving in and us getting our own place was hard for Toni, she never really showed it.

I returned from the gym around 7 a.m. Todd had already showered and Kristopher was perched in his high-chair in front of the TV with his graham crackers and milk. Todd was thumbing through the morning newspaper as I walked over to him to lay a soft kiss on his lips.

"Baby, are you okay?" I asked, trying not to wrinkle his freshly pressed light-lavender shirt.

"I'm good," he said as he continued to flip through the pages, leaning casually against our center island in the kitchen. I hated it when he got this way. It made me worry that he was thinking about her. Todd was a thinker, always had been. A thinker and a peacemaker.

My intuition told me that it was not Alana this time, but despite that, my insecurities got the best of me and I couldn't stop the words before they flew out of my damn mouth. "You're not thinking about Alana, are you?"

Todd looked up and slowly lowered the paper. I swallowed, hoping I hadn't just opened a huge-ass can of worms. He scratched his head and his hand ran down the back of his head to his neck, rubbing it for a minute before taking a long sighing breath. "No, Kai, I am not thinking about that crazy bitch." A feeling of glee shot through my body when I heard his response.

"Sorry, I didn't mean to—"

Todd cut me off. "I have way more to worry about than her ass, okay?"

"Like what? What's going on, Todd?" I was concerned, I'd never seen him like this before.

Todd shook his head and sighed again. He put his paper aside and folded his arms across his chest as he looked up at me, a grim expression on his face. "It's my practice. I may have to shut it down."

"Oh my God. Why? I thought it was doing well?"

"It's doing okay, but not great. I was hoping to get this big client and they ended up going with a larger law firm. Between that and the landlord raising the rent, I can't afford to keep things going. It's either pay the rent at the office or for this place, and you know what will win."

I cringed a bit as Todd said "this place." Our brownstone was definitely out of our price range, but I just had to have it. I told Todd that I would start my event planning business as soon as Kristopher started daycare to help with the rent. Six months had passed and I hadn't even thought about starting. "Well, why can't you just move your practice home? We have an extra room."

"Because I have a family, Kai. I can't bring clients here to the home. It's unprofessional. It doesn't matter, I'll figure something out, I have no choice."

"Wait, wait, first of all, stop saying 'I.' We are a team, remember?" My mind went into overdrive. "I can go and get a job. Maybe my old firm will hire me back. I'm sure Simone can make a call."

"No, I like having you here for Kristopher. I don't want him in daycare all day. The best thing for me is to get a job back in corporate America."

I cringed again. "But you hated working in those big firms. Let's not jump to that just yet. Maybe I can help you out at the office, hustle up some clients or something."

When Todd looked up at me, he started to laugh, shaking his head. "Did you just say 'hustle up some clients'?"

I smiled. I always liked knowing I could get Todd to laugh. "What? So now you don't like my choice of words, huh? Whatever."

Todd continued the joke with me. "Maybe you could also wrangle up a cheaper office space."

"Okay, fine, I am just trying to help. Baby, we're a team and if we don't stay united anything could come between us."

Todd reached out and pulled me in, close. "You're right, and that is why I love you so much."

"How much?" I teased Todd.

"Very much," Todd said, as he planted a long passionate kiss on me. I slid my tongue in his mouth, and felt his manhood start to throb.

I looked down with a broad smile. "I'm glad I can still turn you on."

"Baby, you can always turn me on," Todd said as he went in for another kiss. This time I felt my juices come alive and begin their decent down my canal. Todd's lips began to travel down my neck to my breasts as he pulled back my exercise top to devourer my erect nipple.

"Baby, we can't do this now."

"Why not?"

I diverted my eyes over to our son who was looking like a deer caught in headlights. Barney was no longer interesting to him. Mommy and Daddy were.

"Ah, hello, the wide-eyed two year old in the room is reason enough."

"Baby, he's two, I doubt he even knows where his nose is."

"Don't underestimate our son's intelligence." I gently pushed Todd away. "This isn't gonna happen."

"Damn, Kai, how you gonna get me all worked up and expect me to leave for work now? That could result in permanent damage."

I patted Todd playfully on his chest. "I'm sure you will be fine. Besides, you could always come home for lunch to eat," I said in my flirty I-wanna-fuck-you-so-badly way.

"Done." Todd walked over and kissed Kristopher on his head and grabbed his jacket and briefcase. He looked at me and said in his best Terminator voice, "I'll be back."

"I'm sure you will." I winked at my handsome husband as he attempted to swagger out of the kitchen to the best of his ability while sporting a fresh hard-on. I sat down at the kitchen table and had to wonder what the next chapter of our lives might bring. I just hoped whatever it was, it didn't contain too much drama. I was getting too damn old for all that.

THREE
ALANA

I had an appointment with my parole officer the next morning after I was released. I glanced down at my release paper to see that his name was Randolph Farrow. I adjusted my too-tight, mid-thigh skirt and overly revealing pink cotton top and headed up the escalator at 30 S. Wacker to meet the man who was appointed as my parole officer.

I walked into the dilapidated office and cringed as I looked around at the clientele who surrounded me. Clearly, I was not his typical parolee.

Randolph Farrow sat behind a cluttered desk positioned in the middle of an untidy and filthy office. I knocked on the door and saw Randolph look up at me, back down at his paperwork, and back up again. He motioned for me to come in and have a seat. He carried himself like a man who had been in this job for far too long and taking care of parolees had become more than routine.

His greasy hair was slathered to one side and his pathetic attempt to spruce up his appearance didn't go much further than a questionably clean white shirt and gray pants, with no belt and a coffee stain under his pocket. The disarray was topped by a beer belly and triple chin. Sasquatch in a suit.

"Hello, Mr. Farrow? I'm Alana Brooks."

Randolph looked up and leaned forward in his seat. He rubbed the sweat off his palm on his TJ Maxx pants and stuck it out to shake mine.

"Call me Randy," he said. His eyes did a slow decent from my face to my breasts and back up again. I now had his full and undivided attention.

"Okay," I said.

Randy sat back behind his desk and motioned for me to sit on the metal folded chair in front of him. Randy picked up my file and began to read it. It was clear that he already knew everything in the file since he continued to glance up at me, or rather my breasts, every five seconds.

As Randy continued to pretend to read my file while staring at my breasts, I began having second thoughts about my visit. I scanned the room, making sure if this pervert did anything inappropriate I could easily make my escape or stab him in the neck with my Prada heel, and claim self-defense.

"I'm assuming it's Miss Brooks?"

"Yes."

"It looks like you and I are going to be joined at the hip over the next nine months." Randy chuckled.

Just the thought of being next to the bloated bureaucrat sitting across from me, let alone joined at the hip with someone who looked and smelled like week-old tuna, made my stomach churn. "Yep, looks that way Randy," I responded, trying to stay cordial.

Randy flipped a few more pages through my file and looked back up at me, managing to make eye contact.

"I see here that during your nine months on parole you are not to go near a Mr. Todd Daniels or a Miss Kai Edwards, a distance of one-thousand yards," Randy said and dropped the file on his desk. "Stalking the couple, eh?"

I raised my eyebrow at him, trying to stay calm and cool as I digested his less-than-professional attitude. My phone suddenly vibrated in my purse, breaking the tension in the room.

"Randy, will you excuse me for one second?"

"Of course, sweetheart."

I smiled and stood to answer my vibrating phone. As I turned around with my phone, I noticed Randy's eyes pasted on my ass. I glared at him, thinking I might be able to guilt him into being a bit more professional, but his eyes remained firmly planted on my ass. I also noticed that he was slowly moving his right arm under his desk, but I really didn't want to imagine what it was he was rubbing. I ended my call and moved back to my comfy metal chair. I laid my cell phone on the desk in front of me.

"So, Randy, what is the protocol here? I have things I need to do."

"Ya don't say? The parolee has things to do," Randy said with a sarcastic tone. "Guess what, sweetheart, the meeting is over when I say it is, got it? Randy grinned, showing every single one of his yellow nicotine-stained teeth.

"Of course, right. Whatever you say, Randy." I was starting to lose my patience with his blue-collar, lowlife ass. I tried to remember that I needed to keep my focus on the prize, Todd. The only way I was going to do that was by being able to keep my temper under control.

Randy picked my folder back up. "You have to complete two-hundred hours of community service. There's a list of jobs on the white board in the lobby. I don't care what you pick, just pick one and get it done."

"Fine."

Randy leaned forward in his chair and a piercing squeak echoed through the cramped room as the chair protested its treatment.

"A few ground rules to remember for the next nine months. One, you check in with me every morning, no excuses. If I don't hear from you, I will throw your sexy little ass back in the clinker. Two, if you go anywhere near Mr. Daniels or Miss Edwards, I will throw your sexy little ass back in the clinker. Three, you will complete your two- hundred hours of community service in the next nine months. If you do not," Randy flashed that one-of-a-kind nicotine smile at me, "I will throw your little sexy ass back in the clinker, do I make myself clear?"

"Crystal." I paused, waiting for the other shoe to drop. "Is that it?"

"Actually, there is one last, very important rule. For the next nine months you are prohibited to cross state lines. If you do..."

"You'll throw my little sexy ass back in the clinker," I finished for him.

Randy closed my file folder and revealed his largest nicotine-stained smile yet. "Any questions doll?"

I felt my temperature climb and the hair on the back of my neck stand up. I clenched my jaw, then took a deep breath, reminded myself not to get too indignant with his hillbilly-looking ass. You get more bees with honey.

I revealed a smile. "Randy, as you know I am an actress."

"I did not know that, but it is fitting," Randy said, shooting a wink at me.

"I was just informed by my agent that I have an opportunity to audition for a new show in LA."

Randy leaned further back in his chair and a longer squeak sounded through the room. He clasped his hands behind his head and revealed two equally large sweat stains. "That is fantastic news, Miss Brooks, splendid even. There is one slight problem, if you leave the state of Illinois, I will be forced, and somewhat pleased, to throw your sexy little ass back into the clinker."

In that moment, all I could think about was how much I despised this man sitting in front of me, with his smelly pits, greasy hair and fat pregnant nose—you know the kind of nose that stretches from ear to ear with that line running across the middle.

"So you're saying I can't go to Los Angeles?"

"Unless there is a Los Angeles, Illinois, that is exactly what I am saying, sweetheart."

"Randy, my...my career depends on this. I'm sure you can understand why it's so important that I'm allowed to leave Illinois."

"And I'm sure you can understand that I *will* throw your ass back into the clinker if you do."

Randy and I stared at each other as if we were engaging in a standoff. My heart was beating at an abnormally fast pace and my body temperature was getting hot. I took a deep breath to try and calm myself down.

"So there is no way we can bend the rules a bit? This is my career we are talking about. I'm sure you can make a small exception for me."

Randy sat up and placed his meaty fingers on his cluttered desk and drummed his overgrown fingernails against the glass top as if thinking for a moment.

"Actually, Miss Brooks, maybe there is." A devilish grin danced across his pasty skin and licked his white chapped lips.

"Maybe we can do a small barter?" he stated devilishly. The same meaty hand slipped out of view and back under his desk, probably back to his dick, which I imagined was the size and length of a Vienna sausage.

I continued to stare at Randy, knowing exactly where this was going. "And what exactly are you suggesting, Randy?"

Randy's right hand began to move back and forth again under his desk. "Well, a man's got needs, ya know?"

I decided to play dumb, for once. "Is that right? And what would those needs be, Randy?"

Randy smiled. "Miss Brooks, we are both consenting adults here, right? Evidently, you need something and so do I."

"And what is it that you need, Randy?" *You fat disgusting fuck*, I screamed in my head.

Randy leaned forward as a smile scampered across his thin, chapped lips. "What I'm gonna need are those big blacks lips around my throbbing dick. Now you do that for me and you will be free to go to LA or wherever your little heart desires." Randy ended his sentence with his eyebrow raised and a wink, wink.

Randy and I stared at each other much longer and more intense than we should have.

"That's um... that's quite an offer, Randy."

"I think it's pretty fair."

"How about I sweeten the deal?" I said as I scooted to the edge of my seat. "How about I not only suck your dick, but I let you have your way with my ass?"

Randy's eyes widened like a witch in a broom factory. "Hey, that works for me, sweetheart."

"Then I suggest you take your dick and go fuck yo mama, because the only pussy you're getting around here is the pussy you came out of."

I quickly snatched my phone off his desk, stood up and headed for the door.

"What the fuck did you say to me, you black bitch?" Get the hell out of my office. And if I find out that you've stepped even a centimeter over the state line, I will have your ass. I'm going to be watching you like shit on a baby."

The last thing I heard was Randy scream "your ass" since I was halfway out the building when I laid my last statement on him. Randy was going to be a problem, but I had something for his ass, you better believe I did.

FOUR
TODD

Losing my practice was an all-time low for me.

"So tell me a little bit about yourself, Mr. Daniels." Kenneth Knowles was the managing partner at Jacobs, Knowles and Patterson. He was an older man with a pensive look. He wore a dark navy-blue suit, white shirt and matching blue tie. There was nothing exciting about him whatsoever.

I shifted in my seat before answering his question. It was a question I always hated having to answer at interviews. In fact, it was the question that drove me to start my own practice in the first place. It was a question that if I didn't answer with something that made me sound interesting enough, I wouldn't land this job I so desperately needed right now. My practice in Chicago had done so much better than the one I had opened in New York. There were many days where I wanted to pack up Kai and our newborn son, Kristopher, and head back to Chicago as one big happy family. But the idea of Kai and I having a new start in a new state and avoiding seeing Alana again when she finally got out of jail was reason enough to stay. But New York wasn't panning out and I knew it was only a matter of time before my income dried up.

I cleared my throat, adjusted my tie, took a deep breath and smiled. *Just smile through this; I can do it.* I wasn't usually nervous when I interviewed, but today I was having a hard time holding it together.

"Well, let's see, I'm originally from Chicago, though I obtained my undergraduate and my law degree from Howard University. I had my own practice over the past three years before I went under because of larger, more-established law firms like your own."

We stared at each other for a few seconds before a smile finally emerged from his perplexed look. I guess humor was not his style.

"I see." Kenneth sat up, glanced over my resume, then looked up at me. "So, Chicago, I love that city. What brought you out to New York?"

Yet another uncomfortable question and one I hadn't prepared for. People usually asked about my practice or my experience at Howard Law, not what the hell had brought me to New York.

My mind drifted to the chain of events which brought me to my new life with my new wife. I thought about how my drama-filled relationship with my best friend and my girlfriend had been the key to my sudden relocation to New York. No, that's not right. It had been the catalyst that made me flee New York and try to escape the psychotic arena that Alana created around me and Kai from the very first moment she met her.

Alana's manipulations knew no bounds, from sleeping with Kai in an attempt to manipulate me to choosing her due to a faked paternity test. The final breaking point for me was when Alana followed me to New York, broke into Kai's apartment and threatened not only my life, but the life of Kai and my newborn son—all of this, just to be with me. Justice had other plans for her as her little stunt landed her ass in jail for three years.

Yes, that was what brought me to New York, but telling that story to a white conservative lawyer would lead him to smile, nod and scratch his head and then politely tell me, *Thank you for coming in, we will be in touch.*

I locked eyes with the senior partner of the firm I was interviewing at, as I felt the sweat starting to surface on my neck. I swallowed hard, rubbed my palms down and up the back of my thighs and felt the friction created from the movement. I stopped myself, a nervous tic wouldn't do me any good. I tried to figure out what to do with my hands, so I clasped them together and rested them on the desk in front of me. Apparently, this interview was going to be a lot tougher than I imagined.

"Mr. Daniels? Are you still with me?" Mr. Knowles asked, bringing me back to the present.

My eyes reconnected with his as I pushed out a half-smile. "It's a long story."

"Well, give me the cliff notes."

This man will not let it go. Then again, what lawyer does?

"Okay, long story short, I fell in love and the woman I was supposed to marry, so I followed her here, to New York City," I said with a forced but genuine smile on my face. That was close enough to the truth.

"Ah, the power of true love, or in our case, good pussy."

Upon hearing the word pussy leave his mouth, my jaw damn near slammed to the floor faster than a pull of gravity. What the—? Did Kenneth Knowles, fifty-five, white and very conservative, just say "good pussy" during an interview? I guess it doesn't matter what color, creed or background, a man's common denominator is good pussy. That brought a good laugh out and broke all the ice that had frozen around us.

"Actually, sir, you are right, good pussy is hard to find these days," I threw back with a broad smile on my face. *This corporate-America thing might not be so bad after all.*

The rest of the interview went extremely well. We chatted like old friends reconnecting over drinks and dinner.

"Mr. Daniels, I like you, but most of all I like you for our firm."

Jackpot. Hearing those words made me smile and thank the Lord above. While the thought of going back to corporate America made me feel as if an anchor was tied to my leg. This firm didn't seem to be so bad after all.

"Unfortunately, at this time we are not looking to add any lawyers on our roster here in Manhattan."

Fuck me. "Excuse me?" I had to wonder why I was even brought in for an interview if they were not hiring now. I couldn't afford to wait.

"So, you are not hiring at this time?" I had to get that clarified once and for all."

"No, I didn't say that. We are not hiring in our Manhattan office. However, we do have an opening in our Los Angeles office."

"Oh, wow, did you say 'Los Angeles'?"

"Yes, would that be something that interest you? A competitive salary, signing bonus and a company car."

"That's a nice offer, but..." *Kai is not going to go for that.* "I would have to run it past my wife."

"Listen, I know it's a big move. Frankly, I can't stand LA. I'm a New Yorker myself, but I think it might be a great fit for you. Talk it over with your wife and get back to me by the morning."

I shifted once again in my seat. *How would I break this to Kai?*

"I can do that," I said as I stood.

"Great, we would love to have you on our team."

"It's a lot to digest, but I'll definitely get back to you tomorrow with my decision. It was great meeting you, Mr. Knowles, and I appreciate the opportunity."

"It was great meeting you as well. I look forward to hearing from you."

I headed out of the fifty-floor commercial skyrise on Madison Avenue. I had to think for a moment, *could I really live in Los Angeles?* I had never thought of LA as a home. I was excited and apprehensive all at once, and wasn't sure how Kai would react to the news. Then again, it wasn't like she had anything to lose. In fact, with a move like this we both had everything to gain.

***

"Los Angeles, seriously?" Kai said. She wasn't a fan of the idea by the look of discontent on her face.

"Baby, just look at it as a new start."

"If you haven't noticed, we are in the midst of a new start right here in Brooklyn," Kai said as she motioned to the unpacked boxes. "We aren't even unpacked here yet, baby."

"That's a good thing though. Look at it as having fewer boxes to pack."

Kai started to pace back and forth on the distressed walnut-colored wood flooring as she ran her fingers through her untamed curly hair. I loved Kai's hair; it always reminded me of Freddy from that show *A Different World.*

"Well, how long do you have to think about it?"

"I have until morning."

"Like, tomorrow morning?"

"That would be the one."

"How are we supposed to make a life-changing decision in less than twelve hours?"

"Baby, if you don't want to go, then, we won't go."

Kai stopped pacing and walked over to me. "No, we should at least consider the pros and cons."

"Good thinking. I can think of one pro right now."

"What is that?" Kai asked.

In my *Tony, Toni, Tone* impression, I started to sing, "It never rains in Southern California, they tell me, it never rains in Southern California, they tell me."

"Okay, okay, but that is only one pro. I'm going to go get some paper and a pen," Kai said. She headed for the back to retrieve her negotiation tools. I heard the computer chime and turned toward the desk it was sitting on. Simone was calling over Skype. I hit accept.

"What it do, Simone?"

"Todd, how are you?"

"Can't complain."

"Where is Kai?"

"I'm right here," Kai said as she walked up behind me with pad and pen in her hand. "Todd just dropped a bomb on me."

"That's fine, but I have another bomb to add to that."

"What? What's going on?" Kai asked, shooting me a look as she sat in the chair in front of our laptop.

"Alana was released from jail yesterday."

Kai looked back at me, clearly rattled by the news.

"When?" I asked.

"Yesterday morning," Simone replied.

"I can't believe it. She's out already?" Kai said, her voice troubled.

"Time flies when a bitch named Alana is out of your life," Simone said.

"So, now what?" Kai asked, looking at me as if I had a master plan.

"I doubt she will come looking for us, baby." I said this despite knowing deep down that was probably not the case. I'd known Alana for a long time and one constant was that she didn't give up easily.

"I thought she was serving three years?" Kai said to Simone's image on the screen.

"Yeah, she got out early, maybe due to the open-leg policy," Simone said as she fluffed her hair in the mirrored screen reflection.

"Well, if she comes anywhere near us I'll get another restraining order and throw her ass right back in jail," I said, hoping that would reassure Kai of her safety.

Suddenly, I was struck by the thought that with Alana out of jail, this was another check in the pro column for Kai and I to move to California. We'd be that much further away from her. I could throw that out there, but I didn't want Kai to think Alana was our motivating factor.

"Todd, I'm surprised you didn't get a call from her attorney."

"Actually, Simone, I may have, but my business lines are down right now."

"Why? What's going on?"

I shot Kai a look, and diverted my attention back to the laptop screen. "In a nutshell, I am closing the door to Daniels' Esquire."

"Shut up, why? Wait, does that mean you guys are moving back to Chicago?" Simone asked, suddenly upbeat. "I mean it's time my BFF came back home already. It's been almost three years since you left and I want my turn at babysitting my godson. I say enough is enough, this is getting ridiculous."

"Well, actually that was the so-called bomb Todd was laying on me when you called. He got a job offer in LA."

"You're kidding me, right?" Simone's voice was shriller than I'd ever heard before. "What kind of firm is it?"

"It's an entertainment firm, which was my specialty in Law School. Hell, I just fell into divorce law when I couldn't land a job in that field."

"But we haven't decided yet," Kai chimed in.

"Well, baby, one of the pros is that entertainment law is very lucrative to be in."

"So you're not just moving, you're moving even farther away from me?" Simone fell back into her chair. "Well, isn't that just fan-fucking-tastic I say?"

"But we haven't totally decided yet," Kai reiterated again.

"I was sitting here trying to convince your BFF when you called," I said with a laugh. Simone was good comic relief in my book.

"We were about to list out the pros and cons," Kai threw in.

"Well, here is one big fat con: You will be further away from me. How about that? That con should outweigh the sum of all the pros you might conjure up."

"Nice try, Simone, but no."

"Like Todd said, it is not yet decided."

"What are some of the pros?" Simone asked.

Kai looked up at me as I stood behind her chair.

"That's what we were about to do when you called."

"Okay. I will hold on." Simone sat back and folded her arms.

"Yeah, this is gonna take a little longer than a few minutes. This is our life here."

"Fine, if you gotta get all dramatic about it, call me back."

"Love ya."

"Love ya more if you move back to Chicago."

Kai disconnected the call and turned toward me. "I guess we should get started."

Kai dropped a pad of paper on the desk and wrote *Pros and Cons* at the top of the sheet and a semi-straight line down the middle.

"All right, let's do this," I said with a smile and flopped down next to Kai on the couch.

Although Kai knew as well as I did that I needed to take this job, it was hard for her to see any pros in uprooting our family and moving across the United States. I hated doing this just as much as she did, but my mind kept wandering back to the idea that Alana was now out of jail, which was not a good thing.

I had to find a way to convince Kai that we should move, because now that Alana was a free woman, it was only a matter of time before she tracked us down, and who knew what she had up her sleeve for us this time?

FIVE

ALANA

Emanuel booked me on a nine a.m. flight to LA from Chicago, so I could get into LA with plenty of time to spare before my three p.m. audition. Right before I boarded, I checked in with my jackass of a parole officer, so I was at least good for the rest of the day before his suspisions peaked. I set the alarm on my phone for five a.m. each morning while in LA, which would be seven a.m. Chicago time, to call Randy and check in. That early I was sure I'd get his voicemail. I was pretty sure that Sasquatches didn't roll out of bed before nine a.m. Even thinking about him made my damn stomach turn.

I stepped off the plane at exactly 11:30 a.m. A four-and-a-half hour flight which equated to losing only two-and-a-half hours of my life made for a gold star in my book. I loved gaining time while traveling. It was another good way to keep me one step ahead of the game. I also liked to catch a few winks on the plane, but this time I had to focus on the TV pilot script that was emailed to me just two days before I was to head to LA.

I was determined to nail this part and was willing to do anything that could help me land the role on the CW network. Nothing would distract me, including the tall, handsome, eligible bachelor who sat next to me in first class during the entire four-and-a- half hour flight. I ignored him during the flight because Alana Brooks was on a mission. Besides, I preferred the married kind. Single and looking held no challenge for me.

I arrived at the Beverly Hills Hotel and settled into my room. I quickly ran a nice hot bath, ordered up a bottle of red wine, along with a veggie burger and a side salad. After my bath and quick lunch, I found that I still had some time before my audition, so I pulled out my laptop to check my emails.

I decided to check Facebook, too, to see if Emanuel had reactivated my account. Before going to prison, I had told him to de-activate my profile, not close it down. I didn't want to have to start fresh and add the 4,000 friends all over again—one of whom included Todd. I punched in my password and found myself staring blankly at the new feed. Two years in jail and everything had changed drastically.

After fiddling around with Facebook, trying to familiarize myself with the new controls and layout, I wanted to see if Todd had unfriended me. I typed in his name and there he was, in all his Facebook glory. Men were such fucking idiots. The first thing I would have done if I were him was unfriend me, but not Todd, he probably didn't even think that far ahead.

As I checked Todd's Facebook vitals, I saw something that made me sit up, gasp and nearly lose my damn mind. I threw my laptop to one side, snatched up my cell phone and dialed Emanuel's number, not even giving him a chance to say hello.

"Why the hell didn't you tell me Todd and Kai were married?" I demanded once I heard him pick up the phone.

There was complete silence on the other end.

"I'm waiting," I said impatiently.

"Sweetheart, I didn't want to upset you before your audition. I wanted to make sure you were clear and focused to get this part."

"Oh, don't worry, I will get this part. You can fucking count on that. You NOT telling me upsets me more."

"Alana, you have to admit, it was only a matter of time, especially with you being in jail and all."

The thought of me being in jail and being powerless to stop their marriage sent a galloping rage through my body. This was just one more hurdle I would have to overcome.

"Alana, it's not the end of the world. There are so many men out there who would give their left testicle to be with you. You are a beautiful, intelligent—"

"Oh, save it, Emanuel. Let's not dwell on the obvious. You know what I want, so just stop with the ass kissing. I gotta go."

I hung up the phone, sat back and closed my eyes. How could he have married her? Her? I was supposed to be the one walking down that aisle, honeymooning in Brazil, making love on the beach. Me, not fucking her. I closed Facebook and tried to get Todd and that bitch Kai out of my head. I needed to focus if I wanted to nail my audition. I needed to get my life back on track so I could be ready for Todd.

By two p.m. I was ready to show these producers who was the right woman for this part—Alana "Get It Done" Brooks. Refreshed and prepared to take on the world, well, at least the producers of my new show, *Office Temps*.

I was auditioning for the role of a temp to the star of the series, Jennifer Taylor. I was sure the role was for the generic sassy new temp who kept the boss in check. The part was for a reoccurring role, but I was sure that after the network and producers saw my skills, I would be quickly bumped up to co-star. It would just be a matter of time in my book.

I put the finishing touches of my makeup on and headed downstairs to await the car that would take me to my audition. I preferred to not drive in cities that I was unfamiliar with. Besides, if I drove, I couldn't drink.

I opened a bottle of champagne to calm my nerves and drank a few sips, just to take the edge off. I popped a mint in my mouth and laid my head back on the headrest. My car headed down Beverly Blvd to Crescent Drive, over the canyons until finally dropping me onto Laurel Canyon Boulevard.

Thirty minutes later my black town car pulled up to the CBS Radford Studios in Studio City, California. A pimpled-face young kid greeted me at the car and escorted me into their production offices.

"Can I get you a bottle of water, Miss Brooks?"

"That would be nice, thank you," I said. The young kid scurried away, returning within seconds with a cold bottle of water.

I looked at it and was about to ask for Perrier, but I ignored the impulse, thinking that I'd better not rock the boat until the part was mine. There would be plenty of time for demands and criticism after the show was number one.

The PA escorted me to another room where to my surprise I was met with not one, not two, but a dozen other women waiting. I stopped and felt myself tense up. I had been led to believe it was just going to be me and perhaps a few other women, but then again, this was an audition and the producers had to keep their options open.

I casually glanced around the room at the women and was impressed by the beauty that surrounded me. This was the first time in my professional career that I felt a bit intimidated, just a bit though, not much. I quickly put on my diva-delish face and made my way to an empty spot across the room and felt all twenty-four pairs of eyes sizing me up.

I sashayed over in my navy-blue, small pinstriped fitted pants suit. It was a design I got personally from DKNY when I did a bang-up fucking job at my last photo shoot. Of course giving the photographer a blow job sweetened the deal I'm sure. I had to have this suit, and now, I was glad I went the extra mile to get it. Looking at the other women there for the audition I was sure they were all wondering who I was and where the hell I came from. With that I felt like I had the upper hand on them. I liked to keep snitches guessing.

Forty-five minutes later, someone finally called my name. A bit irritated, I curbed my attitude and followed the frumpy, in-need-of-a-total-makeover, casting assistant into the next room. I quickly switched my frown that had formed while starring at the back of the casting assistant, to a gleeful smile as I walked into the room. Gotta walk in with a smile. No one likes a switcher.

"Good afternoon, beautiful people, how are you all doing today?" My initial spark of enthusiasm got a smile from pretty much every one but one decrepit-looking woman in the back corner, who to my disappointment, was the casting director.

Her name was Kimberly Bryant and she came with a scowl on her face three miles long that lapped into the next. Her skin was in dire need of a nip and tuck and her hairline looked more like a hat that was sliding off her head. I managed to get a slight smile out of her after I turned to shoot her a flirty wink.

"Can we see your head shots please?" The frumpy assistant reached her dwarf-like arm toward me. I reached in my bag and slid two of my best shots into her hand.

"Oh, we just need one. This one is fine."

I wanted to say both were fabulous, but whatever. "Okay, great."

Another woman stood as the assistant passed my head shot back to Cruella DeVille.

"Alana, are you ready?" the assistant asked, bringing me back to her viewpoint.

Ah, no, bitch, I just came to smile and critique you. I tilted my head and gave her a sunny-California smile, "Yes, of course."

"Great, let's start from the top of scene B."

"Great," I said, mirroring her enthusiasm.

***

By the time I left Radford Studios it was almost seven p.m. I had successfully made it through the casting directors and producers. The producer session had included two writing producers, one of whom was Emanuel's booty buddy. He would have fooled me, he didn't look gay at all. I think that was his goal, seeing as how I had sensed he was acting straight. Hollywood at its finest.

We were told that if we made it to the next round of auditions we would hear from our agents by tonight and that the next round of auditions would be held tomorrow. That would be the make-it-or-break-it audition, one I had better be prepared for.

Finally, the last audition was me facing the executive producer—or as he was sometimes known around Hollywood, the Show runner—along with a few network studio executives.

All in all, it had been an exhausting day, but I felt good about my audition by the time I left the building. I said my good-byes to the pimpled-face PA and headed to my car.

On the drive home back to Beverly Hills I made my driver take a detour down Sunset to Gower and slid him a twenty-dollar bill to go into Roscoe's Chicken and Waffles to pick me up the famous #15: three wings, a waffle and side of grits. Of course I would never eat this in public, but that was why I had a driver.

By nine p.m. I was fully bathed, shaved and relaxing on my king-sized bed. All I could think about was Todd and Kai. I wondered what kind of wedding they had. Knowing Kai, they probably had a backyard wedding with paper lanterns and homemade cupcakes. I opened Facebook up and dove into Todd's photo albums. There it was, just as I had imagined it. A backyard wedding, the height of banality. Kai made me sick.

My phone sat just inches away from me. I was awaiting my call from Emanuel. I was beginning to get a bit anxious, since I had not heard anything yet, but I had to remind myself that they did not finish the sessions until at least eight and seeing as how it was only a little after nine o'clock, I thought I should still try and keep hope alive.

I laid my head back, closed my eyes, and tried to forget about all that was going wrong in my life by focusing on what was good. The smooth tunes of Neo interrupted my thirty seconds of silence and I looked down at my phone to see my mother calling.

"Dammit." I knew exactly why she was calling me. I picked up the phone and immediately braced myself for the worse.

"Hey, Mom, I was just about to call you."

"Really, Alana? Where are you?"

I sat up, felt my stress level rise, bit my lip and as they say let the shit hang out for all to see."

"I'm in LA."

Silence on the other end. I was hoping my mother would just hang up out of disgust.

"Did you just say, 'LA'?"

"Mom, I can explain."

"Explain what, Alana? How you got released from jail and don't call or even bother to come by and see your own daughter? Do you realize what I am sacrificing to raise her?"

"It's not like you came running to bring her to visit me when I was locked up."

"I told you I wasn't going to let her see you that way. I am not painting that picture for her, not for my grandchild."

I sat in silence as tears began to swell up in my eyes. My chest heaved up and down, faster and faster.

"Mom, I'm doing the best I can. I'm trying to build a foundation for me and my child."

"Really, Alana? By running after married men and getting locked up in jail? I raised you better than that."

"Just like you raised me to turn the other cheek, right, Mama?" I shot back.

"You damn right. You wouldn't even be in this mess if you had just stayed with Avery."

"Mama, Avery cheated on me like it was his job."

"Alana, marriage has its highs and lows, you just have to wait for the highs to come back around."

"Is that what you're doing, Mom? Waiting for that high that will never come back now that Dad is gone? Now that he finally walked out of your life? Our lives?"

I heard a sigh on the other end of the phone. "We grew apart."

"He left you for his mistress of fifteen years and you just stood there and took it. You didn't even fight for what was yours."

"It's not that easy."

"It's easier than you think, Mom."

"Are you in LA chasing Todd again? You need to leave him and that poor girl alone. You'll find yourself back in jail if you don't learn when to stop and walk away."

"No, that's how you and I are different."

"He made his choice, don't you get that?"

"The only thing I get is that Todd loves me and I love Todd. He is the only man that..." I looked down to see Emanuel's call. "Mama, I gotta go," I said, swallowing back the tears, hoping my voice wouldn't crack from the unspoken emotions building inside of me.

"Alana, we are not done here. I have to talk to you about something."

"I will call Riley back tomorrow."

"Alana!"

I disconnected with my mother, took a deep breath and connected the call with Emanuel, but not before putting on a big fat smile to mask my pain. "Darling, talk to me."

"Hey, beautiful, I have some wonderful news. You made it to network auditions."

Hearing that made me want to cry even harder.

"That is wonderful." I exhaled a relieved sigh.

"Are you okay? You sound a little weird."

I swallowed and tried to calm my trembling body. "Oh, I am fine, just exhausted from the day."

"Well, child, get some rest, your audition is at ten a.m. tomorrow. I have a good feeling about this, Alana. Like I said, if you get this part, it will be a life changer."

"That would be just what the doctor ordered. Thank you, Emanuel."

"Are you sure you're okay?"

I pushed back my emotions, which were trying to make their presence known. "Positive. I will talk to you tomorrow."

I hung up the phone and stared at the peach-colored walls that surrounded me. I wanted to jump up and down, scream, laugh and cry all at once. I was frozen. Neo broke my trance again as his electrifying tune filled the empty space around me and I looked back down at my phone to see who was calling. It was my mother. I slid my hand over the top of the phone, sliding the icon to voicemail.

I leaned back on my pillow and closed my eyes as the tears that had been building up finally rushed to the surface and down my freshly washed and moisturized face. There was a lot on my plate and too much of it was bullshit. I needed to get back on top of my game and getting this part was just the beginning. From there, everything would fall right into place. I just had to find a way to get close to Todd.

SIX

KAI

Just the thought of Alana being out of jail threw a thorn-covered blanket over our lives. After we got off the phone with Simone, Todd and I weighed our pros and cons over the next hour until we decided that moving to LA would be a good move right now, considering our current circumstances. I wasn't working, and well, Todd's last point had sealed the deal for me. The salary and perks he was being offered by this new firm would allow me to continue staying at home to raise our son. When I heard that, it was a done deal. We were LA bound.

Before Todd and I made the move to Los Angeles, I had to close a very important chapter in my life. The last time I saw Toni was five months ago, the day before Todd and I had officially moved out of her building.

Toni and I never really had closure on what went down between us, which was mostly my fault. I had been purposely avoiding *that* discussion with her. It was my awkward way of trying to forget the past and act as if nothing had happened. We occasionally talked superficially over Facebook, email and had a nice game of phone tag running, but I knew before I left New York, I had to go a bit deeper with her, especially since it might be the last time we ever saw each other.

I stopped in front of Toni's brownstone before heading up the short staircase to her front door. I didn't bother with calling first. That would only make the anticipation of me coming over that much worse.

I rang the doorbell and waited until I saw Toni through the glass as she headed for the front door. The moment she realized it was me, her pace slowed and a skeptical smile ran across her face. I was so damn nervous, I could feel my heart beating in my throat. I swallowed, wishing I had brought a bottle of water for the trip.

"Well, hello, stranger," Toni said, swinging the right side of her red-stained double wooden door open. I always loved Toni's building, right down to her beautiful arched entryway. She had told me that she always painted her front doors red, saying it was a symbol of prosperity.

"Hey," I said as our eyes connected. "How are you?"

Toni's head began to nod up and down before a single word left her mouth. "I am well. This is a surprise."

"Yeah, I'm sorry I didn't call first, but—"

Toni waved her hand in the air, as if dismissing my apologies. "Oh, no worries. How are you?"

"I'm hanging in there," I said

"How is the little man?"

"I'm assuming you're speaking of my son, and not my husband," I said, hoping to break the ice a bit.

"You would be correct," Toni said with a broad smile.

"He is wonderful and busy. I hope I'm not interrupting."

"I'm grading papers, but it's okay. I am always looking for an excuse to take a break." Toni took a step back and gestured for me to come in. "Please, come in, come in."

I accepted Toni's invitation and entered her foyer, closing the door behind me. I followed Toni into the kitchen, and took a quick survey of my old place—somewhere where I had found solitude and safety not that long ago as a scared and pregnant single mom-to-be. Toni headed toward the fridge and opened it. I noticed that her kitchen had changed.

"Did you remodel?"

"I sure did. It was time and I didn't want to put it off any longer. I wanted to do it before I rented out the place again."

"It looks really nice," I said, making small talk, which calmed me a bit.

"Have a seat woman. Can I offer you something to drink? Toni asked as she looked inside her fridge. "Actually, I should have looked before I offered. Unfortunately, I just have beer and room temperature water down here. I could run upstairs and get something else?"

"Oh, actually, water would be fine."

"Water it is." Toni closed the fridge, walked through an open passage to her laundry room and came back with two bottles of water. She handed one to me and opened the other one for herself. Then she took a seat across from me at her small bar high table.

"So, how is work?"

"Busy. We are entering mid-terms, so it can get a bit hectic, but I am hanging in there." Toni smiled and I could see her brain turning over why I might've shown up on her porch without so much as a phone call after five months.

"Well, at least you're staying busy."

"I am."

Toni and I shared a moment of awkward silence. This was harder than I thought. I had to just throw it out there before it killed me.

"So, you're probably wondering what I'm doing here."

"A little bit, but I'm sure you will fill me in," Toni said as she took a quick swig from her water bottle.

"You sure you don't want a beer?"

"No, no, thank you."

"You sure? I have plenty."

"If you don't let me get this out I'm going to lose my nerve and flee out of here just as fast as I did five months ago."

Toni was silent and nodded for me to go on. I forgot that when she got nervous over-the-top courtesy was her go-to defense mechanism.

"Thank you. So I um, listen, I um..." This was harder than when I rehearsed. I took a sip of my water and as it ran down my throat I felt my body temperature drop a few degrees. That seemed to help with the intensity I felt building up.

"I just wanted to talk to you about what happened with us. How we ended so abruptly and what kinda altered our friendship."

"Kinda." Toni repeated my selected choice of word with a raise of an eyebrow.

"Okay, strike the kinda."

"Noted." Toni continued to nod.

I shifted uncomfortably in my seat, took two more sips of my water, and gathered my thoughts.

"I guess what I am really saying is that I am sorry I brought you into my mess of a life. Here I was, a pregnant woman, jilted by her boyfriend, alone in a new city, trying to piece my crazy life back together. I should have never involved you or gotten involved with you. It's just I was—"

"Lost, confused, reaching, needy, and a little desperate."

"That...wow, that sounds about right," I said, but thinking, *Okay, Toni, don't hold back, tell me how you really feel.* I continued, "But mostly I was selfish. My motives were selfish and I am so very sorry."

Toni and I stared at each other intensely.   She looked down, then back up at me with a slight smile.

"Listen, stop beating yourself up, I am a grown-ass woman and if you haven't forgotten, it takes two to tangle."

I nodded my head. Even though she had a point, it didn't make me feel any better.

"Kai, I knew exactly what I was getting into and even though all my friends told me to avoid you like the plague, I um, I just couldn't. My intentions were never to...to actually fall for you, but we are all human and well, it happened, ya know? But in the end, I was fine. Do I miss you? Of course, I have to admit, I miss our friendship mostly, but, it is what it is and I will survive."

"I don't know what to say."

"Say you are human and as humans we all make mistakes."

"Can you ever forgive me?"

"Already have."

I stood up to walk over to Toni and hug her. "Thank you."

Toni pulled away, looked me deep in my eyes. "I do appreciate you coming here today and telling me all this. My only question is 'What the heck took you so long, woman'?"

We both laughed. "I was scared, thinking the awkwardness would pass...not to mention my procrastination flaw."

"You thought my feelings would just dissipate into thin air?"

"That was the hope." I smiled at Toni. "I have one other thing to tell you."

"Oh lawd, before you say anything I just have to say, 'It ain't mine'." Toni stepped back as she threw both of her hands up in the air.

We laughed. It felt good.

"Now that's funny. No, it's not that. Todd and I are moving to California."

"Shut yo' mouth. What for? You just settled in here."

"Yeah, but he had to close down his law firm and it's been hard and well, we really had no choice."

"Wow, sunny California. Well, hopefully, **Tony! Toni! Toné**! was right when they said it never rains in Southern California."

"That would be great. I just hope I like it. I'm getting too old to try and make new friends."

"Oh, woman, you will be fine. You actually look a bit like a California girl. With your size-six figure and bleach-blond curly hair, you will fit right in."

When Toni referenced my hair, I insecurely ran my fingers through the overprocessed and dyed strands of hair. "Yeah, that's what you get when you do your own color. Definitely not a professional."

"Oh, please, it looks great. I'm the one who needs to do something with this cocoon up here." Toni rustled through her dread locks that were twisted into a bun on the top of her head.

I heard Toni's front door open then close.

"Hey, babe, you home?" a female voice called from the front of the house.

"In here," Toni answered.

A very attractive woman with dark-mocha skin and a short Halle Berry cut walked into the kitchen and over to Toni. The woman planted a gentle kiss on Toni's lips, turned and directed her attention to me.

"Kai, I want you to meet my fiancé, Jessica, Jessica McCoy."

"Wow, you're...you're engaged?"

Toni looked at Jessica. "Yep, we are."

"Congratulations!" I said to Toni, truly meaning it. "I couldn't be happier for you!" I then directed my attention over to Jessica and extended my hand toward her. "Congratulations to you as well, Jessica, and great to meet you by the way." I smiled, but I was still feeling a bit weird about the whole awkward situation.

"Nice to meet you, Kai. I've heard a lot about you."

"Oh, is that so?" I asked. Though, I wondered privately why Toni would talk about a lover of hers from the past. "I hope it was all good," I said and glanced Toni's way, wondering what exactly she told her new fiancé about me.

"Toni had nothing but great things to say about you, especially how you were such a great tenant."

I smile as Jessica walked over to the fridge and grabbed a beer. She opened it and turned. "You had a baby, right?"

"I did, he is two years old now. What about you guys, any children in the near future?"

"Ha, well, maybe in the distant future. I am just settling back into New York," Jessica said as she gave me the once-over.

"Oh, where did you move from?" I inquired.

"Well, I am originally from New York. I lived in Chicago for the last three years."

"Really? That's where I'm from," I said.

"Yeah, Toni mentioned that."

"Why did you leave Chicago?" I asked.

Jessica shrugged her shoulders a bit, made a noncommittal facial gesture. "It just wasn't working out for me. Besides, New York is where I belong, right, baby?" Jessica leaned over and planted another kiss on Toni's lips.

Knowing Toni had someone made my closure with her all the more easier.

"Kai is actually moving to LA with her husband," Toni interjected.

"Very nice," Jessica said as she sipped on her beer.

"Yeah, my husband got a pretty good job offer, so we decided to take that leap of faith and go."

"What does your husband do?" Jessica asked.

"He's a lawyer. He had a small practice in Chicago before he moved here and opened up one here, although the economy hit us pretty hard, so..." My voice trailed off. I caught myself before I gave away too much information to the virtual stranger in front of me.

"Yeah, that happens. I am a lawyer myself."

"Oh, is that right?" I asked and started to feel like a bit of a third wheel. I stood, looking for a diplomatic transition to leave. "I better get back home. I left Todd to pack the kitchen up and that could be a disaster in itself."

"Your husband's name is Todd?" Jessica asked suddenly. She was about to take a sip of her beer, but had lowered it when she heard my Todd's name.

"Yes, do you know him?"

Jessica looked as if she had seen a ghost, which made me wonder what she knew.

"Ah, no, well, maybe, actually, seeing he's a lawyer, and I'm a lawyer, I was just thinking our paths might've crossed while I was living in Chicago, that's all." Jessica's eyes started darting around the room like a balloon with the air let out of it. *Where the hell did all that come from?* I wondered. I stared at Jessica and could tell she was processing something in her head. What that something was, I had no damn clue.

"Excuse me, I'm gonna go do a little work. It was nice meeting you, Kai," Jessica said abruptly as she exited out the kitchen.

"Yeah, you, too." I directed my attention back to Toni. "Is she okay?"

Toni waved Jessica's weird behavior off. "Oh she is fine, child."

Toni took a few steps closer to me. "Don't be a stranger, okay?"

"Of course not. And if you're ever in LA, please reach out to me."

"I will! Jessica's sister actually lives in LA, so maybe we can try to connect if we ever go out to visit."

"That sounds good."

Toni and I held a stare before we embraced, giving each other a nice long final hug. I am going to miss those hugs."

"Okay, I better go," I said before pulling away.

"Right," Toni said as she wiped away a tear.

"Take care, Toni."

"You do the same."

I turned and walked out of her home, out of her life. As I walked the three blocks back to my brownstone, I couldn't get Jessica's expression out of my head when she heard Todd's name. Something was up with that, and I was determined to find out.

SEVEN
ALANA

As I sat in the small café on Robertson Boulevard, awaiting Emanuel's call, I couldn't keep myself focused. I was anxious to know if I had gotten the part. My last audition with the network executive and showrunner had gone exceptionally well in my opinion, and I was feeling relatively good. Everything was starting to fall into place, despite my rocky start. But as I always say, it's not how you start, it's how you finish and I planned to finish strong.

I was pleasantly surprised at how attractive the showrunner was. In fact, he sort of reminded me of Taye Diggs, but about a foot taller with a leaner build. The moment I walked into the room he greeted me with that *how-you-doing* smile. His dark skin and impossibly straight teeth sent a pleasant chill dancing through my body. We definitely had a connection, or at least it felt that way with the way his eyes traveled up and down the length of my body. Yes, I was feeling good about how this was going to turn out.

I pulled out my iPad and jumped on Facebook, trying to see if Todd updated his page with any new information about his life, but there was nothing. Men are so damn vague and apparently that was just as true online. I clicked on his albums and saw a picture of them—Todd, Kai, and that damn baby who made three. I rolled my eyes with every picture that flashed before me. Kai may have thought it was over, but it was far from that.

I thought back to how I should have been more careful with Riley's paternity test, and kept the original out of the house, far from Todd's prying eyes. I shook my head, and reminded myself not to dwell in the past, and instead look ahead to my future—one with Todd in it. I closed Todd's page, enough drudging up what would not be.

I turned my attention to my profile page and saw that I had a message waiting for me. I clicked on the icon to see a message from Jessica McCoy, titled, *I miss you*. I shook my head. *Really? That bitch will not quit.* You would have thought my pussy was dipped in 24-karat gold the way her ass was stalking me. I contemplated just erasing her message, but what the hell, I had time to spare, not to mention, I was in the mood to be amused.

The way I ended it with Jessica was in my typical Alana style. Diss them before getting dissed, that was how I rolled, preferably when the relationship was on the upswing. Keeps them guessing, longing and wondering what the hell happened. I had to admit, THAT was another reason I wasn't done with Todd. Other than the fact he and I were meant to be together, I wouldn't let him get away with dissing me. The relationship ends when Alana says it ends.

I diverted my eyes back to Jessica's email and clicked it open to read.

Hey, babe, how are you? Long time no hear. I tried reaching out to you a few times, but to no avail. Are you still in Chicago? You still doing your acting thing? I just wanted to let you know that I moved back to New York, but I will be in Chicago for business from time to time. I would love to see your face and catch up. Maybe we could meet for a drink or dinner...or more. ~smile.

Seriously, if my eyes could have rolled any further they would have tumbled out of the back of my head. Jessica McCoy had to be the most annoying woman on the planet, but I doubted she was aware of that. I really should've introduced her to Maceo. Now that would have been an interesting pair. I diverted my eyes back to Jessica's email.

...Anyway beautiful, if you get a chance in your busy and oh so fabulous schedule hit me up on Facebook or better yet, call me, my number is still the same. I miss you.

Xo Jessica.

I closed her message and out of Facebook while sipping my chai latte. I wondered when Emanuel was going to call me about this part. My eyes wandered around the small cafe, and watched the other patrons busy at work on their laptops. I idly wondered what their story was. Los Angeles was pretty fascinating to me. It seemed like everyone was striving for something better, bigger, deferring their life for that big break.

My phone finally rang, and I glanced down to see it was Emanuel calling. I answered it on the first ring.

"Well?" I said, skipping over the unnecessary small talk.

Emanuel was quiet, too quiet.

"Emanuel, are you there?

"Alana, I am so sorry, but you didn't get the part."

My heart sunk to my damn knees. "What? Tell me you're kidding?"

"I wish I was." I heard Emanuel sigh on the other end. Clearly, he was just as disappointed as I was. "They decided to go in another direction."

"Another direction, what the hell does that mean?" I asked as the other patrons in the coffee shop began to stare my way.

"They chose someone else."

"Who?" I said with much aggravation in my voice. Who could they have possibly gone with that was more fabulous and fly than me, Alana Brooks."

"I didn't get that information."

"What do you mean you *didn't* get the information? Did you fucking *ask* for that information?" I felt my blood pressure rise with every word that shot out of my mouth. I rarely raised my voice with Emanuel, but shit, I was pissed. How could they have not given that part to me? I nailed my auditions, not to mention all the flirting going back and forth between me and the showrunner. I was a damn shoo-in.

"Well, get it," I commanded my agent and friend.

"Alana, what does it matter? It's not going to change their decision."

I wanted to tell Emanuel that it was not me, but my ego demanding this information and my ego always wins—always.

"Besides, I bet she isn't as fabulous as you. Honey, Hollywood is all about the politics and…" He sighed. "We just didn't have enough insider votes."

I slumped back into my chair. "Shit. I am tripping. You're right, Hollywood is a big political potluck. They made their decision," I said, my voice trailing in a small whisper.

Then I thought maybe this was a sign that I really should be in New York, closer to Todd. Yes, getting this part would have been a nice boost to my career, but in reality if I wanted to get Todd back I needed to be in close proximity to where he was, and that was New York. I sat back up from the spark of epiphany I was having.

I took a very deep breath. "You know what? Forget it. Who gives a shit who got the damn part?" I said pulling myself together even more. "Let's re-focus here." Of course I didn't dare vocalize to Emanuel that Todd was the focal point of my new plan. He didn't have to know all the details.

"I am all ears, girlfriend," Emanuel said.

"Now that we gave LA a shot, let's re-direct our focus back to New York."

"New York, why am I not surprised?"

Clearly, he knew me better than I thought. "Emanuel, shut it, just hear me out."

"Fine, I am listening," Emanuel said, not bothering to hide the attitude.

"I can sell my condo in Chicago which will give me some money to live off of until you secure me a few gigs in New York."

"Hold on now, let's not rule out LA all together, I have a few more irons in the fire out there."

"Like what?"

"Like a guest-star role on the same show you just went in for, along with a few more shows. Girlfriend, black TV is coming back and they will not want to miss out on Alana Brooks," Emanuel sang on the other end of the phone. He really knew how to cheer a diva up.

"This is true, but if it's not meant for me to be in LA, well, it's just not meant to be," I said, trying my hardest to sound philosophical. Emanuel saw right through it.

"Nice try, Alana, but I know your motivation and it has four letters."

"Emanuel, I don't know what you are talking about."

"Child, if you don't give that a rest, it's gonna put you six feet under."

I didn't want to get into it again with Emanuel about Todd. He would never understand our connection. Frankly, no one ever would. I'm sure to the outside world looking in, I looked insane, but Alana is not crazy dammit, just determined. Ever since I was a child, I always mapped out my life to go exactly the way I wanted. If I hit a wall, I jumped over it. If there was a ditch, I manevoured around it. Nothing ever stopped me from reaching my goals and nothing ever would.

"Listen, I better head to the airport, so I won't miss my flight. I will call you when I touch down in Chicago."

"Yes, we will definitely finish this conversation later."

I hung up with Emanuel and took another deep breath. I caught a reflection of myself as I minimized my Google page and stared into the dark-blue background of my desktop that was creating a mirror image of me.

I looked at my butterscotch complexion and oval face looking back at me and wondered what Todd was doing right now, and if he ever thought about me, us and what we had. I knew Todd loved me, he was just conflicted right now. It was up to me to make him see how much we were made for each other.

I gathered my things, headed out of the small café on Robertson Boulevard and jumped in my car where my driver was waiting to take me to Los Angeles airport.

Yep, the fact that I didn't get that part in LA was indeed a good thing.

EIGHT

KAI

The moment I found out we were moving to LA, I went online and found a rental service in the Los Angeles area to locate a nice home for us. Todd and I decided that renting a house would be the best move before investing in a property in LA. While it was great that Todd got such a great job here, we needed to make sure it was a permanent thing.

It didn't take long for the real estate agent in LA to find a few houses for us in an area called Ladera Heights along with a few houses in nearby neighborhoods like Baldwin Hills and View Park. Since the 1980s these neighborhoods had become a mecca for upper-class black families, so I figured they would be a good fit for us and our growing family.

After a few weeks of looking, we eventually settled on a 3-bedroom, 2-bathroom Spanish-style home in Ladera, a section known as Lower Ladera, just south of Slauson Avenue between LaCienega and Wooster Blvd.

It wasn't long before we moved into our new home, and discovered just how perfect it was for us. With hardwood floors, high-beam ceilings and an updated kitchen, I instantly fell in love when we moved in.

The best part about the home was the finished backyard, equipped with an outdoor fireplace, wet bar and built-in bed, something we utilized the first night we moved in. It was as if this house was built just for us. Todd's office was located in an area called Century City, which was only a fifteen-minute commute.

All in all everything was falling into place nicely.

"Babe, where's my tie?" Todd asked as he came out of the bathroom of our new home.

"Your tie should be in your wardrobe box in the back bedroom," I said, scanning the numerous boxes placed all over the entire home. I tried calculating the amount of time it would take us to get settled and make this house a home. Todd nodded his head as he headed back to retrieve his tie.

The movers had finally dropped off our remaining things, so it was great to finally have everything in one place. Now the real work of unpacking would begin. My sister, Mila, was bringing Kristopher to us in a few days, so we needed to at least get halfway settled before we had a toddler roaming around the place —not mention, my judgmental sister.

"Did you find it?" I yelled to the back, making sure Todd didn't need any assistance.

"Yup," Todd said as he walked into the kitchen as I started to unpack the dishes.

"What time is your meet and greet with your boss?"

"Two thirty."

I looked at the clock that displayed 11:45. "Why are you leaving so early?"

"You know me, I want to make sure I have enough time to get there, park, acclimate myself to the area and not rush, maybe even grab a quick bite to eat."

I smile at my anal retentive lawyer of a husband. "I think you will be fine."

I could tell Todd was a little nervous. After having your own practice for so many years, having to jump back into the rat race would make anyone a nervous wreck. I put down the tea kettle I had just unpacked and walked over to Todd.

He was fiddling with his tie, making it worse than what it was.

I undid it and then started to tie his yellow tie with small blue diamonds. He quickly surrendered, and dropped his arms down to his sides as I tried to create the perfect knot. We were both silent as I did my thing to make my husband look pristine in his blue pin-stripped suit and crisp white shirt.

Despite the welcomed distraction, I couldn't get the way that Jessica woman had inquired about Todd the last time I was at Toni's house off my mind. I wish I could, but I couldn't. Did Todd know her in Chicago when he was with Alana?

Did he mess around with her? Perhaps they met through a mutual attorney friend. My senses were going haywire and the next thing I knew, I was putting my thoughts into words.

"Baby, who is Jessica?" I said as I continued working on his tie.

"Who?"

"Jessica McCoy?"

Todd looked at me with a perplexed look on his face and the right side of his mouth curled up. "I have no clue, honey, why?"

Why? Why? Of course he would ask why, but I didn't think that far, nope, I had run through a thousand different ways he might respond to my question about Jessica, but none of them anticipated him questioning *why*. At the moment I realized if I told Todd how I met her, it might incriminate me, since I didn't tell him that I went to see Toni before we left Brooklyn.

I had to think fast. "Oh, just some woman I met at the market near our old house. She said she was a lawyer from Chicago, so I assumed you knew her."

"Baby, all lawyers don't know each other."

I smiled a smile of relief. "Right." Then finished up Todd's tie. "There, now you are good to go."

Todd reached up to feel his tightly tied knot. "What would I do without you?" Todd smiled at me.

"I don't know, but let's not find out, shall we?" I smiled, putting the last touches on his outfit by lowering his collar. I leaned in and kissed him on the lips.

"I love you and you are going to do just fine. You are an amazing lawyer and they are damn lucky to have you."

"Hopefully, they'll share your sentiments."

"Seeing that they relocated us three-thousand miles here, I have a hunch they do."

Todd pulled me in close as he grabbed my ass, pulling my body against his. I felt his manhood rising.

"I'll take that," Todd said, moving his face close to mine. "Have I told you how much I love you and how happy I am that you're my wife?"

I smiled, inside and out, my emotions dancing on their toes. "I love you more."

We kissed deeply and I felt him rise a bit more. "When was the last time you were licked?"

I smiled. "Baby?"

"What? I have some extra time. Besides, you know you like it."

I always felt Todd isolated my liking for oral fixation, almost as if it was his own passive aggressive way of reminding me of my past with women. I knew he was fine with it now, but for some reason it always hit a nerve and made me feel guilty.

"Tell me you don't want it. We don't even have to get sweaty," Todd said as he started his decent down my body. He began by kissing every inch of my neck from side to side. Todd pulled back, licked his lips and pulled my tank top over my head, revealing my bare erect nipples. Todd shook his head.

"I fucking love your breasts." Todd took my right breast in his mouth, circling my nipple with his tongue, before devouring it with his entire mouth and quickly moved over to the next.

My knees weakened as my wetness began to flow down. I let out a satisfied moan to let Todd know he should keep doing exactly what he was doing. Todd continued to devour my breasts as he expertly slipped off my sweatpants and panties. I stepped out of them and pushed them aside with my foot. I felt a chilled sensation shoot through my naked body as Todd picked me up and placed my bare ass on the ivory quartz countertop.

I let out a soft squeal from the cold shock of the stone. It wasn't long before Todd was slowly licking my inner thighs, quickly replacing that chill with a rush of heat.

Todd steadily made his way to my happy place, kissing my clit then slowly running his tongue around my lips before sliding his tongue in and out of my love box, making me feel like I was losing all my composure. Every inch of me began to twitch uncontrollably as if someone was administering small electrical shocks to my helpless body. Todd was definitely down there on a mission.

I shifted my hips left, then right, then back, then forth, trying to hold on to the overwhelming feeling of ecstasy my husband was giving me in this moment. I closed my eyes, as my head fell back, rocking side to side against our chocolate shaker-style cabinets.

"Oh, baby," I moaned as I placed my hands on his head, raking my fingers through his scalp.

I felt an orgasm rushing to my head as his soft tongue continued to massage my clit and every inch surrounding it. Todd stopped, looked up smiling, "You like?"

"Yes, baby, I like, don't stop!" I said, guiding his head back down.

I felt my body temperature rise and I couldn't help but giggle as I thought of how the coolness from the stone countertop felt refreshing against my bare bottom.

Todd continued to pleasure me with his tongue as it rhythmically moved in and out of my love box, then back up to my clit, circling and sucking with much purpose. I felt my orgasm coming and this time I could not stop it from crashing in.

"I'm gonna cum, baby, I'm going to cum. Oh my God, baby, I'm..." My body tensed with intensity before collapsing from the wave of sensation that engulfed my being. Todd continued to tease my clit as my body was now fighting off his last touches. I finally moved his head from my legs.

Todd stood, smiled as we kissed. He pulled away as I wiped my juices from his mouth. "You better go wash your face," I said with a smile.

"Yeah, good idea." Todd gave me a light smack on my ass, then turned and walked out the kitchen. I sat there on the counter unable to move as I worked to catch the breath he had stolen.

Todd always went the extra mile when it came to eating my pussy. I guess he felt he had to compete with my past female lovers and he was not to be outdone. I had to applaud him for that and the fact that he was definitely a champion when it came to that department. I had to admit after his knowledge of my affair with Alana and Toni, he really upped his game, and I couldn't have been happier.

***

After Todd left to meet with his boss, I had some time to myself. I knew I couldn't relax too much since I had a laundry list of things I had to get done before Mila arrived with Kristopher in a few days. One of the most important was finding a good pre-school. I was lucky to have a parent from Kris' old pre-school in Brooklyn recommend Tender Hands when she found out we were looking for a home in the Ladera Heights area, so that would be my first stop for the day.

I jumped into the shower, threw on a pair of jeans, flip flops and a pink ribbed tank top. I loved that it was fall in LA and that I was able to get away with wearing flip flops and a tank top.

My mind was racing a mile a minute, trying to figure out how I was going to get everything done. Despite Todd's assurances he didn't know Jessica. The idea they might still know each other lingered in the back of my mind. I pulled up Toni's profile and clicked into her photo albums. There she was, Jessica McCoy. She looked a little different in the pictures than how I remembered her. She was a little thicker, not as attractive, clearly she wasn't very photogenic.

I clicked on Jessica's picture and was even tempted to add her as a friend, but I didn't want to rock any boats. So, I did what any wife would do when they needed more information, I logged onto Todd's Facebook account. My heart jumped into my throat when I saw Jessica had sent Todd a friend request. *Who is this woman to him and why was she requesting him on Facebook? Should I accept for him? Although if I do, then Todd would know I was on his account.* I shook my head. Maybe I was thinking too hard about this. I mean they were both lawyers after all. I took a deep breath, logged out of Todd's account, and shut down my laptop. I closed my eyes to get a few minutes of reprieve, focused on my breathing and tried to calm myself. I opened my eyes. It was time to get my day started and stop obsessing over this Jessica chick. Whatever her possible relationship was with my husband, it wouldn't help me get the extensive list of things I needed to accomplish done. I need to put her on the back burner of my mind and move on. I placed my laptop on my ottoman, grabbed my super to-do list and the keys to our Toyota Highlander and hit the road.

***

I pulled up to the pre-school around 2:30 p.m. and noticed a few parents heading in to pick up their children. I loved that the school was only three blocks away from my house, a stone's throw as I like to say. In my mind, I had already convinced myself that Tender Hands was the perfect pre-school for Kristopher.

I parked my truck and jumped out to hear a female voice behind me say, "You do not want to park there." I turned to see a woman walking my way with a beautiful smile.

"Excuse me?" I asked cordially.

"The owner of that business is kind of an ass and hates it when parents park directly in front of his store. He's towed more than a few parents."

"Oh, that sucks."

"Tell me about it, one of those parents was me," the woman said, smiling as she continued to approach me.

"Sorry to hear that, but thanks for the heads-up."

"No problem. I'm Camille Spaulding," she said as she put out her hand.

"I'm Kai Edwards, I mean, Daniels."

A sincere smile stretched accross Camille's face. "Newlywed I take it?"

"Yeah, I'm still getting used to my new name." I smiled back and looked down at her left hand. I noticed she wasn't wearing a wedding ring. Then again, this was LA and people did things differently here. Though, normally, it was the married men who forgot to put their ring on when they headed out the door. Most married women loved to rock their rings and show them off to their girlfriends.

"Are you headed into the pre-school?" Camille inquired

"Yes, do you send your kids here?"

"Yes, and kid, singular, that's all I need right now."

"Oh, I understand, I have just one myself, a boy, he's two."

"I have a girl and she is four, going on forty." Camille flashed her million-dollar smile at me again. I couldn't help but notice how stunning she was, almost model-like.

Her long lean body was at least 5'10" with her light-cashew complexion and her curly, dark-brown, silky hair. I thought I looked like a Cali girl, Camille could be a poster child for this state."

"How do you like it here?" Suddenly, I wasn't feeling as attractive as I did before laying eyes on her.

"Oh, I couldn't be happier. My daughter has been here since she was two, so this is her last year, but I have been very pleased with everything, from the teachers and the curriculum to the parents."

As Camille continued to talk, I realized she looked familiar to me, as if I had seen her somewhere before. Perhaps she was an actress and I had seen her on a commercial, she definitely had the look.

"That's good to hear, my husband and I just moved here from New York, by way of Chicago."

"Oh? I am originally from New York!"

"What part?" I inquired.

"Spanish Harlem," Camille said.

"We actually lived in Brooklyn for a little over two years, then Todd, my husband, got a great job out here, so here we are."

"No way! I have family in Brooklyn. Great place and great schools there, too."

"Yes, something I will miss."

"Tender Hands is a great place. I think your son will love it here."

"I definitely hope so."

We shared a moment before I broke the silence. "I better head inside and talk to the director. It was very nice meeting you, Camille."

"Same here, Kai...Daniels." We both got a chuckle from Camille's call back to me forgetting my new last name.

"Right, I better keep practicing that," I replied. I waved at her and turned to head into the school.

***

After about forty-five minutes and a stack of registration papers later, I felt good about sending Kris to Tender Hands pre-school, especially after meeting Camille and hearing what she had to say. It was always great to get an endorsement from an active parent at the school. Camille and I exchanged numbers when we realized we lived down the street from each other. Though that wasn't a huge surprise, since most of the families at the school lived in the neighborhood.

But most of all, it was nice to make my first friend.

I still had a few things to take care of and there never seemed to be enough time. I headed up Slauson Avenue to Lacienega and down to the Fox Hills Mall. I needed to swing by Target and pick up a ton of things for the house. I was almost there when I found myself sitting at a red light, daydreaming about my life with Todd, thinking of all the great things we could do now, now that Alana was gone for good.

A broad smile trickled across my face when I realized that Alana had no idea where we even were. She probably still thought we were in Brooklyn—the same place she broke in to.

I shook my head. *Stupid bitch! Who breaks into someone's house and then thinks he will take you back?* That was an invitation for jail, which I was pleased to see she got.

Alana may have been beautiful, but no one would accuse her of being the sharpest tool in the shed.

The light turned green and before I could pull away I turned to look inside the car next to me. I got a glance of the woman sitting in the backseat of a black towncar. My stomach churned and I felt instantly nauseated. I could've sworn sitting in the backseat was Alana. I sat there for a minute, dazed and confused as the town car next to me pulls off. The person behind me blew their horn, snapping me out of my trance.

I headed home, thinking how much that woman looked like Alana, but how could it be? She was probably still in Chicago, and besides, why would she be in LA?

I pulled up to the mall, told myself to stop tripping. I still had a million things to do and very little time to get them all done.

NINE

ALANA

Twenty minutes later I was at Los Angeles Airport. I saw Emanuel's name flash across my screen. I quickly picked up his call.

"Talk to me," I said, jumping out of my town car in front of the Delta departure terminal.

"Okay, I managed to get you an audition for an up-and-coming George Tillman film shooting next month in New York, starring Anthony Mackey and Jennifer Hudson."

"Hmm, alright. What's the pay?"

"They are offering five-thousand dollars."

I was walking into the airport when I stopped in my tracks. "Emanuel five-thousand dollars will pay my bills for a month. You have to do better than that. I can't go back to living with my mother."

"Child, just hold onto your Prada purse. Okay, I called in a favor and even though you don't have any credits, the producers liked your look and they're willing to meet with you for a guest spot on that new soap, *The Westons*."

"A guest spot? That's just one day, maybe two."

"It is, but that one or two days could give you great exposure and lead to an extended role. Sometimes you have to crawl before you walk."

The problem was Emanuel had failed to realize my crawling days were over. My head was starting to pound. I couldn't believe my life was taking a turn like this. I had to get back on top of my game. Maybe me not getting the part in LA was a sign, but things needed to start looking up fast.

"Fine, just do what you have to do. Just get me some more auditions, something."

"I'm working on it, girlfriend. You could always go back to print," Emanuel quickly pointed out.

I hated when Emanuel said that. To me, going back to print work was like taking a step backward. But a girl's gotta do what a girl's gotta do.

"I take it you have some print work for me?"

"That I do, honey child. Just say the word and they are ready to point and shoot you."

"Whatever."

"Hey, it's not the end of the world, and it is a paycheck."

I hung up with Emanuel and jumped on my 11:30 p.m. flight headed back to Chicago. Emanuel was right, print was not the end of the world. Not to mention it would keep my shopping habit fed, something I needed to keep up, seeing that looking good for Todd was a priority.

Two hours into my flight, my jackass of a parole officer came to mind. His willingness to screw me over—in more ways than one—got on my damn nerves. I'm sure I would have to deal with him when I got back to Chicago. Alana always came prepared for battle.

My flight touched down at 6:30 a.m. I headed down the terminal and through the baggage claim to pick up my Louis Vutton three-piece luggage set when I noticed flashing blue and red lights outside the glass windows of Delta's Terminal 7. I wondered who Chicago's finest was here to arrest. I headed out the sliding glass doors to get a better view. I always liked to see a little live drama and not just the kind associated with reality television.

I headed to the curb to look for my driver when I was startled to see that Chicago's finest were here for me.

"Alana Brooks, you are under arrest for violation of your parole, leaving the state of Illinois."

This was not my fucking day.

A police officer threw handcuffs on me. I saw Randy, aka Sasquatch, step out of his 1993 green Ford Taurus equipped with brown rust stains, no hub caps and white dice hanging from the mirror. Yeah, this guy was a real class act.

"Hello, sweetheart. Welcome back to Chicago."

"It just got a lot less attractive at the sight of you."

A devilish smile leaped across Randy's face. "I sure am gonna have fun throwing your pretty little ass back in jail." He then turned to the officer standing behind me. "Take the parolee downtown."

It didn't take long before I was booked, fingerprinted and placed in a holding cell. This was not the homecoming I had expected. I was given my phone call, and I called the only lawyer I knew that could handle this type of case, Maceo Smith, Todd's old law partner.

I have to admit, Maceo and I were a lot alike in that we both did what we had to do to get the job done. Plus, there was the fact that we slept together the night Todd found out about the paternity test. I indeed was at my lowest. A perk for Maceo, no less.

I liked to try and forget about that night, but Maceo always held onto it tight, thinking he might be able to come back for seconds, but that wasn't gonna happen.

I gave Maceo an earful with my one call and he was down at my holding cell in thirty minutes flat.

In less than one hour Maceo had rallied up Sasquatch, his boss, Phillip Hernandez and the head of police, Sergeant Alphonso Wilson. By the time everyone showed up, it was 10:00 a.m. and I was tapping on exhaustion's door. I had to hold on though, things were just about to get good.

"I don't understand why we are even here?" Randy said, as he sat across the table from me. "My parolee took an unauthorized trip to Los Angeles which was in violation of her parole. Now she's going back to prison, end of case."

"I understand the actions of my client, although there are a few things that need to be cleared up first," Maceo interjected.

"And what would that be?" Mr. Hernandez, Randy's boss asked.

"My client claims that your employee made a sexual pass at her in exchange for immunity."

"Bullshit." Randy jumped up out of his chair as if he had a spring in his ass. "Your client is a whore and a liar."

"It would be in your best interest to keep the name-calling out of this room," Maceo shot back in a firm tone. I loved Maceo. He was definitely a man-whore, but he could handle the best of them.

"Are you denying these allegations Mr. Farrow?"

"You damn right I am. I specifically told my parolee that under no circumstances could she leave the state of Illinois, end of story."

Randy's boss, as well as the head of the police department, remained silent. I looked at Maceo and gave him a nod. He pulled out my cell phone, opened up my recorder and hit play. Then Maceo leaned back in his chair and folded his arms across his chest.

Voices from the recorder filled the room.

"So you're saying I can't go to LA, Randy?"

"Unless there is a Los Angeles, Illinois your ass is staying right here, darling."

"Randy, my career depends on this, I am sure you can understand why it is so important that I go."

"...And I'm sure you can understand that I will throw your ass back into the clinker if you do."

"So there is no way we can "bend" the rules a bit? This is my career we are talking about, I am sure you can make a small exception for me."

There was a pause and we could hear a faint rustle on the recorder.

"This is ridiculous," Randy interjected. "What the hell is this?"

"Oh, I think you know exactly what this is," Maceo said, reaching for the recorder to turn it off. It was his way of making sure nothing was missed from Randy's outburst.

Maceo looked at the other two parties in the room, Mr. Hernandez and Chief Wilson. "May we continue?"

They both slowly nodded.

Maceo hit play and once again voices from my recorder filled the room.

"Actually, Miss Brooks, maybe there is. Maybe we can do a little bartering."

"A man's got needs, ya know..."

Pause. I looked over at Randy who was turning three shades of red.

"No, I don't know, Randy."

"Miss Brooks, we are both consenting adults here, right? You need something and well…so do I."

Randy's neck now matched his face.

"And what is it that you need, Randy?"

"I need those juicy blacks lips around my throbbing dick, that's all and you will be free to go to LA or wherever the hell your heart desires."

Randy was so enraged he couldn't speak. His nostrils were flaring out of control as his chest heaved up and down. He looked like a time bomb ticking down from ten. When it finally hit zero, Randy sprung up from his seat, slapping the table with his meaty right hand. "This is bullshit."

Maceo turned off the recorder. "I could think of another word for this."

"I think we've heard enough," the chief of police interjected.

Silence blanketed the cramped room with stained-covered walls and metal chairs.

"What do you want?" Randy's boss, Mr. Hernandez, finally broke his silence. The chief of police stayed silent, only shaking his head in disbelief.

"I'm glad you asked," Maceo said as he sat up and folded his well-manicured hands in front of him. "First, I want Mr. Farrow fired, a written apology from him and the restrictions of Alana leaving the state of Illinois lifted."

I jabbed Maceo in the arm. He continued, "Also, we are going to need Alana's two-hundred hours of community service to disappear and her record expunged."

I finally let a smile spread across my face.

Mr. Hernandez just stared at Maceo, then over at Randy who was seething from every possible opening of his body.

"Done."

"You are damn lucky I don't sue your ass for damages and emotional abuse," I said to Sasquatch as he and I locked eyes. I even shot him a quick wink.

Randy lunged for me across the table. I leapt up as the table flew over and the chairs scattered everywhere. Maceo jumped in front of me protectively as three police officers bust into the room to detain Randy.

"You fucking bitch," Randy snarled at me. Saliva spewing from his mouth.

"Yeah, I think you're the one who's the bitch now," I said, peeking out from behind Maceo. My human shield.

"That's enough, Ms. Brooks. Take his ass away," the chief of police said, following the officers and Randy out of the room.

"So, do we have a deal?" Maceo asked Mr. Hernandez.

"We have a deal," he said through gritted teeth. He stood stiffly and left the room without saying another word, closing the door behind him.

Maceo shook his head. "Damn. Alana strikes again," Maceo said, gathering his scattered papers from the floor.

"Hey, a girl's gotta do what a girl's gotta do. You came with a little heat yourself. I knew you wouldn't disappoint me."

"Maceo doesn't disappoint, that's my motto." Maceo shot me a look. "So how long have you been out?"

"A few weeks," I said.

Maceo looked me up and down. "I'm glad you haven't forgotten about me. I was excited when I got your call."

Ugh. I knew I couldn't get out the door without Maceo trying to plant his damn seed.

As much as he annoyed the living shit out of me, he looked good in his tan suit, ice-blue tie and crisp white shirt. He was a decent-looking brother with his clean-shaven head and goatee, but he wasn't who I wanted to spend the rest of my life with. I had my eye on the main prize, Todd Daniels.

Maceo continued to dissect me with his eyes.

"What, Maceo?"

"We had fun that night, huh?" Maceo grinned as he ran his hand down his tie and across his dick.

"No, Tequila and Gin had fun that night. Unfortunately, we were only the victims of their consumptions."

Maceo let out a chuckle. "Cold, oh so cold, but so true. But hey, I ain't complaining, not one bit. So you wanna—"

"Save it, Maceo. I already paid you, so don't think a blow job comes as a tip."

Maceo let out a louder chuckle. "Damn, you're sexy as hell, you know that?"

"Yeah, we already agreed on that. Anyway, thank you for your services, but I gotta get going."

"So, I guess you're moving to LA now?"

"Not quite. I didn't land the part I flew there to audition for. I need to figure out my next move."

"Oh, is that why you were out there? I thought you went out there because you found out that Todd and Kai were living there now."

"What?"

"I have to be honest, I don't know what you see in him, he's a cool brother and all, but damn, he's kinda on the corny side," Maceo said, oblivious to my shock.

"Hold up, did you just say Todd *lives* in LA?"

"Damn, baby, you're losing your stalking skills. I guess jail time will do that to ya. Yeah, he and Kai moved there a few weeks ago. He got some job at an entertainment firm and..."

"Let me get this straight. *My* Todd lives in Los Angeles, California?"

Maceo laughed. "Well technically he's *Kai's* Todd now. Between me and you, the whole lying on the paternity test and breaking into Kai's apartment, that pretty much sealed the deal for him. Haven't you learned your lesson yet?"

"For the record, that's none of your business and you're not anyone who can pass judgment on anyone," I said, attempting to tune Maceo's ass out. I stood up and paced back and forth in the tiny room. "This changes the whole game, the whole entire game," I said to myself.

"Aww shit, better alert the authorities," Maceo joked. "What are you about to do now?"

"How about you don't worry about what *I'm* going to do, okay? Like I said, thank you for your services, but I'm out."

I turned, grabbed my jacket and headed for the door.

Maceo kept laughing. "Damn, so that's it? I mention Todd's name and you jump into action? How you just gonna leave me like this? Alana? Alana?"

I wanted to turn around and let Maceo know that groveling only amplified his loser-like qualities, but instead I ignored his pleas and headed for the door. I picked up my phone and dialed Emanuel's number with a quickness.

"Hey, Emanuel it's me, I need to be on the next flight back to LA and one more thing, I need the phone number and address for Kurt Lawson, the executive producer of the show I just auditioned for."

The moment I heard that Todd moved to LA, everything changed for me, everything. If I was going to set up residency in LA I needed a nice-paying job and I knew just the one I was going to get.

TEN

ALANA

It had been less than twelve hours since I found out about Todd moving to LA when I found myself standing in front of Radford Studios where Kurt Lawson had his private office. I was on a mission and there was absolutely nothing that was going to stop me…nothing.

"Alana, how did you get in here?" Kurt asked, looking up at me.

"Your assistant wasn't at her desk, so I took the liberty to let myself in," I said, sauntering his way. I took off my half-jacket, and revealed my assets for him to see. I was wearing my Calvin Klein form-fitted cotton white dress with extra cleavage, black 3-inch Jimmy Choo heels and no panties. Panties were so overrated.

Kurt's eyes scanned me up and down and I smiled as my outfit had its intended effect on the man. His mouth dropped open as he took in everything I was showing. It was obvious that Kurt and I had a definite connection, and now that I had his undivided attention I was sure I could change his mind about the part.

"I hope you don't mind me dropping by unannounced, but—"

Just then Kurt's assistant burst into the office out of breath.

"Oh my God, Mr. Lawson, I had no idea she was here, I am so sorry," his assistant said, shooting me a shitty look. I gave her a casual smile, but didn't move one muscle. It was apparent by the way Kurt was salivating that this intrusion by his assistant was the one that was unwelcomed.

"Don't worry about it, Sara, I'm sure this will only take a few minutes." Kurt gave his assistant a half-smile. "Close the door behind you."

Sara did what she was told as I gave her a finger-roll good-bye wave then directed my attention back to Kurt.

"Thank you for seeing me, Kurt."

"It wasn't like I was given much of a choice. So, tell me, what can I do for you...?" Kurt struggled to think of my name, and I was slightly disappointed, clearly our connection wasn't as valuable as I thought.

"Alana Brooks"

"Ah, you beat me to it." Kurt said, snapping his fingers. He looked me up and down once again as I watched him close the Apple Powerbook that was laying in his lap.

"No problem, you gotta be quick to keep up with me," I said, hoping that my joking manner would help make things more comfortable between us. I sat in the chair directly opposite from him and looked directly into his eyes, even as he kept staring at my body.

"Kurt, I don't mean to intrude on your work, but I got a disturbing call from my agent a few days ago and I just had to come here personally to see what I could do to right a wrong decision." I uncrossed and crossed my legs, revealing my complete lack of panties.

Like a dog salivating for a bone, Kurt's eyes ogled my uncovered jewelry box. I figured if Sharon Stone could get away with it, I sure as hell could. I watched Kurt's eyes as they stayed glued to my honeypot.

"Kurt?" I said, snapping him back to attention. As focused as he was on my goods, I wondered when the last time he had gotten laid.

"Yes, sorry." He shook himself back to reality. "Actually, Alana, it wasn't personal, we just thought that the other actress brought a little more spice to the part—not that you aren't spicy yourself, of course." Kurt smiled broadly while his eyes did another lap around the curves of my body. "At the end of the day, it was a unanimous decision.

"Right, unanimous, but I'm betting the final decision was yours," I said, licking my lips from the right side to the left.

Kurt took a deep breath. "It um, it may have been…sort of," Kurt added.

Now I was getting somewhere. I stood and made my way over to the couch where Kurt was sitting and sat next to him, leaving barely enough room between the two of us. Kurt didn't move and only smiled slightly at my sudden presence beside him. I placed my hand on his leg as Kurt moved his laptop off his lap and onto the desk.

"Do you do this a lot, Alana?"

"Do what, Kurt?"

"Come into executive producers' offices to seduce them to get what you want?

"Only the cute ones," I said, my hand sliding up his leg and only pausing when I let it get snuggly between his thighs.

Kurt adjusted in his seat, but didn't move away.

"I'm not one to beat around anyone's bush, Kurt." I slowly moved my hand closer to Kurt's penis that was already showing signs of life and steadily straining the material of his jeans.

"You're a businessman, and you can appreciate directness I'm sure," I said, continuing to massage Kurt's thighs. "So, I am just gonna come out and say it. I want that part and I am willing to do anything to get it." My hand continued to travel toward his belt buckle as I clumsily fiddled with its clasp.

Kurt adjusted himself again, pretending to move away, but really doing his best to aid me with this so-called seduction. It was clear that he was not about to stop me from doing what I had set out to do.

"That's nice to hear, but the part *is* taken."

"Perhaps you didn't understand me the first time," I said as I finished with his buckle and unzipped his pants. "I am willing to do anything to get it."

Kurt chuckled. "You think giving me a blow job will make me change my mind and get you the part?" He laughed even harder. "I hate to tell you this, Alana, but I have been in Hollywood a long time and blow jobs are like fist bumps, they are pretty common around these parts."

I inched closer to Kurt, slipped off my right shoe and began to rub my bare foot up and down his calves while simultaneously rubbing his nipple through his black T-shirt. "Well, I don't know if you've heard, but I'm not from around these parts."

I looked down to see Kurt's penis steadily pushing past its barrier that was once his zipper. I reached down and guided him out in the open. Kurt had a nice-sized penis. It wasn't too small or too big, just right.

I felt my mouth salivating with the idea of how I was going to make him squirm. and the fact that I could control a man with the movement of my tongue in compilation with a simple suction technique of my jaws. Yep, a technique I learned while in high school, only to master in college. As a grown-ass woman I had pretty much made it an art form.

"Goddamn, you are, oh my God, you are so *fucking* good," Kurt screamed between his grunts and moans. It had only been thirty seconds since my mouth had made contact with his yearning dick and it seemed as if Kurt was about to explode like a ten-year-old volcano. I felt his hand pushing my head to take in more and more of his throbbing penis as I licked, sucked and curled my tongue around every inch of him. I sat up as I continued to massage his nut sack and his shaft with my right hand.

"So, like I was saying, I really, really want that part, Kurt," I said as I continued to massage his nuts, then slid just the tip of my middle finger slowly in his ass. That was an erogenous place for most men, and by Kurt's reaction, the doorbell to heaven for him.

"Oh, God, okay, listen, it's not one-hundred percent my decision."

"Kurt, that's not what I want to hear." I squeezed his balls a bit more as my finger explored a bit deeper. I topped it off by running my tongue under the tip of his shaft as I sucked the tip of his penis with all my might. I called this my trio teaser.

"Well, it is my sole decision to stop right now." I slowly sat up, wiped the pre-cum from my mouth and motioned to gather my belonging for my exit.

"Fuck, okay, okay, listen, hold on, let me make a call."

I reached over with my free hand and retrieved his cell phone sitting next to him, slapping it in his right hand.

"Now?" Kurt looked at me in amazement. I looked up and withdrew his penis from my mouth to make the conversation go easier.

"No better time than the present as I like to say."

"How about I call after we are done here?"

I slowly shook my head from the right to the left as I relaxed my hand off his penis. Pulled my finger out his ass.

"Okay, okay, fine, shit." Kurt picked up his phone and dialed a number. The moment I heard confirmation of another voice on the other end I smiled and slid my mouth back down on his hard thick shaft.

ELEVEN

KAI

I needed to run over to Tender Hands in order to turn in the last of Kristopher's medical records for his admission. That's where I saw Camille heading out of the front door.

"Well, hello, fancy running into you here," Camille said as we met on the steps of the school. Camille had a cheerfulness about her that was infectious. She made me smile whenever I saw her.

"Hey yourself," I responded, a broad smile breaking out all over my face.

"Where is the little one? I'm dying to meet him," Camille said, looking on either side of me as if Kris were hiding behind me.

"He's still with my sister in Chicago. I'm just dropping off some paperwork before he starts."

"Nice, so what are you up to today?" Camille asked. She twirled her dark coffee- colored curls with her index finger. I couldn't get over how attractive this woman was, and I felt myself staring at her more than I should have. She was wearing green cargo pants and a white fitted T-shirt that hugged her body so close I could see every inch of her perfect figure. I wished I knew someone I could hook her up with, but being new to LA, I didn't know anyone who might've been interested.

"Today I'm doing a lot of nothing. Trying to get myself some me-time."

Camille smiled, and looked me up and down. I got the feeling she was taking me all in with one big swoop.

"That sounds nice. If you want to take a break from your 'me-time' we could meet me for lunch."

Lunch would be nice, I thought, also I could get to know Camille a little better. "Sure, where?"

"Have you been to Simply Wholesome on Slauson Avenue?"

"I haven't been anywhere but to Target, and Bed, Bath and Beyond," I said with a laugh.

"Of course, well, it's a Jamaican spot, and the food is amazing. They have the best jerk chicken patties around."

"That sounds good."

"How does noon sound?"

"Sounds like a plan."

"Great, then I will see you then. Call me if anything changes," Camille said.

"Of course."

We gave each other one last smile good-bye as we both headed in our intended destinations, me into the school and Camille to her car.

Camille was a sight for sore eyes. Todd wasn't the only one having a tough time adjusting to a new city. I was having a difficult time as well, though finding a new friend to talk to with Camille would make things a bit easier.

***

When I arrived at Simply Wholesome, Camille was already sitting at a table. We spotted each other and she waved me over to her.

"Hey you!"

I sat down across from Camille at the table for two. "Hey. Thanks for the invite again. I don't know a whole lot of places to eat yet, so it's good that you told me about this place."

"I love it. It's a little on the pricy side, but the food is healthy and close to home, so it's a gem in my book."

I smiled and picked up the menu to scan the selection of what they had. There was a lot to choose from.

"I hope you don't mind, but I already ordered a few plates of food—some of their more popular dishes. I thought you could get an idea about the food and taste a little bit of each."

"Oh no, I don't mind at all. I was just about to ask you what I should order," I said as I settled in across from Camille.

Camille's hair was parted down the middle as her brown curls framed her heart- shaped face. As I stared at her caramel-colored skin, full lips and oval eyes, her face had a very familiar look to me.

"Do people tell you that you remind them of Rosario Dawson?" I said, finally putting my finger on why she looked so familiar.

Camille took a swig from her iced coffee. "Oh, all the time girl. I even get stopped from time to time and asked for autographs. I think my hair is a bit lighter than hers, but I guess that doesn't matter."

There was a small silence as we each found ourselves at a loss for words. We stared at each other for a moment before I broke the silence. "How long have you been in LA?" I asked, leaning back in my chair.

Camille looked up toward the sky then back down again. "Going on five years now."

"Do you like it?"

"I have adjusted to it. LA is so different from New York, as I'm sure you know, coming from Brooklyn and all," Camille said. She took another sip from her iced coffee.

"What was it that brought you out here originally?"

Camille shook her head as she leaned back in her chair, crossing her arms across her chest. "I wish I could say it was a great opportunity or even the year-round perfect weather, but it was a man. A man I'm not even with anymore. But that's a good thing."

"Really?"

"Definitely. I was married for exactly one year, three months and eight days, but who's counting?"

"Clearly, not you," I said, hoping to keep the mood light.

"I tell you, girl, men can be something else. I used to have this theory about men and women: We were designed to be put on this earth, procreate, then leave each other the hell alone."

I laughed at Camille's relationship theory. If everyone knew about it, it would probably benefit eighty-five percent of mankind. "That's pretty funny and painfully truthful."

"If you have a good man, Kai, hold on to him, there aren't that many out there. Believe me, I've looked."

"Oh, wait a minute, if you are having a hard time finding a man, there has got to be something wrong with the male species of the world! You are too beautiful to be single." I was shocked with how open I was being with her.

"Well, aren't you sweet! But I'm not looking for just any man, I'm looking for a good man. Those, my dear, are hard to find. Believe me, I've searched high and low. I honestly thought I found him in my daughter's father, but, boy, I was wrong," Camille said. She shook her head and rolled her eyes up then back down.

"What happened?" I paused, thinking that I should probably pull back a bit. After all, I barely knew this woman and I was asking her to spill her entire life story to me. "If you don't want to tell me I completely understand."

"Oh, it's no big deal. Four years and one-hundred-fifty hours of therapy helped me get over it and him, so let's just say, how you get 'em is exactly how you will lose 'em."

I thought about Alana for the first time and how she got Todd with deceit. Deceit was exactly how she lost him, too.

"That is so true."

"My ex is in the music industry, and, well, I used to dance in videos."

Upon hearing dance and videos my left eyebrow shot up before I had a chance to mask my expression.

Camille laughed out loud. "Before you even go there, I was actually a trained dancer before I hung up my jazz shoes for stilettos. I studied at the Harlem school of dance for four years."

"Oh, wow."

"Yeah, wow is right, had my dreams set on being an Alvin Alley dancer."

"What happened?"

"I got hurt, tore my Achilles, and my dancing was never the same again. My window of opportunity shut down before I had a chance to climb through it." Camille looked down at her coffee shamefully and then back up at me.

"So after I dusted my ego off, I realized I needed to make money somehow and a friend recommended doing music videos." Camille took another sip from her iced coffee. "One video led to two, and then another, and then the money was good, but the hours and the people sucked. I was on the verge of getting out, going back to school when I met my ex-husband."

Camille smiled at the memory and she shook her head. "I was so in love with that man, and thought I would ride or die for him, but he took me through it. It wasn't until we were married that I found out I was pregnant and I found out he had an entire *other* family in New Jersey. I guess he thought he'd get away with it since he moved me to California and into a nice home, all the while playing house in New Jersey."

"How did you find out?"

"Facebook."

I shook my head. That damn Facebook had done in its share of people. "Wow."

"When I confronted him, he didn't even bother denying it. He just walked out the house and never returned. At the time, I was eight months pregnant with my daughter, Natalie."

"Oh my God. Why didn't you go back to New York?"

"Too ashamed to face my family I guess. Plus, it just felt better out here, ya know? Besides, he's a pretty big name now in the music industry so my child support check keeps me comfortable," Camille said as she perked up a bit. "I can be miserable by myself."

"Well, I am sure you will find someone."

"That's my plan," Camille said with a half-smile. It dawned on me that it wasn't a lack of beauty that kept Camille from finding another man, it was her choice to go after one. There was definitely a difference. I watched Camille slip into her own private flashback, then quickly snapped herself out.

"How long have you and Todd been married?" she asked.

"A little over a year now. We broke up for a while and after we got back together we didn't want to rush things, but we both knew that marriage was right around the corner."

"Is he a good man?" Camille asked. She was watching me to see what I had to say about him, probably gauging how honest I was going to be about Todd's flaws.

I thought for a minute. "I do believe I have a great man. We have been through our bit of drama ourselves. But at the end of the day...Well, he's a keeper," I said, thinking about the day that Todd proposed to me.

Kristopher had been almost a year old when Todd came home with two tickets to Chicago, saying we should fly home to see my parents and friends. The night we got in we dropped Kristopher off at my mom's and we went to Blackbird for dinner and drinks, the location of our very first date. When dessert came, there it was, sitting right on top of my chocolate truffle cake, a princess-cut diamond ring. It was as if the time stopped as Todd picked it up, licked off the frosting and slid the ring on my finger. It was the second best day of my life after the birth of our son.

"Kai?" Camille asked, bringing me back to reality.

"Yeah."

"Our food is ready. I'm gonna go get it."

"Okay, great, do you need any help?"

"I can handle it," Camille said, shooting me a wink. She stood and headed over to the pickup counter with every man's head in the place turning to watch her walk across the floor. Camille definitely had a body that made men cheat and women worry. I made a mental note to think twice about bringing her around Todd.

What I thought would be a quick lunch turned into two hours of good conversation. I hadn't clicked like this with a woman in a long time and it felt good to have someone to relate to again. Camille was cool and real and the conversation between us flowed nicely.

I put the last bit of food in my mouth and leaned back in my chair. "Oh, my goodness, that food was amazing. I loved, loved the jerked chicken patties and the tofu scramble with the home fries"

"Stick with me. I will escort you to the promised land of good food."

We shared a laugh.

"I will definitely be back."

"We should come back on Wednesday. Matter of fact, if you aren't doing anything Wednesday night, I have a girlfriend who invited me to a listening party for a new up-and-coming artist. You want to come with us?"

"Oh, wow, a listening party, I have always heard of them, but have never been to one."

"Then you need to go and have the full LA experience. I'll RSVP for the two of us?"

"Oh shoot, wait, did you say Wednesday?"

"Yes, do you have plans already?"

"Sort of, my sister Mila is flying in from Chicago with my son, she was supposed to come Friday, but she switched it to Wednesday. Rain check?"

"Of course. Now that we are neighbors and our kids will be going to the same school, I am sure we will be seeing a lot of each other," Camille said as she reached out and touched my hand. Her touch sent an unexpected sensation through my body. I smiled back and slowly pulled my hand away.

"This is true." I glanced down at my watch it was now 2:20. "You better get going. Don't you have to pick up Natalie at two-thirty?"

"Two-forty-five, but yes, I better get going." Camille picked up her iced coffee to finish the last bit of it. "I had fun, Kai."

"Yeah, me, too."

Camille stood. "Enjoy the rest of your day and don't be a stranger."

"Of course not."

Camille gave me one last look that sent a second tingling sensation through my body before she turned and walked out of the restaurant. I couldn't believe it was happening again—I was attracted to this woman.

TWELVE
ALANA

"Hello, darling." I sang as I swung open my door to see Emanuel's smiling face beaming my way. I had been back in Chicago for less than eight hours and was anxiously awaiting word from him about the part in Los Angeles.

"Girlfriend, whatever you did, you did it well." Emanuel entered my condo, snapping his fingers with his famous two snaps with an upswing.

"Did the bitch get the part?" I asked with every ounce of enthusiasm I could muster.

"The bitch got the part!" Emanuel chirped back to me.

"That's what I'm talking about!" Emanuel and I embraced as I closed my door behind him then proceeded to do a small happy dance around my small quaint condo. While I knew I had the part before I left the studio, it was nice to hear the official call.

"Honey child, I never heard such earnest in one man's voice. The showrunner called me personally to let me know you were the perfect person for the part. It was as if you were the second coming."

"Well, a-coming he did and did and did again."

"Ewww weeee, girlfriend. Tell me you didn't?"

"I would, but then I'd be lying," I said with a broad smile on my face.

"Can I get an 'Amen' and a hip bump? I ain't mad atcha," Emanuel squealed back at me. We bumped hips twice in synch. "A girl's gotta do what a girl's gotta do," Emanuel continued as he took a seat, crossing his legs on my white plush king chair with matching ottoman.

"My sentiments exactly." Some women took pride in themselves with baking the best cake or knitting the perfect sweater, but my skills lay in giving a damn good blow job. It may not be up there in the top ten skills everyone should have, but we all have our crosses to bear.

"When do I need to be back in LA? I have a few things I need to wrap up in Chicago," I asked, sitting on the edge of the matching ottoman close to Emanuel.

"Two weeks. They need you there for promotional shots."

Two weeks wasn't a lot of time to do much of anything, but I could make that work. "Sounds good."

I couldn't believe it was all coming together. I had a sense of accomplishment dancing through my veins, I felt that getting this part was one step closer to my ultimate goal of getting Todd back.

"Oh, one more thing. Now that you will be on a new show, you will need an entertainment lawyer. Emanuel reached in his cherry-colored Jack George designer briefcase and revealed a hot-pink folder. He would have hot-pink folders in his office.

"I highlighted the ones that I think you should really consider, but the choice is ultimately yours," Emanuel said as he stretched the hot-pink folder my way. When I grabbed the folder, my cell phone rang. I looked down to see that it was my mom.

I swear she had to have some sort of tracking device on me. I couldn't wait to tell her the good news.

"Mom, hey." I stood as I threw up my pointer finger to Emanuel, letting him know this would only take a second. I slowly walked into my bedroom to talk to her.

"Alana, I have been waiting for you to call me back. Now this is getting ridiculous. You have been out of jail for one week now and you still have not seen Riley."

"Mom, I know and I am sorry, but I have some amazing news. I got the part in LA, on a new television show." I waited to hear my excitement mirrored from my mom, but all I got was a deep sigh.

"What does that mean for Riley?"

"She can come live with me now, but I just need one more month and I will—"

"No, Alana, you need to come get her today. She misses you."

"Mom, I have to go back to LA. It will only be for a little bit longer."

"I don't care what you have to do. Riley needs you and you have been out of her life long enough. Come and pick her up today, you hear me?"

"Please, Mom, everything is working out just the way I planned. Todd is even in LA and I just need to get settled, get him back and then I can send for Riley. One more month, that is all I need and then we can all be a family again."

I heard another loud extended sigh on the other end. "Todd already has a family, Alana. When are you going to get that through your head? He does not want you."

I took a deep breath. "Mom, please do not go there again with me."

"You need to wake up, Alana. Riley is your family now, not Todd."

I could not continue this conversation with my mother, she was making my head throb out of control. "Mom, I'm going to have to call you back."

My mom was still in her hyperactive talk mode. "Oh no you will not. Not until you can tell me what time you'll be picking up Riley."

"Fine, I will pick her up in a few hours."

"I will have her packed. Listen, Alana, I am only doing this because—"

I deliberately hung up on my mom, not trying to hear the whole I'm-only-doing-this-because-I-love-you speech. I wasn't in the mood at all.

I headed back out to the living room to finish my meeting with Emanuel.

I flopped down on my white leather chaise that faced my bay window, overlooking Chicago's South Loop. Emanuel stood from the king chair he had made himself very comfortable in and walked over to me. "Are you okay? You walked into that room on cloud nine and came out in a deep dark valley, what happened?"

I felt like the air had been let out of my balloon. I now felt torn, confused and frustrated. "It's my mom."

"What about her? Is she okay?"

"Yes, she is fine. She wants me to come pick up Riley today."

"Did you need me to go get her?"

"No, it's not that. It's just I needed her to keep her a little while longer until I get settled in LA and..." I stopped myself before I accidentally revealed my other plan of action, which included getting Todd back. Something I needed to start keeping to myself.

"Where's her daddy?"

I threw my arms up and gravity pulled them back down to my sides. "Hell if I know, and honestly, I don't care."

"You could always get a nanny."

"Ah, hello, I haven't shot one episode yet. Where am I gonna get the money for a nanny?"

"Yeah, you do have a point."

Silence fell over the room. Emanuel was sweet for trying to help, but I knew I was on my own with this one. I picked up the hot-pink folder that contained a list of entertainment law firms.

"How many firms are here?" I inquired as I pulled the stack of papers out of the folder.

"Just three," Emanuel replied. "The one I recommend is McClendon and Dixon. I haven't had a chance to really review the other two as of yet, but all three are good."

As I began to flip through the different firms, something caught my eye. I gasped as I saw a name that made me sit up so straight, you would have thought someone shoved a rail up my back.

"What is it?" Emanuel saw my expression.

"Nothing, I will go with this firm."

"Which one?

"Jacobs, Knowles and Patterson," I said.

Emanuel scratched his head. "Actually, you would be a better fit at McClendon and Dixon."

I ignored Emanuel's advice. "No, I made up my mind. Also, I need you to book me on a flight back to LA tonight?"

"Tonight? But you..."

"Yes, tonight."

"That'll be expensive, Alana."

"Must you fight me on everything?" I barked at Emanuel. "Take it out of my first check. It won't be long before I will be back on top."

Emanuel paused for a minute and folded his arms while twisting his lips in defeat. "Fine, whatever you want. Listen, I gotta run." Emanuel reached for his pink folder. I handed him the folder, but not before putting the paperwork for Jacobs, Knowles and Patterson aside.

"Actually, I'm gonna hold onto this one if you don't mind."

"That's fine, I have a copy at the office." He paused, gathering up the rest of his paperwork as he gazed at me. "What are you going to do about Riley?"

I stood, walking over to my front door with him. "I will figure it out."

"You sure you're okay?"

"I'm fine. Don't forget to text me about my flight information."

Emanuel slowly nodded then looked me over from head to toe. It was his way of trying to detect the unknown from me. "Okay, well, call me later, superstar. I am so happy for *us*!"

I smiled at Emanuel as he swished out my house. I quickly closed the door behind him as I picked up my iPhone and typed in my mother's email address.

Hey Mom,

I hope you can understand that I cannot take care of Riley right now. I will be back to get her in 1-2 months tops, I promise. Thank you for all you have done for me. Please tell Riley I love her and I will be back for her before she knows it. I love you, Mom, and I know you will understand when the time is right.

Love, Alana.

I dropped my cell phone down onto my chaise and picked up the papers to Jacobs, Knowles and Patterson's law firm and stared at the name that had leapt out at me: *Todd Daniels.*

"Yes, this is definitely a sign." I paused, mentally correcting myself. "THE sign that we will be together again."

I dropped the papers down onto the cocktail table and headed to my bedroom to pack my bags for Los Angeles.

THIRTEEN
TODD

I settled into my new office and loved every minute of it. It had only been a week, but I knew that I'd made the right decision the moment I stepped into the firm. Work was a little slow since they were still deciding who to place me with as my front clients, but so far, it had all been good.   I wanted to ease my way back into corporate America anyway, and this was the perfect firm to do just that.

It was nearing lunch time and I was trying to decide where I should go grab some food. A few colleagues had mentioned Houston's Restaurant and that sounded pretty good right about now. Houston's was one of my favorite eating spots in Chicago and I had a craving for their Chicago-style spinach dip.

I pulled out my phone to make a reservation for me and my colleague when I noticed I had a message on my Facebook account from Maceo Smith. I opened the message and read it quickly:

Yo, T. Daniels, heard you moved to LA, don't have your digits, hit me up asap. I got some shit for you. 312-555-4682

I hadn't talked to Maceo since he closed our practice in Chicago after all the sexual assault suits had hit him. That brother was a good lawyer, but he had his issues with women, and they had issues with him. I dialed his number, and he answered with a professional tone.

"Maceo Smith speaking."

"Hey, Maceo, it's Todd."

"T. Daniels! What is up my brother?"

"Nothing much, just settling into my new gig in LA. Sorry I lost contact with you, but—"

"Yo, not to cut you off, we'll get to the necessary small talk and all, but *yo*, Alana is either on her way to LA or already there."

I felt my body immediately tense up. "What are you talking about?"

"Your girl, Alana, got wind that you and Kai are in LA now."

"What? Are you serious? How did she find out?"

"Who knows? Motherfuckers talk yo. Listen, that bitch isn't wrapped tight at all, so I wanted to give you a heads-up so you can prepare for the worst. Alert the authorities, clean out your safe house, or do what you got to do. I am sure she is on her way out there now, so you might want to hunker down."

As Maceo talked, I glanced up through my glass walls that separated me from the rest of the office, and couldn't believe what I was seeing. I started to breathe a bit faster as the image I had laid eyes on rapidly approached me. It was none other than *Alana Brooks* coming through my office door with my boss, David Johnson in tow.

I slowly pulled the phone away from my ear, and I could still hear Maceo slightly, but I didn't care what he was saying. All of my attention was focused on Alana.

"So do what you got to do my brother! I just wanted to give you a heads up." Maceo continued talking while Alana and David—now standing in front of my desk— waited for me to wrap up my phone call.

"Yeah, yeah, thanks, listen, I gotta call you back," I said as I slowly hit end, laying my phone on my desk as Alana and I stared at each other.

"Todd, I want to introduce you to one of our newest clients, Ms. Alana Brooks. We were lucky enough to sign her fresh from Chicago," David said, oblivious to my shocked expression at seeing Alana for the first time in two years.

I sat frozen in my damn seat. Was I fucking dreaming? This couldn't be happening right now.

"It is so very nice to meet you, Todd, is it?" Alana said, taking two steps closer to me, her hand extended my way.

What the fuck is happening right now? Is Alana really standing in front of me?

"Todd, are you okay?" David asked, snapping me out of my internal confusion, bringing me back to the present nightmare.

"Yeah, I, um, I'm good," I said, standing as I looked at David.

I directed my attention back to Alana and took her hand. "Alana, it is very nice to meet you."

Our hands locked as I felt the softness of her skin that I remembered. Alana gave my hand a little squeeze as she winked at me. I pulled my hand back, shoving it into my pants pocket.

"Alana just landed a part on a new CW show, *Office Temps*, and we were lucky enough to sign her. Treat her well, Todd. This one's gonna be a superstar!"

Alana laughed out loud. "Oh, David, you are too kind. I'm sure Todd will roll out the red carpet for me," Alana said, tilting her head at me. "Isn't that right, Todd?"

I wanted to knock that fucking smile off her face. I don't know why I was so surprised, like Maceo said, and I saw firsthand, Alana was one crazy bitch.

"We're going to need to start going over all her contracts. I figured you could get started with that, since they are pretty basic. I'm going to leave you two to get to know each other." David placed his hand on Alana's shoulder. "Again, welcome to the family, Alana. Todd is gonna take real good care of you. Isn't that right, Todd?"

I smiled and nodded at David. He gives me the thumbs-up.

"Oh, I'm sure he will. Thank you so much, David," Alana said, dazzling the senior partner with her perfect smile.

David returned the smile and left my office, closing the door behind him. Before saying anything, I made sure my boss was out of earshot.

"What the fuck are you doing here?" I said, trying, and failing, to not let my temper get the best of me.

"Wow, is that the way to treat an old friend? Not to mention a new up-and coming client. How about a hug?" Alana stepped forward to hug me and I took two big steps back.

"You are not my fucking client, and you damn sure are not my friend. I should have your ass thrown back in jail."

Alana walked over to my bookshelf and looked through my things as if it were the most natural thing in the world that she was there. "I'm not breaking any laws here, Todd. I have a right to be here just as much as you do. You work for me now, so in essence," Alana swung back around to look at me, "you are *my* bitch."

My phone buzzed. My assistant's voice came through the speaker.

"Mr. Daniels, your wife is on the line for you."

Alana smiled and walked closer to me. "Oh, the wifey is calling. Please give her my regards."

I picked up my receiver. "Tell her I'll call her back."

"Of course, Mr. Daniels."

I hung up the phone and turned my attention back to Alana. "You need to leave, now."

"What will David think? He wanted us to get to know each other," Alana said, easing down into my black leather couch, crossing her legs and shooting a smile my way. "Don't worry, I actually wore panties today." Alana chuckled. "'Cause you know how I roll, right?"

I sat back down in my chair, trying to calm my jangled nerves. I was not going to let Alana get the best of me. I would play her little game.

"Pretty resourceful of you, figuring out where I was."

"You know me, resourceful is my middle name. Besides, did you think you could get away from me that easily? And LA of all places? But, hey, I'm not complaining, I think I will love it here. LA agrees with me."

I folded my hands together, placing them deliberately on my desk. "What do you want?"

"You know what I want, for things to go back to the way they were, before you lost your damn mind and scurried back to that vanilla bitch, Kai. What do you see in her anyway? Seriously? She is such a nothing."

"Yeah, that's not gonna happen."

"Yeah, we'll see."

"You are crazy, you know that?"

"Crazy about you and I know you feel the same. You were always slow to realize your *true* feelings, Todd. I can be patient. I did wait for the last two years in prison. Thank you very much for that."

Alana uncrossed then crossed her opposite leg. "So this is going to be fun, me and you working together in LA. The parties, the stars, the threesomes. I'm getting all tingly and wet just thinking about it." Alana smiled devilishly as she wiggled on the couch. "I guess it is a good thing I wore panties. I wouldn't want to mess up your brand-new leather couch."

"Yeah, fat fucking chance. Don't get comfy. I'm putting an end to this right now," I said. I headed out of my office and down the hallway toward David's office. This was about to stop, right the fuck now. I pulled it together before knocking on David's door.

"Excuse me, Mr. Johnson."

"Todd, what's wrong, is everything okay with Alana?"

"Actually, no."

"No?"

"I don't believe I'm the best fit for her, sir."

"Why is that?

I stood for a moment, trying to find the right words but nothing rational came to mind. Everything sounded off the wall, bizarre, downright crazy or out of a sexual thriller movie.

"Todd?"

"I just think someone else could service her better, I um—"

"Don't be ridiculous. You will be fine. Besides, she requested you."

"She what?"

"Yeah, the day we signed her she requested that you be her front lawyer."

"I thought the entire firm represents each client."

"Oh, we do, but each client is given a front lawyer who handles their day-to-day affairs."

I rubbed the back of my neck, and felt that familiar feeling of anger at Alana rising again. "Right."

"My hands are tied. We like to keep our clients happy, the last thing we want to do is lose them to another firm."

"Of course." I didn't know what else to say to plead my case without giving my crazy tumultuous past with Alana away. I needed this job, which meant I had to suck it up.

"Speaking of, Alana is in the running for the co-host spot on that *Good Morning Gossip* show. Her agent already arranged it for her. I'll need you to fly to New York to meet with the producers and make sure her contracts are in order."

"When?"

"This Wednesday. It will be a quick trip. You will be back by Friday. Alana's gonna tag along with. Might give you a good way for you two to get to know each other."

"Is that necessary, sir?"

"Yes, it would be for the best."

I took a deep breath. "Okay then," I said, sounding less defeated than I actually felt. I quickly came to the harsh reality that fighting a senior partner would very well jeopardize my job. This in turn could lead to a choice to keep me or Alana, and in this town, talent always wins.

I headed out of David's office. When it rained, it fucking poured. I felt my stomach turning, as knots were multiplying faster than baby rabbits.

Before reaching my office, I took a detour to the men's bathroom. I tried throwing some cold water on my face, hoping it would help me focus. Alana being back in my life felt like a bad dream, and all I wanted to do was wake up.

I headed back to my office, but when I got there Alana was gone. *Thank God.* I slowly closed my door and sat back down at my desk.

I took a deep breath and tried to figure out what the hell I was going to tell Kai. This was so typical Alana showing up like this.

My mind began to race and I started to contemplate if I should even tell Kai. Fuck, I had to tell Kai. As I sat at my desk, my mind continued to go back and forth on what to do, like a champion match at Wimbledon. Unfortunately, in my case, there would be no winners here.

This couldn't have come at a worse time, after Kai was already questioning me about Jessica. I knew that threesome would come back and bite me in the ass. *Shit.*

I took a deep breath. Maybe I could wait to tell Kai later. There was no sense in stressing the both of us out. Besides, I really needed this job and Kai knowing that Alana was here right under my nose would just add to the drama. But, on the other hand, if I didn't tell her, she could find out and then... I stood, started to pace. *Fuck me.* Why wouldn't this bitch just go away? *Fuck!*

My phone buzzed. "Mr. Daniels, it is your wife again."

"Thank you."

I sat back down behind my desk, took another deep breath and ran my hand down the back of my head to my neck where I squeezed it. *Damn, damn, damn.* What should I tell Kai? I looked down at the flashing light on line two, waiting for me to pick it up. My hand reached for the receiver, but stopped short before picking it up. As my hand hovered in limbo my mind jumped back and forth about what to do. *Shit.* The phone let out three short beeps, an indication that the call had been on hold for three minutes now.

"Ahhhh, fuck it," I said out loud as I reached for the phone, I have to tell Kai everything.

"Hey, babe, how's work going?"

"It's going. Listen babe-" When I heard Kai's voice everything took a drastic turn.

"What's up?"

"There's something... that came up at work, so I'm going to be home later that I planned."

I dropped my head in frustration. I would just have to tell her when the time was right.

FOURTEEN
KAI

"I cannot believe how much I missed you," I said as I stripped my baby boy out of Mila's arms the moment they walked off the plane. I kissed his soft tender face all over.

"He looks so much bigger," I said to my twin sister, beaming at the sight of my son.

"It's only been seven days, Kai," Mila said as she straightened out her peach silk shirt, twisting her mouth up at the jelly stain Kristopher planted on her during the flight.

"Seven days is an eternity in toddler years," I said, continuing to kiss my sweet little man's face. "Thank you so much for keeping him while we got settled. And thank you so much for flying him here."

"Of course, but I'm sending you my dry-cleaning bill," Mila said, continuing to scratch off the dried-up jelly on her shirt. "Where is Todd? I thought he was going to be with you."

"He had to fly to New York on business this morning so..."

"So soon? Didn't he just get that job?"

"Yes, but they needed him to fly to New York to go over contracts for a new client they just signed."

"Humph." Mila's smirked as she gave me a cross-eyed stare.

"What is that supposed to mean?"

"Just weird how they have to send him, the new associate, to New York. You sure it wasn't his idea to go?"

"Okay, Mila, you just got to LA, why are you already trying to tap dance on my last damn nerve? Todd is away on business, end of story," I said as we headed out of the United Terminal toward baggage claim.

Mila's accusation couldn't have come at a worse time, being that I still had that Jessica woman on my mind ever since she had lost all composure after I mentioned Todd's name. Then, with the way Todd had reacted when I mentioned her name to him, it all added up to someone not telling me the truth. Dammit. Maybe Todd wasn't in New York on business, maybe he went there to see that Jessica woman. I knew she was with Toni now, but hell, I was sleeping with Alana when I was with Todd. If I have learned anything from Simone, don't put anything past anyone, especially a man.

I tried to dismiss the seed my sister had planted into my head moments after seeing her. I hated when Mila always thought the worst and made it her mission to dwell on it.

It's no secret that my twin sister and were like oil and water, hamburgers and caviar, pizza and mashed potatoes—we just didn't mix. I was happy as hell to have my little man home, but then I thought about how that came with the price of Mila staying with me for the next four days. All I could do was pray for a miracle that we both came out on the other side of it alive. My goal was to be the bigger person and take the high road.

"Todd wouldn't lie to me, Mila, okay?"

"Kai, it's not like you two have a squeaky-clean track record. Hell, it's a blessing you two even managed to get married after that fight you had with that what's her name woman." Mila looked at me. "What was her name?"

I took a deep cleansing breath, rolled my eyes and reminded myself to take the high road. "Her name was *Alana*." I completed my sentence with a forced smile. I felt my body temperature nearing its boiling point.

"Right, Alana."

Mila chuckled as she slid into the passenger seat. I tried to tune her out as I buckled Kristopher into his car seat and gave him one last kiss on his little lips before closing the door and jumping into the driver's seat. The moment I sat down, Mila continued her rant, not missing a beat.

"Talk about a love triangle with a twist. I remember the first time I laid eyes on that woman, I thought she was attractive, although you *really* thought she was." Mila chuckled, shaking her head.

I stared straight ahead as I drove toward the exit of the parking garage. Mila happily continued to chatter along. I even turned on the radio to give her a hint, but that didn't even faze her.

"And just think, I thought it would be Todd to stray first with her, funny that it was you who ventured over to the other side."

I thought I better use something else to calm me down. Counting might work, hopefully.

Mila shifted her body toward me in the car. "Do you ever talk to her anymore?"

I ignored Mila's question, and instead concentrated on my counting. *One, two, three, four, five.*

"How does that work anyway? Can you still be friends with a woman after you did the deed with her? Kai, are you even listening to me?"

I stopped my counting and slowly turned to Mila.

"Why would I talk to her anymore, Mila? She set me up to steal my man," I said in a slow methodical tone.

"Well, from what I remembered you had your own little fun in the interim."

I smiled, bit my lip, looked straight ahead and continued to count. *Six, seven, eight.*

Mila turned back forward and shook her head. "I will never understand that girl- on-girl thing. If you ask me, it's just downright disgusting. I don't know how you can live with yourself."

Nine, ten, eleven.

"How does that work? Are you like a part-time lesbian?"

Screw the high road. I stopped the car, put it in park and turned to my sister.

"Okay, I am only going to say this once, so I hope you have on your goddamn listening ears. There will be no more talk about my past. About Alana or me and Todd's encounters with her." I stared her down, ignoring how uncomfortable she was getting. I continued berating my sister.

"Yes, I slept with a woman. As a matter of fact, I have slept with two, okay?" Mila's head jerked back after hearing me mention another encounter with a second woman.

"So if you want to continue to judge me I can just as easily drive up to the departure terminal and dump your ass out there on the curb. I'm sure there will be another flight leaving very soon to take your judgmental ass back to Chicago."

I stared at my sister. "Have I made myself clear?"

Mila's eyes were as wide as her white china saucers in her fancy display cabinet. "Yes, yes, very clear," she said in a soft, trembling voice.

I put my car in drive. "Fantastic." We drove the rest of the way in silence. Mila looking straight ahead, and me humming to the sounds of Alicia Keys, 'Girl on Fire'. No matter how satisfying it was to put my sister in her place, in that moment, all I could think of was Todd and if he was really in New York on business or pleasure.

***

After getting Mila settled in the guest room, I bathed, fed and cuddled with Kristopher, trying to make up for our lost time.

After I got him down for a short nap, I tried calling Todd, but his phone went straight to voicemail. I looked at the clock and it was 1:00 p.m. LA time so that meant it was 4:00 p.m. in New York. His plane probably had not landed yet.

I walked into the kitchen and found Mila sitting at the table sipping on a glass of white wine. It was a bottle of Moscato I had picked up for Todd and I to drink, but what the hell, I had to choose my battles wisely.

"When did you start drinking in the middle of the day?"

"It's been a long week," Mila said, continuing to sip her wine. "Now who's being the judgmental one?"

I raised an eyebrow and ignored Mila's comment as I opened the fridge and pulled out some chicken for dinner. The tension was thick in the room and I had to find a way to cut it.

"Listen, Mila, I am sorry for snapping off on you earlier, but sometimes you can be…"

"A bitch," Mila finished. While I was going to try and sugarcoat it a bit, she took the word right out of my mouth.

"Since you said it, yes."

She looked at me and we both chuckled. A silence fell between us.

"So how are Charles and the twins?" I said, hoping to steer the conversation to happier topics. "The twins are great. They started kindergarten and they are loving it more than I expected."

"You have them in Montessori school, right?" I asked, already knowing that answer.

"Of course, I wouldn't have it any other way," Mila said as she topped off her glass.

I never remembered Mila drinking as much as she had in the last few hours she had been at my house. It threw up a red flag for me and I was not one to brush it under the rug.

I grabbed some crackers, cheese and grapes and headed over to the table. "Mila, is everything okay?"

"Of course."

"Going through a bottle of wine in less than an hour is normal for you?" I said, lifting the half empty bottle of wine that sat between us.

"My wine consumption is none of your business, Kai," Mila said, looking away, then back at her glass.

"It is when you are in my house and the fact that I trusted you with my child over the last seven days."

"Oh please, Kai, are you serious? Can we just drop it? Your son is here safe and sound. I felt like unwinding from a stressful week. Let's not make a big deal of this, okay?"

"Fine," I said, dropping it. I reached out to retrieve a few crackers and spread some cheese on them. I popped one in my mouth. "So has anyone heard from Raymond lately?"

Mila rolled her eyes as she squirmed a bit in her seat.

"Corrine didn't tell you?"

My body tensed up, "Tell me what?"

Mila lifted her wine glass and took a few more sips. "Maybe she told me to tell you. I guess I forgot." Mila waved her hand in the air as if she was dismissing something of non-importance.

"Mila, what is it?"

Mila locked eyes with me. "Raymond's in jail."

"What? When?"

"A few weeks now, maybe a month, I can't remember."

The fact that Mila was being so damn evasive with what I thought was a huge deal was pissing me off. "What happened?"

"Apparently, he discharged himself from rehab, went to some girl's house and beat the crap out of her."

"What?" Who?"

Mila shrugged her shoulders. "No one knows. But the girl slipped into a coma from the beating and eventually died from an aneurism. They gave him twenty years in prison. Nice huh?"

She swirled the liquid within her glass, staring down at it, and continued. "So now he's not just a crackhead, he's a woman-beater and a murderer. That should look great on his resume."

I couldn't believe what I was hearing. This was typical Mila to hold this kind of information from me.

"Mila, why are you just now telling me this?"

"Because I have more important things to think about than to give you a daily update on our crackhead-turned-murderer brother, that's why," Mila said as she hiccupped from the wine.

"Oh my God, you are unbelievable, you know that? Seriously. Just because Raymond doesn't fit in your elitist mode of what a person should be, you act like he is less than human."

"Raymond had just as many opportunities as we did, he just chose to screw his life up. He made a choice and now he's living with the consequences."

"Really? And you've done such a great job with your life?" I said, shaking my head in pure disgust of my sister's take on my brother's spotty track record.

"I'm sorry you feel that you have a dark shadow hanging over your head that you constantly have to hide from your bourgeoisie friends. Newsflash, Mila, he is your brother and will always be your brother, okay?"

Mila didn't respond and kept drinking her wine.

"So you have nothing to say?"

"At least now I don't have to worry about him showing up at my house when I have friends over." She rose her glass in a mock toast. "Now that I will drink to."

"You are unbelievable." I stood and walk out of the kitchen. I felt myself hyperventilating as I picked up my phone to call Todd. Straight to voicemail. "Dammit," I said, throwing my phone to the ground.

I really needed to talk to him. I couldn't go back to face my sister. All I could think about was my brother Raymond. Why would he do such a thing? How had his life turned out so badly? How was it that me, Mila and Raymond had turned out so differently from each other?

I picked the phone up from the floor and moved toward my room. I closed the door behind me and laid across my bed. I was waiting for Todd to call me back. Life was starting to pile up right now and I wasn't sure how much more I could take without him.

I was in a state of numbed confusion and I needed to hear Todd's voice. I needed to be reminded that he was my one and only constant in my unraveling life.

FIFTEEN
ALANA

I finally had Todd all to myself and I couldn't be more thrilled.

"How long are you going to keep this whole, not speaking to me act up?" I asked, as we headed up to the front desk to check in at the Roosevelt hotel on East Forty-Fifth Street in Manhattan, New York. Todd hadn't said a word to me during the entire five- hour flight. He had always been the king of silent treatments. It was one of his cuter attributes if you asked me. He'd get over it. I was always able break him out of it.

Todd shot me a shitty, almost exasperated look. "We are here on business, Alana, so when it is time to talk business, I will talk."

"You're so cute when you're mad, you know that?"

"Stop talking. I'm serious about what I said." Todd turned his head away from me, gazing straight ahead, looking as if he was trying to tune me out.

"Fine." I looked straight ahead as well, then back at him. There were four people ahead of us in line to check in. Todd stood a few feet over from me.

"So you didn't miss me...at all?" I said as I stared at him, taking in every inch of his beautiful profile, including his strong cheekbones and light mustache.

Todd took a deep breath and continued to ignore me. He shifted his weight from right to left and put his hands in his pockets, remaining stubbornly silent.

"I missed you a lot. I mean I had a lot of time to think about you while I was in jail. Did I thank you for that, by the way? It was a splendid experience to say the least."

That made Todd turn his attention back my way. "No one told you to violate your restraining order and break into Kai's house, so don't thank me, thank yourself."

See, I had a way of getting Todd to talk, I always did. I prided myself in knowing that I was smarter than him. Always had been, always will. Todd was a man and men don't think five steps ahead like women do. That's their major downfall and our way of gaining the advantage.

"Okay, you're right. I let my emotions get the best of me, but I was hurt. You just went off and left me, fleeing to New York to be with Kai."

Todd swiveled around on his right foot and looked me dead in my eyes. "I can't believe I am even hearing this. You fucking lied to me Alana, and you used me and you used Kai, so don't come to me with this 'you hurt me' bullshit, okay? Everything that happened to you, you brought onto yourself."

"Todd—"

Todd threw up his hand. "Alana, stop talking, okay? I don't want to hear anything else about our past, leave it where it belongs. We are here on business, period. Don't make it anything more than that."

"Okay, fine," I said, watching the vein on the side of Todd's forehead pulsate faster than normal.

"Thank you."

Todd turned back around, and looked down at his watch. His phone rang again and he hit a button on the screen silencing the ringer. He slid the phone back into his pocket.

"Was that Kai?" I asked, a jealous urge cascading through my body.

"Yes, as a matter of fact that was Kai, my *wife*." Todd stressed the word wife and I had to admit, that stung. I took the hit, and let him have that one jab.

"How did she take the news? You and me here in New York, together?" I asked, knowing damn well he didn't mention this little getaway to his *wife* nor the fact that we were now working together.

Todd shook his head and I believe rolled his eyes. Then he turned toward me, "She was fine, okay?"

The one thing I knew about Todd was whenever he lied or was stressed, he ended his sentences with *okay*. I chuckled.

Todd shot me a look out the corner of his eye. "What's so damn funny?"

"You didn't tell her."

"Yes I did."

"No you didn't." I looked down at my black signature Gucci boots, then back up at Todd. "I see nothing has changed."

"What the hell does that mean?" Todd asked, turning back toward me.

"Keeping secrets from each other. Kai did it to you and now you are doing it to her. There is hope for me yet."

"Please, in your over-flattered dreams."

"Hey, if that's what works for you two, the more power to ya."

"Yes, Alana, more power to me, because you know what, I don't have to justify shit to you."

"I'm not asking you to. I am just observing what's in front of me, that's all." I bit my bottom lip, and felt my body heat up from the exciting exchange between us. If he didn't care about me, he wouldn't even be engaging me right now, and wouldn't be giving me the time of day, but he was.

"Alana, I see right through you, you're not fooling me one bit. I see your game. I see what you are doing and guess what, that shit isn't gonna fly this time. You came to LA unexpectedly and thought in that twisted mind of yours that I would actually consider taking you back?" Todd shook his head. "You are crazier than I thought. So, I'm going to say this loud and clear, Kai is the woman I want to spend the rest of my life with, not you. Whatever master plan you have magically conjured up to change that, is not gonna work, got it?"

The woman at the counter waved for the next person in line as Todd continued to stare at me. He cocked his head. "What no comeback?"

"Yeah, you're next," I said.

Todd dropped his eyes, picked up his carryon bag and stepped past me and up to the helpful reservationist as I stood a few steps behind him. I watched him from behind in his double-breasted blue suit, baby-blue shirt and burgundy tie.

Todd retrieved his hotel key from the clerk.

"Hey, do you want to grab a bite to eat later?"

"No, Alana, I *do not* want to grab a bite to eat with you later. I *don't* even want to be here in New York with you."

Todd turned and started to head toward the elevators. I looked up at the woman waving me over and instead of going to the counter, I dropped my bag and followed Todd for a few steps. "Todd, wait."

"What now?" Todd looked at me. I'd never seen him so irritated before in my life.

"Listen, I know you are not a fan of me right now, but damn we could at least be cordial since we are now working with each other, right?"

Todd looked down, then back up. Still irritated.

"I promise I will not bring up the past or anything related to our little threesome. We will keep it strictly business. I know you have to be hungry, because I am starving."

Todd took a deep breath, looked around the hotel lobby and back at me.

I put my hands up as if to surrender. "Dinner and a drink, that's it," I added. "Besides, I need to get some clarification on what we are doing tomorrow," I said, lying through my teeth. "I mean, I would hate to tell David that my own lawyer didn't make any time for me while he was in New York with me, right?"

I stood there waiting for Todd's response, hoping what I said did the trick to smooth things over between us momentarily. Sometime you have to play dirty, and I was pretty good at that.

Todd clenched his jaw and I saw the muscle flex on the side of his face. "Fine, I will give you forty minutes."

"Fabulous! I'll take it. Let's convene here at say six p.m. That's exactly one hour from now. I hear the Madison Club Lounge is a great spot for dinner and drinks."

Todd didn't respond, only gave me one last irritated look before turning and heading to the elevator.

I smiled and thought to myself, *Game on.*

SIXTEEN
TODD

I headed down to meet Alana for dinner, much to my chagrin. I would have preferred room service, a couple of brews and a Skinamax movie, but Alana had a point, if we were to work together, we could at least be cordial. Don't get me wrong, I had known Alana for far too long and knew she probably had something up her Chanel-laced sleeve, but I wasn't falling for it, not this time. I couldn't be more happy with Kai and I'd be damned if I let Alana mess it up again.

I stepped out of the elevator and headed toward the Madison Club Lounge in the Roosevelt Hotel. The lounge was soaked in the quintessential ambience of a classic, old- school New York City hotel lounge. I walked into the sight of rich mahogany paneling, stained-glass windows and deep-cushioned leather chairs. This spot was definitely sexy, but, unfortunately, I was there with Alana, not Kai.

I spotted Alana sitting at a table for two on the right side of the lounge. I preferred to sit at the bar, but since she beat me to the punch, I would roll with it. Besides, my plan was to only have a few drinks, a small bite to eat and then head back up to my room to prepare for my day tomorrow. I'm sure Alana had a different agenda, but she was in for a rude awakening.

"Hey, handsome," Alana said, beaming at me as I sat down.

"Hey," I said in the driest tone I could muster. I glanced down to see Alana had already ordered our first round of drinks. *Figures.* "I see you didn't waste any time getting started."

"When in Rome..." Alana said, picking up her wine glass and taking a sip.

I sat across from her and glanced up at the 50-inch television, catching the highlights of the earlier football games.

I glanced back at Alana and noticed she was watching me.

She shot me a smile. "You have always been a football fanatic. That's one of the things I love about you."

I tried to ignore Alana's niceties and picked up the menu to see what kind of food I could order.

"Oh, I already ordered your favorite, fillet mignon with mixed vegetables."

I slowly put down my menu. *Here we go.* I needed to put her ass in check with a quickness.

"Listen, Alana, I only agreed to come down here to show you I can be the bigger person and that I can be cordial when needed. So before you start taking us down memory lane, let's get a few things straight between us. We are not friends. I am your lawyer, period. We are here on business and nothing else. I don't need you ordering my drinks or my damn food, okay?" I shook my head, threw down my menu, picked up my Jack and Coke and threw it down. I felt my body tense up, so I took a deep breath to calm myself down.

Neither one of us spoke for a few seconds. Alana finally broke the silence.

"I'm sorry. I was just trying to be nice, nothing more." Alana looked away. "I've just been going through a lot since I got out of jail. Between Riley, her dad and my mom, it's been hard." Alana looked away as she took her napkin that was on the table and pressed it to the corners of her eyes.

I looked away from her display and took another deep breath. I tried to focus on the couple across from us and briefly wondered what kind of life they led. I brought my focus back to Alana who was still looking down.

"How is Riley?" I asked. Despite having found out that Riley wasn't my daughter, a day didn't go by that I didn't think about her.

"She's good. I'm sure she misses you," Alana said, putting the napkin back down on the table.

"Yeah, I miss her, too."

"You should call her."

"Alana, you know that wouldn't be a good idea."

"Right, of course.

"Just tell her I said hi for me."

"Okay," Alana said. She looked back up at me and gave me a quick smile. I didn't return it. Instead, I looked away again.

More awkward silence.

The waitress brought our food and neither of us made a move toward it. I wasn't as hungry as I thought. Finally, we both started to eat in silence. After a few uncomfortable moments, Alana tried to restart the conversation between us.

"Listen, Todd, I...um...I'm sorry. I didn't mean to put you through so much drama and..."

"And what? Make my life and Kai's life a living hell?"

"Well, those weren't my exact words, but okay."

"I don't believe you," I shot back and took another small bite of my steak.

"Fine, whatever, don't believe me. At least I got it off my chest."

I threw my fork down. "Really? So you saying 'I'm sorry' is somehow supposed to erase all those years of what you did?" I shook my head. "You are a piece of work, Alana."

"Forget I even said anything, okay?"

"I will, Alana. Honestly, I don't think I could ever believe anything that came out of your mouth anymore."

"People change, Todd."

"Yeah, but you're not people."

"Whatever, Todd.

"Yeah, whatever." I knew that dinner was a horrible idea, and our conversation so far had confirmed just how much of a trainwreck I thought it would be. Alana continued to sip her drink, then out of the blue started to chuckle to herself. I waved our waitress down, motioning for another drink. If I was going to get through this forty minutes I would need some more assistance.

"What the hell is so funny, now?"

"Nothing." Alana chuckled a bit more, and shook her head again. "I was just thinking of that time in college when I first met you. How I let you drive my car and how you pulled over so I could go pee."

A half-smile emerged on my face, the memory from college coming back to the surface. "Yeah, on the steps of someone's home no less. I couldn't believe you did it."

"Hey, I had to go."

We both laughed about that. I had to admit, Alana and I had some fun times in college. I hated how our relationship had taken such a turn for the worse, because in all honesty, we had been pretty good friends.

"Also, I couldn't believe that you didn't even tell me that I had tucked my skirt into my damn panties and you had me walking into that Kappa Party like that."

"Hey, you always yearned for attention, and you got plenty of it that night. Just ask Brett Montgomery."

"Okay, you did not just bring up his name. He was so gross."

"Yeah, but he loved some Alana Brooks. I took another sip of my drink. "You never gave that brother some?"

"Nope"

"Not just a little bit?"

"Ah, hell to the no. I may have fucked a lot of guys in college, but he wasn't getting anywhere near this."

I didn't know if it was the alcohol seeping into my bloodstream that was having an affect on my attitude, but the more Alana and I cruised down memory lane, the more my defenses began to relax.

After about two hours later and our fourth round of drinks, I was pretty faded. I didn't even notice my phone ringing. I finally saw I had missed three calls from Kai.

"Shit."

"What?"

"I missed three calls from Kai, fucking around with you," I said, pulling myself up to call her back. My head spun and I realized I was probably drunker than I first thought.

"Tell Kai I said hey."

"See, there you go, there you go," I said as I chuckled. "Now zip it, remember, this is our secret."

I dialed Kai's number and she picked up."

"Baby, where have you been? It's three a.m. there? Did you fall asleep?"

"No, I um, I ended up having drinks with Al...a lot of people."

"A lot of people. Todd, are you drunk?"

"I may be a little inebriated, yes, but I am in complete control," I said, falling into the bar seat next to me.

"But it is all good in the hood."

Silence fell over our connection. "You still there, Kai?"

"Why did you just say that?"

"Say what?"

"It's all good in the hood. Alana used to always say that."

"No she didn't. Baby, you're tripping," I said. Alana walked over to me and placed a fresh drink in front of me. I picked it up and threw it down. "Listen, baby, let me pay my bill and get out of here and I will call you the moment I get into the room," I said, shooting Alana a thumbs-up.

Alana then leaned past me to retrieve a glass of wine from the bar. Her hand brushed against my dick and I got an instant hard-on.

"Oh shit."

"What?"

"Nothing, baby. Listen, I-I gotta go. Ima call you later."

"Todd, wait—"

I hung up before Kai had a chance to throw out a rebuttal."

"What the fuck are you doing, Alana?"

"What? I was merely reaching for my glass."

"You touched my dick."

"Did I?"

"Yes."

"I may have grazed it. I mean, it's *hard* to miss, being so nice and thick, and..." Alana looked down. "And growing as we speak. I see *someone* has missed me."

"Okay, stop. Seriously, I gotta go. I'm going to bed before we both regret something or someone," I said as I heard the words repeat in my head. I was seriously fucked up and I needed to get to my room fast. I stood up as the room began to spin. I fell back down in my seat.

"Oh my God!" How did I let myself get so damn drunk?" I looked at Alana who seemed tipsy, but not as fucked up as I felt.

"Shit, I needed some water," I said.

"Here, let me get you some," Alana said as she flagged down the bartender. He slid a glass my way as I chugged it down. Great, now I felt like I was about to throw up.

"Fuck me."

"Come on, I'll walk you to your room," Alana said, grabbing my arm. I pulled away. My intention was to quickly whip my arm away from her, but it felt as if everything was happening in slow motion. That movement almost had me on my ass, if the guy next to me hadn't caught me mid-fall.

Alana jumped in. "I'm sorry, he's had his limit for the night, as you can see. We were just heading upstairs, thank you." The man released his hold on me and I fell into Alana's arms.

"Come on, Willie Wino, let's go."

"Hey, I am not that damn..." *Burp* "...drunk."

"Yeah, right." Alana smiled. I could have sworn she was getting her kicks out of seeing me like this. We headed to the elevator. Once inside I felt as if I was losing consciousness.

"What's your room number?" Alana asked.

"What?"

"Your room number?"

I couldn't remember my last name, let alone my damn room number. I ran my hand down my face, felt it turning numb. "I can't remumber my womb mummer." When I started to not make sense, I knew it was close to curtain time.

"Fine, let's just go to my room."

"Oh no you don't, I'm not falling for the banana in the tail pipe."

Alana laughed loudly. "Listen, you may be fine and all, but right now you are not all that fuckable. This is not a good look on you, boo."

"Just leave me in the elevator. I'll sleep here." I felt my body sliding down to the floor, only to be helped back up by Alana.

"Todd, just come to my room, sleep it off for a few hours then go back to your room. If of course you remember your *womb number* by then." Alana chuckled.

The elevator door opened and I stumbled out, leaning on Alana as we headed down the hall and into her hotel room, shutting the door behind us. That was the last thing I remembered until...

***

A knock at the door startled me as I heard a woman's voice yell from the other side of the door, "Maid service."

I managed to yell back, "Come back later." My eyes were still closed, but that didn't stop those internal drums from banging on every inch of my membrane. I grabbed my head with both hands in an attempt to make it stop. I slowly opened my eyes and tried to focus on where I had ended up after having too much to drink the night before.

Where the fuck was I? I felt a moment of displacement as I scanned the tan velvet painted walls and chocolate curtains, the flat screen TV and the black modern furniture. After a few seconds of soaking in my surroundings I remembered I was in the Roosevelt Hotel in Manhattan.

My mouth was dry. I felt like I could have drank the entire Manhattan River right about now. I felt movement beside me and when I turned, I saw Alana asleep right next to me. My eyes sprang open and as I jumped up, I noticed I was completely naked.

"What the fuck?!" My outburst woke Alana and she turned over with a satisfied grin on her face.

"Morning, baby," Alana said, belting out a yawn, followed by a smile. That's when I noticed she was naked, too. This was not good, not good at all.

"What the hell did you do to me?" I asked, jumping up from the bed. I grabbed my head as it continued to pound harder. I searched the floor for my Calvin Klein shorts, and quickly put them back on.

"The question is what did *you do* to me."

"Don't fucking play with me, Alana. What the fuck happened last night?"

Alana sat up and leaned against the white-cushioned headboard. "Are you saying you don't remember, Todd Daniels?"

"That's what the fuck I'm saying." I kept looking around the floor for the rest of my clothes and belongings. "Tell me we *did not* have sex last night. Tell me."

Alana only gazed back at me with that stupid smirk on her face and I felt like throwing up all over again.

"Got dammit, Alana, I'm fucking waiting."

"Okay, we didn't have sex last night."

"Is that the truth?"

"Of course not."

I felt the bourbon churning in my stomach, getting ready to make a return trip through my esophagus.

"Hey, I can't help it if you are still attracted to me. I mean, I don't fault you, you're a man, and..." Alana pulled back her sheet to reveal her naked body. "I am a sexy ass woman." Alana smiled.

"You're a fucking bitch, you know that? And for the record, I am not attracted to you," I said, looking away from her exposed body.

"Actually, I think your sidekick would beg to differ," Alana said as her eyes dropped back down to my penis.

"Stay the hell away from me, you hear me? Fucking crazy bitch." I grabbed the rest of my belongings and finally located my phone. Thirteen missed calls from Kai. I was so fucked right now.

"Shit, shit, shit." I headed out of Alana's room, slamming the door behind me. I headed toward the elevators and finished buttoning up my shirt and tucking it into my pants. I walked in the elevator and just stood there. I couldn't even remember my damn room number.

I hit the lobby button and the elevator took me back downstairs to the front desk. I now understood why key cards didn't display your room number, but it didn't help when you were drunk out of your mind and you ended up in your ex's room naked and confussed. That was when I had a big problem with it.

I got my room number and jumped back onto the elevator. My phone rang; it was Kai. I took a deep breath, shook my head and prepared myself to face the firing squad.

"Hey, baby," I said in a nonchalant tone, hoping her anger didn't match what I conceived it could be.

"Where in the hell have you been? And don't fucking lie to me."

Kai's words sliced through my head like a hot knife through a cold stick of butter. "Baby, I am so sorry. After I got off the phone with you, I headed upstairs to my room, only to realize I left my phone in the bar. I only got it back right now." I swallowed hard, and hoped that Kai bought that. My lie would quickly fall apart if I had to explain any further. I was so damn pissed at myself, I couldn't even see straight.

"You left your phone in the bar? Really?"

"Baby, I know it sounds crazy, but I drank a little too much last night and I am so sorry." I repetitively hit my head on the elevator wall behind me. I wished in that moment I could have cloned myself and beat the shit out of me. Kai was silent.

"Okay, I'm not going to sit here and give you the tenth degree. I just needed to talk to you this morning. Mila was getting on my last nerve last night and I just needed to hear your voice."

"I know and I am so sorry, baby. Listen, I have to get to my meeting, but I promise I will call you afterward and we can talk."

"Fine, okay, I love you."

I held my breath and my whole body tensed up with guilt from her words.

"I love you, too, baby."

I hit end on my cell phone, as the elevator door opened back up. I slowly moved toward my room. As I entered, I clutched my head in my hands and slid down to the floor. My head was pounding as I struggled to remember what happened last night. Alana had to be lying, but there was no way of me knowing what had really happened. I was drawing a complete blank. No matter how hard I tried, I could not remember a thing.

I leaned my head against the hotel door and Alana's naked body popped back in my mind and my dick instantly got hard.

What was wrong with me? I started banging my head against the door over and over and over, saying out loud to myself, "I love Kai, I love Kai, I love Kai."

But if that was true, why did I still feel attracted to Alana? Alana's naked body popped in my head again and I felt my dick start to throb.

"Shit, stop it!" I dropped my head into my hands. "What the fuck am I going to do now?"

SEVENTEEN
KAI

"Surprise," I said, lightly knocking on Todd's new office. I thought I'd come down and see if he could break away from lunch, but the look I got when I walked through the door was closer to pure shock rather than the happy surprise I expected.

"Baby, what, what are you doing here?" Todd asked, leaping to his feet.

"Well, I can't say I was in the area, since I wasn't, but I woke up this morning missing you and thought, I wanna go see my husband since apparently you came straight here from the airport.

"Yeah, I um, I had to finish up some things, but I had planned to cut out of here early to come home."

"Really?"

"Seriously."

I didn't know if I believed Todd or not. He'd been acting pretty weird lately. "Well, I am here now." I wrapped my arms around Todd's waist, pulling him close.

"Baby, if you haven't noticed, my walls are glass. I'm trying to keep it professional."

"Oh right," I said, pulling away a bit. "Sorry, sorry. So are you hungry? I thought we could go grab lunch."

Todd headed back to his chair, but not before shooting a look past me to the other side of his glass walls.

"Actually, baby, I don't think I will be able to get away."

"Why?" I asked, walking over closer to his desk, picking up the framed picture of our family. We were so cute.

"I um, I just have too much to finish here," Todd said, typing up a few lines on his computer. "Rain check?"

I flopped down in front of him. I needed to figure out what the heck was going on, period. "Okay, why are you acting so secretive lately? I gotta say, you are really starting to make me question our move here."

"What? No!" Todd closed his laptop, stood and walked back around his desk toward me. He moved a stapler and a pencil holder over before he sat on the edge of the desk.

"Baby, I am just so stressed with this new job. I want to make a good impression. Besides, if I mess up, I could be out of a job and right now, I am the sole breadwinner."

I didn't like Todd's comment about him being the sole breadwinner. I know we made a collective decision for me to stay home and him to work, but hearing it out loud made me feel less than him and I didn't like the way that felt.

"Yeah, I know, but I just miss you and I wanted to spend some time with you. Mila was driving me nutty."

"Oh right. How long is she staying?"

"She actually left on a red-eye this morning"

"Wait, I missed her?"

"Stop with the fake disappointment."

Todd smiled. "How about I finish up here as fast as I can and head home? Maybe we can get a babysitter and I can take you out to dinner."

"Now that sounds nice," I said, sliding my foot up Todd's leg.

"Okay, you need to stop. You're getting me all excited at work," Todd said and once again his eyes diverted past me and out to the exterior office. I turned to look for what he was looking at, and then back at him.

"What are you looking at?"

Todd's head snapped back toward me. "Nothing, why?"

"Then why do you keep looking past me?

"What? What do you mean? I'm looking at you."

"No you're not. It looks like you are looking for someone or looking *out* for someone. What's going on?" I was becoming even more irritated than before.

"Actually, I have an appointment coming in, so I was on the lookout for them. We don't have real secretaries here, they're all virtual. So people can sometimes wander through the halls aimlessly," Todd said, raising his left eyebrow to make his point.

"So nothing is wrong? Nothing you need to talk to me about?"

"No..." Todd looked away, then back at me, as if he was collecting his thoughts or maybe his lies. "No, not at all."

I continued to stare at Todd, hoping to detect whatever unspoken nugget of information he was trying to hold back.

"Seriously, Kai, everything is fine, it's just my job."

"Fine, then I will go, go have lunch by my lonesome. Oh, by the way, Camille took me to this amazing restaurant by our house."

"Who is Camille?" Todd asked. His eyes continued to drift off of me and then back again. I sucked my bottom lip, telling myself to just let it go.

"Camille is the new parent I met at Kristopher's school, remember? I told you about her."

"Yes, of course, right."

I stood and grabbed my purse. "Nice try, cowboy, but I know you don't remember."

"What? I do, really."

I ignored Todd's attempt at convincing me. I knew him way too well. I stood and grabbed my purse.

"Where did you want to go to dinner? My treat," Todd said, smiling.

"Oh, wait, we can't go to dinner. Tonight is the parents' potluck at Kristopher's school."

"Potluck?" Todd questioned.

"Yes, it's a great way for us to meet the other parents. It starts at six."

"Great. I will meet you there."

"I thought you were leaving early?"

"Six is early," Todd said with a quick smile.

"Fine, then you can meet Camille. I've told her all about you."

"Sounds like a plan," Todd said. His eyes slid past me for the third time, and this time they stayed on something, so naturally I decided to turn around and see what was capturing my husband's attention. The moment I turned my head, Todd grabbed me and planted a kiss on me. It felt good, but was totally weird and out of place. I pulled away.

"Todd, what happened to being professional?"

Todd looked at me. "Oh, sorry, babe, I um, I just wanted to kiss you."

"No you didn't. As I turned my head around, I didn't see anyone but an elderly woman wandering the halls as if she was lost or confused.

"Sometimes I just get a little jealous when you mention you've met a new girlfriend."

My head jerked back. "What? Are you serious? Really? You think every woman I meet I'm going to jump in bed with?" I said frustrated.

"I don't know, maybe?"

"Todd, would you stop it? I told you I was done with that phase of my life, okay? So please just let it go."

"Fine, I'm sorry, baby. You just make me so crazy."

"That's good to know," I said, heading toward the door. Todd followed behind me.

"Hey, let me walk you out."

"That's very nice of you," I said in a playful tone.

"It's the least I could do since I'm blowing you off for lunch. I'll definitely make it up to you tonight."

"You better."

I followed Todd out of his office and noticed he was going a different way than the way I came in. "Baby, why are you going this way? Is this like an escape route or something?" I said jokingly, though my intentions were serious.

"No, actually, this is just a faster way to the front—less turns."

Before I could declare that I was onto his game, Todd planted a kiss on my lips as the elevator doors opened. "I will see you later," Todd said as he made his way back to his office, not the way we came either.

I rode the elevator down to the lobby and could smell a familiar perfume. I couldn't put my finger on where I had smelled it before.

Just when I thought I had figured it out, the elevator doors opened and the smell dissipated. I headed out into the lobby, past the security desk and Starbucks Coffee Stand and out into the beautiful 70-degree California sunshine. I pulled out my cell phone to call Simone. I needed to get her handle on what had just happened.

"Hey you, what's going on?" Simone said, picking up the phone.

"Nothing much. Just leaving Todd's office. I tried to surprise him and he damn near shoved me out the door before I even had a chance to say hi."

"Was he on the phone?"

"No."

"In a meeting?"

"No."

"Did he have Monica Lewinsky under his desk?"

"Simone, really?"

"Listen, he was just probably in the middle of something when you stopped by."

"It's not just that, he's been acting weird ever since we got to LA. Then there was that whole charade in New York where he supposedly forgot his phone in the bar. Plus, let's not forget that Jessica woman who is still a mysterious open case."

"Kai, you are starting to sound like a real *bored* housewife of California. I love you, but stop it. Go sign up for a yoga class and be done with it."

"Oh gawd, am I? I don't want to turn into one of those needy, overly sensitive housewives."

"A few more of these phone calls may get you your membership card in the mail."

"Oh geezus."

"Hey, I told you to move back to Chicago with me."

"Yeah, and maybe I should have pushed more for Chicago. I am not getting a good vibe in California so far. Well, when it comes to Todd anyway."

"Listen, don't think too much into his little idiosyncrasies. Men can't adjust as fast as we do." I could imagine her grinning over the phone. "Their little brains have a hard time processing large amounts of new things shoved into a small space."

"Yeah, you're probably right."

"Go enjoy yourself. Get a massage! Take one of those Hollywood tours. Hell, if I were you, I'd veg out at the beach all day."

"Yeah, you're right, I need to chill out a bit."

"Yes, you do. Listen, I gotta take this call, talk soon?"

I disconnected from Simone, and stood looking back up at the 20-story high-rise where Todd's office was located. I thought about going back upstairs to apologize and I even took a few steps toward the door before stopping and turning around.

"Ah, I will tell him later. For now, I think I will just head to the beach."

EIGHTEEN
TODD

"Now that was a close call," Alana said, sauntering into my office. It had only been minutes after Kai had stepped onto the elevator. "For a second I thought Kai saw me. Good job diverting her with a kiss." Alana took a seat across from me in my office.

"Then again, she probably wouldn't have known it was me until her brain registered it. I'm sure I am the last person she would expect to see in Los Angeles, let alone in your office."

"Alana, what do you want?"

"Do I really need to answer that? Because I think we both know the answer to that," Alana said, shooting a flirtatious wink and air-kiss toward me.

My patience was slowly wearing thin with this woman. I stood and headed toward my office door. I didn't care what went down in New York, she wasn't going to get the best of me. I'll be damned if I let this little setback ruin the rest of my life with Kai.

"I have work to do so if you don't want anything, kindly get the fuck out of my office," I said with a smile and tilt of my head.

"Is that any way to treat the woman you made love to the other night? By the way, I didn't appreciate you jumping on the red eye this morning without letting me know. I was looking forward to our flight back together. You know, to cuddle and recap our night together."

Just the thought of what I did to Kai made me slip back into an internal rage. How in the hell did I let Alana get the upper hand on me? I never should have met her for drinks. That was my fault, and I needed to figure out how to fix this shit if it was the last thing I did.

"Alana, first of all, I don't remember a thing about that night. So, technically, it didn't happen."

"Oh, it happened, and happened and happened."

"Okay, shut up."

My head pounded as I tried to remember that night, but every time the memory surfaced, all I could remember was going to the bar to answer Kai's call. After that it was all blank. And then I woke up completely naked next to Alana.

I had only blacked out once before when I was pledging Kappa Alpha Psi fraternity and my brothers kept giving us tequila shots delivered by turkey basters.

My phone buzzed and I prayed it was not Kai calling or my secretary telling me that she was on her way back. I headed back around my desk and hit speaker on my phone.

"Yes?"

"Mr. Daniels just wanted to remind you of your one p.m. meeting with Bobby Carter. He's going to meet you at the W Hotel on Beverly."

"Great, thank you."

I was just about to disconnect when I heard her say, "You also have a six p.m. dinner meeting with Alana Brooks."

"What?" I looked up to see Alana giving me a five finger roll wave. I picked up my cell phone and selected the calendar app.

"I don't have a meeting with Alana at six."

"Oh, I know, she just texted me a few minutes ago saying she needed to meet with you."

"Alana is in my office now, I'll discuss it with her."

"Oh, okay. Hi Miss Brooks!"

"Hi Sherry! Thanks a million for squeezing me in his schedule."

I hung up the phone before my receptionist had a chance to respond. Damn virtual assistants. She was probably at home, taking calls in her damn panties.

"Where's a good place for us to meet tonight? I've been hearing great things about Crustaceans in Beverly Hills, which isn't too far from your one o'clock meeting."

"I have a previous engagement, Alana, so we're going to have to reschedule," I said as I grabbed my jacket and briefcase to head out for my one p.m. meeting.

"I guess you'll have to change it."

"Yeah, okay," I said. I was seconds from heading out my door when Alana spoke up again as she flipped lazily through my *Men's Fitness* magazine.

"It would be such a shame if Kai found out about what happened while we were in New York. I mean, what would she think, or in your case, do? God forbid she leaves you, since she'd never be able to trust you *ever* again." Alana smiled.

I stopped, took a deep breath, pulled myself together, and reminded myself that Alana would stop at nothing to be back on top, no matter who she hurt.

"Alana, it's my word against yours and Kai wouldn't believe you for a second."

"That it may be, but how will you explain you keeping our working relationship from Kai? And before you tell me that she knows, I know you haven't told her yet." Alana raised her right eyebrow. "Todd, honey bunny, I know you too well."

Alana and I locked eyes. I stayed silent, and felt the guilt consume me. I was feeling like a trapped rat.

"I guess you didn't think that far, now did ya?" Alana diverted her eyes back to my *Men's Fitness* magazine.

I took a few more steps and opened my office door. "Alana, if you think this little game you're playing is going to work in your favor, think again. We will never be together again."

Alana looked up from the magazine and smiled. "May I remind you, it's not how you play the game." Alana threw the magazine down on my cocktail table, stood up, straightened out her skirt and walked up to me. She was standing only inches away from my face, and I could smell her scent. It was that same smell that she knew used to drive me crazy. She ran her finger up and down my button-down shirt. "It's how you finish."

"I will see you tonight, pumpkin, six p.m., don't be late." Alana let her hand glide down my canary-yellow tie with blue diamonds before dropping it and heading out the door.

***

I arrived at Crustaceans at six p.m. sharp. I figured if I could go over whatever Alana wanted to discuss, I could still make it over to Kristopher's school for the tail end of the potluck.

Six-fifteen rolled around and still no Alana. I ordered a beer, drank it down, played a bit on Facebook, returned a few emails and finally glanced at my watch. It was now six-thirty-five. I felt my frustration building as I dialed Alana, got her voicemail, and ordered another beer.

Six-forty-five.

"The hell with this," I said. I grabbed my jacket, briefcase, and threw forty bucks down on the table. I nodded to my waiter and made my way toward the door. I stepped outside to see Alana stepping out of her white rented Audi Q5 SUV.

"Leaving so soon?"

"Alana you are forty-five minutes late."

Alana looked down at her rose-colored Diamond Michael Kors watch. "Really?"

"Yes, really. I told you I had a previous engagement, so I'm leaving."

"Oh, that's a shame, I invited David."

"What? I asked, my face falling when I saw my boss David pulling up to the valet.

"He wanted to join and I couldn't say no."

David jumped out of his Mercedes-Benz E-Class. "Todd, I hope you don't mind me joining you and Alana tonight. I wanted to get an update on what we've got working for her and since I was in meetings all day this seemed like the perfect time."

I looked at Alana, then back at David. "Of course, that's not a problem, sir."

"Great, let's head in, I'm starved." David moved his way into the restaurant and was followed by me and Alana. I pulled Alana back out of earshot from my boss.

"I don't appreciate this shit. You had me waiting for forty-five minutes and then you invite my boss without telling me, I told you I had something to do tonight."

"Next time try keeping your dick in your pants and all will be good in pleasant-ville," Alana said with a wicked smile on her face. David walked back over to us.

"They've got a table for us upstairs," David said with a broad smile on his face.

"Great, I heard the garlic noodles here are to die for," Alana said, shooting me a smile.

***

Two hours later I found myself racing down LaCienga toward my son's school, hoping and praying I didn't miss the Potluck Meet and Greet. I turned down Slauson to La Tiera then made a sharp right onto 64th Street before turning into the parking lot of the school.

I jumped out of my car and as I was running toward the front door, Kai walked out with Kristopher. *Dammit.* The moment my eyes connected with Kai, I slowed my pace. I had a strong feeling that this was not going to be good. Thank goodness a woman walked out right behind Kai with her daughter, which may have been my saving grace.

"Baby, hey, listen, I am so sorry, my meeting ran late," I said. I moved to give Kai a kiss and a hug, hoping my tenderness would help lessen the blow that would come later.

Kai pulled back as her eyes shot left then right.

"Baby, are you okay?

Kai gave me a weird smile. "Um, sure, I'm good." She turned her attention to a woman—a very attractive woman I might add—who resembled Rosario Dawson. "Baby, this is Camille who I told you about," Kai said with a smile surging across her face. She looked at Camille and then back at me. I wasn't sure if Kai was mad or just waiting until we got alone to lay into me.

"Nice to meet you, Camille," I said and extended my hand her way.

"So this is the Todd I've heard so much about from Kai."

I slowly pulled my hand back. "I hope it's all good."

"What other way would it be?" Camille said with a half-smile.

I felt my left eyebrow shoot up. "Right," I said, drawing out the word. This woman was fine, but she wasn't as friendly as she first appeared.

"Kai, I better get going, call me later."

"Of course."

I watched as Camille gave me one last once over before heading to her car. I looked back at Kai.

"What's up with her?"

Kai looked at me, then back toward Camille walking to her car, then back at me. "What's up with what?"

"That woman totally wants you."

"Todd, don't start."

"What? If she isn't a lesbian, then I don't know..."

"She is not a lesbian."

"Listen, I think I have been around enough lesbians to know when one is diggin' you and she is diggin' you," I said, smiling.

"Really, Todd, you're going to go there? I think instead of focusing on who wants to fuck me you need to focus on coming home to your wife. Especially considering how you've been MIA ever since we got to LA. Now you show up two hours late to something that was important to me and you give me the ninth degree about having a new friend that you *claim* is a lesbian. I cannot believe you right now."

I wasn't sure what to say or if I should even bother saying anything at all. I definitely stepped knee-deep into that one.

"I am taking our son home, join me if you wish, I don't give a damn."

I watched as Kai walked off and got into her car. I guess that wasn't the best line of defense to use with her, seeing as I had been hanging out with Alana. I took a deep breath and figured I better think of a good way to apologize when I got home.

NINETEEN
KAI

The fact that Todd thought Camille was into me brought the guilt back for being friends with her. It never crossed my mind that Camille could be into me, let alone be a lesbian. She didn't come off as a lesbian, just a very friendly person.

I had to admit, the thought of it made me a little more than a little excited. I guess my explosion toward Todd had a lot of different emotions behind it—one being that I was over him not being at home, and two, well, my guilt of being attracted to yet another woman. That was a territory I promised myself as a married woman I would never venture into again.

When I finally got home, it was already nine p.m. I knew Todd would be right on my heels, so I had to pull it together before he walked through the door. By turning the tables and laying the guilt back on him for being out of sight most of the time, I knew he would come in apologizing, having forgotten entirely about the Camille thing.

"Baby, I am so sorry, I didn't mean to insinuate anything. I should be flattered that she is attracted to you," Todd said, dropping his briefcase on the couch. His suit jacket quickly followed as he moved over to where I was standing. "Lets me know that my woman is still sexy."

Todd pulled me close and kissed me on my forehead, moving to my cheek and finally my lips. I moved my head to the right as he continued down to my neck.

"Can you forgive me?" Todd pleaded.

"I guess, but why do you think every attractive woman is a lesbian?"

"I don't know, baby, I guess I am just a little weary, you know?

I pulled back. "Weary? Seriously, we made a pact, no stepping out on each other, right?" I said, staring deep into Todd's eyes, hoping to detect the undetectable.

"I know, I know," Todd said, his eyes diverting away from mine. I lifted his chin with my hand, and forced him to make eye contact with me.

"Listen, I told you I've been there done that with a woman, and frankly, it was just a phase for me, okay? Yes, Camille is attractive, and if she is attracted to me, well, that's her problem."

"Oh my God, baby, you are making me so horny. I love it when you get all feisty and stuff." Todd began to kiss my neck some more. I was getting turned on until I looked down to see Kristopher staring and smiling at us. Todd looked down, too. I gave Todd a look.

"I got 'em." Todd picked up Kristopher. "Come on, little man, it's bath time."

Todd headed to the bathroom to give Kristopher his nightly bath, and I headed to the kitchen to pour myself a glass of wine.

After retrieving my glass, I moved back to the living room where I kicked off my shoes and flopped down on the couch. Camille passed through my mind, and another warm sensation danced in my stomach. Damn, was it really just a phase? *Yes*, I thought. I shook her out of my head and grabbed my laptop off our cushioned ottoman. Perhaps wasting some time on the Internet would help push her face out of my head.

I hit Amazon, eBay, Babies R Us and Pinterest.

My concentration was interrupted by a scent I was picking up in the air. It was a familiar scent. In fact, it was the same scent I smelled in the elevator at Todd's office. I stopped typing and looked around, wondering where it was coming from.

I shook it off and I started to type again, but the smell kept bothering me. I set my laptop beside me as I stood, and did a 180 when I noticed Todd's suit jacket draped across the couch a few inches from where I sat. I found the culprit of the mysterious scent. I reached out and pulled the jacket toward my nose, getting an up-close-and-personal sniff. I sniffed again and yes, it was definitely a woman's scent.

I could ask Todd, but I was sure that he would tell me that he had women clients in his office all day. The scent being a woman's perfume wasn't what was bothering me. It was the *familiar* smell of it that was driving me crazy. I had smelled this perfume before.

My mind started to churn as I listened for Todd and Kristopher. I heard them in the bathroom, so I started to snoop around in Todd's pockets. I was not one to snoop. Well, maybe just occasionally. But Todd was acting so weird since we moved to LA and if he wasn't going to voluntarily tell me what was going on, it was within my jurisdiction to find out for myself. Unfortunately, my search came up dry. Other than an old peppermint and half stick of gum, Todd's pockets remained frustratingly empty.

I threw Todd's jacket back over the couch and flopped back down. The scent cascaded through my nose again and began to drive me a little crazy. I shook my head and tried to forget about it. It was probably some random scent I smelled before. That was my fault for always making it a point to visit perfume counters in the department stores.

I started typing again when it hit me like a brick flying through the air— ALANA! That was Alana's scent! I swung around and grabbed Todd's jacket again, this time taking a deep breath of his top right lapel and my eyes widened as I took it in. Yep, that was how Alana smelled. How could I have forgotten that smell? I had tried to block a lot of things out about her, maybe that was one of them, but it all came rushing back to me like a tidal wave.

I sat up, my back totally straight as my mind started to race. Could Alana be in LA? Was that her I saw in the car the other day? And now her smell on Todd's jacket. Oh my God! Was Todd with Alana tonight? My breath started to quicken the more I created this horrible scenario in my head of them hooking up again. Would he actually do that to me? Contact Alana and not tell me? Holy crap. We had a pact, our makeshift truth circle.

I tapped on the space bar on the keyboard, making the screensaver vanish. I opened up another Safari tab and typed in Facebook pulled up Todd's page and searched for Alana Brooks in his friends' list. I found her profile quickly and my eyes focused in on the tab that said where she was living. Next to it I saw with a sigh of relief it still listed Chicago as her place of residence.

I sat back, breathing a sigh of relief. I stared at Alana's profile picture, which was one of her glamorous, overzealous poses.

I wondered where she was and who she was doing right about now. She was one person I did not miss in my life, not at all. I often wondered if Todd missed her, seeing as they had known each other for so long. Could you just cut someone off like that? Could he?

"Hey." Todd's voice startled me. With two quick clicks I closed Facebook and opened up Pinterest.

"Hey, you done with the bath?"

"I am. What are you up to?" Todd stood in front of me, rolling his sleeves back down.

"Nothing, just doing some pinning," I said. I was sure that Todd could hear my heart beating against my chest.

Todd looked past me and headed my way. He reached over me and grabbed his suit coat off the back of the couch.

"I gotta drop this off at the cleaners," Todd said, draping his jacket over his arm.

I stared at his face, trying to detect anything abnormal about his body language and tried to stay calm. "Why? It doesn't look dirty," I said. I hoped my prying came off like disinterested conversation.

"Oh, yeah, I've worn it a few times and believe me, it's time. Todd leaned back down, and gave me a peck on the lips. "Ima go read Kristopher a story."

"Okay," I said and watched him leave the room. I leaned my head back and thought about what Simone had told me. Perhaps I did have too much time on my hands. I laughed at my conspiracy theory.

My phone chimed, announcing that I had a text. I checked it and it was from Camille.

Hey chica, good hanging out with you tonight.

I texted her back.

Same here, sorry you didn't get a chance to get to know Todd, maybe next time. Have a good night.

I placed my phone down, slid my mouse over Facebook and logged out of Todd's account. My phone chimed again. When I picked it up I noticed it was Camille again.

Actually, I'm glad he was late, I liked having you all to myself. Nite.

I stared at the text and couldn't come up with a good way to respond to that. Being attracted to Camille was one thing, her having feelings for me could turn everything into a big problem.

***

"I liked having you all to myself?" Simone repeated what I told her as she peeked above her Oliver Peoples glasses. "And you have to question whether or not this woman wants to fuck you?"

"So you think she does?" I asked, feeling a little giddy inside, but I masked it for Simone.

Simone removed her glasses, and slowly placed them on top of her iPad. She leaned forward and smiled. "Kai, it shouldn't have to take a women's head between your legs to give you a hint that she wants to eat you."

"I don't know, Simone."

Simone flopped back into her seat. "Okay, here we go again. Listen, I love you to pieces, but saying 'I like having you all to myself' isn't going to come out of my mouth. You do the math. We both know you can be a bit tardy to the party when it comes to this kind of stuff."

"Ha ha."

Simone gave me one last look, threw back on her glasses and grabbed the menu sitting in front of her.

I was meeting Simone for lunch at Sandwiches, a new restaurant on the Santa Monica Pier. This was my first time down here and it was amazing. The water, sun and energy of the pier all combined into one of my favorite new places to visit while living in LA.

Simone called me last week and told me she wanted to discuss something in person with me. I didn't argue with her since I was happy to have my best friend come visit me in LA. I hadn't seen her in six months and for me that was five months too long.

"So what is it that you had to talk to me about in person?'

"Well, ever since you and Todd decided to take the leap into la-la land, I have been thinking."

"Okay?"

"Why not open a boutique agency out here and have you run it?"

"But I am a stay-at-home mom now."

"Kai, you're a stay-at-home mom with a son in school five hours a day, so tell me what you are staying at home and doing," Simone said, twisting her mouth to the side, waiting for a response.

Simone was right, Kris had been in school for two weeks already and I was bored. Besides, there were only so many lattes and yoga classes I could take.

"Plus, I'm sure you guys could use the extra income."

I started giving a lot of thought to what Simone was proposing. "When were you thinking of opening it?"

"Not for a few months. I have a few contacts out here and I want to follow up with them first. You could even start out by working part-time."

"Can I think about it?"

"Of course, take all the time you need. If you don't do it, then I won't open here. Can't let just anyone run the company and I know you would do the damn thing justice."

I was pleased to hear that Simone had so much confidence in me.

"Thanks, Simone."

"Also, when you are ready we should sit down with the few clients that I have and…"

Simone's voice began to fade as my mind went back to Camille. I looked up to see Simone staring at me.

"What?"

"What's this woman's name?" Simone said pulling me back to the here and now.

"Who?"

"The woman who has clearly stolen your attention away from our meeting."

"No, I wasn't thinking of Camille. I was just, um, thinking of Kristopher, so…"

Simone looked at me as she took off her glasses. "You're not thinking of going there again are you?"

"Oh God, of course not. Come on, don't you think I learned my lesson with Alana? I worked too hard getting Todd back from that evil bitch, I'm not going to lose him again. Besides, Todd and I made a promise to be one-hundred percent honest with each other."

Simone sucked air through her teeth and sat back in her chair. "One-hundred percent huh?"

"Yes," I said. I wasn't sure if I was trying to convince myself or Simone.

"Heartwarming. Almost made me cry. Almost."

"Would you stop it? Have a little faith in me, okay?"

"I don't know, Kai. You tend to teeter. I just hope you don't teeter right into her lesbian clutches."

"No, there will be no teetering here. It is flattering that someone so attractive as her could be into me, but at the same time, I told you, me being with Alana and then Toni was just a phase. It's been almost three years since I have been with or thought about being with a woman, why? Because it was a *phase*."

"Hey, if you say so."

"I know so. I will prove to you that I am not into this woman. Plus, I am convinced that Todd will be truthful with me as well."

TWENTY
ALANA

"Tell me why I have to be here for you to try on some stupid outfits again?"

I poked my head out of the dressing room of Neiman Marcus. "Seriously, Todd, you are ruining this for me." I pulled the curtains back to reveal my new Ann Klein black and red halter dress. I took two steps out to see Todd pacing back and forth and mumbling something to himself.

"Oh would you stop it already? You used to enjoy doing this with me in college."

Todd stopped, turning to look at me. "No I didn't. In college you were my only means of transportation, I had no choice."

I ignored Todd's comment and headed his way. "Whatever! Can you zip me up please?" I slowly turned my backside to Todd, but kept a close peripheral view on him. I noticed how his eyes diverted to my nice tight ass that was accentuated in this dress. I smiled to myself. Men were so damn easy. Todd continued to stare as if he forgot why I walked over to him.

"Todd?"

"What?"

"My zipper."

"Oh, right," Todd said, snapping out of his trance as he zipped me up.

"Thank you." I headed over to the full-length mirror across the room. "Besides, I needed a male opinion on what to wear to the show's launch party tonight."

I noticed Todd was ignoring me. I needed to divert his attention back to me. "So what do you think?"

Todd looked up. "About what?"

"The dress." I turned his way, and gave him a full view of what I was working with.

Todd tilted his head, shrugging his shoulders while giving me and my new dress a once-over. "It's fine."

I turned to show him my nice round high ass again. I knew what he liked. "And now?"

Todd looked up again, back down to his phone, then quickly look back up with his eyes locked on my ass, then quickly back down. "Yeah, it's um, it's fine."

"Just fine?"

"What do you want me to say, Alana?" Todd blurted out in annoyance.

"You are even more handsome when you are irritated." I smiled and walked back over to him.

Todd turned his attention back to his iPhone. He looked up when I was inches away. Our eyes locked. I could smell the mint gum between his masculine breath. It was intoxicating. We held each other's eyes in an intense stare before Todd took a step back from me.

"What are you doing, Alana?"

"I need you to unzip me," I said, gazing into his eyes then down to his lips. I wanted to kiss those lips, those nice juicy lips, but I refrained, the time wasn't right. I turned my back to him once again so he could unzip me.

Todd took a deep breath until he finally unzipped my dress.

"Thank you, darlin'." I let the dress drop to the floor where I stood, revealing my white lace bra and panties. I took two steps away and waited for his reaction.

I turned slightly to see Todd trying *not* to look, but in his mind I knew he was drooling. I looked down to see a small bulge forming in his pants. A slight smile of satisfaction spread across my face as I walked slowly back into the dressing room. I added a cherry on top by bending over very slowly to pick up my dress.

Todd turned away from me to hide his bulge as I moved back into the dressing room.

"Are you free tonight?" I asked through the curtains. I peered out to spy on Todd who was desperately trying to adjust his unexpected hard-on.

"Not for you, Alana."

"Great, because I need a date for the party tonight," I said, heading out of the dressing room with the red cocktail dress in my hand. I had decided this would be my purchase for the party.

Todd was standing there with his face curled up. "Yeah, that's not going to happen. I have plans with Kai."

I shook my head. "Todd, Todd, Todd, how many times do we have to go over this? You work for me, and as your client, I need you to accompany me to this affair tonight. I am sure Kai would understand. Oh wait, Kai doesn't even know you work for me now because you didn't tell her."

I could see Todd's mind racing, and I assumed that he was trying to figure out how to tell Kai the truth now after the fact. He'd try to make it seem like it was an oversight or misunderstanding. I knew Todd like the back of my hand. He always thought he could handle everything on his own.

"I plan on telling Kai when the time is right."

"Right, of course you will."

I smiled at Todd. "Besides, this is a good networking opportunity for you. There are going to be tons of actors, writers and producers there. You should be thanking me for even allowing you to tag along. Consider yourself lucky."

"Alana, save it, okay. I will go as your lawyer, period, not your date."

"Tomato, toma-toe. Pick me up at seven?"

"I will meet you there at seven and will be leaving by eight."

"Fine. Oh, and wear your black small pinstriped suit with the red tie. It'll complement my dress fabulously," I said, and shot Todd another good-bye wink.

Todd swiveled and headed for the door. "Good-bye, Alana."

"Bye, handsome."

I watched Todd head out the door and smiled to myself. Getting Todd back was going to be easier than I thought—like taking candy from a baby.

TWENTY-ONE
TODD

I arrived back at my office around four, dreading the call I would have to make to Kai telling her I would have to work late again. I honestly thought that after New York and Alana breaking into Kai's apartment, that this brand of drama was out of my life. Apparently, I was mistaken.

Sometimes I wished that Alana had never stepped into my life. Our friendship had been weird from the beginning. I was registering for the fall semester of my second year, and she walked up to me and planted a kiss on my lips without a word. While I didn't mind an unsolicited kiss from a beautiful woman, I didn't know her from a can of paint.

Later, I discovered that she was trying to send the starting running back at our school a message that she was not available. It was the sort of challenge that most men loved, and it turned into a chase for Alana throughout our four years in college. She later married Avery Anderson, but as it goes with most pro-football players, the wife isn't the only piece of ass they have. That was something that didn't sit well with Alana, naturally.

The first time I slept with Alana was in college. It was after a fraternity party and Avery and Alana were on a so-called break. She was too drunk to drive, so we ended up walking to my dorm and crashing in my room. I don't know if it was the alcohol, the warm body next to me or just the fact that I hadn't gotten any ass in two months, but I made a move on Alana that night, even knowing in the heat of the moment that it was a mistake. Just like I knew choosing Alana over Kai fifteen years later was an even bigger mistake. Doing that gave Alana hope, hope that I think drove her obsession for me to this day.

I shook my head, hoping to shake away the past memories. I picked up the phone to call Kai, and then placed it back down.

I had to find a way to get Alana out of my life for good. I wasn't sure how, but this couldn't continue.

"Hey baby."

"Don't tell me, you have to work late again?"

"Just for an hour or so, the paperwork is piling up here and—"

"Save it, Todd, it's always something. We haven't spent any time together since we moved here. I'm starting to think this move wasn't such a great idea after all."

I cringed hearing the hurt radiate from Kai's words. Maybe she was right, maybe this had been a bad move.

"Baby, I promise, it will get better."

"Yeah, I hope so. I guess I'll see you when you get home," Kai said and hung up the phone.

I sat back in my chair. "Dammit."

I had to find a way to tell Kai about Alana. This was not what I had signed up for when I took this job in LA. My phone buzzed and it was my assistant.

"Yes?"

"Alana Brooks is on line one for you."

"Tell her I'm not here."

"Yes, Mr. Daniels."

I clicked my phone off and sat back again. Before I had a chance to close my eyes, my cell phone was ringing. I shook my head and sent Alana to voicemail. I felt my body tensing up as if I were drowning in a sea of sand, going deeper and deeper. I had to find a way out fast before it killed me and my relationship with Kai.

***

I got to the party around 7:15 p.m. I stopped off at a lounge on Labrea to have a quick drink and clear my thoughts of all the harmful things I wanted to do to Alana. The party was on the lot on Stage 45, the set of Alana's new show, *Office Temps*. The moment I stepped onto the stage and saw the masses of Hollywood people, I knew this was not a party for me.

When Alana and I were dating, I hated these types of events. They were filled with people willing to do anything to get what they wanted. I glanced over and saw Alana laughing and talking with two men and a woman. There was no doubt, she was definitely in her element.

"Hello," I said, walking over to Alana and her mini-entourage. Alana was wearing the red lace dress she picked up earlier today and as much as I hated to admit it, she looked sexy as hell.

"There you are," Alana said as she grabbed my arm. "This is my handsome lawyer I was just bragging to you all about."

Everyone smiled, giving me the Hollywood once-over. I wondered what Alana could have possibly said about me."

"Alana tells us you just moved here from New York.

"I did. About a few months back."

"How do you like Los Angeles?"

"It's an adjustment, that's for sure," I said, trying to be as social as I could.

"How long have you guys been together?" a petite blonde woman I hadn't seen asked.

"Oh, we aren't together. Alana is just my client," I said, feeling more than a bit annoyed at the assumption. I didn't think I was giving the vibe that we were dating.

The woman looked a bit stunned. "Oh, I'm sorry, it just seemed like you two were a couple."

Alana placed her hand gently on my arm. "Well, we *were* a couple once. It just didn't work out. But who knows what the future will hold, right, honey?"

I looked away, annoyed, and then back at Alana and the three people standing there. "It was nice meeting you all. I'm going to grab a drink at the bar."

"Oh, get me a pomegranate martini, please. I will be over there to join you in a bit," Alana said as she shot me a sexy smile.

I turned, grating my teeth together, and moved to grab Alana's drink. I considered how badly the martini would stain her precious new dress, not to mention cause an un necessary scene, so I decided against it. I took a few steps away from everyone, but not before hearing one of the women in the group say to Alana, "You were right, he is delish."

I shook my head and headed for the bar. I downed a Jack and Coke before I heard Alana walking up behind me.

"Why are people here thinking we are a couple?" I said the moment Alana was in earshot.

"I don't know, maybe they see our ridiculous chemistry?"

"We don't have chemistry, Alana."

"Clearly, we do. It's not just me that sees it, but the world. We really should stop fooling ourselves and just go for it."

I downed yet another drink, felt my head start to get light as the alcohol settled into my bloodstream. I glanced down at my watch. "Well, I'm out of here."

"Already? You have only been here fifteen minutes."

"Thirty, it took me fifteen just to find the damn stage."

I set my drink on the high table next to me, turning to leave.

"Wait, don't leave yet, at least come see my dressing room. Please? It will only take a second, then you can leave, I promise. Besides, I have to grab something."

I looked around the set, made sure no one was clocking our moves. If this would get me off the hook and out of here faster, then so be it. "Fine."

I followed Alana as she led me to her dressing room. I looked down at Alana's form-fitted dress and had to admit how amazing her ass looked. This bitch was crazy but she still had a banging ass body. I felt my dick getting hard as I imagined that ass belonging to Kai as I bent it over and fucked the shit out of it.

We got to her dressing room. It was nothing special. There was a tan leather couch, flat screen television and two matching ugly-ass green chairs. I turned around to take in the whole room. "So what's so great about this?"

"That's the point, wanted to get your input on how I could change it...put my stank on it," Alana said with a smirk as she sat down on the couch and crossed her legs. She patted the seat next to her, but I ignored the invite.

"I'm not an interior designer, Alana."

"Well, duh, but I wanted to hear what you would do if this was yours."

This was ridiculous. "Alana, do you think I am stupid? I know why you lured me here."

"Why is that, Todd?" Alana adjusted herself on her tan leather couch and looked up at me.

"To try and fuck me, again," I said, tugging my collar, and feeling a surge of heat on my neck.

Alana leaned back on the couch, folding her arms. "My, my, aren't we full of ourselves tonight?"

I shook my head. "Good night, Alana."

"Wait, okay, the real reason why I brought you here was to give you this." Alana picked up a large folder from her desk, opened it, pulled out a piece of paper and handed it to me.

"What is this?"

"It's an invite to my birthday party."

"Why are you giving this to me?"

"Because you're invited, silly. I would say bring Kai, but that probably wouldn't go over so well." Alana smiled, playing with her hair.

"I'm not coming to your party, Alana," I said, taking a few steps toward the door. Alana stood and followed me.

"Now that's just silly. You've always come to my parties ever since we first met."

"It's not gonna happen this year."

"I don't know why you are being so difficult, Todd."

"I don't know why you don't get that we aren't friends."

Alana and I stared at each other, neither one of us giving up any ground.

"Fine, don't come, your loss."

"Thank you, I will take that loss. Good night." I turned toward the door, but not before hearing a knock.

I opened the door and a man stood there wearing tan khaki pants, a white shirt and a black jacket. "I am looking for Alana Brooks."

Alana stepped up behind me. "Can I help you with something?"

"Are you Alana Brooks?"

Alana looked at me, then back at the young guy. "Yes, why?"

He pulled out a white envelope and as Alana grabbed it he said, "You've been served."

"What the hell are you talking about?" Alana replied as the man turned and walked down the hallway, disappearing as he turned the corner. I closed the door slowly and Alana looked at the white envelope, then back at me.

"It's not from me," I said. Though knowing Alana's track record, it could have come from anyone.

Alana walked back over to the other side of the room as she slowly opened the envelope, and gasped out loud. "Oh my God." She turned and looked at me, then back down at the paper and read it to herself.

"What is it?" I stepped a few feet closer, trying to see what devastated her so much.

"It's a petition for guardianship. My mom is trying to take Riley away from me." Alana let out another loud gasp. "She is asking the court to terminate my paternal rights for good."

Alana dropped the envelope, collapsed onto the couch and sobbed.

I stood there, unsure of what to do. My heartstrings were being pulled now that I had Kristopher and I could never imagine someone taking him away from me. I walked over to where Alana was sitting and sat down next to her.

"I can't believe she is doing this. I told her I just needed a little more time to get myself together. I am trying as hard as I can," Alana said through her tears.

"Can she do this?" she asked me.

Before I could pull it back, my lawyer instincts jumped in. "Let me see what I can do."

Alana stared at me. "You would do that for me?"

"For Riley."

"Thank you so much," Alana said, collapsing into my arms. I sat erect on the couch again, not knowing what to do, and attempted to see through her tears. Could this be another one of her stunts?

I glanced at the paper sitting beside her and saw *State of California Courts* stamped on the bottom. I sighed and wrapped my right arm around Alana. She began to sob harder and looked up at me.

"I can't lose her. I know I haven't been the best mom, but that's why I am out here trying to make a life for me, for us." Alana looked up at me. "That is why I need you, baby, you can't leave me. *We* need you."

Alana pulled in closer to me and I felt my body tense up. I attempted to pull away but Alana began to hug me tighter. Before I knew it she was kissing my neck and working her way up to my face.

"Alana stop, stop." I continued to pull away from her.

"I need you." Alana continued to push into me.

"Alana, stop."

"I need you so much." Alana began to claw me, her aggression was overpowering and before I knew it she had my pants unzipped and her hand was inside my pants massaging my dick through my underware.

"Oh shit."

Alana continued to massage me. I felt my hardness rise. I tried to stand, but my legs felt weak. I looked down as Alana pulled my *entire* dick through my zipper section of my pants and wrapped her mouth around it, almost in one simultaneous movement. Her warm tongue sent a hot sensation of pure ecstasy through my entire body.

"Oh fuck," I gasped.

Alana started licking and sucking my dick with the same aggression that got me here in the first place. I tried to push her head away, but the more I pushed the harder she persisted and the harder she sucked. I couldn't believe I was here, *again*.

First in the hotel in New York, which I do not remember at all, I was totally out of it, but now, now I could stop her, but I didn't. My body was overpowering my mind, my rational. *You are sooo fucking up right now.* I was being forced to do something against my will, but I could not stop her.

Alana continued to work me as she swirled her tongue around my dick's head. I could see her look up at me with determination in her eyes.

"Oh my God," I moaned out loud, trying to catch myself. I couldn't let Alana see how much I was enjoying this. Shit! I forgot how good Alana was at giving head, something I wished Kai knew how to do better.

Alana continued pushing me deeper within her mouth. I felt my dick sliding down her throat as she ran her tongue up and down my shaft, counteracting the motion with her hand. I felt my toes crisscross in my Marc Jacobs shoes. My mind began to jump back in time, back when we were dating, back when Alana and I would have the wildest sex I could have ever have imagined. Pop, a flashback of me fucking Alana from behind as I pulled her hair and she yelled out loud. Pop, Alana giving me head in my car as I finger fucked her.

"Aw fuck, Alana," I said bringing myself back to the present.

Alana pulled up and looked at me with even more determination in her eyes. "I love it when you say my name."

I saw an opportunity to push back and find the strength to stand to get the hell out of there. I pushed myself up, but Alana latched back on, sucking harder and faster like I was a tootsie pop and she was trying to get to the center. I felt my body drop back down to the couch, surrendering to her oral power.

New weakness flowed through my body and I felt my climax coming fast and strong. My testicles began to tighten, letting me know it was all about to come to an end. I pushed up *again* on the edge of the couch as a surge of heat rushed through my body. Alana pushed my dick even deeper into her mouth. It felt as if my dick was halfway down her throat again. "Fuck," I gasped, as my adrenaline pushed me to finally stand as I came so damn hard in Alana's mouth. "Ohhh, shiiiiit!"

I heard moans coming from Alana.

I grabbed on to the bookshelf for support, trying not to fall back down. My legs were weak, I was breathing as if I had just crossed the finish line of the LA marathon.

"Yummy yum yum." Alana smiled as she pulled my dick out her mouth. "See, baby, you could have this every day if you just come back to me. Every day."

I stumbled, falling into the table next to the couch, but successfully stood.

I managed to stagger to the door.

"Don't go, please." Alana was still on her knees, looking up.

I ignored her remark as I opened her door.

"Todd, I love you."

I turned and locked eyes with her. "You only love your damn self." Those were my last words as I slammed the door behind me. I took two steps then lost my balance and fell into the opposite wall. I managed to tuck my dick back into my pants and zip myself back up as I saw a guy coming down the hallway.

"Are you okay, buddy?" he asked.

"Yeah, I'm fucking fantastic," I said, slowly regaining my composure. I felt the strength flow back into my legs and my body. I headed down the hall and out of the stage.

I took in the fresh air, and breathed in deeply. I couldn't believe what had just gone down. I thought of Kai and cringed at the idea of what she would do if she had any clue about what had happened. I didn't want to go home; I couldn't face my wife.

I shook my head, adjusted my pants and belt to make sure I was presentable. I headed for my car and when I got there I just sat there. I knew I was digging a deeper hole every single day I allowed this secret to fester.

TWENTY-TWO

KAI

"I was surprised to get your call," Camille said, giving me a warm smile and placing the glass of red wine in my hand.

I shifted to get a bit more comfortable on her brown leather couch and I glanced around her soft-cream-colored living room with earth accents. I couldn't get what she texted me out of my head. Even though Simone was usually right about these things, I had to see for myself.

"Yeah, Todd is working late *again* and I hate to be in the house alone."

"Oh, so you're using me? Ah ha!"

That phrase sounded much better in my head. "No, no, it's not like that, believe me, I just..."

"Kai, I'm just messing with you. Believe me, I used to hate being alone when my ex was on the road. I get it." Camille winked at me as she headed back to the kitchen to fetch a plate of cheese, crackers and grapes.

"I hope I am not intruding...last minute and all," I said.

"Oh God no! I love the company. Besides, I was actually gonna give you a call to see what you were up to tonight, so it worked out perfectly."

Camille sat down next to me on the couch and crossed her legs Indian style. She had on an oatmeal-colored V-neck T-shirt and matching linen pants. She looked very comfortable. Her hair was swooped up in a bun on the top of her head and I noticed she was wearing princess-cut diamond earrings, one carat at least. Made me wonder just how much she was getting every month from her ex huband.

I picked up my wine and sipped on it, and Camille did the same. Silence fell between us and the only thing we could hear was the sound of our kids having a toddler conversation in the back room.

"I think our kids play well together," Camille said, curling her legs up under her chin as she wrapped her arms around them.

"Yeah, they do," I said, feeling myself getting nervous being with Camille. I took a sip of my wine to help calm my nerves. Camille was hard to read. One minute she was into me, and the next, nothing.

"So you said Todd is a lawyer?"

"Yes, an entertainment lawyer."

"Oh nice. Is that what he did in New York?

"No, actually, he was a divorce attorney there."

"He could clean up here as a divorce attorney. No one stays married in LA."

I felt a warm sensation cascade through my body from Camille's comment. Not exactly what I wanted to hear right now. I looked down.

"Oh, I wasn't referring to you and Todd," Camille added quickly, picking up on my awkwardness from her off-the-cuff comment.

"Of course," I said with a smile. I drank a little bit more of my wine.

"Either way, all attorneys work too much in my book. My sister is a lawyer and she's always working. I was surprised when she told me she was engaged."

"That's your sister in Brooklyn, right?"

"Yep. She is actually engaged to a woman."

"Oh, she's gay?"

"I guess. It all depends on the day with my sister," Camille said as she grabbed a few crackers and some cheese from the plate. "So, Kai, what do you like to do for fun?"

"Not that much anymore now that I have a kid. It's kinda hard to find the time."

"It's not that hard. You're just not trying hard enough. Hang around me, I'll show you some things." Camille looked at me hard then eased out a smile.

There went that tingly sensation again. I took a deep breath and smiled, taking another swig of my wine.

"I would never want to wear out my welcome," I said, deflecting her comment.

"You could never wear out your welcome with me, Kai. I love having people over here. I'm an Aries, it's in my DNA, we thrive off of social interaction.

"Oh, you're an Aries? I'm a Sag."

"There it is, our signs are compatible. That's why I like you so much."

"Right," I said, breathing a sigh of relief. That was it, Camille was an Aries. She wasn't attracted to me, she was just a social butterfly, which most Aries were. I immediately felt calmer hearing that.

Camille started bobbing her head as I heard the faint sounds of house music escaping from her speakers.

"Is that house music I hear?" I asked as I struggled to make out what song that was.

"Yes it is."

"Oh my God, you like house music?" I continued with the utmost excitement in my voice.

"Yes I do. Love it in fact. That was all I listened to growing up in New York. That's where it originated."

"Ah, excuse me, Miss New York, but house music originated in Chicago, thank you very much."

"Oh no, here we go, another Chicagoean claiming the origin of house music."

"Well, you are looking at a house head. You don't know anything about Farley "Jackmaster" Funk, Mr. Fingers, or Frankie Knuckles."

"Yep, I know them well. Camille walked over to her iPad, hit a button and the song "Love Can't Turn Around" filled the room.

"Wow, I love love that song," I said, and felt my body starting to move involuntarily.

Camille started to dance along with the music and I watched her sway, turn and bounce to the sound. She looked so damn sexy, dancing to the music. She reached out for me to join her.

"Oh no, I hung up my dancing shoes years ago."

"Come on! You're already dancing in your seat." Camille pulled me up from the couch and I quickly fell into step with her. We held hands and grooved to the music. She started to turn me as we ended up doing the cha-cha.

"Wait, you can cha-cha, too?" Camille said, as we smiled at each other.

"Of course, I am from the Chi, remember where house music originated," I said with a knowing smile.

"Right," Camille said as she gave me a playful wink.

We continued to dance when a new song came on, titled "Heavenly Father." This song was more spiritual and sensual. We both got lost in its lyrics.

I turned my body and began to groove when I felt Camille behind me. She placed her hands on my hips as she guided them left then right. I closed my eyes and leaned back into her and my butt-pressed against her pelvis. We swayed to the music as I felt her breath on my neck. I closed my eyes and became lost in the music and her scent.

I turned to face her, my eyes still closed, and my body still grooving. I felt Camille wrap her arms around my waist as my eyes opened to see that we were only inches away from each other. We both stopped dancing and stared at each other.

I felt my body start to tingle everywhere and I quickly realized something in that moment—I missed the touch of a woman. I breathed in the soft smell of Camille's skin and hair and I lost myself in her for that moment. I lost myself so much that before I knew it, we were in a serious lip-lock. Our tongues danced a familiar dance as her kiss was soft, sensual and slow. Something I had missed.

I felt my body open up as my juices flowed down, soaking my panties. Camille pulled my shirt up as she rubbed my erect nipple, sliding her hand into my pants as her finger massaged my clit. I was wet and so fucking turned on I didn't even realize what I was doing, until I came to my senses as I jerked away, wiping her wetness from my lips.

"Oh my God, what am I doing?"

I stared at Camille and she smiled at me with her head tilted to one side, wiping the moisture from the sides of her mouth as well as off her fingers.

"That should not have happened."

"But it did," Camille said, smiling.

"I um, I have to go."

"Don't tell me, you've never gotten with a woman before?"

I ignored Camille's comment, pissed she even pegged me as someone who *got* with women.

"Kai," Camille said as she stepped close to me and placed her hand back on my leg.

I stepped back from her, moving her hand off of me. "You don't get it. I am not bi-sexual, okay," I said giving Camille one last stern look.

"You could've fooled me."

I felt my body tense up and I stormed out her living room. I heard Camille right behind me.

"Kai, wait, listen, I'm sorry, really. I was out of line and I don't want you to be mad at me. I don't know what came over me.

I headed down the hallway and grabbed Kristopher.

"Kai, please don't go," Camille pleaded.

I didn't look at Camille before heading out her front door.

I walked home, and thought about how much I enjoyed that kiss from Camille. I felt the wetness in my panties. What was wrong with me? It had been three years since I was with a woman and I thought this shit was over for me. Why now? Why was I so damn attracted to Camille?

***

"Kai, you awake? I turned to see Todd sitting on the side of our bed, looking down at me. The moment I saw him, I felt a wave of guilt engulf my whole body.

"Hey, I must have dozed off." I turned to look at the clock that displayed nine-forty-five.

"Yeah," Todd said as he stared deep into my eyes. "I missed you." His voice was soft and breathy.

"I missed you, too." I sat up on one elbow. I then noticed Todd had on shorts, a T-shirt and was freshly showered.

"How long have you been home?" I asked.

"About thirty minutes or so?"

"You showered?"

"Yeah, I had a long day and I wanted to get the day off of me. I'm sorry again about tonight. I left my meeting as soon as I saw an opportunity," Todd said, and he started rubbing my stomach. I felt my body respond to his touch. I am sure kissing Camille earlier that night helped give me a good start. I had to tell Todd what had happened. I had to stay true to our pact.

"Baby, I have to…" I said, stopping as I noticed Todd looking at me with this look, this weird look.

"Todd, what's wrong?" I sat up, thinking what I needed to tell him could wait.

Todd just stared at me, and then he laid his head in my lap. I rubbed his head. "Baby, are you okay?"

He was silent as he began kissing my stomach, lifting my shirt to touch my bare skin. His lips made contact with every inch of my stomach before moving up to my breasts. I closed my eyes as Camille crossed my mind once again. I tried to shoo thoughts of her away. This probably wasn't the best time to tell my husband I had been intimate with a woman *again*. Though to be fair, he wasn't making it easy to fit it in. Todd made his way to my neck and I felt myself starting to get very turned on.

"Baby, wait."

"Shhh, Kai, don't talk just…just let me make love to you," Todd said with his puppy-dog eyes.

"Are you sure you're okay?" I asked one more time.

"Yes, I just want to be with you." Todd closed his eyes as he climbed on top of me and that night we made love with the most passion I could remember in a long long time. It was amazing, but it also made me wonder what the hell was going on in his world.

TWENTY-THREE

TODD

"This is nice, huh?" Kai said as she laid across a blanket with her head in my lap, looking up at me.

It was early Saturday morning and we finally had time to spend it together as a family. My guilt was starting to eat away at me at a faster rate while I attempted to analyze my situation. I still had to tell Kai about everything that had been going on since Alana stepped into my office.

I looked down at Kai, stared at her smooth caramel complexion and almond eyes. I ran my fingers through her thick, curly locks. "Yeah, this was very nice. We need more of this."

Kai turned as she sat up on her elbows. "Now that's the pot calling the kettle black." Kai smiled at me.

"Don't start none, won't be none," I joked back.

"Yeah, yeah."

"Listen, I told you things were going to change and, well, this is my attempt at it. So slow your role, relax and enjoy the moment. The beautiful park we are sitting in, the seventy-degree weather, our son playing nicely in the sandbox."

"I know, I know. Oh, don't forget tonight we are going to dinner with my mom. Her flight gets in at five and she is meeting us at six for dinner."

"We don't have to pick her up from the airport?"

"Apparently, she rented a town car. You know how Corrine does it."

"Nice, I like your mom even more. It's all about being self-sufficient."

Kai smiled then flipped onto her back, laying her head in my lap once again, staring up at the sky.

"So last night, wow. What brought that on?"

I knew my overpowering lovemaking session was going to raise a red flag for Kai. I guess that was one of my fatal flaws, I tended to overcompensate when I knew I was fucking up.

"What brought what on?" I asked, knowing exactly what she was insinuating.

"You were pretty intense with your lovemaking last night."

"Are you complaining?" I challenged.

"No, it was just different." Kai opened her eyes. "But is everything okay?"

I shrugged my shoulders. "Yeah, everything's fine. Is everything okay with you?" I thought I'd throw the question back in her direction, and pull some of the heat off of me.

Kai was quiet for a few seconds as she closed her eyes. "Yes, everything is good, baby." She began to rub my leg.

A silence fell over us as my eyes started to wander around the park. I looked over at Kristopher in the sandbox, and then over at another family eating lunch at the park's picnic tables. Then I glanced to my left, and saw a woman with a child walking in our direction. As the woman got closer I soon realized who it was.

"Isn't that your friend from the school?"

Kai's eyes popped open. "Who?"

"The woman I met the other night."

Kai sat up and looked in the direction I was staring.

"What's her name?"

Kai began to fix her shirt, running her fingers through her hair. "Camille."

"Right, is that her?"

"It is."

Camille was now less than ten feet from our picnic blanket.

"I thought that was you two," Camille said, approaching us with a smile.

"Yep, it is us," Kai said, and I couldn't help but notice that her tone was weird. I couldn't swear to it, but it almost sounded like she didn't want Camille around us. I figured Camille didn't pick up on that since she kneeled down on the corner of our blanket.

"Camille, you remember my husband, Todd?"

"Sure do," Camille said, giving me a quick nod. She scanned me from head to toe. "Todd, this is my daughter, Natalie."

"Hi, Natalie, you sure are beautiful."

Natalie smiled and headed over to the sandbox where Kris was.

Camille looked a little different than I remembered. She almost looked full Hispanic even though I knew she was mixed with black. I think it was her silky hair.

"Nice to see you again, Camille. I know when we met it was pretty brief. I got caught up in a late meeting that night," I said, shooting Kai a look. I was trying to reaffirm my story, even if it was a meeting orchestrated by Alana.

"Hey, I understand, my sister is actually a lawyer, and her hours can be crazy."

"Oh, does she practice here?"

"No, she actually lives back in Brooklyn now where you guys moved from." Camille directed her eyes over to Kai, who was looking a bit uncomfortable. "I told you about her, right, Kai?"

"Um, yes, you did," Kai said with a half-smile. Why was Kai so uncomfortable with Camille? My phone rang and when I looked down I saw it was Alana calling. *Dammit.*

"I gotta grab this," I said, standing up with my phone in my hand, making sure Kai didn't see the display screen. "This will only take a second."

"Okay, babe," Kai said.

I walked about eight steps out of earshot before I picked up Alana's call. "Why are you calling me on a Saturday? I am with my family?"

"Hello there, handsome, how are you?"

"What do you want, Alana?" I said in my most deadpan tone I could muster up. I felt like shit about what had happened the other night in Alana's dressing room—mostly because part of me enjoyed it.

"I see someone rolled off the wrong side of the bed this morning."

"I'm fine, okay? I thought we agreed no calls on the weekend."

"I know, but I was just calling to remind you about my birthday dinner party tonight. I'm having it at Seasons 52 in Century City, eight p.m.," Alana said with a tinge of excitement in her voice.

"Have fun, Alana, I'm not coming."

I heard Alana sigh on the other end of the phone. "But you always come to my birthday parties," Alana whined.

"Well, not anymore, things are different now or haven't you been paying attention?"

"Oh, come on, it will be fun. We can even slip into the bathroom and—"

"Alana."

"What?"

"I have to go."

"That was fun in my dressing room, huh? I think I need another taste of you." Alana continued disregarding my sign off.

"I have to get back to my family, okay?" I was about to hang up on her when she grabbed my attention.

"Wait, I was also calling to let you know that you left your wedding ring in my dressing room the other night."

"What?" I said and looked down to see my ring was gone. *Fuck me.*

"Yeah, it must have slipped off during our little tussle on the couch."

"Dammit," I said. How could I have not noticed my wedding ring slipping off?

"Yeah, that sucks for you, but yay for me. It all works out. You can pick it up tonight when you come to my party. Has Kai noticed it gone yet? Probably not, I don't remember her being the most observant one."

I ignored the dig. I wasn't going to engage her.

"So I will see you at eight?"

"No."

"What about your ring?"

"I will get it Monday when I come to the set. Just leave it in your room, in the drawer of that side table."

"Too late, I have it with me. I tucked away for safekeeping."

I shook my head. "Good-bye, Alana."

"What about tonight?"

I hung up on Alana and stood there for a minute, trying to think of what I could tell Kai if she noticed my ring was gone. I looked over toward where Kai and Camille were sitting. I couldn't hear what they were talking about, but their body language was saying a lot. I watched as Kai continued to look uncomfortable during her conversation with Camille while Camille did all the talking.

There was something up with that, something Kai wasn't telling me. I shook my head, maybe I was jumping the gun like I did the other night when I met Camille. Maybe I was trying to find guilt in Kai since I was neck-deep in it myself. I shoved my phone back into my pocket, took a few steps only for it to ring again.

"Dammit."

"What?" I said in a harsh tone.

"Todd, it's David Johnson"

"Mr. Johnson, how are you on this Saturday morning?" I quickly changed my tone when I heard the voice of my boss.

"Doing well, Todd. Listen, I just got a call from Alana Brooks and she is requesting your presence tonight at her birthday party."

I felt my anger escalate by the second.

"Is that right? Funny that you called, Mr. Johnson, I actually just got off the phone with Ms. Brooks and I gave her my regrets on not being able to make it tonight."

"Why is that?"

I paused, didn't expect David to investigate further, but just take my reason and be done with it. "Well, actually, sir, I have a previous engagement tonight. It's my mother-in-law's birthday and my wife and I are taking her to dinner."

"Well, we can't disappoint the mother-in law, now can we?" David said with a laugh.

"No, sir, we cannot." I was happy to see that David was on the same page as I was.

"But I'm sure your dinner won't last all night? Just swing by Alana's party afterward and make a quick appearance. Bring your wife and the mother-in-law as well, I am sure Alana wouldn't mind one bit. We like to keep our clients happy. I am sure you can agree with that."

I felt my teeth clenching together in an unnatural way. "Of course."

"I can count on you to be there tonight?"

I swallowed hard, kept my emotions in check. "I will be there," I said, forcing a smile, hoping it could hide my dismay.

"Great. Sometimes you have to take one for the team, right?"

"Oh yeah," I said, though he couldn't know how big this hit would be.

"See you on Monday."

"Yes, have a good weekend, sir," I said and hung up the phone and shook my head as I looked back down at my bare ring finger. How could I have been so damn stupid to lose my wedding ring, in Alana's room of all places?

TWENTY-FOUR
KAI

"You did it, didn't you?" Simone hit me with a left-field question as we chatted over Skype mid-afternoon.

"Did what?" I asked innocently, looking away from my screen. I knew exactly what she was referring to. I looked back to my computer screen to confess. Sometimes I think my best friend is psychic.

"Fucked her?"

"Simone, I didn't *fuck* her, and why do you have to be so crass?"

"Then what happened?" Simone continued with her interrogation.

"She, well, she fingered me, okay."

"Okay, that's much classier, much classier indeed." Simone's sarcastic tone rang loud and clear.

"But it's not going to happen again."

Simone shook her head. "If I had a tube of lipstick every time I heard that…" Simone then leaned toward her screen with eager eyes.

"So how did it go down and don't skip the details. Wait, am I going to need a bag of Doritos for this? I had to go on Weight Watchers after those stories about you and Alana. I'm thinking I'm gonna need to re-up my membership."

"I don't know why you think my life is so entertaining."

"Talk to me after fifteen years of marriage and you'll understand."

"Can we just drop it? I feel bad enough as it is that anything happened."

"Fine, maybe it's for the best. I can't afford to gain any more weight right now anyway." Simone began to analyze her face and body from her reflection on Skype. "I seriously need to lose some damn weight. Maybe I could get one of those surgeries, you know the one where they attach your throat to your ass."

"Simone, stop it, you're fine."

"You say that because you don't have to see me naked," Simone said. She pulled out a folder and opened it.

"Okay, let's get down to why I'm calling this afternoon."Have you thought about my offer about running my satellite company out there?"

I sat back in my chair, folded my arms. "I have."

"And?" Simone said with enthusiasm in her voice.

"I think I want to do it. I mean between Todd working late almost *every* night and Camille making moves on me, I need a distraction. So, yes, I will. But only part-time, right?"

"Yes, just part-time. If business picks up, we can always hire another associate."

"Okay, sounds good."

"Todd is still working late, huh?"

"Yeah, and it's taking a toll on us. I mean if he brought his ass home once in a while I wouldn't have to hang out over at Camille's house."

"And get finger-fucked, huh?"

"Simone!"

"Sorry, I couldn't help it, you left that door wide open. Are you going to say anything to him?"

"I have to, ya know?"

"Why? It's not like you are in a full-blown relationship with this woman. She grazed your clit, and it's not like Todd is an angel. Who knows what he is doing 'working late'?" Simone said emphasizing "working late" with air quotes.

"I believe him. Besides, Todd and I made a pact."

Simone sat up in her seat and leaned toward the screen. "Excuse me, a what?"

"A circle of truth—a pact."

"Right. Pardon me while I guffaw my fat ass off. Screw the surgery, just keep those comments coming."

I rolled my eyes at Simone's sarcastic comment again.

"I am sorry, Kai, but making a truth pact with a man is like asking the pope not to pray.

"Todd and I have come a long way and I think we can say that we're at a point in our lives where we can be truthful with each other." Although I have already failed by not revealing to him about Camillie.

Simone made a sour face, scratched her head, and then looked away from the screen.

"Now what, Simone?"

"Okay I wasn't going to say anything, but you pushed me with all your truth-pact and kumbaya comments."

"Tell me already."

Simone took a sip of her coffee, which was sitting on her desk. "Well, I talked to a colleague who reached out to Alana's agent for a print job and, well, they told him that Alana had moved to Los Angeles."

"Alana is out here in Los Angeles?" I sat up in my seat."

"Apparently, she got a role on some new sitcom coming out on BET."

"Oh shit."

"Oh shit is right. When did anyone tell that bitch she could act?"

I shook my head. "No, the other night Todd came home late and his jacket smelled like her."

"Alana?"

"Yes, and before that, I could have sworn I saw her in the car next to me. Oh my God, do you think he is seeing Alana again?" I asked, feeling panic rising up in my chest. So much for our fucking truth pact.

"I'm not gonna say yes, but if she is out here, I wouldn't put it past her to reach out to Todd. She is obsessed with him."

"But how would she know we are here?"

"Anyone with half a brain can do a little research and find out things, including Alana, despite how small her brain may be."

"Oh my God, what should I do? Should I ask Todd?"

"You could, but be ready for a lie. Your truth pact should trump the male *lie* gene in your case."

"Simone, please, I can't take the jokes now."

"Okay listen..." Simone put on her serious tone. "Forget about asking him, he will lie."

"You think?"

"Kai, stop. It's been proven time and time again that anything with a penis can't help themselves. What you have to do is approach it in a way where he thinks you know something, but isn't sure exactly what it is. That will weaken his defenses and allow the guilt to flow."

"How do I do that?"

"You casually mention fact as fiction."

"Okay"

"Let me give you an example. Todd walks into the room and before he has a chance to say anything, casually throw out how the other day you thought you saw Alana in a nearby car, and follow it up with, but that couldn't be true since she's in Chicago, right? Then stop talking and see how he responds. Notice his body language and the choice of words he uses."

"Like what?"

"Well, for starters, does he look away? Change the subject? Act irritated? All of those are telltale signs of a *man*, sorry, I mean a *liar*."

"I cannot believe this is happening."

"Where is he now?"

"He went to the gym.

"Did he?"

"Oh God, I don't know anymore. Dammit, Simone!"

"Don't get all worked up because he'll see it. If he is hiding anything, then he'll make it a point to hide it even harder. Just relax and do what I said, don't just come out and ask him."

"Okay, fine. The timing couldn't be worse. My mom is here and we are going to dinner with her tonight. And you know how my mom is."

"Yeah, you may want to postpone your 'nonchalant' interrogation until she leaves."

"All this time I was worried about some woman named Jessica."

"Who is that?"

"Oh God, it's a long story. I don't want to get into that right now. I gotta stay focused on this Alana thing. Why won't she just go away?"

"I say the same thing about roaches. Listen, call me if you need to talk more, but I've got to run."

"Okay, thanks, Simone." I disconnected from Simone and sat back, taking a few deep breaths. I closed my eyes, only to be jarred by the doorbell ringing. Who could that be? I moved to the door and opened it, hardly believing who was standing on my front stoop.

"Hey." Camille smiled at me.

I wasn't totally shocked to see her standing there, seeing how earlier that day she had invited herself to sit down with Todd and me at the park.

"Hey," I said. I didn't want to invite her into my house, I didn't want to add part two to our little escapade.

Camille lifted up a small bag of avocados. "I thought you'd like some. I just picked them from my avocado tree."

"Oh, thanks," I said, reaching for the bag, still standing in my doorway.

"Can I come in?" Camille asked in a sweet voice.

"It's not a great time," I said. I was still focused on the Alana bombshell that was just dropped on me. "I have a lot going on right now." I wasn't trying to hurt her feelings, but I needed to stay firm on my decision to keep Camille at a distance.

"Oh, right, no problem." Camille looked down then back up. "Listen, Kai, I, I don't want it to be weird between us. I like you and I don't want what happened to ruin our friendship. So maybe can we start over?"

I stared at Camille as she stood in front of me on my porch. She was such a beautiful woman, and I hated the fact that I was so attracted to her. Truth be told, I liked what happened the other night, but unfortunately where I was in life, it had to stop there.

"Yes, I would like that."

A broad smile spread over Camille's face. "Great, so I will talk to you later?

"Sure."

"Okay." Camille smiled once again before she turned and headed back toward her house. I watched her until she was out of my view before I closed my door, headed to the kitchen and placed the avocados in a ceramic bowl on the counter. I went to the fridge and poured myself a half of a glass of white wine, and checked on Kristopher who was napping peacefully in his crib.

I turned to head for my bedroom and sat down on the edge of the bed. I ran my right hand over our white down comforter while holding my wine in my left. I took a small sip followed by a deep breath.

My desire to tell Todd about what had happened with Camille had passed, especially since I knew that he might be sleeping with Alana again. I took two larger sips of my wine before placing it on the nightstand and dropping back onto the bed. I stared at the white ceiling fan above, with the sound of a ticking clock filling the room.

I closed my eyes and prayed that all of this with Alana was just a stupid coincidence, but deep down, in my gut of guts, I knew that there was no such thing as coincidences.

TWENTY-FIVE
TODD

After our brunch and trip to the park, I needed to hit the gym to release some stress that had been building up with this whole Alana thing. I couldn't believe I let things get this far. I needed to get a handle on this and quick. The last thing I needed was for Kai to find out before I had a chance to tell her. If that were to happen, well, that might spell the end of our marriage and I refused to let it.

I headed into the locker room when my cell rang. I looked down to see that it was Maceo calling, just the person I needed to talk to. Maceo always seemed to call at just the right time and I needed his advice more than ever right now. I heard after I left Chicago Maceo got into a bit of trouble with a few sexual assault suits, so I heard he was contracting out most of his jobs until he was able to rebuild his reputation.

"What's going on, Maceo?" I said into the receiver.

"You, brotha," Maceo said, his chipper voice already making me smile. "I was calling to see what has been up since Alana checked into LA. I haven't heard from you and wanted to make sure everything was cool. Make sure no one was back in jail."

"Not yet."

"Aw shit, that doesn't sound good, talk to me," Maceo said, reading me perfectly through the phone call.

"Things couldn't be more messed up right now," I said, sitting down in front of a row of lockers in the men's locker room, tossing my bag to the side.

"That doesn't surprise me one bit, " Maceo commented. "What's the crazy bitch up to now that she's in LA?"

I quickly filled Maceo in on everything that had happened since Alana stepped into my office. It was good to actually talk to someone about it, get the shit off my chest, hear another guy's perspective, even if it was from someone with Maceo's questionable judgment.

"Damn, that is some psycho almost baby mama drama." This was Maceo's response to everything I told him.

"Now she wants me to come to her annual birthday party tonight, something that I told her wasn't going to happen. "

"Good move, good move. You don't need to go to that, giving her false hope."

"Exactly. So she goes over my head, plays her little games and pulls my boss into it."

"Fuck that. I wouldn't go, stand your ground. Send that bitch a message, a strong one. I hate to say this, bro, but you gotta pull your ball out from under the bed. Don't let that bitch push you around, not a good look for you, not at all."

"I know. Half of that is my fault since I didn't tell Kai from the jump, but now if I tell her it will look like I was hiding this on purpose."

"Well, you are," Maceo said

"Yeah, but it's a little more complicated than that."

"How so?"

"I have to find the right way to tell her."

"How about, 'Babe, they just hired that bitch Alana unbeknownst to me. I can't quit because you ain't working and we need the cheese, so Ima deal with it.' Cool?"

I chuckled, imagining how that conversation would go with Kai. "Yo, it's not that simple."

"Simple as simple does, *yo*. Personally, I think the fact that you didn't say anything to Kai tells me you're still attracted to Alana."

I wasn't sure if I heard Maceo correctly, but it hit a nerve, since this was something I wasn't ready to accept yet. I knew there were feelings there, so I did what anyone would do in my situation, I denied it. "The last thing in the world I am is attracted to Alana."

"Yeah, okay."

"What does that mean?"

"Yo, I get it, been there done that. Maceo Smith is the king of wanting to bang out a bitch who two weeks prior set my car on fire. But you gotta separate yourself from that, cut that shit out, or else a bitch like Alana will ruin your life."

"Maceo, I know where you're coming from, but I'm not that guy."

"Okay, well, maybe I didn't hear you right the first time, but what was your reason you hadn't told Kai yet?"

I didn't have a response for that. I closed my eyes and opened them again. I saw a few guys walk by, headed for the showers then focused back on my phone conversation. I asked myself why I hadn't told Kai.

"Exactly," Maceo said, filling in the silence between our connection. "You haven't told Kai because deep down you're thinking, just maybe, under all those layers of fucked- up craziness that she is, there could be a normal, sophisticated, fine-ass bitch named Alana, who we all know is fun, spontaneous and adventurous and happens to give the best head this side of the Mississippi River. Which by the way brother, for most guys, that would make her a goddamn keeper in a perfect fucking world. But we all know Alana will never be normal. That bitch Alana is far from it, in fact, she is deranged, unstable and at times over-the-top psychotic. She's already stalked you two once already and those types of tendencies run deeper than hell itself. So you tell me, is that really someone you want to deal with for the rest of your fucking life?"

I just stared blankly, unable to say a single word. Maceo had a damn good point. I was just too damn stupid to see it. What was there about Alana that I was holding on to? Was I really just hoping that her craziness would just go away? I hated that after all that had happened between us I was still attracted to her in some crazy fucked-up way. I felt sick to my stomach, and thought of Kai. I thought of how leaving her would cut her to the core. I thought about how something like that could never be redeemed, ever.

Maceo's voice pulled me back to our conversation, my harsh reality and out of my internal battle. "Listen, I know you two have been friends forever and it's hard to cut that off, but yo, you have GOT to let that shit go, period. There's no kind of future in her, none. Zero. Nada. Zilch. Let her know that ship has sailed, adios, done deal."

I dropped my head in my hand, ran my right hand through my hair. "Yeah, you are right, Mace, you are so fucking right."

"Damn straight I'm right, son. You gotta let her know that *you* are running shit, not *her*. I hate to keep beating a dead horse, but pull your damn balls out from under whatever rock you left them and put that bitch in her place and walk the hell away. Point fucking blank."

"Mace, you have never been more on point."

"If it was me, I would just choke the bitch out and be done with it. Tell her if she says anything to Kai there will be more where that came from, but I know you handle things a little differently than I do."

"Putting hands on anyone can't result in anything good," I said to him. I didn't admit to Maceo that the thought had crossed my mind once, or twice.

"Maybe not, but it would definitely send a final message. Just my opinion. I know you're going to do what you're comfortable with, but I wouldn't wait too much longer if I were you."

"I hear you."

I hung up the phone, and let what Maceo said sink in deeper and deeper. What the hell was wrong with me?

I sat up and told myself to pull it together. Kai was the best woman and best thing to ever happen to me. No matter what I thought of Alana, no matter if she still made me hard, no matter if I thought there might be something worth saving about her, none of it was worth the pain, craziness and drama Alana brought into our lives. Not anymore, not one fucking bit. Give people enough time and they'll always show you who they really are, and how they'll always be.

I stood, grabbed my gym bag and decided to forgo my workout. It was time to put Alana in her gotdamn place and I knew exactly how I had to do it.

TWENTY-SIX
KAI

I woke to the sound of Kristopher's voice through the baby monitor. I realized I must have dozed off for a few minutes. I sat up, looked at the clock, and saw it was 4:30 in the evening. Kristopher had probably been up for a while from his midday nap, but he tended to just sit in his crib and entertain himself these days, which I loved.

I rolled over onto my stomach and laid my head on top of my crossed arms, thinking about my conversation with Simone and the fact that Alana might be here in LA. Just knowing that Alana was in the same state made my skin crawl. I couldn't even begin to imagine what my reaction would be if she were having any sort of contact with Todd. I turned my head over, and took a deep breath. Simone was right. I shouldn't just ask Todd, that would never materialize into anything concrete. Despite our pact, or circle of truth.

I heard the front door open then close. I sat up knowing that it had to be Todd coming home from the gym.

"Babe." I heard him call my name out from the front.

"In the bedroom," I yelled back. I heard Todd come down the hallway and watched him enter our bedroom.

"You sleeping?" Todd asked.

I propped myself up on one elbow. "I managed to take a short nap since we'll probably be out late tonight. By the way, we are meeting my mom at The Village around six."

"Right," Todd said, dropping his gym by the door.

"How was your workout?" I asked, trying to make small talk before I started in on what Simone deemed my nonchalant interrogation.

"Good, good, you know me, in and out, no socializing," Todd said.

I sat up as I leaned back on our ivory-colored padded headboard, crossing my legs Indian style.

"What are you going to wear tonight?"

"What do you want me to wear?" Todd shot back, unlacing his shoes.

I wanted to come right out and ask him about Alana, but I stuck with Simone's advice and instead continued to throw out feelers.

Todd continued undressing, pulling off his shirt and throwing it in the dirty clothes basket. It was quickly followed by his shorts and socks. Todd stood in front of his dresser and took off his watch, laying it down. I needed to start my interrogation before he got into the shower so I could watch his body language closely.

"So a funny thing happened..." I started, nervous.

"What's that?" Todd said, slipping off his Calvin Klein boxers. My eyes diverted all over his body. I was distracted by his naked form.

"The first week we were in LA, I was driving down Slauson and I could've *sworn* I saw Alana in the car next to me."

I crossed my arms, and did what Simone said, watching his body language closely. Oddly enough, the second I mentioned Alana's name, Todd's dick jerked.

"Is that right?" Todd asked, opening the dresser drawer. He pulled out a fresh pair of boxers and slipped them on.

I sat up a bit. *What the hell was that about?*

"I thought you were getting in the shower?"

"I will. I just got a little chilly. So you thought you saw Alana, huh?"

"Yeah, now wouldn't that be crazy if Alana were here in LA?"

"Pretty much yeah. Although I doubt she is here," Todd said as he avoided eye contact with me.

"How could you be so sure? I mean, she is an actress, sort of anyway, and LA is the place to be if you are an actress after all."

"I guess. Where are you going with this?"

"Well, I Skyped with Simone today while you were at the gym and she said that a colleague of hers requested Alana for a print shoot and Alana's agent told her that she was in LA shooting a new sitcom."

"Huh. You sure it was Alana?"

"No, but that's what Simone said."

Todd's eyes shifted from left to right as he quickly looked at me then back away again. He shrugged his shoulders. "Honestly, I wouldn't put anything past her."

Todd grabbed a T-shirt from his top left dresser drawer before turning toward the bathroom. "I need to jump in the shower if I'm going to be ready by six."

"Yeah, of course." I watched Todd head into the bathroom and jump in the shower. I pulled out my phone to text Simone.

You were right, Todd is hiding something.

Simone texted me back almost immediately.

Momma is always right. Keep working on him, he will break eventually.

TWENTY-SEVEN

TODD

I left Kai in the bedroom and jumped in the shower, letting the hot water cascade like a waterfall down my head, face and body. What the fuck was that from Kai? Did she know something? Was she trying to see how I would react to her questions? Or did she really see Alana in that car?

I leaned my head back and let the water hit my neck and chest. Dammit, I had to come clean with Kai tonight. I knew her mom was in town, but this shit had to stop. Fuck.

I dropped my head back down, letting the water slide down the back of my neck again. I thought about what Maceo schooled me on earlier, and reminded myself that Alana was a twisted bitch who only had loyalty to herself.

I tightly squeezed my eyes shut. Alana, Alana, fuck, why couldn't I get her out of my head? The mere thought of her named triggered my relentless manhood. It was if her name was attached to a sexual trigger of a loaded gun, my loaded gun. My dick started to get hard thinking about that day in her dressing room. The way she worked me, my dick, my mind.. Fuck. I slammed my fist against the blue tiled wall, felt the pain vibrate through hand and up my arm. My dick continued to grow, getting harder and harder with each passing thought of her. Taking on a mind of its own. Leaving me with no choice but to follow. Fuck. I opened my eyes, reached up and grabbed some of Kai's hair conditioner, squeezed a palm full in my aching hand as I reached down and grabbed my throbbing penis.. I began a rhythm. Slow then fast. Fast then slow. It felt so good, too good. The hot water falling over me took me into a momentary utopia, one I didn't want to leave.

The sight of Alana's lips around my dick kept me going as my hand slid up and down my shaft faster and faster as I squeezed harder and harder. Fuck. I tried to push her image out of my head, but it kept popping back in. I was reaching my climax, climbing, stroking, mmmm. Climbing, stroking, shit. Climbing, stroking, ahhhh. I exploded all over the shower wall and my body went limp, my legs felt weak. I shook all over.

"Todd?" Kai's voice shot through me like a bullet at close range and I nearly hit the ceiling. *Dammit.*

"Yeah, yeah what's up?"

"You're going to use up all the hot water."

"Oh, right, sorry, babe," I said. I quickly washed the rest of my body and jumped out of the shower. Kai stood by the sink washing her face. I couldn't even look at her. Guilt ravished my body.

"Remember when Mila was here and I told you how weird she was acting, drinking up all the wine?"

"Ah, yeah, why?"

"According to my mom, she and Charles are getting a divorce."

"Oh, wow, why's that?"

"Apparently, he's been cheating on her for the last four years."

My stomach did a quick double back flip upon hearing the word 'cheating' come out of her mouth. I slowly turned and finally looked at Kai. "They've only been married for five years."

"Exactly. Clearly, he shouldn't have gotten married."

"Yeah," I said as I finished drying off, scooped up my underwear and T-shirt and headed out the bathroom to finish getting dressed.

***

"Why are you so quiet?" Kai asked as we drove together to the restaurant. I was not looking forward to dinner with her mother with all this tension between us.

"Am I?"

"You haven't said a word since we left the house."

"It's nothing. Just tired I guess." I looked at Kai and gave her what I hoped was my best reassuring smile.

Kai looked away, then back at me as her body followed a bit with her head. "Is there something you need to tell me, Todd?"

Her question struck a deep emotional cord in my soul. It was the perfect opportunity to come clean with Kai and tell her the whole truth and nothing but... but...I couldn't.

My chest started to tighten and I felt the beads of perspiration gather in unison on my neck. I turned to look at Kai, really look at her, deep into her eyes. I loved her more than she knew. But I couldn't tell her because I couldn't hurt her. Instead, I tucked the truth back under my pallet of guilt, for now. We were minutes from seeing her mom, now was not the time.

"No, I'm good, just a lot on my plate, with work and all. I'll probably perk up when we get to the restaurant and get a few drinks in me," I said, smiling at her again. I even threw in a quick wink. "You look beautiful by the way," I added before focusing again on driving.

"Thanks," Kai said, scanning her outfit as if she'd forgotten what she was wearing. She leaned back against her headrest.

We pulled up at 5:45 and entered the LA trendy restaurant. It was Saturday night and I guess everyone had the same idea as we did. Corrine was already there, which did not surprise me at all. She was always early to gatherings. As we walked into the restaurant I felt my cell phone vibrating in my jacket.

"Hey, babe, I'm gonna run to the bathroom really quickly, you want me to grab a few drinks from the bar when I come out?"

"No, I'm good," Kai said, rubbing my arm from shoulder to elbow before dropping her hand down to her side. She moved over to where Corrine was seated. I turned and walked in the opposite direction as I pulled out my phone, to see I had a text from Alana.

Just making sure you will be coming to my party tonight. Dinner is at 7 p.m., followed by dancing. Will be fun, fun, fun.

I quickly texted her back.

Running late, not sure if I will make dinner.

Then I erased the whole text thread off my phone. I stood by the men's bathroom, cursing myself. Why did I even respond to her? Earlier after hanging up with Maceo, I had made up my mind that I wasn't going to go to Alana's party.

I leaned against the wall, tapped my foot on the terra-cotta Spanish tile flooring, and a thought ran through my head. *I could go just to tell her this shit stops now.*

I shook my head, vetoing that thought as quickly as it came. No, fuck it, I am not going to even give her the satisfaction that I left my dinner to come to hers. My phone vibrated again. I looked down to see another text from Alana.

Well as long as you come it doesn't matter what time, just come. I have a surprise for you. :)

I didn't bother to respond this time. I erased the thread, shoved my phone back into my pocket and headed to my dinner with Kai and her mom.

***

"So how are you liking Los Angeles so far, Todd?" Corrine asked between bites of her Cajun-style salmon dinner.

"It's no Chicago or New York, but it's definitely growing on us."

"Us? Well, thank you for speaking for me, honey," Kai said as she playfully jabbed me in the side.

"That's what husbands are for, right, Corrine?" I shot Corrine a knowing smile.

"Hey, don't drag me into the middle of what you two have going on," Corrine joked back.

I had to admit, I was having a good time with Kai and her mom. I forgot how entertaining her mom was, especially with a few drinks in her. Mixing that good company with a little alcohol, time was flying by. We were having so much fun that I hadn't noticed it was already 8:45.

I wasn't sure if it was because the restaurant had gotten louder as the night went on or that I was just enjoying myself, but I didn't notice my phone vibrating off the hook. Kai was leaning against my chest and I guess she felt it.

"Baby, your phone is ringing like crazy, don't you feel it vibrating?"

"Aw, baby, I thought that was our love vibrating."

Kai rolled her eyes at my corny comeback. Corrine smiled, content with the idea that her daughter finally had a good man and a baby.

"Don't quit your day job, honey," Kai shot back. "Who's blowing you up?"

"It's probably just the office. I'm going to take it outside since it is so loud in here. Excuse me, ladies, I will only be a minute."

I stood and walked toward the front of the restaurant. I made my way past the sea of tables and patrons out the door. I pulled out my phone and noticed I had eight missed calls from Alana.

"Where the hell are you?" Alana screamed through the phone. She picked up immediately after I dialed her number the second I stepped outside. The restaurant she was in sounded just as loud as mine, but apparently she didn't think to step outside when she saw me calling.

"Listen, Alana, I'm stuck here, so I'm not going to make it."

"Well, get unstuck and get your ass over here, now!" Alana's voice slurred. She was definitely drunk.

"Yeah, that's not gonna happen, so have fun," I said.

"Todd Daniels, if you are not here at my party in twenty minutes I will be forced to send Kai a nice little text, including all the details of the juicy blow job you enjoyed the other night along with our night in New York."

I felt my anger rising up from my gut. I replayed what Maceo said to me, plus all the shit I had been putting up with from Alana since New York. Coupled with Kai's look of concern on her face as we drove into the restaurant tonight, it all seemed to have come to a head for me at that moment.

"You know what, Alana, you and all your idle threats can go straight to hell."

"What?"

"You heard me," I said, my voice strong. My intentions stronger.

"Well, well, well. Looks like someone is trying to grow a pair."

My eyebrows shot up to my hairline. "What the fuck did you say to me?"

"Todd, just tell your pansy boring wife and her uppity-ass mama that you have a better party to go to and get over here pronto."

"How about I tell you to go fuck yourself because I am not coming."

There was a pause.

"Are you seriously forcing my hand? Because I will send Kai a text right now," Alana threatened.

"You know what, do it, it doesn't even matter, Alana, Kai knows everything, okay?"

"You're lying. You don't have the fucking balls."

"Apparently, I do because you sucked on them. Happy fucking birthday bitch!" I said, slamming my open palm against the screen, ending the call. I took a deep breath, squeezing my fists so tightly together I thought my hand would explode off my arm.

Shit! Now I had to tell Kai before she got that text from Alana. What the hell had I done?

I raced back into the restaurant, past the front hostess, the bar and sea of tables. My knees felt weak as I carelessly bumped into a dozen people along the way.

I saw Kai and her phone sitting on the table next to her as I approached them. I didn't even bother to sit down, but gently grabbed Kai's arm, all the while keeping my eye on her cell phone.

"Baby, can I talk to you for a second?" I said, pulling Kai's arm up, hoping her body would follow. I felt my adrenaline pumping faster and faster as I knew time was of the essence.

Kai looked at me, perplexed. "Baby, we're about to sing happy birthday to my mom, can it wait?"

I looked at Kai's phone and noticed it was flashing with a text on her display screen. Shit.

"No, it will only take a second, I promise."

I continued to hold onto her arm, and attempted to ease her up so we could talk privately and out of her mom's prying ears. I needed to tell Kai everything before she read Alana's text. Full disclosure.

"Baby, it's going to have to wait," Kai said as she sat back down. "The candles are already lit."

I swallowed hard, and pushed my temper back down. I had to keep a check on my emotions. I looked down once again at Kai's text alert flashing on her phone sitting on the table.

I said to her in a firmer tone. "No, Kai, it cannot wait."

I pulled her arm up with a little more force, indicating again for her body to follow.

Corrine watched our interaction with a touch of concern. "Is there a problem, Todd?" Her voice had the sound of a mother bear protecting her baby cub.

I locked eyes with Kai's mother and wanted to tell her to mind her own damn business, but I kept a check on my temper.

"No, Corrine, I just need to talk to Kai alone for one second, just a second," I said, the words falling out of my mouth in a rushed tone.

"About?" Corrine shot back, as she kept her eyes locked on me.

I felt a rock forming in my throat, felt the perspiration dripping from my underarm. "Actually, it's nothing that you should be concerned about," I said as Kai's phone flashed for the fourth time. My eyes shot to the phone then back to Corrine. "It will only take a minute. One minute."

"Well, whatever it is, so long as no one is dying, it can wait. Right?" Corrine glared at me once again as Kai released her arm from my grip. I had to accept a temporary defeat. It was clear I wasn't going to win this battle.

I took a deep breath and surrendered.

"Of course, right, it, um, it can wait," I said, sitting back down at the table. Waiters crowded around our table and every one began to sing, "Happy Birthday."

I didn't join in with the singing. Instead, I kept an eye on Kai's phone, watching the text alert that continued to flash. I ignored everything else around me. The flashing LED became my world as I focused on that goddamn phone.

My body was tense and I had to strategize a new plan. I needed a distraction, something that could help me get Kai's phone away from her and give me a chance to erase that text from Alana before she read it. I glanced up to see Corrine smile as she blew out the candles and everyone around us cheered. It felt as though I were watching a silent movie in slow motion. My focus was only on Kai's phone. I finally heard Kai's voice break me out of my trance.

"Todd, Todd?"

"Yeah, sorry."

"Do you want a piece of cake or not?" Kai looked at me with the cake knife in her hand.

"No, I um, no thank you."

Kai turned her attention back to her mom.

"What's that beeping noise?" Corrine asked, an annoyed look on her face. "Where is that coming from?"

Kai turned and was now focused on her phone for the first time. "Oh, sorry that's my phone, I have a text message. I better check it. Could be the babysitter."

I watched Kai place down the knife then reach for her phone. To me, everything looked like it was moving in slow motion. I had to do something, *anything*. She could not be allowed to read that text.

The moment before Kai grabbed her phone I inadvertently swung my arm into a glass of water knocking it over right on Kai's phone. The noise of the glass hitting the table brought me back to real time as everyone jumped from their seats.

"Todd, what the hell?" Kai screamed, dodging the water flowing toward her.

"I am so sorry," I said, scrambling to grab the extra cloth napkin on our table, hoping to catch the cascading water before it hit the floor.

Kai reached for her wet phone, examined it, and attempted to turn it back on. "Seriously?" She looked at me. "Great. My phone is ruined."

I breathed a sigh of relief and I grabbed Kai's phone out of her hand to verify that her phone was dead for myself. Yep, it was indeed toast. *Thank God.*

"Sorry, babe, I didn't even see that glass of water in front of me. I'll get you a new phone tomorrow, okay?"

"An iPhone would be nice." Kai looked at me with her puppy-dog eyes.

"Then an iPhone you will get," I said with a relieved smile on my face.

"Really?" Kai shot back with pure excitement. "I thought you said iPhones were overrated?"

"Yeah, but I'm not the one who needs the new phone."

"Awww, thank you, baby," Kai said, swinging her arms around me.

"Now that's a great husband. You got a keeper, Kai," Corrine chimed in.

I smiled a broad smile as I tucked Kai's phone in my pocket for safekeeping.

TWENTY-EIGHT
ALANA

"Cut! That's lunch everyone," the director of my new show, *Office Temps*, yelled to the cast and crew. This was my third taping and I was starting to get the hang of things. I had never done comedy and trust me on this, comedic timing looks a lot easier than it really is. That was something I had to find out for myself on the first day of rehearsals. Lucky for me, Emanuel had an acting coach lined up the day I stepped foot on set.

I headed over to the craft table to grab a cup of coffee. I was still nursing my Saturday-night hangover. I don't normally get that drunk, but I was so damn pissed at Todd. How dare he not come to my party? How dare he talk to me with that kind of disrespect?

I scanned the stage looking for him through the sea of cast and crew members who were lingering on set. I was expecting Todd today since he needed to retrieve his wedding ring. Then again, he could be at home trying to save his sorry-ass marriage with Kai since I sent her that juicy text message.

I could only imagine the look on her face when she received it. I kept getting excited thinking about how it must have all went down. Damn, I wish I could have been there. It was the perfect justification for when her ass dropped the 'pregnancy bomb' on me at my movie premiere. That still pissed me off and the memory was as fresh as if it had happened yesterday.

I took a deep cleansing breath and attempted to calm myself down. That smug look on Kai's face was seared in my memory like a damn brand on a cow's ass. I took solace in the fact that the tables would be turned on her now that Kai was aware of everything going on between me and Todd.

I had been imagining the scenario all weekend, but my favorite version went like this: Kai picks up her phone and sees my text revealing everything to her. An argument ensues and it escalates with a few choice words thrown in there. Todd flees the scene and begins to try and figure out how to mend the situation and plot revenge on me.

He didn't know that whatever pathetic revenge he could come up with didn't scare me in the least. I was the queen of revenge. It would only be a matter of time before their marriage started to break down like Kirstie Alley in an Ironman competition. The fact that Todd kept our dalliance from Kai all this time without saying one word to her should've been especially damaging to their relationship.

That would be the moment I could step in and comfort the wounded Todd to make him mine again, which I knew would be a walk in the park. The two things I knew about Todd, were one, he was easily swayed, and two, he could not stand to be alone.

I finished making my coffee and turned to head toward my dressing room to grab my things and head home when I saw Todd across the set talking to the show's executive producer, Kurt.

I stopped in my tracks as my Gucci heels pushed into the ground like brakes on rollerblades. I watched them talk and laugh, which made me wonder when the hell they got so damn chummy? The bigger question was, why was Todd so damn happy?

After Saturday night and my surprise text, he should've looked like a beaten man. Something wasn't right, I thought as I folded my arms, tilted my head and stared at Todd's body language. Uh huh, something was definitely off.

I placed my hands on my hips and waited for Todd to notice me staring a fucking laser beam through him. He finally turned and our eyes connected. I gave him a raised- eyebrow look, hoping he got my gesture and ended the conversation pronto. I needed to know the status of his relationship with Kai.

Todd turned back to Kurt and they continued to talk and laugh. My annoyance meter was jumping out of control. Todd finally broke away from Kurt and he sauntered, yes, sauntered over to me. An arrogant smile danced across his face to the tune of his arrogant walk. The sight of him so freaking happy right now pissed me the hell off. Todd stopped just inches from me.

"Why are you so damn happy?" I said, irritated.

"It's a beautiful day in Zamunda, don't you think?"

"Really, Zamunda?"

"What? You know *Coming to America* is my favorite movie."

"Whatever, Todd," I said, turning to head for my dressing room. I noticed Todd following behind me, continuing to throw out his sarcastic comments.

"What, no snappy comeback, no demands or requests?"

I continued down the hallway, then headed into my dressing room as Todd closed the door behind us.

I tossed my script down on the couch and turned back to him. "Oh, I get it, this is your whole defense mechanism tactic. So tell me, how did Kai react to my text? Are you homeless? I have room at my condo."

Todd shook his head, laughed, looked up at me and back down.

"I have no idea because she never saw your text."

We held another stare as I processed what he had just said. My eyes narrowed to the size of a coin slot on a Vegas slot machine. Todd's smile grew even larger, if that was at all possible.

"What? You think I'm lying? Todd asked. "Go ahead and call her, ask her for yourself."

I wasn't sure what angle Todd was playing, but I was not the one to be fucked with right now. I had a pounding headache and a master plan he was fucking with.

I pulled my phone out from my purse and dial Kai's number, the number I had since I knew her in Chicago. My head whipped back as I heard, "The number you called is not in service at this time." I looked up at Todd.

"Oh, that's right, I forgot to tell ya, that number has been changed as of," Todd looked down at his watch, "a few hours ago. Like I said, it's over, Alana."

Todd walked over to me and shoved his hand down my shirt. I tried to pull back and block his hand. I knew exactly what he was going for. He pulled out his wedding ring.

"Some things never change I see. Thanks." Todd slipped the ring back onto his ring finger. By the way, nice try on the custody claim. You seemed to have forgotten that I have your mother's number. Next time you want to use your mom in your little schemes you may want to let her in on it."

"You don't know who you are fucking with."

"Really? I think I have an inkling," Todd said as his face morphed into a more serious look. "Stay the hell out of my personal life, you hear me? Come near my family again and you will regret it. That's a goddamn promise."

Todd headed to my door and out of my dressing room, leaving my door wide open. I walked over to the door and yelled down the hallway to Todd, "She will find out eventually, you can't hide it forever!"

I stood there in silence, processing what had just happened. I felt my rage building up from my toes and I slammed the door behind him. I paced the small dressing room.

Moments later a knock at the door startled me. I opened it to see a man standing there.

"What do you want?" I asked, irritated by the interruption.

"You told me to meet you here. You wanted me to follow up on that custody suit you got going on? The one with your mom?"

My frustration was now at full throttle. "Just forget it. Your services are no longer needed." I closed the door, only to have him stick his foot in it.

"Yeah, that's fine and all, but I came all the way from LA to the valley, so you need to compensate me for my time. Gas isn't free."

I rolled my eyes, grabbed my wallet and gave him ten bucks.

The guy looked at the money, then back at me. "Ya know, it would be a shame if TMZ found out that the whole custody suit was all a fraud, not a good look for a rising star like yourself."

"Are you trying to blackmail me?"

He looked at me and shot me a, *of course I am*, grin.

I took a deep breath, grabbed two more twenties from my wallet and slapped them in his sweaty hands. "Get lost, loser."

"The way it looks, you're the one that lost."

I slammed the door on him, infuriated, and I heard him laughing on the other side.

I walked over to my couch and slowly sat down, leaning my head back. I threw my feet up on my cocktail table. Todd might've thought it was over, but please, like I always say, it ain't over until Alana says it's over.

TWENTY NINE
TODD

I decided to take Kai out to dinner to break the Alana news to her. It had been three days since I laid into Alana in her dressing room and I knew it was only a matter of time before a ticking bomb named Alana would go off.

Kai's mom had left town the previous night, so this would be the best opportunity to finally get this off of my chest and out in the open. I played out a few scenarios in my head, and was constantly changing my mind on what to do.

I knew the best way to tell Kai was to come from my heart. I never wanted to hurt my wife or allow myself to intentionally keep this from her.

I just hoped it all went over okay, but I had to be honest, I didn't have a great feeling.

"You okay, babe?" Kai's voice pulled me out of my internal conversation and back to her as we sat at Toscanova Italian restaurant on Santa Monica Boulevard.

"Yeah, I couldn't be better," I said with a smile as I glanced down at my menu, then back up at Kai. "What are you in the mood for?"

I twisted in my seat, feeling my nerves getting the best of me. I kept trying to think of ways to calm me down without using my favorite crutch—alcohol.

"I think the ravioli filled with spinach and ricotta cheese looks good, what are you getting?" Kai said, reading off the menu.

I closed my menu, and figured I wasn't all that hungry. "Probably the margarita pizza."

"You always get that."

"I can't help it, I'm a man of habit," I said, placing my menu on the table. I rubbed my hands together.

"Yes, you are, and that is one of the things I love about you," Kai said. She picked up her phone, read a text as her expression changed to one of annoyance, then she placed her phone down, taking a sip of her wine.

"What was that about?"

"What was what about?"

"That look. You got a text and had a look."

Kai shook her head. "Mila."

"What about her?"

"I don't get it, she is getting a divorce, but wants to act like everything is just fine."

"Babe, Mila wants you to think her life is perfect. If she thinks you know the truth how can she justify being judgmental about your life?"

"Please, this is Mila we are talking about." Kai shook her head. "Whatever, I don't want to talk about it."

Kai took another sip of her wine and avoided eye contact for a few seconds. I scratched my head, scanned the restaurant, and noticed a couple across from us engaged in what seemed like a deep and somewhat awkward conversation. I guess I wasn't the only brother who took their significant other to a public place to drop unwanted news on her.

I glanced back at Kai who was texting again. My senses told me that she was not texting Mila, but I wouldn't say anything. I needed to stay focused on why I was here.

I had not heard anything from Alana since I put her in her place down at the show. That wasn't necessarily a good thing. One thing I'd learned about Alana was that she could strike at any time.

I adjusted myself again in my seat. I was ready to say what I had come here to say. "Um, baby, there is something that I—"

"Good evening, I am your waiter, Christine, I'm gonna be your server tonight? Can I tell you about our special?" The perky red head appeared from nowhere.

"Sure." I looked at Kai, who looked at me with an assuring look. "Actually, I think we already know what we want," I said.

"Okay, great. Did you want to start with an appetizer?"

I noticed Kai had picked up her phone yet again. I looked back up at the waitress. She smiled at me. "I can give you two a few more minutes."

"Thank you. That would be great," I said with a polite smile.

Our waitress walked away and I glanced back at Kai who looked upset.

"Oh no," Kai said.

"What? What's wrong?" I asked, my heart jumping into my throat. Did Alana find a way to track Kai's number down?

"Oh my God." Kai put her hand over her mouth as she gasped.

"Kai, what? What is it?" My body started to tense up with the damn anticipation. Who was texting her?

"It's Kristopher, he fell off the arm of the couch."

I breathed a sigh of relief from hearing that it was not a text from Alana. I also felt concern about my son, of course, but Alana was still at the forefront of my mind.

"Is he um, is he okay?" I asked, my whole world a roller coaster of emotions going from anxiety to concern.

"You think we should just go home?" Kai asked, worried.

I knew I needed to get this out, but now of course Kai couldn't concentrate on anything other than our son.

"How bad is it?"

"I'm gonna call," Kai said as she stood. "Gonna go to the front where it's not so loud." She quickly walked away from the table.

I dropped back in my seat, and scratched my head. I tried to think of another time to tell Kai and shook my head. No, I have to tell her tonight, regardless of what is happening with our son. I couldn't hold on to this any longer.

I saw Kai heading back my way, looking even more stressed than before she left.

"He busted his lip, we should go. I already told our waitress what happened."

"Okay." I jumped up, grabbed my coat and followed Kai out of the restaurant.

***

Forty-five minutes later, I found myself sitting on the living room couch waiting for Kai to come back from checking on our son.

"How's he doing? I said as Kai settled in next to me on the couch.

"He's fine. I think the sight of his own blood was the worst part."

Kai breathed a sigh of relief and laid back into my arms. "You never expect these things, you know. You try your best to protect your children, but sometimes things just happen that are out of your control, you know?"

Kai's last words hit home for me. "Yeah, I know."

"But that's life, right?"

"Right." I had to get this off my chest and I had to do it now.

"Kai, I need to talk to you about something."

"Okay," Kai said, her eyes closed.

"A few—"

"Are you hungry? I just realized we didn't even eat." Kai opened her eyes slightly, interrupting my flow. "I could make us something if you want."

I knew she was exhausted—we both were—and coming down from an adrenaline high produced by the fall of our son.

"No, I um, I'm okay right now." I sat up a bit, although the weight of Kai's head on my shoulders didn't really allow me to move too far.

"I um, I need to..." I felt my voice shaking as the words fell out of my mouth. I took a deep breath as I felt my heart picking up its pace, the sweat forming on my skin. Kai opened her eyes and slowly sat up to look at me.

"Baby, what is it?" Kai said as she placed her hand on my chest.

I stared at her, finding myself unable to speak. My words were jammed up in my throat. I felt my body tense up and I even started to believe I was about to hyperventilate.

"Baby, what's going on with you? You're starting to scare me."

I looked across the room to our mahogany bookcase, then to the clock on the wall, over the dining room table, then finally back at Kai. "I um..." I reached up and rubbed the back of my neck, feeling its wetness. "I know where Alana is."

Everything stopped. Kai's mouth slightly fell open. "What, what do you mean you *know* where Alana is?"

I swallowed hard, and continued to rub the back of my neck, the heat from the friction between my palm and my neck building. "I know where she is because she's a client at my firm."

I watched as what I said fell from my mouth to Kai's ears and channeled through her thought process. The sound of my heartbeat was so loud it felt as if it were about to push out of my ears. I watched Kai's eyes flicker and then narrow even more. Her body posture collapsed as she ran her fingers through her hair.

Everything was quiet, too quiet. I needed Kai to say something, anything.

I looked away only to turn my head back into an incoming full-fledge slap to my face. My body jerked back as Kai leaped to her feet.

"You fucking asshole. How long has that bitch been your client?" Kai's voice was loud, too loud.

"Kai, listen, I can explain."

"How long has that bitch been your client?" Kai repeated, even louder.

I stood, needing to put some distance between me and Kai just in case she had another hand spasm. *I will give her one blow, but two, there might be a problem.*

I swallowed hard again, took a deep breath. "A few months now."

I looked up to see Kai's hand careening through the air towards me again. This time I intercepted it half-way pulling her body into mine.

"Calm down, Kai."

"Get off me."

Kai jerked away then began to pace, looking down at the ground. She stopped and looked up at me. Her breath was fast, heavy. Her eyes piercing.

"It all made sense now. You working late all these days, your phone blowing up all day and all night, you coming home smelling like her."

Kai stopped, looked away. I could see her mind thinking, processing. "So that was her I saw that day in the car. Oh shit."

Kai looked back at me, and I could see that her eyes were filled with tears.

"Did you fuck her?"

I opened my mouth to speak, but nothing came out.

"Oh my God. I can't believe this, I feel like the worlds biggest idiot."

"Kai, I can explain, it's complicated, but…"

Kai walked over to the couch.

"Oh my God, I can't breathe." She looked as if she was about faint. I ran to grab her, but instead she started swinging at me like a wild woman. I put my arms up to block each blow.

"Don't you fucking touch me, don't you *ever* fucking touch me," Kai screamed, clutching her stomach. "Oh God. Oh my fucking God."

I heard Kristopher begin to cry in the bedroom. I was sure we were scaring our poor child to death.

"Kai, please, it's not like that, I can explain, if you just calm down, I can explain."

"Explain what? How you fucking lied to me and you kept her from me?" Kai's voice was choked with tears. "All this time I thought I was crazy or that my mind was playing these sick tricks on me. I was hoping and praying that maybe, just maybe my hunches were wrong, but here you are not only confirming Alana is here in LA..." Kai grabbed a lamp off the table next to her and flung it across the room at me. "...but you were fucking her all along!"

I jumped to the right to dodge the flying lamp as it slammed against the wall, breaking into two large pieces.

"Kai, calm down!"

"No, you calm the fuck down." Kai was shaking all over. "How could you keep this from me with all she's done to hurt us?"

"I was trying to protect you! Kai, I love you, and I..."

Kai shook her head repeatedly, "Really, Todd? Protect me how?"

Kai and I stared at each other. I didn't know what else to say. I felt myself sinking as if I were standing in a box of quicksand. The clock was ticking and I was out of answers.

"Exactly." Kai turned and walked out of the living room. I sank down onto the couch and dropped my head into my hands. I felt my emotions unleash as tears filled my eyes. A few minutes passed and I looked up to see Kai with Kristopher and a small bag in her hand. I stood up.

"What are you doing?"

"I'm leaving, that's what I am doing."

"Come on, Kai, seriously, we need to talk about this."

"I can't even look at you right now," Kai said as she headed for the door.

I cut her off and grabbed her arm.

"Don't do this, Kai, please. I don't mean to hurt you, you have to believe me."

"Well, it's too late for that," Kai said as she pulled her arm back with a swift jerk and headed out the door, closing it behind her.

I stood in the middle of my living room as my frustration turned to rage, rage at myself. I turned, slamming my fist against the door as hard as I could without breaking anything, including my own hand.

"Fuuuuuuck! I yelled as loud as I could. "What the fuuuuck!?" I yelled again. I walked back over to the couch and sat down, felt a cold chill as it flushed through my soul. My body went numb as I leaned my head back and slipped into a state of unspoken misery.

THIRTY

KAI

When my eyes opened the next morning, I found myself hoping that everything that had happened last night had been a bad dream. I turned my head and saw Camille sitting on the edge of the bed staring at me. I turned to my left and noticed that Kristopher was gone. I instantly jumped up.

"It's okay, I've already taken them to school," Camille said in a soft tone.

My body relaxed a bit. "Thanks."

"You wanna talk about what happened last night? You kinda scared me when you came over."

I looked down at her white down comforter that I was under and back up at her.

"Yeah, sorry about that. Maybe we can talk later?" I wasn't in the mood to talk about everything yet, especially with Camille.

"Okay, no worries. You hungry?"

I shook my head, "No, I um, I think I just need to lay back down."

"Of course." Camille stood. "If you need anything, I'll be downstairs on the computer."

"Thanks," I said and gave Camille an appreciative smile.

Camille headed for the door.

"Hey," I said, stopping her before she left.

"What's up?" She glanced back at me.

"Thanks for letting me crash in your guest room last night."

"Hey, that's what friends are for, right?"

I nodded, "Right."

Camille walked out the room and closed the door behind her.

I laid my head back onto her white down pillow and thought about Todd, Alana and what he told me last night. I let out a deep sigh, grabbed my phone, and saw that Todd had called eight times. I threw my phone to the side. I couldn't believe this was happening all over again. Why wouldn't Alana just leave Todd alone? Leave us alone?

I started to play the What If...? game in my mind. What if I had never slept with her? What if I had never met her? What if I had told Todd about our relationship from the get-go? What if...? What if...? What if...?

I shook my head. I needed to get out of the past, and to be present in the now. I needed to figure out what the hell to do. I threw my hands onto my face. What was I going to do?

I stood, headed to the bathroom and stared at my face. My puffy eyes, bare face and untamed hair did not make for a charming reflection.

I splashed my face with cold water, hoping that would magically change my appearance, but unfortunately, that only made it worse.

I turned and headed back to bed. I crawled underneath the white down comforter, and pulled it over my head. I breathed deeply and felt the heat rise. I came out from underneath and felt the cool air hit my face. I sat back up, grabbed my phone and Skyped Simone.

"Where are you?" Simone asked, her eyes darting around behind me, trying to figure out my location from the interior.

"I had a fight with Todd last night. No, correction, Todd told me some very disturbing news which turned into me lashing out and leaving last night."

"Okay, so what happened?" Simone asked, continuing to eat her lunch at her desk. "Perfect timing by the way," Simone said as she bit into her sandwich.

"Of course it has to do with Alana."

Simone placed her sandwich down. "You're kidding. What the hell happened?" She picked up a napkin and wiped her mouth.

"Apparently, your suspicion was right. Alana is indeed in California."

"Is that right?"

"Oh it gets better. Alana is a client at Todd's new firm and has been for the last three months. A fact he has conveniently kept from me."

Simone turned, scratched her head, looked away from the screen then back. "He slept with her, didn't he?"

"Oh my God, Simone, how did you know?" Well, he's a man and she's Alana, so it's not that hard to piece together."

Simone let out a loud sigh. "Wowzer. So where did you end up?"

"I'm at Camille's," I said, holding my breath.

I heard a loud clanking sound as Simone dropped her fork onto her desk. "You're where?"

"Simone, don't start."

"Oh, I'm going to start alright. Let me make sure I have this straight. You had a fight with your husband, which is justified considering the circumstances, and then because of that fight, you move in with your girlfriend?"

"She's not my girlfriend."

"Oh right, she's not your girlfriend, she's your lova! Say it with me, lova, L-O-V-A, lova."

"Would you stop it? I know this isn't the best situation, but I had nowhere else to go, but to…"

"Ya lova's house." Simone finished my sentence for me.

"Simone!"

"Why don't you and Kristopher check into a hotel?"

"We can't afford a hotel. We are barely living off of one salary as it is. Besides, Camille and I talked and I told her that I wasn't getting down like that. We are actually just friends, really."

"Well, whatever you have with this Camille woman, you ought to cut off ties with her for good."

"That's a bit drastic, don't you think?"

"Not at all. Listen, you've got bigger issues than dealing with some single mother looking to fill an emotional void. Get rid of her before I do." Simone gave me her firm momma look over her Burberry designer glasses.

"Okay, okay," I said, hoping to appease Simone. In reality I had to do it at my own pace.

"Back to Alana." Simone shook her head. "I swear, that woman is worse than flesh-eating bacteria, just eating away until there is nothing left. Someone seriously needs to put a hit out on that bitch."

"Yeah, that would be nice." I shook my head. "I can't believe Todd would do something like this to me. So much for our truth pact."

"Yeah, don't get me started on that."

"Simone, I don't know what to do. I feel so paralyzed right now. I feel like I'm back at square one, you know?"

"First of all, you'll never be back at square one, you and Todd have a long history, so I know you can fix this."

"So do Todd and Alana."

"True, but your history is a lot healthier than anything the two of them ever had. Besides, you two have a baby together and he's your husband; that counts for a lot. You guys aren't dating anymore."

I nodded my head and took in all the advice Simone was breaking down for me. This was exactly what I needed to hear.

"Listen, Kai, shit happens and I know it hurts, but you can't let it get you down. You are a strong woman, but somewhere down the line you let Alana steal away your power. You have to take it back and I know you can do it."

Simone took a sip from her ice water. "What you need to do is pay Alana's ass a visit."

"You mean confront her?"

"Yes, pretty much, but not in a hair-tied-up-vaseline-on-your-face-no-earrings kind of way. Leave that ghetto shit for Tammy on *Basketball Wives*," Simone said firmly. "What you need to do is let her know woman to woman, in a calm but firm voice, that you know what the fuck is going on, and let her know that you are not fazed by her one iota. Let her know that you are one-hundred percent in control, not her. Alana expects you to be all hurt and crying and hysterical, but no, give her some shock treatment instead. Show that bitch you are not the one to be messed with. You have to take control back."

I didn't say a word while Simone was preaching to me. I knew she was right. I couldn't let Alana know that I was affected by this. That was exactly what she wanted and how she managed to get the upper hand in the first place.

"Kai, you and Todd are a unit, a team. There is no I in team, we all heard that familiar statement from high-school PE class."

"So I should forgive Todd?"

"Yes, but make his ass sweat a bit. Don't let him off so easy."

"Todd told me last night that he didn't tell me about Alana because he was trying to protect me from her and handle things his own way."

"And we see how that ended up. Kai, he's a man, and they make stupid decisions on a daily, almost on the minute basis. Believe me, I know the score after years of marriage to a serial cheater." Simone checked her watch. "Hey, I gotta jump on this conference call, but call me tomorrow and let me know how you're holding up."

"I will, and thanks, Simone. I don't know what I would do without you."

"I love you, Kai."

"Love you more, girl," I said and hit end on our Skype call.

I leaned back, stretched and processed all of what Simone told me. Even though I was damn pissed about Alana and Todd, I couldn't let Alana know it. Simone was right. I had to show her that I was not fazed and that I was in control. I took a deep breath as I stood and walked over to the mirror across from the bed. I looked at my reflection starring back at me.

Yep, it was time to pay Ms. Alana Brooks a visit.

THIRTY-ONE
ALANA

The more I thought about it, the more I knew it wouldn't do me any good if Kai found out about Todd and I. Like I always said, everything happens for a reason. So, the fact that Todd hadn't told Kai yet was a great thing. Right now I needed to keep Todd under my beck and call.

My plan was simple; keep him near, wear him down, show him what a real wife should be. Todd might've thought he had one up on me by coming into my room, flexing his muscles, and telling me it was over, but pu-lease, he had no idea what was about to come his way. I was going to save my big surprise for him when the time was right.

We ended rehearsal early, which made me happy because that meant I had the rest of my day off. I was in dire need of a deep tissue massage and a mani-pedi.

I dialed Todd's number and got his voicemail. No worries. I was gonna need him to accompany me to an award ceremony this weekend, so I would leave him a message to give him the heads-up.

"Hey, handsome, give me a call. There is this little soiree this weekend that I need you to attend with me. Business of course, but we can turn it personal if you like. Anyway, call me back to confirm. Byeee."

I disconnected the connection and turned the corner of the set to head back to my dressing room. I opened the door and nearly dropped my phone and everything else in my hands when I saw none other than Kai fucking Edwards chilling on my damn couch.

I scanned the room to make sure she was alone and that this wasn't going to turn into a two-on-one ambush. Once I saw it was only Kai, I put on my game face. I made myself ready for whatever she had to offer. I slowly closed the door behind me and walked closer to where Kai was sitting.

"You don't look happy to see me," Kai said, smiling at me.

I kept calm. "To what do I owe this unexpected visit?"

"Oh, I think you know why I'm here, Alana."

I shook my head. All I needed to do was play dumb and let her do all the talking while I gathered information. "No, I can't say that I do, Kai."

Kai stood and crossed her arms against her chest. My eyes drifted down to her ring finger as I stared at her wedding ring, white gold-princess cut-one carat. Rage began to stir up inside of me. I looked back up at Kai, who was smiling even bigger now.

"Did you really think you were going to get a ring from Todd? Seriously, Alana?"

I swallowed hard. I had to admit seeing Kai wearing a ring from Todd didn't sit well with me, not at all. I took a deep breath and forced out a smile.

"It's not over until the last woman is standing, don't you think?"

Kai let out a small chuckle. "Wow, you are a piece of work. I've never met someone more determined to make such a fool out of themselves. It's kinda pathetic, don't you think?"

"I think the only thing pathetic is you thinking that you've won," I said

Kai raised her ring finger toward me. "Oh, I have." Kai placed her hand on her hip. "Which brings me to why I am here."

Kai took a few steps closer to me. "Let me be clear about what it is I am about to say."

"Please do," I said with a small grin.

"I'll be damned if I let you come between me and Todd again." Kai took another step closer to me. "I know everything, Alana, every single thing and guess what? It stops now."

I continued to stare right back. I couldn't believe this bitch was trying to intimidate me.

"I may have let down my guard down back in Chicago when I first met you, but that Kai, is long gone and forgotten."

"You look pretty much the same to me. All the way down to your knockoff designer shoes," I said.

Kai let out a small chuckle. I felt my body tense up as her gaze got even more aggressive. "Well we all know the saying, fool me once shame on you, fool me twice shame on me, fool me a third time Alana gets a visit from yours truly."

Kai took yet another step closer, bringing her face within inches of mine. I wasn't going to back down, never have, never will. I just wish I didn't have on my Marc Jacobs hoops just in case this bitch wanted to go all Love and Hip Hop crazy on me.

"Stay away from my man if you know what's good for you." Kai sucked her teeth as her mouth then turned up in the corners.

I laughed. *This bitch must think she just met me.* "Eat much pussy lately, Kai?" I knew that would hit a sensitive nerve.

Kai pulled back a bit. "Screw you, Alana."

"No, I would rather screw Todd, oh, right, I did." I stepped away and retreated to my corner, hoping to put a little distance between us after my statement.

Kai folded her arms across her chest once again, and nodded. "That's right, that's what you do best, fuck other women's men, and *women* for that matter."

A smile stretches across Kai's face. "You're a ho, Alana, and, that's what hos do. But here's a little nugget for ya, nobody wants to marry or associate with a ho." Kai sucked her teeth again, a habit I was finding to be quite annoying. She turned and walked over to my bookcase, looking at my personal knickknacks and then turned back toward me.

"One thing I've learned, is that no one is perfect. God knows that goes double for you, but at the end of the day, what really matters, is who you go home to."

Kai walked back over to where I stood as a devious smile stretched across her face. "Who are you going home to, Alana? I mean, you don't have a man, and I doubt you have someone you can call a *real* friend. I would bet my last dollar that you conveniently dumped your daughter onto your mother. So that leaves," Kai looked up in the air and then back down at me, "nada, zilch, nobody."

Kai's words were beginning to provoke emotions in me that I could not control nor figure out where they were even coming from. All I knew was that I was getting more pissed off by the second. A slow burn was igniting inside me and I didn't know why.

"You're like cancer, Alana, you eat away at everything you touch. You're a disease that no one wants to see coming because we all know the outcome."

"I think you better leave, now!" My words shot out as my voice started to tremble.

"I'm already gone." Kai turned and headed for the door, then opened it. "You may want to consider picking up a cat or a gotdamn ferret on the way home since those are the only companions you will be lucky enough to have. Animals love you no matter how fucked up you may be.

Kai smiled just before slamming the door behind her, shaking the thin walls of my dressing room around me.   I felt my world around me go dark and then I felt nothing.

THIRTY-TWO
TODD

I couldn't sleep, I couldn't eat, and I certainly couldn't function. I tried numerous times to reach out to Kai, but she wasn't returning my calls. I missed her—her smell, her voice, her touch. I missed my son. But most of all I missed us.

Only twenty-four hours had passed since Kai stormed out of the house after I dropped the news on her about Alana, but to me, in my state of depression and frustration, it had felt like an eternity. I was still wearing the same clothes the night Kai walked out. I was trying to find the energy and motivation to move.

I jumped to the sound of my cell phone ringing. I was quick to grab it, hoping it'd be Kai returning one of my many calls, but once I saw the display and who was calling, I dropped it back on the table with a groan. It was Alana, *again*.

I sat up, dumped my head into my hands and slapped my forehead numerous times with the palms of my hands. How could I have been so damn stupid? I stood and grabbed my dick through my pants, and yelled at it at the top of my lungs. "It's your fucking fault!"

I dropped back down onto the couch, knowing full well that in reality it had been a compilation of things that had gotten the best of me. I should have kept my eye on the bigger picture and not let these small details change my course of action. I was an idiot and I needed Kai to know that.

I leaned my head back, and listened to the ringing of my cell phone again. I glanced at it to see that it was Alana and shook my head. I forwarded her call to voicemail. Will this ever end?

Silence fell over my living room, with nothing but a ticking clock in the background. I thought of Kai and how much I loved her and how much I wanted to tell her that over and over again.

My mind drifted back to the first time I saw Kai. It had been when I was in Curt's Café on Michigan Avenue in Chicago. A smile made its way across my solemn face and I chuckled to myself thinking how that moment played out. Kai tried playing hard to get, and I didn't take no for an answer.

Our connection was instant, and our chemistry undeniable. I knew that moment I would marry her and she would be mine forever. She had that something that made her different, unique and safe. I couldn't help but ditch my soon-to-be ex-girlfriend along with my unordered cup of coffee and follow Kai out of the cafe and up the street.

I watched from behind as she walked with purpose, weaving in and out of the oncoming bodies who were making their way in the opposite direction of her, of us. It was a hot and sticky day in Chicago, but that didn't matter, not one bit. I pushed my way through the heat and humidity like a forty year marriage in Hollywood.

Kai finally stopped at the corner newsstand and I knew that was my chance to claim what would be mine. Seeing her up close, her eyes, her lips her undeniable essence, only confirmed that our chance meeting was meant to be. I was on the fence of what I wanted to do with my current girlfriend, Adriane, of four years, but the moment I saw Kai in that café, my mind was set to walk the other way, and walk the other way I did. I still remember the butterflies dancing in my stomach while we exchanged our flirty banter and how I couldn't wait to see her again.

When we parted ways and I headed back to my office, I was still thinking about her caramel skin, full lips and amazing calves—all things I noticed while looking her way.

The moment I settled back into my office, I grabbed my cell phone and dialed her number. People always tell you to wait two days before calling, but I knew I didn't want to waste any time where Kai was concerned. In that moment I didn't care, I wanted to hear her voice once more before I finished my day.

I opened my eyes and was brought instantly back to reality and my depressed state. I glanced around my empty house, sighing, thinking about how it mirrored the emptiness within my heart. I had to do something. I couldn't live like this. I needed to get Kai back.

I decided to head into my office around eight a.m. It didn't make sense for me to just sit around the house, I needed to do something to take my mind off of my problems. I tried Kai twice on my drive in, but continued to get her voicemail.

I walked into the lobby and noticed my boss David was already there. I stopped mid-stride in the middle of the hallway, halfway to my office when I had an epiphany. I needed to make a change and there was only one way to do it. I made my way into my office, turned on my computer and started typing. Ten minutes later I hit print, grabbed my document off of my printer and headed down the hall to my boss' office. I lightly knocked on his slightly opened door.

"Todd, you're here bright and early this morning," David said, looking up from his computer.

I slowly walked into his office and settled in. "Yeah, I have a lot on my plate and well, I wanted to come in and sort out a few things out, one being Alana Brooks."

"Alana Brooks? Is there something wrong?" David asked, giving me a concerned look.

"Actually, sir, I'd say there are a lot of things wrong."

David motioned with his hand. "Have a seat, please."

"Actually, sir, I think I should stand for this one," I said, swallowing hard. I laid the piece of paper in my hand on his desk.

"What is this?" David reached for the letter.

"My letter or resignation. I am sorry sir, but I don't think I am suited for this company."

"I'm confused, Todd. Our clients love your work and Alana—"

"Alana is the problem, sir."

"Alana? How so?"

"With all due respect I would rather refrain from discussing my issues, but suffice it to say, I can no longer work with her and if that means me losing my position here, then I am one-hundred percent okay with that," I said firmly, holding my ground. We stared at each other for a moment before David nodded his head at me.

"Well, this is unexpected," David said, folding his hands neatly on the desk.

"Why didn't you come to me with this earlier?"

I shifted, contemplated my next thoughts. "I thought I could work it out myself, trying to keep my personal issues out of the office. A huge mistake on my part, sir."

David slowly nodded his head. Tood a deep breath. "I don't want to lose you, that's for sure. You've proven to be a valuable asset to this firm so far. To be honest, I see a lot of potential in you."

"Thank you, sir."

"So, instead of losing you, I'd prefer to reassign Alana to another colleague effective immediately."

"Thank you, sir. Thank you very much," I said. It felt as if a small weight had been lifted from my chest.

I gave David one last thank-you nod before turning out of his office, down the hall and into my office.

I sat down at my desk and leaned back as far back as the chair could go. This was a start I thought. I sat up, grabbed my phone and called Kai's voicemail.

"Hey, Kai, it's me. I did something today that I should have done months ago. Call me, please."

THIRTY-THREE
KAI

I picked Kristopher up from Tender Hands, grabbed a bite to eat, then headed back to Camille's house. I pulled up in front of her house and sat there for a minute. I had to laugh at the irony of being mad at Todd for doing the exact same thing to me as I did to him. Though, he took a step back, doing his with Alana.

I shook my head, with Alana of all people... How did she still have a hold on him? I knew that Simone said I should make Todd sweat a bit, but the truth was, I missed him. I looked down to see that I had five more missed calls from Todd and one voicemail message.

I headed in the house and found Camille watching Steve Harvey on *Family Feud*. Kristopher immediately ran to the back to play with her daughter Natalie while I closed the door behind me.

"Hey."

"Hey, where did you disappear to?" Camille asked, looking my way.

"I had to go take care of a few things," I said. I didn't want to give away the fact that I went to pay Alana a visit.

"You hungry?"

"No, I stopped to eat after I picked up Kristopher from school." I sat down on the two-toned gray chair across from her. "Thank you again for letting me and Kristopher stay here, but I think we will go home tonight."

Camille sat up a bit taller. "Oh, okay. You know you can stay here as long as you like, and I promise, no funny business."

I shot Camille a look and we both laughed.

"Did you just say no funny business?" I asked.

"I did, and don't judge me," Camille said, still chuckling. "At least I got a smile out of you."

"Yeah, I'm sorry I have been a bit out of it, but..." I stopped myself, not wanting to go any further about what was going on in my life.

"Kai, what is it? You can talk to me, you know."

I took a deep breath, thought for a minute. "It's complicated."

"Life is complicated," Camille said, staring at me. She wasn't going to let this one go.

"Yeah, but this is the complicated, almost unbelievable at times."

"Kai, I just want to help. I am not here to judge you, seriously."

"I know. It's just such a long drawn-out story, and..." I looked at Camille and thought about what Simone said to me, but in this moment I needed another person to talk to.

"Okay, well, the gist of it is I made a really big...huge mistake, and, well, now I am living with the consequences." I looked away then back at Camille who was all ears. "A few years back when I was just dating Todd, I slept with his best friend—his female best friend."

"Okay. Now that is different. I'm listening."

"And since then, my life has been one big cesspool of hell. It started with Todd leaving me for her when he thought her child was his, which by the way, he later found out was a lie, a way to get him to marry her and not me.

"But you two are married," Camille said.

"Yeah, but that didn't happen until after all the lies came out and he finally saw her true colors and who she really was..." I paused.

"Why am I sensing a but?" Camille said.

"Because there is a big-ass but. In essence, this woman will not leave us alone. She pretended to be mugged. Then she broke into my house in

Brooklyn, threatened Todd and my newborn son's lives and now, now, she magically appeared out here in LA on a quest to get Todd back. This woman is manipulative and will stop at nothing to get what she wants." I looked at Camille who was at a loss for words. I couldn't blame her. "Hey, you wanted to know and there ya go. Pretty crazy, huh?"

"That's um, that's some story there. Sounds like a Lifetime movie of the week."

"Yep, that's what I have been living, a Lifetime movie."

Camille shook her head. "This woman sounds like a piece of work. She also sounds like a woman my sister used to mess around with back in Chicago. The stories she would tell me about her I couldn't believe. Ever since my sister came out of the closet back in college, she's made horrible choices in women. Fortunately, I think she may have found a good woman back in New York, some professor at NYU or someplace."

"So you *and* your sister are into women?"

"Well, yes. Technically, she is my half-sister. We have different fathers." Camille ran her fingers through her coffee-brown hair. "I'd tell my sister to leave that crazy woman alone, but she was obsessed with her," Camille continued. "She was so desperate to be with this woman that my sister agreed to do a threesome with the girl's boyfriend."

"Do you remember her name, the woman's name?" I asked. I wasn't sure what made me ask her that, but I couldn't stop myself.

"Gosh, what was that woman's name, something like Alicia, Anna, no wait, *Alana*."

My mouth fell open upon hearing Alana's name, as I bent over like someone had just sucker punched me straight in the gut. I managed to sit back up, even though I felt dizzy. Thank God I was sitting down. "Camille, what is your sister's name?"

"Jessica."

"Jessica, what?"

"Jessica McCoy."

"Oh my God."

"Kai, what's wrong?"

In that moment, everything became clear. All of it flashed before my eyes like a horror flick on fast-forward. First, I remembered Jessica's facial expression back in New York, standing in Toni's brownstone and her saying to me, "Todd is your husband?" Next, I remembered seeing Jessica's friend request to Todd on

Facebook. Finally, I remembered Todd's expression when I asked him who Jessica was. It all came together in one quick swoop.

I stood, not knowing what to do or what to say. Everything was happening so fast.

"Kai, are you okay?"

"I um, I have to go. Can you watch Kristopher for a little while?"

"Of course, but where are you going?"

"I just need to get some air. I need time to think." I felt like my brain was about to explode.

"Are you sure? I can…"

"I just have to go," I said, grabbing my purse and heading for the door. I jumped into my car and drove off seconds after my last words to Camille.

I rolled down both of my windows and took several deep cleansing breaths in and out. I felt my emotions getting the best of me and I started to cry uncontrollably. What other lies were there for me to discover beneath the surface of this woman called Alana? What else would I find out?

I pulled my car over while the tears started to accumulate in my eyes. It was so bad, the tears were beginning to impair my vision.

I put my car in park and looked up to see I had driven to my house. I stared across the street at the house where Todd and I attempted to make a home together, but it felt far from a home right now. I started to cry again and I couldn't help but think that this drama would never end so long as Alana was walking the face of the earth.

I took a deep breath and contemplated going into the house to tell Todd about my latest revelation. His threesome with Alana and Jessica. It was the cherry on the top of our fucked-up seven-layered cake of drama. Will this ever end? I kept repeating that phrase to myself without a definitive answer. I didn't know what to think anymore, who to trust or where to go. It was all beginning to be too much. I was coming undone.

Thirty minutes later I found myself still staring at the house I shared with Todd and the memories we attempted to create, the more my hurt turned to anger. I was angry that he even introduced me to Alana in the first place, angry that he left me for her, angry that he hid the fact that she was in LA and angry at his continued lies and deceit when it came to *her*. I hated both of them. They deserved to be together.

I shifted my car into drive, pushed down on the accelerator, and sped down the street. If this was how Todd wanted to play it, then fine, two could play that game.

A few minutes later I was back in front of Camille's house. I jumped out of my car, heading back into her house. I walked in to see she was not in the living room. I headed to the back to see her coming out of Natalie's room.

"Hey, I just put a movie on for the kids and got them down for a while. Are you okay?"

I didn't say a word, but just gently grabbed Camille's hand and lead her into her bedroom and closed the door.

"Kai—"

"Shhh, don't say anything, please." I looked at Camille, then leaned in and started to kiss her passionately on the lips. She pulled away. "Kai, what are you doing?"

"What I should have done two days ago?" I said, pushing Camille against the door. I laid my body against hers and as we kissed, our tongues did a familiar dance as our bodies slid to the floor together.

If this was how Todd wanted to play it, so be it.

THIRTY-FOUR
ALANA

"Can I get another glass of wine, please?" I signaled to my bartender and he delivered another glass of Merlot my way. I was on my third glass of wine as I sat at the Whisky Blue bar in the W Hotel in Westwood. I figured if I wanted to get drunk it would be at a place where I could get a room if need be.

I glanced at my watch and noticed it was almost 5 p.m. Kai's visit earlier today was unexpected, but I never backed down from a challenge. Not ever. My cell phone rang and I noticed it was Todd's office number. I smiled from the inside out. I knew Todd couldn't stay away for long. He needed me.

"Well, hello, darling."

"Alana, this is David Johnson," David said in a professional tone.

"Oh, David, hello," I said. I felt my buzz drop down two notches. "I'm sorry, I thought you were Todd calling me."

"Actually, Alana, that is why I am calling you." I heard David clear his throat. "We've decided to move Todd over to another client, one that is more suitable for his expertise, and—"

"Move Todd? That is unacceptable, David," I said, starting to feel my rage start an uphill climb.

"Alana is there something going on between you and Todd that I need to be aware of?"

"No, um, why would you ask that?" I felt my breath become shallow. "Did Todd mention something to you?"

"No Alana, he did not."

"Then why--"

"Alana, I understand that you are not happy with our decision, but in this case our hands were tied. Believe me, Alana, your new associate, Anthony Matthews, will be just as suitable for you as Todd Daniels was," David said cutting me off.

"I highly doubt it. David is there a way we can all sit down and talk about this?"

"Not at this time. Believe me, Alana, it's for the best. I give you my word that Anthony will be a great fit for you."

"But David—"

"Listen, Alana, I have to grab this other call. Let's talk a little later. Thank you for being so understanding," David said, quickly hanging up the phone.

I sat there for a minute and wondered what Todd could have told him. What made David so damn quick to take Todd away from being my day-to-day attorney? I wondered if Kai got to him as well.

I took another big gulp of my wine, polishing off the glass and waved to my bartender for another. I felt every inch of me start to tighten up and my breathing began to pick up its pace. I felt like everything was slipping out of my control and I didn't like it, not one bit.

I grabbed my cell phone and dialed Todd's number. This time when his voicemail came on I didn't hang up. Instead, I gave him a piece of my mind.

"I just got a call from David that I'm not pleased about, about you being reassigned. Let me just say this once and for all, you are *my* lawyer and if you can't deal with that then get the fuck over it." I took a deep breath, taking my anger down a level.

"Todd, I need to see you now and I don't appreciate you sending your little bitch down to my set either." I took another deep breath.

"I am at the W Hotel in Westwood and expect you to be here in the next hour, please." I hit end and tossed my cell phone back down on the bar. The sound of my phone hitting the marble top made a clattering sound, making more than a few people look my way.

"What the fuck are you looking at?" I snapped at them.

Two guys just chuckled to themselves and turned back around.

"Assholes," I said under my breath. I turned and found Emanuel standing inches from me.

"How long have you been here?" I darted my eyes over at my gay-gent.

"Oh, long enough to see that you need to be cut off."

"What are you doing in LA?"

"I am here with a new client, trying to get him a few guest-starring roles on your show. Something we discussed in length last night."

"Oh, right. How did you know I was here?" I asked. Clearly, I was drunker than I thought, since my memory was failing me.

"You texted me and told me you were headed here because you had a bad encounter and needed to drink the feeling away."

"I said that?"

"Those were your exact words." Emanuel slid into the bar seat next to me.

"So what is going on with you? You look like hell, you're loud and destructive and don't think I didn't hear that off-the-cuff comment you just made."

"You heard that?"

"The whole bar heard you."

"I've had the worst day ever. I'm so glad you're in town. I could really use a friend right now," I said, as I felt my emotions getting the best of me, hoping they didn't reveal my true feelings right now.

"Well, maybe this will cheer you up. You just booked a principle role in a feature that shoots in Canada opposite Anthony Mackey.

"What? Seriously?"

"Yes, girlfriend. The director saw some of your dailies from your pilot and loved your energy. Plus, he dug your hot looks as he called 'em. He wants to meet you and go from there. In Hollywood terms that means you've been handpicked."

Emanuel pulled out his black day planner. "Should I book you and Todd a ticket to Canada?"

"Please, Todd doesn't deserve to go with me. Matter of fact, he doesn't deserve me, period. He's a fucking prick and Kai's a bitch. I can't believe I even went there with her," I said, feeling the venom shoot through my veins with each syllable I spat out. "As far as I'm concerned they deserve each other."

"Okay, I definitely think it's time to exit stage left and away from the alcohol."

"Please, I am fine. Besides, I can just get a room upstairs. You wanna join me?"

I saw Emanuel's face wrench back in disgust. "Yeah girlfriend, you're drunker than you know. I'm going to the little boys room and when I get back, I will drive you home."

"Fine." I watched as Emanuel left. I sat there and surveyed the room. I turned to see a woman walking with her daughter in the lobby of the hotel. I stared at her, my eyes trailing through the bar area and into the adjoining lobby. I continued to watch and admire the mother bending down talking to her little girl. I studied their body language as the little girl smiled then wrapped her arms around her mom. I swallowed hard, thinking about how I missed Riley so very much, how I needed to stop trying to make things perfect and just go and get my baby before it was too late.

I picked up my phone and dialed my mom's number."

"Hey, Mom, can I speak to Riley?"

"You have a lot of nerve calling now after that little email stunt you—"

"I know I know, please spare me the lecture right now, just put Riley on the phone, please."

"She's not here, Alana."

" Where is she?"

"She's with Avery."

"What do you mean, *with* Avery?"

"He came and got her a few days ago."

"What? And you just let her go?"

"He's her father, Alana."

"He only got her so he can extort money from me! Don't you see that? I can't believe you let him take her."

"Whatever you and Avery have going on is between you two. Apparently, he is getting remarried."

"Oh my God, really? How devoted of him."

"Also, what is this about some custody suit I filed against you?" My mother continued ignoring my mini rant.

"What?"

"Yeah, I got a call from Todd. Alana, what are you up to out there? You abandon your child and now you're faking a paternity suit?"

I dropped my head into my free hand. *Geezuz*. I had completely dismissed this in my mind, forgetting the fact that I would have to hear about this from my mom as well.

"Why would you lie and tell him I was suing for custody of Riley?"

"Mom, I can't get into that right now."

"Well, whatever scam you're trying to pull backfired on you, Alana, because right after he called me, he called Avery."

"What?" I placed my hand over my mouth. This was turning out to be a freaking nightmare.

"When will you learn to leave well enough alone?"

I hung up on my mom, and my mind started to race. The foundations of my life seemed as if they were being knocked out from under me. First, Kai walked in my dressing room and demanded shit, acting like she was running things. Then Todd changed up the game by calling my mom, Avery and now Riley. I was enraged with Todd, with Kai and with anyone else who was happy and content right now because I, Alana Brooks, was so far away from it. This was all about to change.

I glanced over to see Emanuel's car keys laying on the bar. My mind began to race, contemplate, create. With no sign of Emanuel anywhere I grabbed his keys, and jumped out of my seat, rushing out of the bar. I was determined to come out on top no matter what. They had no idea who the hell they were screwing with.

THIRTY-FIVE
KAI

My eyes popped open the next morning to see Camille's master bedroom. It was much larger than her guest room I had been taking up residence for the last few days. I scanned her peach-colored walls and vertical white blinds before I reached over to grab my phone to see what time it was. I focused on the small digital numbers on my iPhone, 7:16 a.m. to be exact.

I sighed and placed my iPhone back down on the bedside table and turned to see Camille still sleeping beside me. I closed my eyes then quickly opened them back up. What had I done?

I quietly slid out of Camille's bed, hoping to avoid waking her. I slipped on my jeans and T-shirt, located my shoes and headed out of her bedroom. I closed the door only to realize I had forgotten my damn cell phone on her bedside table. Dammit. I contemplated just leaving it until after I had taken Kristopher to daycare, but thought twice about it, knowing I might not come straight back.

I slowly turned the doorknob and re-opened the door. I took a few soft steps into Camille's room and moved quietly through the space to pick up my cell phone. Grabbing it, I slid it into my pocket and Camille turned over. I froze, holding my breath, but she continued her deep sleep and I let out a silent exhale. I shook my head and headed out the room once again.

I gently picked up my son who was still half-asleep, grabbed his clothes, food and toys. I dropped Kristopher off at daycare, changing and feeding him there.

I jumped back in my car and began to drive. My plan was to keep going until I saw the waters of the Pacific Ocean, felt the sand under my feet and the sound of the seagulls in my ears.

I found a spot near the water and sat down to look out at the waves. I threw my hood on from my sweatshirt and pulled my knees to my chest. The cool air felt good on my face. I reflected on everything that had happened to me—from the night before, to the days before, and the years that passed, all the way back to when this whole thing started and I met Alana Brooks. I allowed time to pass while I sat quietly on the beach. Finally, I reached into my jacket and pulled out my cell phone.

"Hey, what are you doing up so early? Are those waves I hear?" Simone asked after picking up my call.

I finally worked up the nerve to call Simone and confess what I had done. "I slept with Camille." I bit my lower lip and waited for her reaction.

I reached down, drawing circles in the sand with my index finger and talked through her silence. "Go ahead and say I told you so, and that you knew it all along. But you know what? I don't care. I did it because I wanted to hurt Todd just as much as he hurt me."

"What did he do now?" Simone asked.

"While we were apart, when I was living in New York, he had a threesome with Alana and some woman named Jessica."

Simone was quiet.

"What, nothing to say to that? Because I have tons to say," I said, hoping to fill the silence.

"Listen, if you think I, Simone 'Eye For An Eye, Tooth For A Tooth" McCormick, is going to sit here and judge you for sleeping with Camille to get back at Todd, that damn sure isn't gonna happen, but we both know there is a lot more to it than that."

"What are you talking about?"

"Kai, you know I love you to pieces, but there is something that you have not come to grips with in your life"

Silence fell between me and my best friend. I heard Simone take a deep breath.

"Okay, and what is that?" I said.

"Your sexuality."

I sat there feeling numb. I wasn't sure how to respond, but mostly, I didn't want to respond. I didn't want to know the truth, because the truth was about to force me to accept something I wasn't ready for.

"Kai, your revenge sex involves a desire for women."

"But it was only a few times," I said not ready to throw in my white towel.

"Yes, but those few times were a few too many times for your best friend not to sit up and take notice. Now don't get me wrong, I totally get revenge sex. Hell, sometimes it can be better than real sex. If I was in your situation, I probably would've done the same thing, but I'd go straight for a brother or even a sexy-ass father if one existed. That's the kind of cold bitch I am. But I would never go after a sister or female friend. You see where I am coming from? You see the difference?"

I stayed silent.

"Kai, it isn't a secret that you enjoy sleeping with women, but you have to remember how you got into this whole situation in the first place."

"By sleeping with a woman," I said, knowing what was about to come out of Simone's mouth.

"Now although that woman was a psychotic and very unstable woman, she was still *a woman*, and lately your pattern has been to rebound with just that."

"Simone, do you think I am gay?"

"No, I think you're bi-sexual and there is nothing wrong with that, Kai, but you have to own up to that side of you."

"You don't think I am just bi-curious?"

"I think you crossed that line when you met Toni. Now, Alana I would have given you that as being bi-curios, but Toni and now Camille, you have crossed over."

"But I love Todd and I want to be with Todd."

"Of course you love Todd and I know you want to be with him no matter what. But you two have to be on the same page. This whole running to a woman every time you have issues has got to stop. Remember, you two are a unit and you can work these issues out together without involving a third party."

I felt cold air hitting my face as I sat in the sand, unable to move. Simone was right, I had to come to grips with who I was before I could move on. I needed to talk to Todd.

"Do what you have to do to make it right, Kai. Remember, you two have a child together now, so the game is different, the rules have changed. Figure out what you want and what is best for your family unit and work that shit out once and for all."

"Okay."

"But remember, at the end of the day, it's what's going to make *you* happy."

I sat on the beach for thirty more minutes after disconnecting my call with Simone. I thought about Todd, Alana and everything that had transpired since she walked into our lives. It was funny how things happened and how we dealt with those problems as people. The choices we make today have a tremendous effect on how the rest of our lives play out.

I stood and headed back to my car as my internal monologue said to me loud and clear, *It's time to make some better choices and it need to start with Todd.*

***

I slowly walked back into Camille's house to find it empty. I breathed a small sigh of relief, as I was not ready to face her the morning after. I knew my anger mixed with desire fueled my so-called sexual escapade with her last night and once again, I found myself in the same awkward place that I had with Toni.

I shook my head as Simone's words rang clear in my head. As I began to collect my things I heard the front door to Camille's house open then close. Everything tightened inside of me because I knew what was coming next.

"Hey you." Camille stood in the doorway of her bedroom as I zipped up my bag full of mine and Kristopher's belongings. "You're leaving. Why am I not surprised?"

I felt a sense of deja-vu swirling through the room as I turned to face my lover from last night.

"I'm so sorry, Camille, I was out of line last night and what happened..."

"Shouldn't have happened." Camille threw her arms up in defeat. "Of course. But it did, Kai, and guess what? You orchestrated it," Camille said, the annoyance in her voice dripping off of each word she spoke.

"I know. I'm sorry and, well, bottom line is..." I took a very deep breath. "I know I am bi-sexual, *but,* I also took an oath with my husband and that is something I have to honor."

"Right, and fucking me would throw a monkey wrench in that, I get it." Camille shook her head, looked away then back at me. "Listen, it's cool, you had a moment and I was in the right place at the right time."

"Camille, I'm sorry."

"Me, too," Camille said, and we held a stare. A small smile emerged from her lips as she slowly shook her head.

"What?" I said.

"I knew it. I knew you were bi-sexual. Can't fool me, no you cannot."

"Whatever."

"It's all good. I'm not gonna lie and say I didn't enjoy it, but I knew it wasn't going to materialize into anything and that's fine with me, really."

"Really?"

"No, but I will get over it."

That was good to hear coming out of Camille's mouth. I wasn't sure if that was her defense mechanism kicking in, but I wasn't going to question it.

"Do you think we could still be friends?" I asked hesitantly.

"Oh you did not just go there!"

"I'm sorry, but I am really bad at the whole girl-on-girl-after-we-have-sex protocol."

Camille laughed and shook her head. "Yes, you are, but it's cool. Let's just take it one day at a time. How about, I'll see ya when I see ya?"

"Right." I figured that was Camille's way of nicely saying *no, we cannot be friends.* Message received. I finished zipping up my bag and walked past Camille and out of her house. I picked up my phone and dialed Todd's number. He picked it up on the first ring.

"Hey it's me, can we talk?"

THIRTY-SIX
TODD

I saw Kai pull up in front of our house. I stepped out onto our porch and watched her car slowly come to a stop, turn off the engine and step out.

We locked eyes and a cold sensation shot through my body. I didn't know what this visit could bring. I swallowed hard as I watched Kai walk toward me. I didn't move, not one step. I wanted to see what she would do first. As Kai got closer I noticed she had tears in her eyes and that was when my feet became unglued. I dropped my defenses, ran over to her and hugged her so tight. I breathed her in as I felt her arms around me.

"Baby, I'm sorry, I'm sorry, I'm sorry, I'm sooo sorry," I repeated over and over then pulled back to look into Kai's eyes before I planted a kiss on her lips, followed by another long hug. "I am sooo sorry."

"Me too, baby. Me too."

Kai and I held hands and we walked into our house together. I didn't say anything else since we were both at a loss for words. Each one of us was waiting for the other to speak.

"I missed you," Kai said, as she sat next to me on the couch.

"You have no idea what I've been going through, baby," I replied, fighting back my emotions as they fought to overtake me.

"I have to tell you something," Kai said, looking down and away, then back at me.

"What? Tell me."

"The last few days have been hard for me and...and I have had so many different emotions going through every part of my body."

Kai squirmed a bit in her seat. "I was so mad I wanted to hurt you just as bad as you hurt me and—"

I grabbed both of Kai's hands, held them tightly, looked into her eyes, stopped her from struggling with what she wanted to say, from what I already knew. I took a deep breath, thought carefully about my next words. "Baby, I know you are bi-sexual, first Alana then Toni, the writing was on the walls. I love you and it doesn't matter how many women you have been with.

Kai looked up at me. "I'm sorry," Kai said as embarrasement washed over her face.

"Don't be. All that matters is that we are together again. I wouldn't have married you if I had a problem with it."

"But you do."

I paused, coming to terms with my truth. "I do, but I love you more."

I squeezed Kai's hands a bit harder, feeling the guilt dissipate from her body. "I just wish you would let me in a little bit more. Let me know when you are having those feelings and we can work it out together."

Kai smiled at me. "I can do that."

I took a deep breath. "So I did something, something I should have done months ago," I said.

"Okay?"

"I told my boss that I could no longer represent Alana one on one."

Kai slowly pulled her hands out of mine. "Is she still with your firm?"

I felt my jaws clench together. "Yes, but she is no longer *my* client."

Kai was silent as she took a deep breath.

"Listen, if you want me to wear a tracking device I will wear a tracking device, but if that's not good enough, then I will just quit my job. Baby, I know I fucked up. I should have told you about Alana the moment I found out."

"Then why didn't you?" Kai asked, fresh tears in her eyes. Those tears made all the guilt I had inside re-surface.

"I was just scared of losing you, my job and everything that we worked for."

"But how could you sleep with her?"

I stood, throwing my hands up in frustration. "That's the thing, I don't even remember that night in New York. I swear it was as if I wasn't even there. One minute we were having drinks and the next, I woke up in her bed. I never intended to hurt you, you know that." I sat back down. "Let me just say right here and right now, I want to put all things Alana in the past for good. That means everything."

"Everything?"

"Like she never even existed," I said.

"Seriously?"

"Yes. We can't let her get the best of us again."

Kai looked down. I put my index finger under her chin and lifted her head back up. "We have to stay strong, strong enough so that nothing can penetrate what we have. We are a unit, a team, the dynamic duo." I continued trying to convince Kai, as much as I was trying to convince myself. I thought back to the moment in Alana's dressing room when she got the best of me. The one thing I did remember, the one thing I had to take to the grave. The one thing I could never explain.

"Okay?"

A broad smile fell across Kai's face. "Okay."

We fell into each other's arms right there on the couch, holding each other as if it was the very first time and the last.

***

A few hours later I woke up with Kai still in my arms. Emotional exhaustion was victorious over the both of us. I looked down at her face and smiled. I kissed her on the forehead and then softly on her lips as her eyes slowly opened and she focused back on me.

"Hey, we fell asleep," I said, looking down at her.

"What time is it?"

I pulled my arm from behind Kai's head and glanced at my watch. "It's one o'clock."

Kai sat up. "I have to go pick up Kris." Kai held her head.

I sat up next to her, noticed her looking extra fatigued. "You okay?"

"Yeah, I um, I'm just really tired. I didn't sleep well last night."

"Do you want me to go get him?" I said.

"No, I can. I'll be fine once I get moving."

Kai stood and I remained on the couch. She walked over to the door and picked up her purse, turning to me. "Can I take your car, mine is low on gas and I don't feel like stopping right now."

"Yeah, of course," I said, reaching in my pocket, pulling out my keys.

"So are we good?" I shot Kai a look, waiting for my final confirmation.

"Yeah, we're good." Kai shot me a reaffirming nod back. "See you in a few."

Once Kai had left, I decided not to go into the office. Half the day was gone, so I didn't see the point of going in. I was excited, relieved and energized all at once. I felt that Kai and I had drug ourselves through the fires of hell and made it out unscathed on the other side. It was such a great feeling. One I will never trade ever again for the unnecessary drama that once filled and suffocated our lives.

I wanted to surprise Kai with something special, something that she could remember for a lifetime. I could think of nothing better than a pair of two-carat diamond earrings.

I jumped in the shower, threw on my favorite jeans and button-up olive-green shirt and headed out the door to the jewelry shop. It wasn't long before I was holding the perfect pair of princess-cut earrings. I smiled at the thought of Kai's face when she opened the box. She had been wanting a pair like this for a while now and I had been taking my sweet time to give them to her, pushing it off every day, waiting for that one special occasion. I couldn't think of a better time than the reunion of our love.

I got back home, expecting to see Kai and Kristopher when I walked through the door, but to my surprise they were not there. I tried Kai's cell phone, but it went straight to voicemail. I glanced at my watch and saw it was almost three. Kai had left just after one o'clock, what could be taking her so long? I tried her cell phone again, voicemail, and again, voicemail again. I shot her a text and waited, nothing. I finally called the daycare center.

"Tender Hands, this is Trina, how can I help you?"

"Hey, Trina, this is Todd Daniels, Kristopher's father.

"Oh hi, how are you?"

"Not great, by any chance has my wife been by to pick up Kristopher?"

"No, she hasn't."

I was silent, unsure of what to say, as my mind started to race.

"Is everything okay?"

I scratched my head. "Actually, I'm sure it is. What time do you close?"

"We close at six p.m."

"Okay, then someone will be by to pick up Kristopher by then."

"Sounds good, Mr. Daniels."

I hung up the phone and tried Kai's cell again, and again, I got her voicemail. "Shit, where could she be?"

Camille came to mind, but why would she go by her house? Did I read into our conversation all wrong? I began to pace, thinking of my next step. I didn't want to call Camille, maybe I could drive by her house. I grabbed my keys and suddenly remembered I didn't even know where she lived. I jumped back in Kai's car as my cell phone rang. I saw Kai's name flash up and picked it up immediately.

"Baby, where are you?"

"Good afternoon, I'm calling from the UCLA Medical Center emergency room. I'm afraid to inform you that your wife has been involved in a serious car accident. Is this her husband?"

"Yes, it is. Is she okay?"

"You need to get down here as soon as you can."

THIRTY-SEVEN
TODD

I stared at Kai as she lay still in her hospital bed. I looked at my surroundings and the sterile white walls, ceramic floors, simple blue curtains and the sound of the beeping machine next to her bed. I focused on the bandages on her head and arm. I noticed the peacefulness on her face. I hadn't slept since they brought Kai into the hospital six hours ago. When I didn't show to pick up Kristopher, they called and said Camille was willing to watch him for us. I was grateful for her in that moment since I needed to be with Kai.

I leaned my head back and closed my eyes, only to be startled as the hospital door opened and the doctor walked in.

"Hi, I'm Doctor Ng. Are you her husband?"

"Yes, I am. How is she?" I stood, taking two steps toward the doctor.

"Your wife will be fine. She was fortunate. Just a few bruises and a fractured arm. Frankly, it could have been much worse."

I nodded my head. "Thank you, Doctor."

"The baby was not harmed either."

"Baby? Kai's pregnant?"

Dr. Ng looked at the chart in her hand, flipped a page up. "Yes, she is ten weeks." Dr. Ng then looked back at me with a smile. "Congratulations"

I stared at Kai, still sleeping, then back over to the doctor. "Thank you."

"Your wife should be okay to go home in a few days." Dr. Ng gave me one last half- smile and then exited the room.

I walked over to the side of Kai's bed, bent over and gently kissed her on the cheek. When I stood back up, Kai opened her eyes and looked at me.

"Hey," Kai said in a soft tone.

"Hey, you're awake," I said, smiling down at her.

"What happened?" Kai asked, trying to sit up.

I stopped her. "Baby, relax. You had a car accident."

"I did?" Kai reached up to feel the bandages on her head. Then quickly to her stomach.

"The baby is fine."

Kai breathed a sigh of relief, then smiled as she reached out and touch my hand. "Thank God."

"Why didn't you tell me?"

"I wanted to wait until I got a blood confirmation back before I got you all excited, or freaked out. Are you happy?"

"Yes, of course! God, yes! This is great news. We're having another baby."

"Looks that way."

"Wow. How do you feel?"

"Not great, considering I just had a car accident. What exactly happened, anyway?"

"A witness said you sailed through a light and slammed into the car in front of you."

Kai looked up to the ceiling as if she was recalling the incident. "Yeah, I remember trying to stop, but I couldn't. It was weird, but that was the last thing I remembered."

"Good news is, the doctor said you and the baby will be fine."

"Okay." Kai settled back into her bed just as a police officer walked through the door.

The officer looked at me. "Mr. Daniels, can I speak to you for a minute?"

"Sure." I looked at Kai. "I'll be right back." I kissed Kai on the forehead and followed the police officer out into the hallway.

The police officer held a piece of paper in his hand and looked down at it before speaking. "Mr. Daniels, we got the report back from where your car was towed."

"Okay?"

"It appears as if your brakes were cut."

"What?" I ran my hand through my hair and down the back of my neck, trying to stay calm. "Okay."

"We've looked into it and found a report of a woman around your home late last night—sometime around 10:30 p.m."

"Did you get a description?"

"It wasn't great, but we did manage to obtain the license plate of the car she was driving."

"And?"

"And it was registered to Hertz Car Rental under the name of Emanuel Vaughn."

"Emanuel Vaughn?"

"Yes, do you know him?"

"No, not directly," I said. In my head I knew exactly who did know him, which pointed to exactly who did it.

***

I headed out of the hospital, rage building beneath each step I took. My intention was to go home, grab a change of clothes, and head back to the hospital. But, the moment I jumped behind the wheel I found myself heading straight to the office, hoping to find Alana.

I parked my car in the visitors' parking space and headed for the elevator that would take me to the 11th floor. I stepped out of the elevator and walked down the hallway, not speaking to any of my colleagues. Instead, I stayed focused on why I was there. My mind was thinking two steps ahead, already deciding that if I didn't find her here, I would leave and try her dressing room on the lot. I was on a mission to find her and nothing was going to stop me know..

I scanned the front conference room, my office and the small kitchenette with no sign of Alana. I couldn't think straight. I felt my body losing control with the thought of what could have been done to Kai and my unborn child.

I continued down the hallway, turned the corner and found myself in front of the main conference room. There she was, laughing as if she didn't have a care in the gotdamn world.

I stood there staring, contemplating, plotting. My rage was at its peak and suddenly, I found that I couldn't control it. I swung open the door with so much fury it slammed against the opposite wall, startling everyone in attendance. I zeroed in on Alana like a snipper to its intended target, didn't allow anytime for a reaction as I charged her like a raging bull with a freshly stamped brand.

I headed straight for her neck as I made instant contact, wrapping both of my hands around it with extreme power and vengeance. I didn't miss a beat as I squeezed her neck as tight as I could with both hands. We tumbled onto the floor with me landing on top of Alana as I straddled her body with my legs.

We locked eyes as her mouth opened, but nothing came out. I continued to squeeze Alana's neck as her face turned three shades of red. Alana pressed her hand hard up against my chin, trying to push me off, but my wrath was just too strong. Alana tried to talk, but I just squeezed harder. I couldn't let go. My hands had a mind of their own. My body and my soul wanted Alana to feel the amount of physical pain and emotional turmoil I felt seeing Kai laying in that hospital bed.

I watched as Alana's eyes began to close as sweat fell from my face to hers. She was dying and I didn't give a fuck. I was in the moment, this moment of pure hate and revenge and hurt when an unknown arm wrapped around my neck, yanking me off of Alana's body with a hard jerk. I felt myself being overpowered by not one, but four men. I resisted as much as I could before I surrendered to their leverage. I was thrown across the room and knocked into two chairs and fell to the ground. I quickly stood, out of breath, still full of rage while two of the men continued to restrain me, one on each arm. I tried to pull away, but they held on tighter, making sure I didn't go after her again.

David ran to see if Alana was okay as I watched Alana cough and gasp for air, trying to regain the breath she had lost in that few seconds I stole from her.

"Are you fucking nuts!?" I heard David Johnson yell.

I felt my chest heaving out of control while I tried to catch my breath from the adrenaline rush. "No, she is the crazy one."

"What the hell is wrong with you?" David continued.

"What's wrong with me is this crazy psycho bitch cut the brakes of my car, that's what's wrong."

I watched as everyone fell silent and turned their attention to Alana, looking for an explanation.

Alana managed to raise her head. "David, he's lying. He's just saying that because I turned down his advances," Alana said between coughs still grasping for air.

"What? What the fuck?" I lunged back toward Alana, only to be stopped by the two guys restraining me.

"You gonna believe this bitch? This manipulative lying bitch?"

"Get the hell out of here, you're done here, you're fired." David stood as we locked eyes.

I jerked away from the two guys holding me. "You don't have to fire me, because I quit. I don't want to work with someone who intentionally tried to kill me or my family."

I locked eyes with Alana one last time. "Kai was driving my car and she was pregnant. I bet you didn't know that, you crazy bitch. You almost killed my unborn child and my wife."

Alana continued to stare at me while she held her injured neck and looked away. I felt my emotions getting the better of me. I turned and noticed the whole room just staring at me. I headed for the door, slamming it behind me so hard I heard the glass rattle.

THIRTY-EIGHT
ALANA

As I examined the bruises on my neck in the mirror I could see Emanuel standing behind me with his arms folded and lips curled up over his head.

Tap, tap tap. His black prada dress shoe, with a white tip, made the sound bounce off my caramel-colored walls, in addition to my nerves. I tried my best to ignore his obvious dismay, but he was making it pretty darn hard.

"What in Sam Hill were you thinking, honey chile? Cutting that man's brakes with his pregnant wife behind the wheel? And I'm not even gonna go there about how you stole *my* car to do your little dirty deed."

I turned to look at Emanuel, rolled my eyes up and around and back again. "Will you stop with all the dramatics already?"

"Dramatics? If Kai would have died you would've never seen daylight without the silhouette of black bars."

"Well, she didn't, and I won't, so can we just drop it please?"

"Whatever," Emanuel said as he walked into my kitchen and grabbed two bottles of Perrier water.

I turned to examine my bruised neck again and couldn't help but replay the horrible scene of Todd attacking me. I always knew Todd had a temper, but he took things entirely too far when he attacked me. They do say there is a thin line between love and hate. That line was definitely crossed.

Emanuel made his way back over to me as he handed me a bottle of Perrier water for myself.

"Todd and Kai agreed not to press charges if you agreed to stay five-hundred yards away from them, and move out of LA the moment the show is done, or cancelled. The way the rating are looking it will probably be the latter."

I took a long sip of my water. "Is that right? I should be the one filing charges." I turned to face the mirror again and my injuried neck. "I look like a damn raccoon. How am I supposed to shoot a movie looking like this?"

Emanuel waved his hand in the air. "Oh, girlfriend, that is what makeup is for."

"Well, thank God for Bobby Brown and her magic brushes." I headed over to my couch and sat down. Emanuel followed behind me and sat on the other end as he sipped his sparkling water.

"So is it safe to say that this whole nightmarish charade with Todd has finally come to an end?"

I turned my head, ignoring Emanuel's reminder of what I did. In all fairness, Todd was the one who pushed me to the edge. No, I thought, this was not over, it was over when Todd was mine. Period.

"Well?" Emanuel glared at me, waiting for my confirmation.

"I really don't want to talk about it, please," I said, hoping Emanuel would get the hint that this was one thing I did not like discussing with him, or anyone else for that matter.

"Emanuel shook his head as he continued to sip his Perrier water, then stood. "Fine. Don't forget, you leave tomorrow night for Canada."

"How long is this shoot for, again?"

"Thirty days, after that you have to be in New York for your guest-star spot on Good Morning Gossip and after that I got you a re-occurring role on that new daytime soap, The Westons.

"Did you book anytime for me to breathe?" I asked, shooting him a playful look.

"Negative, girlfriend, you will be sooo busy over the next six to eight months, you will be like, Todd who?"

I doubt it, I said to myself and I slowly shut my eyes. Suddenly, they popped back open when a thought appeared in my head. "Hey, why don't you come with me?"

"To Canada?" Emanuel said with a scrunched-up expression.

"Yes. It will be fun. We can go shopping and hit up all the clubs. It could be like a girls' getaway with work weaved in of course."

"I can't just pick up and go to Canada."

"Why not?"

"It's not a good time." Emanuel gave me a half-smile as he looked away. It was obvious that a trip with me was not on his priority list.

"Right, of course. It was a stupid idea anyway, I said, feeling a bit dejected, in addition to somewhat lonely. "Well, I better start packing, so..."

Emanuel placed the remainder of his water on my cream leather coaster that sat on my cocktail table and slowly stood.

"I better get going myself. I'm heading back to Chicago tonight, so I will call you tomorrow to make sure you are all set for your flight tomorrow." Emanuel made his way over to my front door.

"Sounds good," I said as I laid back on the couch."

"Talk to you then."

"Okay," I said as I gave Emanuel a quick wave good-bye.

I then heard my front door open then shut. I basked in the silence of my condo, but it was just too quiet. I grabbed my remote and turned on the television, flipped through a few channels before muting it and tossing the remote onto the couch.

I sat up, glanced around my condo, it felt empty. *I* felt empty. I grabbed my phone and dialed Avery's number. I wasn't totally shocked when a female picked up his phone.

"Hello, who is this?" I said with an underlining attitude.

"Excuse me, but you called my phone."

"Well, the last time I dialed this phone number it belonged to Avery Anderson."

"It still does, so now that we got that clear, who is this?"

"This is Riley's mother," I said, not trying to provoke a fight, not really in the mood. "I would like to speak to Avery."

"He's not here."

"Well then I need to speak with my daughter?"

There was a pause. "Riley is taking a nap."

"Well, wake her up, please." I felt my jaw tensing up as I spit out those words between clenched teeth.

"Like I said, she's sleeping."

"And like I said, wake her up, please."

There was another long pause on the other end of my phone.

"I could, but that would make me a bad mother, oh, but you know all about that, now don't you?"

"Bitch, if you don't put my daughter on the—"

Click.

"Hello? Hello?" I pulled the phone away from my ear and saw that I was no longer connected. I dialed the number again and of course got voicemail. I threw my phone across the room. My emotions were fighting to take over, but I battled them back tooth and nail. I closed my eyes and held my breath until they subsided.

I slowly stood, walked across the room, picked up my phone and dialed another number. I smiled when I heard my father's voice.

"Hey, Daddy?"

"Alana, is that you?"

"Yes, Daddy, how are you?"

"Alana, what can I do for you?" My dad said in his best businesslike tone.

"Daddy, I...I just called to say hi."

"Alana, listen, I just teed off, can I call you back?"

"Sure, of course. Hey, Dad, I'm shooting a movie in Canada, maybe you can come up, we can spend some time together?"

"Actually, Alana that probably wouldn't be a great idea, with Barbara and all."

"Oh right. Well, she can come, too. I mean, I can get you guys a suite and we can--"

"Alana, I don't think that would be a good idea. You know how Barb feels about you and frankly, I can't blame her. You've never been very nice to her."

I swallowed hard, felt my emotions stirring again. I wiped away a tear that fell down my cheek. "Maybe you can just come?"

"Alana, I really have to go, I will call you later, okay?"

"Of course." My father disconnected while a few more tears fell from my face. I took a deep breath, sat in the midst of my silence and dismay, feeling lonely, mad and frustrated. Frustration began to take over where hurt and loneliness once resided. I shook my head, and thought, this was ridiculous. I grabbed my phone and dialed Todd's number. I heard his voice from his voicemail.

"Todd, hey, this is Alana, um, give me a call. I need to discuss something of great importance with you." I hung up the phone and began to pace around the apartment while glancing down at my phone after every turn. My breathing started to increase while my heartbeat doubled.

After a few minutes, I stopped and dialed Todd's number again.

"Okay, listen, I know what I did was out of line, but you left me no choice, Todd. Regardless of the circumstances, I think we have been friends as well as lovers long enough to look past this hiccup in our relationship. So with that said, call me and let's put this in the past and move on," I said, not able to control the shakiness in my voice or the rapid beating of my heart.

I hung up the phone and continued to pace. After about ten laps around my cocktail table, I dialed Todd's number again. This time my body had broken out into a cold sweat and I felt myself losing control by the second.

"Okay, Todd, I will not be ignored. All I'm asking is for a simple call back, that's all. I think that is being reasonable at the very least. So please *fucking* call me back, we can work through this, please! Thank you."

I felt my breathing become even more erratic as I began to hyperventilate. At this point I couldn't even think straight. It felt as if I was on the top of a roller-coaster ride about to have to the chain pulled out from under me as I cascaded down the first steep hill. My ears started to ring as my vision became blurry. I grabbed for my water and took a huge gulp. In my head it sounded as if I was in the subway system of New York next to a moving train. I placed my hands over my ears as I sunk to the floor, only to have it all stop when I heard my cell phone ring.

I glanced over to see Todd's name on my screen. My heart jumped as a broad smile leaped across my face as a feeling of hope wrapped around my soul like a warm blanket on a cold winter day. "Todd, hey," I said as I heard the sound of breathing then...

"How dare you have the audacity to call Todd after what you did to me, to us." Kai's voice sliced through my emotions like a hot knife through a stick of butter.

"Where...where is Todd? I need to talk to Todd." I looked down at my hand as it began to shake uncontrollably.

"Well that's not gonna happen."

"Put Todd on the phone!" I said in a slow methodical voice.

"Game over, Alana. You lose."

"You don't tell me when it's over, I do!" I felt my voice rise with each word that spewed from my mouth. "He doesn't love you, he loves me."

I heard Kai laugh on the other end of the phone. "I'm only going to say this once, restraining order or no restraining order, if you come anywhere near me or my family again, I will kill you. That's a gotdamn promise."

Kai hung up.

"Hello, hello? Don't you fucking hang up on me, don't you fucking hang up on me! Ahhhhh!" I hurled my phone across the room, and watched it crash against the wall. I thought about what had all gone down, thought about how it was all coming to an unfavorable end, thought about how I could fix this in my favor.

I became overwhelmed by my thoughts. I felt trapped, stuck and defeated. I grabbed my head as I felt the sweat escaping from my pores at a fast and furious rate. This was not how it was supposed to end. I heard an internal click in my brain, a click that turned off all rational thinking as I stormed over to my bookcase and with one vicious swipe I cleared everything off, shelf by shelf, each frame, every piece of fine china and souvenir went crashing to the floor. I didn't care, not one bit.

I felt myself losing control of all that was right, all that made sense. I ran over to the kitchen and began to pull plates, cups and bowls out of the cabinets, smashing them on the floor. One at a time. Two at a time. Three at a time. Blood seeped from my bare feet as the sharp edges of the dishes sliced into them. I didn't care. I couldn't feel the pain in my feet, only the pain in my heart. I was lost in my frustration and misery, my lack of control and the outcome of what I saw to be right.

I dropped to the floor in the chaotic mess of my life and wept and wept until I couldn't weep anymore.

THIRTY-NINE
TODD

Ten Months Later

I stared into the most beautiful pair of hazel-brown eyes I had ever seen, my two-month-old daughter, Charlie. She was perfect, amazing and nothing could have made me happier. The smell of her baby breath sent chills up and down my spine as I picked her up to get ready to feed her. I walked into the kitchen, opened the fridge and grabbed a small bottle of pre-pumped breast milk, next to four other bottles neatly labeled with time of feeding and expiration dates. I smiled to myself at how efficient Kai was at making sure everything was at my fingertips.

I cradled Charlie's 15-pound body in my left arm and held the bottle and burp cloth in my right, only to hear my cell phone ring across the room. I quickly set the bottle and burp cloth on the counter and headed over to grab the call.

"Hey, babe, you checking in on us again?" I said. I positioned my cell between my ear and my shoulder, then scooped back up Charlie's breakfast and headed to the living room to feed her.

"Of course not, I just wanted to call and say hi."

"Kai, you left for work an hour ago."

"Okay, fine. How is my princess? I miss her. And you, too, of course."

"Yeah, yeah, we're fine, okay. I got this whole stay-at-home daddy thing down. Now, get back to work before Simone gets on you for not getting things done."

"I will. I may swing home for lunch. Do you want me to bring anything home for you?"

"I think I'm good," I said.

"Okay, love you. Oh, and Todd, don't forget to pick up Kristopher from school at one p.m. today, not two p.m. Today is his early day."

"I know, I know. Can I go now, so I can feed your princess?"

"Yes, sorry. Bye."

I hung up the phone and laid Charlie in her bouncy that sat on the ottoman as I fed her her milk. A lot of things had changed over the last ten months of my life since that insane day with Alana. Since then, Kai and I put an offer down on a house just two blocks away, Charlie was born and I was now the stay-at-home dad while Kai was the breadwinner.

After I was fired for choking Alana and temporarily disbarred, Kai took Simone up on her offer to run her advertising firm full-time. Staying at home with the kids was an adjustment and I definitely had a new appreciation for the stay-at-home mom and that was no joke. I did miss practicing law, but I knew in due time I would be back out there once my babies were a bit older. As far as Alana, her show was cancelled and she was instructed by a judge to move out of California if she didn't want to face jail time again.

I finished feeding Charlie as her eyes became very heavy. I picked her up as she drifted off to sleep. I held her close to my chest and felt her warmth. I took a deep breath and inhaled her baby goodness, then closed my eyes for a quick reprieve. I felt myself drifting off into my own utopia. A few minutes passed before I contemplated either staying right where I was or putting Charlie in her crib.

The latter decision won as I opened my eyes, stood and headed to the nursery to lay Charlie back down. I walked back to the front, caught a glance at what I was wearing, a black V-neck T-shirt with baggy gray sweat pants and day-old B.O. The thought of taking a shower crossed my mind, but I quickly vetoed that to veg out in front of the TV instead. Hours of watching football and my favorite shows soon became a thing of the past now with the presence of two children, but at the end of the day, it was all well worth it.

I flopped back down on the couch, winched as I pulled out Kristopher's dinosaur from under my ass and tossed it on the floor. My eyes trailed around our living room that looked more like a child's playroom than a true living space. Cleaning the house was on my to-do list, something that I would get to a bit later. Right now I needed to catch up on some me-time.

I flipped on the television and began to channel surf. I continued to scan the channels until I spotted a familiar face, none other than Alana.

Her show, *Office Temps*, was running re-runs on BET. I watched as Alana did her thing on the screen and my normal breathing began to quicken with each inhale and exhale as past images of everything Alana had done began to flash before me like a highlight reel without the glory. I continued to stare at her face as I rubbed the back of my neck, feeling a sheen of sweat on my chin and forehead. I told myself to calm down, just relax, but it never failed each and every time I thought about Alana or saw her damn face, I was brought back to that day, that day when I received that call from the hospital about Kai, the day I almost lost everything that meant anything to me, the day I fucking lost it and attacked her, Alana.

I fought back my newly created anger as I drudged through the memories of the manipulation and the deceit. My breathing became louder and faster and I shook my head and repeated a familiar saying, almost a daily mantra, *I thought I was different, but I guess I was the idiot.*

I began to pound my fist against my thigh, feeling like the biggest moron to think Alana would spare me, me? How could she go so far as to want to hurt me, her supposed best friend?

I grabbed the remote and turned off the TV, tossing the remote to the side. I swung my legs up on the couch, laid back, propped my head up with a pillow and stared at the ceiling while I felt the left vein pulsating in my head. I had to get a grip on my emotions before it ruined everything I had worked for up until now. I had to find a way to relieve this anger I had inside of me for Alana before it destroyed me and my family.

I hated how just the sight of her or even the mere thought could change my mood from an amazing high to a shitty low—lower than a sunken valley. I clenched my teeth, balled my hand into a fist, and felt my jaws become sore from the pressure of biting down. I tried to think about things that made me happy, my children, Kai, my family.

I stood and began to pace, felt my heart racing faster than normal. Why was I feeling this way after ten months, especially since after the incident there hadn't been any attempts to contact me, regardless of the restrictions that were put in place. Why then, why did I still feel this sense of anger every single time her face, her name or a mere memory popped in my head? Why?

I slowly sat down again, and lay my head back onto the pillow. I closed my eyes and tried to block out the negative thoughts floating all around me, felt my mind drifting, wondering, thinking as a tear fell from the corner of my eye and down my cheek.

FORTY

ALANA

"Alana over here!" *Flash.* "Alana you look amazing, one shot over here." *Flash. Flash.* "Alana what are you wearing? Can I get a pose?" *Flash.*

I smiled and continued to dazzle the reporters, cameras and the fans while walking the red carpet for my latest film *Seize the Day*, premiering in New York that night. I decided to wear my lavender Vera Wang asymmetrical jersey dress that stopped mid-thigh accompanied with my just as fabulous Jimmy Choo lavender three-inch heels. Of course I also had my black wool shawl to cover my arms as the weather in New York was a crisp twenty degrees that afternoon.

I had been living in New York for the last year after I was forced to leave sunny California. But it was either move back to New York or serve more jail time for cutting Todd's brakes and that wasn't gonna happen.

I had to admit, I was truly enjoying the hustle and bustle of the big city. I lived in New York briefly right out of college while I was pursuing my modeling career, but I was so damn broke the experience was less than spectacular, it was downright depressing at times. Although it was much different now, very different. I was making around eight grand a week and had money to burn if I chose. Emanuel had successfully gotten me a producer's audition for the new soap *The Westons*. I initially went in for a guest-starring role, but later landed a re-occurring role on the daytime soap. On top of all that, Emanuel even hooked me up in his apartment complex in Chelsea with a fabulous view to boot. I had come a long way in my life and, well, I was living what people would say, the fabulous life. But I won't lie, everything that glitters isn't gold. I had my highs and my lows.

I missed Todd and I missed my daughter, Riley. You never realize how much you miss someone until they are gone.

It had been six months since I lost total custody of Riley to her father, ex-football player Avery Anderson. He claimed he desperately wanted Riley to complete his growing family. New wife with a new baby on the way. I called serious bullshit on his entire game. The moment Avery found out I was on a sitcom as well as staring in a new movie with Kevin Hart, all he saw was dollar signs and my checkered past of being a single and negligent mother did not sit well with the judge. Avery quickly won custody and a fat child support check. The fight wasn't over and once Todd and I were back together everything would change, just you wait.

"Alana! Anything on what you will be shooting next?" another reporter yelled my way. I just smiled, waved and continued toward the theater for the start of the movie.

I headed into the theater and pulled off my black shawl. The warmth of the 500- seat complex theater was a welcomed invitation. I spotted Emanuel across the room, while he talked and flirted with the director of my movie, Xavier Clark. Some things never changed, or at least in his world they didn't.

"There she is," Emanuel sang as I approached him and my fabulous director.

"Darling, you are lucky I have a beefy part in this movie to drag my butt out in this frigid cold weather of New York."

"Is that so? Coming from the ice princess herself," Emanuel shot back.

"Watch yourself," I said with a smile as I tossed Xavier a flirty wink.

Xavier and I kissed as he looked me up and down. He was a very attractive man, six foot two, mocha-colored delight with chiseled features and a magnetic smile. The verdict was still out on whether or not he was on the down low, which in my opinion kinda made my skin crawl. I had no problem with gay men, not one bit, but don't try and trick a sista, exposing her to all your issues like AIDS or whatever your dick carries to me on the day you decided to like women and men simultaneously.

"Alana, my dear, anytime you want to grace me with your presence I would be honored," Xavier said as he sipped on his scotch on the rocks.

This was Xavier's third independent movie and it already had the buzz to be a huge hit in Sundance and several other film festivals. I was just honored that he asked me to be a part of it. Emanuel told me that he admired my work on my BET show and requested me personally. Then again, how could he not be impressed by moi? I was pretty fabuloso, if I don't say so myself, so I will.

***

Three hours later I found myself at the Sky Room in Times Square having cocktails with Xavior and Emanuel and enjoying a fabulous view of the city. I had a feeling Xavier wanted it to be just us, but Emanuel conveniently tagged along. I'm sure he was positioning himself for bigger and better things.

"So, I was thinking about my next film," Xavier said to us as we sat at the bar surrounded by patrons of all different kinds.

"Ewww, do tell, darling," Emanuel sang out as I shook my head at all his gayness just oozing all over the place.

Xavier took a sip of his scotch on the rocks, a favorite I was noticing, and leaned back, folding his arms across his chest. "I wanted to do a more, sex and erotica type movie for my next project, something that people will walk away talking about for days."

"You had me at erotica," Emanuel chimed in as he beamed at Xavier from ear to ear.

"So what's the movie about?" I asked.

"I'm not completely sure yet. I'm still in the brainstorming phase, but I want the story to be exciting, erotic and have an element of surprise. Maybe tie in something pertaining to the world of swingers."

I sat back, crossed my legs and took a sip of my butterscotch martini. "I have an idea for a movie, something that may be along the lines of what you are looking for," I said, interrupting Xavier.

"Really?"

"Yeah, would you like to hear it?" I said with a seductive smile.

"I would, very much so." Xavier sat up a bit.

"Me too," Emanuel added.

"Okay, I am picturing a couple, married, newlyweds, maybe living a simple life in the suburbs of let's say, New Jersey, for geographics sake. Now the husband has a best friend, not just *any* best friend, but a drop-dead gorgeous best friend who happens to be a female."

"Intriguing," Xavier said.

"Now, of course, the wife is sick with jealousy when she lays eyes on this woman and thinks her man cannot possibly be attracted to his so-called best friend. So, what does the wife do?" I took a sip of my martini and then continued. "She starts spending time with the woman to keep her away from the husband. But here's the twist, the wife and the best friend end up having an affair behind the husband's back.

"What the?" Emanuel started to say something, but I cut my eyes at him, letting him no to keep it zipped.

"I love it." Xavier sat up, erect in his seat. "How does it end?"

"Well, how I see it is the wife ends up falling in love with the best friend, then again how can you blame her, the best friend is beautiful, smart and oh so talented."

"Ha!" Emanuel blurted out. He curled his lips to the side and sipped on his drink. I shot him an if-you-don't-shut-your-ass-up look. Then I turned my attention back to Xavier.

"So of course the wife breaks up with her husband, files for divorce and he is devastated, and he leans on the best friend's shoulder for comfort. In the end, the best friends end up falling in love and getting married, because deep down inside they have always been in love with each other, but never took the time to explore the possibility."

Emanuel rolls his eyes up in the air and then back down again."

"Hmm, so what happened to the wife?"

"Oh, she went off to become some overweight lesbian, and do whatever lesbians do well."

Xavier nodded his head, processing the whole pitch. "What would you call it?"

"I would call it, *My Man's Best Friend.*"

"Oh my Jesus!" Emanuel's head hit the bar.

Xavier downed the rest of his drink then glanced at his watch. "Not bad, not bad at all. Why don't you swing by my office next week and we can maybe beat out the details?"

"Sounds like a plan, my dear."

"Listen, I have to get going. But it was a pleasure and you look stunning as always."

I smiled at Xavier's compliments. Xavier looked over at Emanuel who was sitting in his chair with a permanent smirk on his face. "Emanuel, we'll talk."

"Yes, toodles."

Xavier gave me one last body scan before heading out the bar. I turned my attention back to my overly dramatic agent. "Okay, just spit it out."

Emanuel slowly shook his head from left to right. "I don't even know where to begin," Emanuel said to me.

"It was just a pitch."

"Yeah, only of the last five years of your life."

"I can't help it if I make for good cinema. Besides, if I get Xavier to shoot the movie, I can tell it like it really should have happened, with the *real* ending yet to be determined."

"Please tell me you haven't tried to contact Todd?"

"No, I haven't. I have been too gotdamn busy to even breathe, let alone seek out what is mine, but all that will change soon."

"Should I remind you of the restraining order in place?"

"I am aware of that. Besides, that will expire in twenty-two days."

"Alana?"

"Oh don't worry, those days of showing up unannounced are over. I have no plans of showing up at his home. They moved and I don't know where they are, not to mention I think he changed his number. Anyway, at the end of the day, Todd will come to me."

"Is that right?" And how do you suppose that will happen?"

"Let's just say, the movie ain't over until Alana says curtains."

FORTY-ONE
KAI

I decided to pick up a few things from the store on my way home for lunch. Being the boss had its perks, including two-hour lunch breaks. I headed into Ralph's Grocery Store on La Tijera Boulevard, just down the street from where we lived.

I turned down the produce aisle when I saw Camille walking my way. My body tensed a bit at the sight of seeing her again after that night I left her house. It was as if she felt my true intention to make it work with Todd and she never reached out to me again, even as friends.

"Kai, I thought that was you." Camille smiled at me as we closed in on each other.

Camille was with a woman who looked fairly familiar to me, but at that moment I couldn't place where I knew her from.

"How are you?" I said, fiddling with my hair. I was a little nervous and a bit at a loss for words.

"I am great, just a bit busy with my move and all."

"Oh you're moving?"

"Back to New York, yes."

"Wow, that's…that's big? What brought this change on?" I said, feeling my nerves subside a bit.

"It was just time, you know, and I missed having my family around. Oh, speaking of family, this is my sister, Jessica. I told you about her, right?"

Jessica and I stared at each other. *I instantly* put two and two together. Toni's fiancé and Todd's threesome buddy.

"Yes, you are Toni's fiancé."

Jessica's head jerked back on hearing my statement. "Um, have we met before?"

"I'm Kai. We met over a year ago, at Toni's Brownstone in Brooklyn."

Jessica's eyebrows shot to the top of her head as her mouth parted. "Right, right, you were on your way to California?" Jessica let out a knowing smile filled with much more than what she was revealing.

"Exactly. So you and Toni, have you guys tied the knot yet? I haven't talked to her in a while," I said, prying for information. I was curious to hear this answer now that I knew a little history behind Miss Jessica McCoy.

Jessica and Camille exchanged a knowing look, which didn't surprise me one bit.

Jessica smiled, looked down then back up. "Actually, that didn't quite work out the way I thought it would."

Of course it didn't because you're into threesomes with whores and married men, I wanted to say, but I smiled and gave her the polite response.

"I am sorry to hear that. Toni is an exceptional woman."

"Yep, that she is," Jessica shot back with a half-smile.

Just then Jessica's phone rang. An electronic voice announced the caller. *Call from Alana Brooks.*

There was an awkward moment. A very awkward moment. Why in the hell was Alana calling Jessica now? *I swear this world is just too fucking small for my taste.*

Jessica held up her phone. "I have to take this." she steps away.

I looked at Camille. "Oh my God. What's up with that?"

Camille shrugged her shoulders. "I don't know. I think they may be seeing each other again."

"Are you serious?" I ran my hand through my hair. Felt my body shutter at the thought.

"Apparently, Alana called her out of the blue and asked her to fly up to Canada where she was filming some new film and Jessica dropped everything, including Toni and went. Like I said, my sister is on her own thing."

"Clearly." I just shook my head and let out a small chuckle at the power Alana possessed over individuals. I wished I wasn't included in that harem. I thought about Toni and how she must've been feeling. I wanted to call her immediately, but I just couldn't go there anymore.

"Hey, I hope this isn't awkward for you." Camille pulled me back in. "She's in town for a few days and of course I didn't think we'd actually run into each other."

"It is what it is," I said as I shrugged my shoulders, not trying to make such a big deal out of it.

"How is everything? I see Todd all the time now at the school," Camille said, changing the subject.

"Yeah, we kinda switched schedules and roles for that matter after Charlie was born."

"Right, he said you guys had a little girl. Congratulations," Camille said as she touched my arm, sending a chill through it.

"Thanks." Camille and I fell into a silence. I felt like I should say something, anything, but again, I just couldn't go there anymore. I had come to a place in my life where I was secure about my sexual preferences and it felt good. I still felt an attraction to Camille, but just because the attraction was there didn't mean I had to act on it. I was married now and I needed to start acting like it.

"Well, listen, I gotta get home and give Todd a little reprieve from the little ones."

"Okay, we gotta get back as well," Camille said, damn near tripping over my exit line with hers.

"When are you heading back to New York?" I said, not sure why I asked her yet another question after successfully signing off. Apparently, my nerves were getting the best of me.

"Next week."

"Well, have a safe trip and take care of yourself."

"Thanks, Kai, you do the same."

We gave each other one last good-bye smile. Camille then headed past me and I did the same as we walked in opposite directions. I wanted to look back, but I didn't. I kept my eyes straight ahead. I rounded the corner to see Jessica on her cell phone laughing and carrying on. I rolled my eyes at the knowledge that she was on the phone with the devil.

I stopped in front of the meat section, just a few feet away from Jessica. I look over her way and we locked eyes, she turned her back to me, said a few more hushed words then her good-byes and turned back around. I looked down at the ground turkey, trying to ignore her, thought about how Alana had roped in another victim and started to chuckle to myself. I didn't let the past affect me, not one bit. It was nice being on the outside looking in for a change.

"What's so funny?" I looked up to see Jessica standing closer to me. She had a sarcastic smirk stretched across her face, one I wanted to slap off, I really did. I turned and held a stare with the woman who had a threesome with my husband and my ex-lover. The woman who is caught up in Alana Brooks, something bigger than she could ever imagine.

"Alana's not worth it," I finally said out loud.

"Excuse me?" Jessica shifted her weight from left to right. As she slid her cell phone into her back jean pocket and folded her arms in front of her chest.

"Toni is a good woman and if she went so far as to propose to you then she must really love you. Don't throw it all away for Alana. She's not worth it."

"What makes you think I did it for Alana?

I shook my head, looked back down at the Jennie-O Turkey on sale for 3.99 then back up at Jessica. "Because I know how she works and I know how she can manipulate someone, that's why."

Jessica looked at me and smiled. "She had you whipped, huh?"

I shook my head, let out a small chuckle. "No, she had me fooled, there's a difference. I hope you will see that before it's too late for you. You look like a smart woman. I hope your intelligence doesn't fail you." With that I was done. Done with the drama and done with the nonsense. I reached down and grabbed the Jennie-O Turkey meat for 3.99, turned and walked away from Jessica. I proceeded to the front cashier to pay for my groceries, then out the store and headed home to my family.

***

As I pulled out of the parking lot my cell phone rang. I looked on my console to see that it was Kristopher's school calling, which was weird since Todd should have picked him up thirty minutes ago.

"Hi, this is Kai?" I said clicking on my hands free button.

"Hi, Mrs. Daniels, just wanted to let you know that your husband has not picked up Kristopher yet."

"Oh, okay, I'm actually in the area on lunch so I will swing by and grab him. Thanks so much for calling."

I hung up the phone and immediately called Todd's cell and it went straight to voicemail. I felt myself breaking out into a cold sweat as the worst thought entered my head. I drove a bit faster to get Kristopher so I could get home and make sure nothing was wrong with Charlie or Todd for that matter.

The moment I stepped in the house my body immediately felt a sense of relief as I saw Todd and Charlie asleep on the couch. Although Todd was still in hot water since he totally forgot to pick up Kristopher, it was good to see that they were okay.

As Kristopher ran by his dad and into his playroom, I walked over to where Todd and Charlie were sleeping and carefully picked up my daughter, gently kissing her on the lips. The sudden absence of Charlie in his arms woke Todd up. Todd's eyes popped open, followed by his body springing off the couch.

"Oh, shit, what time is it?" Todd said as he jumped up, glancing at the wall clock then back at me. "Damn, I must have been more tired than I thought." Todd rubbed his eyes then neck.

"Todd, you have to be more on top of things. Thank God I was headed home for lunch and could go pick up Kristopher, because they couldn't get ahold of you. Why was your phone off?" I was working overtime to stay calm, but seeing that nothing was drastically wrong helped out my emotions tremendously.

Todd reached down and grabbed his phone off the couch, he then hit the side button and looked up at me. "It's dead. I guess I forgot to charge it last night and it powered down when I fell asleep."

I shook my head at Todd's display of irresponsibility as my eyes glanced around the house that was in a state of sheer disaster. "And the house, why is it such a wreck?"

Todd put up his hand? "Okay, just chill out, Kai, I was getting to it. I can't do everything at once."

"Well, you could do something."

Todd took a deep breath. "It's just been one of those days, okay?"

"Todd, you have responsibilities now and you can't allow these things to make you forget things like picking up your kid from school."

"You know I'm doing the best I can."

"When it comes to our kids you have to do better!" I felt my blood pressure rising as those last words came out of my mouth because I knew what his issue was and it was becoming a problem—a big one.

Todd looked up at me as he nodded his head, then turned and walked out of the living room and into our bedroom and shut the door. I continued to cradle Charlie in my arms as I gently rocked her. I took a deep breath and headed to the bedroom, right after I checked in on Kristopher.

Todd was laying on the bed with his head propped up on the headboard, channel surfing. I laid Charlie down in her bassinet and sat on the edge of the bed across from him.

"It happened again, didn't it?" I said as I reached out and touched Todd's hand. He slowly pulled it away and continued to channel surf.

"Baby, this is becoming a problem, you know that right?" I continued.

Todd clicked off the television, threw down the remote next to his leg and turned toward me. "Kai, I don't need you to tell me what my problems are, okay?"

"Yes I do when they are affecting our family."

"This is my problem and I have to deal with it my way."

I looked away, then back at Todd. "Baby, it has been ten months and yes, it's a blessing that she has not come around or even made another attempt to try and destroy us, but you have to let go of whatever anger you have for her."

"So you're just fine with her and all that she has done to us? Not to mention the attempt on your life and Charlie's?" Todd said as he looked deep into my eyes, trying hard to understand why I was not displaying as much anger as he was.

"Of course I am, I am fucking pissed, there's not a day that goes by that I don't think about her or what she's done. But by holding onto that anger, she wins. Don't you get it? You're only hurting yourself. You gotta let that go."

"Kai, I'm trying."

"Then try harder because there are days where you can't even function, and it scares me. I don't—" I stopped myself, not wanting to cross any lines.

Todd looked at me as his left eyebrow went up. "You don't what, Kai? You don't trust me with the kids, is that it?"

"I'm not saying that, I'm just concerned about you, about us."

A silence fell between us. "Maybe you could see a psychiatrist?"

"What?"

"I mean it couldn't hurt."

"So now you think I'm crazy?" Todd jumped off the bed in defense of his insanity.

"No, of course not, I just think talking to someone may help you resolve your issues, that's all."

"Well, crazy motherfuckers go to see shrinks, and I'm not crazy, okay?

"Wow." I looked away as Todd realized his implication reflected on me when I was seeing my shrink.

"Sorry. Like I said, Kai, I'll work it out myself." Todd turned and headed out the bedroom, closing the door hard behind him. I flopped back onto the bed, throwing a pillow over my face, letting out a stressed-filled scream.

FORTY-TWO

TODD

It didn't take long for me to realize that Kai was right. I needed to talk to a psychiatrist. Between the dreams, the mood swings and the general forgetfulness, it was time for me to put all of it behind me for good.

I set up an appointment with Dr. Carol Tanner at UCLA hospital. This was extremely out of my comfort zone, but I knew that we all needed to get a bit uncomfortable from time to time when we wanted to make a true change.

My first few visits to Dr. Tanner's were pretty informative. I had never been asked so many questions about my childhood, my likes, dislikes, fears and life challenges. I guess in order to help a person get better, a psychiatrist had to know what made a guy tick.

By the fourth visit I could tell that my doctor had gathered all the information she needed to study me inside and out and was ready to start peeling me back like an onion with its many layers.

"You look very nice today, Todd."

"Why thank you, Doctor," I said, taking a seat across from Dr. Tanner. I had decided to wear a suit today. It had been a while since I felt good enough to wear one. My wardrobe lately had only consisted of baggy sweat pants and T-shirts with visible signs of baby food and spit up splattered all over them. Today, I wanted to feel like the confident lawyer I was, and the suit helped me get myself back into a successful mindset.

"How are you feeling?"

"I'm good. Kids and wife are healthy."

"Good to hear." Dr. Tanner uncrossed, then crossed her legs. She glanced at her notebook and began delicately. "Today, I wanted to talk about Alana if you're up for it."

I took a deep breath, rubbed my hands together, and felt a surge of adrenaline run through my body. "Whew, Alana Brooks, that there is a lot to talk about."

"Yes, and the primary reason you decided to start seeing me."

"Right, this is very true." I adjusted in my seat, tugged at my tie a bit and smiled. "What do you want to know first?"

"Let's start with why you didn't confide in your wife the day you found out that Alana was going to be a client at your firm?"

I took another deep breath, continued to rub my hands together. "Okay, I um, I didn't want to upset Kai after all we had gone through to put our lives back together."

"But you would agree that not telling her upset her just as much or more."

"I guess. I'm not exactly sure how to respond to that.."

"It's okay, Todd."

Dr. Tanner wrote a few words on her yellow pad, then looked back up at me.

"Maybe the reason why you didn't tell Kai was because you may have still been carrying around feelings for Alana. Telling Kai would only complicate things for you in your mind and how you should handle Alana being a presence in your life again."

"No, no, you make it sound so complicated, it wasn't like that."

Dr. Tanner put down her pen and leaned back in her chair. "Okay then simplify it for me."

I stared at Dr. Tanner for a few seconds before standing. "I couldn't-" I began to pace back and forth in her office as Dr. Tanner followed my movement with her eyes.

"Are you okay?"

"I'm good. I just need a minute to process what you just told me."

"Take your time."

I continued to pace, struggling to find the right words to say. Realizing I had none.

"Todd, having feelings for Alana does not make you a bad person, it makes you human."

That statement made me stop in my place, turn and look at Dr. Tanner once again.

"What you must learn to do is separate yourself from the urges to act on them," she continued.

I thought about my past actions and how I may have been giving Alana false hope. A reason to keep up her charade.

"You mentioned that you two had been friends since you were teenagers?"

"We met in college."

"She was your best friend?"

"Was, being the key word," I said, feeling my anger rearing its ugly head.

"Other than the fact that Alana had been manipulative in your life, what do you think is the driving force of your anger toward her?"

I started to breathe faster and faster as more memories of Alana and all that she'd done began to flood through my mind.

I took a deep breath. "I just thought... I just thought that... ahhh ..."

"Take your time."

"I thought I was different. I've always known that Alana was the way she was from the day that I met her." I stopped to gather my thoughts.

"But..." Dr. Tanner gave me a verbal nudge.

"But for some insane reason, I just... I just thought she would never cross that line with me."

"With the one she called her best friend," Dr. Tanner added.

"Yes."

I just stared at Dr. Tanner gathering my next thoughts. "I mean everyone has someone that they're one-hundred percent loyal to, right? I thought I was that guy to her." I dropped back down in my seat, and placed my head in the palm of my hands. I looked back up at my therapist. "I thought I was that guy. I guess in the end the only person she was loyal to was her damn self."

Dr. Tanner paused and looked at me, drawing herself up before her speech to me.

"Todd, the reason why you cannot move on with your life is because you have not had any closure with your life with Alana. You have to go to her and tell her how you feel, tell her how you felt betrayed, how you thought you were different than all the rest and how you are devastated by how she could go so far as to try to hurt your wife and your unborn child, which in turn was hurting you. You have to tell her everything. Then let her know that from this point on there will not be any more contact between the two of you."

I looked up at Dr. Tanner and laughed out loud. "You must not know Alana. If I go anywhere near her she will latch on like deranged pit bull and never let go, ever."

"Todd, the only reason Alana was able to come back into your life and stay was because *you* allowed it. *You* made it happen, not her. No one can penetrate your life unless you allow them to."

"What?" I looked away then back at Dr. Tanner. I hated that I was even thinking this, but I was having an "Oprah aha moment." She was right, I created the problem. I did it, not Alana.

"No one can penetrate my life unless I allow them too." I repeated Dr. Tanners pearls of wisdom.

"Exactly."

"So you think I should see Alana face to face?"

"Yes, and like I said, you will have complete control of what happens and how everything would transpire. You not her.

"Wow, this is too deep," I said as I shook my head.

"If that is too tough for you, some people can successfully find closure by not coming face to face with the person, but by writing them a letter."

"A letter?"

"Yes, this letter isn't written for the person to see it, but to get everything off your chest. A lot of times just writing down all your feelings can give you the same relief, closure and forgiveness you would have if you chose to do it in person."

"A letter?"

"Yes...a letter."

"One that she will never see?"

"If you choose, yes. If that seems better for you give it a try and let me know how that turns out for you."

I slowly nodded my head. "Okay, I will try writing her a letter first."

Dr. Tanner glanced at her watch. "I believe our time is up."

I stood. "Thank you, Doctor."

"You are very welcome, Todd. Remember, you are the one who controls your life and all that transpires, not Alana, not anyone."

"Got it." I did an about-face as I headed out of Dr. Tanner's office and back to my car. I sat there for a few minutes and thought about what she told me concerning closure and how I should go about it.

Maybe a letter to her would be the right thing, not to mention I wasn't sure how to even get in touch with Alana. I wasn't even sure if she had the same cell number. Though most people in the entertainment business rarely changed their numbers, and Alana was probably no different.

I leaned my head back onto my headrest and tried to think of what I could say, writing the letter with the blank canvas in my mind. I closed my eyes and talked it out in my head. As I did, I felt myself getting angrier, more frustrated and fed up.

I stopped, opened my glove compartment and pulled out my legal pad, reached into the inner pocket of my jacket and produced a black felt tip pen. I stared at the blank paper, took a deep breath and wrote across the top:

Dear Alana, we need to talk.

I tore off the paper, crumbled it up and threw it on the floor. I stared at the blank yellow pad again then wrote:

Alana, I fucking hate you.

I clenched my jaw then tore that piece of paper off, crumpled that one as well and threw it on the floor next to the first one. After a few minutes of repetitive paper crumbling and throwing business I dropped my pen in my lap.

Maybe the doctor was right, maybe I should've just faced her one last time, have my closure, then never see Alana again. I stared out the window and watched the people pass by. I admired how happy they looked, and wondered if they were putting up a front. I wondered if they felt the way I was feeling at this moment.

I reached in my pocket and pulled out my phone, pulled up Alana's name. I thought about how I should just text her right now. I wasn't even sure where she was, Chicago, New York, she could have moved anywhere over the last ten months. I looked down at my phone and started typing.

Alana, I know it has been a long time, but we need to talk.

I looked up. Maybe I could just type it into my phone and save it, maybe that would make it more real than writing it down on a sheet of paper.

My phone started to ring, so I went to hit save on Alana's message and accidentally hit send. "Shit, shit, fuck," I heard myself proclaim out loud. I couldn't believe I had just sent that damn message. "Shit." I let the call coming in go to voicemail as I sat frozen wondering what I just did and what would be the result of my careless actions, not to mention the consequences.

I sat in silence and just stared at my phone. Nothing. Maybe her number was different, maybe she would never even get the text. I continued to stare at my phone and swallowed. I felt my mouth become dry as it lay agape. Still nothing. I waited five more minutes, which turned into ten, still nothing.

I finally breathed a sigh of relief and threw my phone in the middle console and started my car. I pulled out of my parking space and headed out onto Santa Monica Boulevard when I heard three beeps coming from my cell.

I slowly reach for my phone and as I turned it over I read the text from Alana.

Is this Todd?

FORTY-THREE
ALANA

I was on my way to Park City, Utah in the morning for the Sundance Film Festival. Sundance was the largest independent film festival in the world created in 1978 by none other than Robert Redford. The movie I had shot with director Xavier Clark in Canada was a fan favorite this year and I couldn't be more excited to be a part of the whole experience. Not to mention the idea of seeing myself on the big screen was a plus as well.

I had just let my housekeeper in when I noticed a text from an unknown number. I opened it to read:

Alana, I know it's been a long time, but we need to talk.

I wasn't sure who this was. When I looked at the 323 area code I knew that it had to be a California number, but this text couldn't possibly be from Todd, could it? After the incident I called Todd daily until one day I discovered that he had disconnected his phone number. Changing his number didn't come as a total surprise to me, I'm sure Kai had her hand in that one.

I quickly texted him back.

Is this Todd?

I stared at my phone, waiting to see if I was right, if my prediction that Todd would eventually come to his senses and come back to me, was finally coming true. That was why I would never change my number, ever.

A few minutes later, although it seemed like a lifetime, my cell phone finally chimed and I smiled to myself when I saw what was typed.

Yes.

I felt a fluttering effect in my stomach as if twenty little butterflies had been turned loose. I texted Todd back.

Well, hello stranger. This is a pleasant surprise. What is it you need to talk to me about?

I set my phone down and thought back to my conversation with Emanuel telling him that Todd *would* eventually reach out and well, here he was. I knew trying to outwait Todd would eventually fall in my favor and it was in this moment that the tables were about to turn.

My phone chimed and I looked to see that Todd had texted back.

Us.

A much broader smile danced across my face and I stood, doing a small twirl in place. I noticed my cleaning lady was giving me a strange look as she headed toward the bedrooms to begin her day.

I thought about my schedule as it immediately popped in my head. I maneuvered a few things around in my head before texting Todd again.

I am headed to Utah tomorrow Saturday on a private jet but I could head to California first and meet you, then swing back around to Utah. Are you still in California?

I was fairly positive he was still in California, but I wanted to get a confirmation for my own sake. A good three minutes passed, and there was no response from Todd. I was beginning to get a bit nervous and anxious, wondering if me saying that I would come to him made him uncomfortable. Maybe Todd wasn't in California, maybe he was back in New York, or maybe he left Kai, finally. Maybe. All these possible scenarios were racing through my head. My mind was moving so quick that I didn't even notice that nearly five minutes had passed without Todd texting me back. What was taking him so long?

My phone finally chimed and I quickly looked at it and breathed a sigh of relief to see Todd's text.

Yes, I have to run. I will text you later to see where's a good place to meet tomorrow.

That sounds great.

I texted back as I clutched my phone extra tight.

I held my phone for the next two minutes wondering if there might be anything else from Todd, but there was nothing. I tucked my phone into my back pocket and immediately went into my room to pick out a new outfit for my trip. I would no longer be wearing my comfy brown velour sweat suit, nope, that outfit got ditched the moment I received Todd's text. I eagerly searched through my closet and pulled out my sexy form-fitting, royal-blue V-neck dress with matching shoes. Yep, if I was going to see Todd again, I wanted to look my best.

I pulled out my phone and placed it on my bed, continually glancing at the display screen. I laughed at how I had heard from Todd even earlier than I'd expected. Then again, I wasn't going to complain, not one bit. I wondered what caused him to reach out to me now. Regardless, I knew I would prevail in the end and get Todd because he knew as well as I did that we were meant to be together.

I began to fantasize about how everything would go down when we saw each other. Todd and I always had a special connection, that undeniable pull I couldn't explain. I knew it, and as much as he tried to fight it, he knew it, too. I was so ecstatic that he finally came to his senses and would finally be mine.

I glanced back down at my phone yet again, still no text from Todd. I walked into my kitchen, placed my phone down on my marble countertop and poured myself a glass of red wine. I took a deep breath as I sipped on my wine, continually taking peeks at my phone.

I took a few more sips of my wine then placed it back on my counter and swiped up my phone. I couldn't contain my excitement as I pulled up our conversation thread and shot Todd yet another text.

Looking forward to seeing you. Don't forget to text me the location and I will be there.

I headed back into my bedroom to continue to piece together the perfect outfit. I couldn't keep my eyes from constantly darting over to my phone's display, hoping there would be some response from Todd, but my phone remained stubbornly silent. I was okay with that, just the mere fact that he was thinking about me had me on cloud nine.

I wanted to call Emanuel and include him in on this new revelation and gloat that I was right all along, but I was positive this sort of news wouldn't sit right with him, or with anyone else for that matter. It was just more reason to keep this to myself until the wedding announcements went out.

I flopped down on my king-sized pillow top bed and let out a long and satisfying sigh. In less than twelve hours Todd and I would be together again and the best part was, he reached out to me.

FORTY-FOUR

TODD

I wasn't sure how Kai would take the idea that I was going to see Alana one last time to get my so-called "closure" with her. I was a tad nervous, but deep down I knew this was what needed to be done.

That last incident between us really showed Alana that I was not to be messed with. Or maybe she just came to her senses and had decided to move on. Whatever it was, it was time to close this chapter of my life and be done with it. And most of all, it was the right thing to do.

I walked into the house from my therapy session to see Kai feeding kids at the kitchen table. I took two more steps when my phone beeped three times. When I looked down at my phone I saw another text from Alana that read.

Looking forward to seeing you. Don't forget to text me the location and I will be there.

My heart skipped a beat since I was standing just a few feet away from Kai. I quickly pressed the side of my phone powering it down, then I shoved my cell back into my pocket.

The longer I stood in front of Kai, the more I thought my interaction with Alana may have been a huge mistake. I needed to talk to my therapist, tell her what I did, ask for her sound advice, and pray that she would tell me it wasn't the end of the world and that everything regardless of the outcome would end up fine. I really needed everything to be fine.

"Hey, how was therapy?" Kai snapped me out of my reverie.

"Huh?"

"Therapy, you had a session today, right?" Kai looked up at me between spoon- feeding Kristopher his oatmeal and holding a bottle up to Charlie's mouth.

"Yeah, I did, right. It was um...it was good," I said, walking over to kiss my kids and then Kai. Kai looked exhausted, but with a toddler and a newborn in the house, sleep wasn't on the top of our priority list. I loosened my tie, and shifted my weight from my left foot to my right. "I think I am making progress."

"Do you want to talk about it?" Kai asked, standing. She headed toward the sink to grab Kristopher's sippy cup. I saw it on the counter and reached over to grab it and hand it to her, to help shorten her travel time.

"In a bit. I need to go change and make a quick call," I said, unbuttoning the top buttons of my white business shirt.

Kai headed back over to the table, and gave me a second glance. "Okay." Then she sat back down. "You okay? You seemed a little weird."

"No, no, I'm good. I'll be back, I'm just gonna go and change," I replied hurriedly, headed to the bedroom. Once there, I pulled off my jacket, shirt and pants. I then reached into my jacket and powered back on my phone. I held my breath, hoping there would be no more texts from Alana.

I took a deep breath and called my therapist. I got her answering service.

"Hi, Dr. Tanner this is Todd Daniels." I paused, not really sure how to describe my situation over voicemail. "Could you please call me back? I really need to speak with you. In fact, if you could call me back tonight, I would really appreciate it. Thanks!"

I pressed end on my phone, setting it down on my dresser and reaching into the drawer below to grab a pair of gray sweats pants and black T-shirt. I was just about done slipping on my shirt when my cell phone rang.

I saw it was Dr. Tanner's office, so I picked it right up and began without preamble.

"Thank you for calling me back, Doctor. I'm sorry to have bothered you, but after I left your office, I sort of accidentally reached out to Alana. Definitely a bit premature, and now I am having second thoughts about it."

My therapist paused, letting the information I told her sink in for a moment. "It's perfectly normal to have second thoughts. Did you try and write the letter like I suggested first?"

"I tried and for some reason it wasn't really working for me."

"Okay, well, meeting is definetly an option if that is something you feel more comfortable doing."

"That's the thing, I am not 100% sure about that either."

"I understand completely. But remember Todd, what ever you chose to do, you have to stay in control of your meeting. She can only do what you allow."

"Right," I said. I thought how that statement could have changed a lot for me if I had heard it sooner rather than later. "Thank you, Doctor."

"Todd, if you need anything else, please do not hesitate to call me."

"I won't. Thank you."

I hung up the phone and thought about texting Alana. I needed to let her know that tomorrow would not work for me. I stood in my bedroom contemplating what to do. I hated the indecisiveness that was ruling my life lately.

No matter what happened, I had to tell Kai. I couldn't let part two go down without her knowing. That would definitely be the end of us. I took a deep breath and headed out to tell Kai exactly what I planned on doing.

***

Twenty minutes later I watched as Kai just stared at me. She was staring at me with a confused and almost unbelievable expression on her face. "Your therapist told you to do this?"

"I know it sounds crazy, but I really think if I have one final conversation with her and really get everything that went down off my chest, I can move on with my life," I said not only trying to convince Kai but myself.

Kai was leaning against the kitchen countertop and she dropped her folded arms, lifting herself up to sit on it. "Baby, that sounds crazy. Do you even know where she is?"

"Not really, but if I had to guess, I think she's probably in New York now. I'm not sure, but she is headed this way and was okay with meeting me in a public place."

I noticed Kai's body tense up. "You talked to her?"

"No, we only texted. Listen, Kai, I don't want any more secrets. I told you I want to start with a clean slate.

Kai shook her head, looked away. I walked over to Kai who was still sitting on the counter. I slid my hands between her thighs and separated her legs, stepping between them. I wrapped my arms around her waist and pulled her close to me.

"Baby, it will take thirty minutes tops. If you like, I will call you right before we meet and leave my phone on so you can listen in."

Kai looked away and then back into my eyes. "Closure, huh?"

"One final meeting. Dr. Tanner said that telling Alana exactly how I felt about everything that went down will somehow release the anger I have inside of me and help me be able to forgive her and move on with my life…our life."

Kai was silent, thinking, digesting all that I was throwing her way. She rubbed her hands against her thighs.

"Fine, I mean if that is the final thing that needs to be done..." Kai looked me in my eyes. "Then I guess I am okay with it. I want her gone for good."

"Are you sure? I want you to be one-hundred percent okay with it."

Kai let a tiny sigh. "I am if this is the only way.".

I leaned in and kissed Kai on her forehead, cheeks and then lips. She leaned her body into me. We embraced and I prayed that I was doing the right thing.

FORTY-FIVE

KAI

Simone stared at me with her lips twisted and her right hand on her hip and her left wrapped around the stem of her wine glass.

"So let me get this straight. Todd, your husband, went to meet Alana, your ex-lover, his ex-lover and certified psycho bitch, to have closure that his therapist told him he needed in order to move on with his life?"

"Yes."

"For the last time?"

"That's correct."

"Alone?"

"Uh huh."

"And you just let him go?"

"I did"

"After all that she has done?"

I took a deep breath, and started to feel even stupider than before now that Simone was shining a huge, I'm-An-Idiot spotlight on the situation. "Yes."

Simone nodded her head, turned and took two steps over to the counter, poured herself a little more wine, faced me again and raised her glass in the air.

"Welp, here's to another five years of drama, because you two just gave a new meaning to the saying 'opening up a can of worms'."

Simone put the glass to her lips and downed the rest of her wine. Simone then put her glass onto the counter and grabbed the wine bottle and offered it my way.

"You may want to get in on some of this, you're gonna need it." I took her advice and grabbed a glass from my wine tower. Simone poured me a full glass.

Simone was in town for a few days to help me jump start a big media campaign I landed a few weeks ago. I loved having her in town, but I hated how she put everything into perspective, especially since it wasn't necessarily in my favor.

I dropped down into my kitchen chair as I slouched over my table. I sipped methodically on my wine. "Shit."

Simone moved over to sit down across from me. "The good news is I can now see the drama unfold in real-time. I think I just found a reason to extend my trip."

I glanced at Simone, and didn't find her humor all that funny in my moment of despair. "So, what should I do?"

"What you shouldn't have done, was let him go meet that crazy witch in the first place. But since he's gone now, I would call and tell him to turn around and bring his ass home, pronto."

I nodded my head, feeling more and more like an fool for letting him go now. I thought about how his therapist's suggestion had sounded like such a good and proactive idea in the moment, especially since the initial seed was planted by me to start seeing a therapist. But now, I was watching it morph into a train wreck waiting to happen the more I let the logical side of me think about the whole situation.

"By the way, Todd's therapist…white?"

"Yes."

Simone smiled, shaking her head. "Thought so."

I took a much-needed gulp of my wine and leapt up from my seat. "Okay, I'm going to call him. You're right, this is bullshit."

"Good idea, I will be in the living room looking for something good to watch. Let me know how that turns out."

I shot Simone a look. Her sarcasm was going to be the death of her and probably me.

I headed to the bedroom to retrieve my phone while Simone headed to the living room. I heard the television set turn on as I raced down the hallway. Just the thought of Todd in the same room as Alana again created a nauseating and unsettling feeling in my gut. What the hell was I thinking? I was so mad at myself, I couldn't even think straight.

I tried to remember where I had placed my phone when I got home earlier that day. I felt so unorganized and disheveled, that I couldn't remember where I had put my phone.

I entered our bedroom and looked at the obvious places first—my dresser, our side tables, and finally our adjoining bathroom. But there was nothing.

I grabbed my purse laying on my vanity and dug through the main compartment, side and front. I stopped, took a deep breath, and then it hit me, I had left it in the kid's room when I was changing Charlie. I rushed out my bedroom and down the hall. I felt my heart beating faster as if I was racing against time. When I thought about it, I guess I was.

I entered my kid's room and saw Kristopher watching his favorite movie with Charlie right beside him in her bouncy. I spotted my phone then snatched it up and heard Simone call out my name.

"Kai."

"What?"

"Come here, now!"

"Hold on," I yelled back. I turned on my phone and started to dial Todd's number.

"Now!" Simone yelled back.

"Okay, Okay." I placed the phone to my ear, only to hear Todd's phone ring three times then go to voicemail. Why did his phone go to voicemail?

"Shit."

I hit end and was about to dial Todd's number again when I heard Simone call out again, and the urgency in Simone's voice made me rush out of the kids' room, as I attempted to dial his number yet again.

Todd's phone rang and rang until his voicemail came on again. What the hell was going on? I started to feel my anger rising. Why wasn't he answering the phone?

I hit end once again and walked into the living room to see Simone with her left hand over her mouth, right hand gripping the remote and her eyes the size of saucers glued to my flat screen television. Her face was displaying an array of shock, horror and suprise.

"What's wrong?" I said, unsure of what the hell to expect. My stomach did a small flap jack flip as I walked closer to Simone and the television.

"Simone, what is it?" I said in a concerned voice.

Simone looked at me then diverted her eyes to what had her up in arms on the television set. "You may not need to call Todd after all."

I walked around the couch as my eyes now caught what had Simone up in arms about. I froze and the moment my mind registered exactly what I was seeing, I let out a large gasp and dropped my phone to the floor.

FORTY-SIX
TODD

Alana and I had decided to meet at the bar inside the Hampton Inn near the Good Year Blimp Airport in Carson, California. It was nearing five-thirty and I was feeling incredibly nervous and apprehensive about seeing Alana in person again. I had to keep replaying in my mind what my therapist simply told me…it was me, not Alana that allowed her back into my life. I wouldn't give her that control again.

I headed into the hotel restaurant and grabbed a seat at the bar and ordered a beer. The bar was pretty empty, although that wasn't a big surprise since not a lot of people came to LA to hang out in a hotel bar. I checked my phone and saw that it was now five- thirty-five. We agreed to meet at six p.m. and depending on what time her flight arrived, that could change.

I continued to drink my beer as I rehearsed what I would say to Alana, staying firm and to the point, not letting her take control of the conversation or trying to lure me into anything unwanted.

Five-forty-five. I was on my second beer and needed to take a piss. I told the bartender that I would be right back and that I was waiting for a female to join me. He gave me a reassuring nod and I stood and headed to the bathroom. I entered the bathroom and stood against a stall relieving myself.

I felt my buzz beginning to wane somewhat. I took a deep breath, flushed and headed over to the sink. I caught a glimpse of myself in the mirror as I washed my hands and started to have second thoughts. What was I doing? Would this meeting really give me the closure I needed? It was too late to back out. Or was it?

I finished washing my hands as I grabbed two brown paper towels off the wall dispenser. I stood in the bathroom, wondering if Alana would be there when I got back to the bar. I thought about ducking out the back and standing her up. I stood in front of the sink contemplating my next move. I thought about what she would think or do if I didn't show. I also thought about what she would think or do if I did end up showing up.

"Ahhh dammit." I let out a long sigh as the door of the men's bathroom opened and an older man walked in. By the way he looked at me I was sure he heard my last word.

I grabbed the door before it had a chance to close and stepped outside the bathroom. I turned and before I knew it I was walking back toward the bar. As I approached my seat I noticed Alana was still not there. I pulled my phone out of my pocket, glanced at it and had no calls or texts from Alana, although I did have two missed call from Kai.

It was now 6:05. Alana was officially late, then again she was always late, always. I think some people were just born that way and she was definitely one of them.

I ordered a glass of water as my eyes wandered around the bar. I did a double-take as a woman walked through the door. My body tensed then relaxed when I realized it wasn't her. I drank down half of my water and started to think, maybe Alana wasn't coming, maybe she changed *her* mind. I picked up my phone once again, thought about shooting her a text.

I pulled up her name, then started typing.

Hey, Alana, I am here at the Hampton Inn. What is your ETA?

After I hit send, I set my phone back down on the bar and just occupied myself with the people coming and going. About ten minutes later I was starting to get annoyed, thinking this was typical Alana. I was beginning to wish I had not accidentally sent my initial text to her that had opened up this whole can of worms in the first place.

Twenty more minutes passed, it was now 6:30. Still nothing from Alana. I would have thought if her plane was delayed she would've had the courtesy to at least let me know, but nothing.

I checked my phone again before I waved my bartender down and got my check. I wasn't even going to bother sending Alana a text. In the sixty minutes I spent waiting for her, I had convinced myself that writing a letter was good enough. There had to be a reason she didn't show which meant it was the right thing.

I stood and started walking out the bar. I hit the lobby when my cell phone rang. *Really? Now she calls?*

I reached in my pocket and saw that it was Kai calling again. I quickly picked up the call.

"Hey, baby, I am headed home. Alana was a no-show. I am sorry I should have listened to you. In fact, I'm sort of relieved. Turns out that now that I am here I don't think that I really needed to actually talk to her to get closure. Just knowing I was going to have it gave me that calming feeling I needed, so I think I'm just gonna leave it at that," I said, prattling on.

"Todd, Todd, are you near a TV?"

"What?"

"Is there a TV near you?"

I looked back to where I just was. "Ah, yeah, I think there's one in the bar I was just in, why?"

"Go back in and tell them to turn to channel five."

"Why?"

"Just do it, okay," Kai said. I was surprised by the intensity in her voice.

I turned and headed back into the bar and noticed there was a flat screen on the back wall.

I walked up to the bartender who was waiting on me earlier. "Hey, my good man, could you turn on the TV to Channel Five, if you can?"

"Sure."

I waited patiently as the bartender reached under the bar, pulled out the remote and clicked on the television. ESPN was the selected channel.

"What channel again?" the bartender asked to re-confirm.

"Channel Five," I repeated, directing my attention to the television.

The moment the picture became clear I saw something that made me sit down in the chair beside me.

"Can you turn that up? Thanks."

I was still as I saw what looked like some kind of wreck, to what nature I could not tell yet. A very attractive female reporter stood in view as she spoke into her microphone.

"And if you're just joining us, recapping our top news story of the hour. Approximately, one p.m, eastern time today, a small jet carrying sitcom star Alana Brooks crashed just thirty miles after takeoff."

"Oh my God," I heard come out of my mouth.

I slowly stood, intensely listening to the reporter's every word. "It's been reported that Ms. Brooks along with her flight crew of three, including two pilots and one flight attendant were all killed on impact."

"Oh my God." I heard the same phrase repeat out of my mouth.

The reporter continued to talk, turning to point to the wreckage behind her. It was clear that the wreck I was seeing before me was a small jet plane.

"Just a few hundred feet behind me lay the remains of the wreckage. The black box had not yet been located to tell exactly what had happened."

"Alana Brooks was one of the stars most recently seen on the BET show *Office Temps* cancelled earlier this year. She was said to be headed to the Sundance Film Festival in Park City, Utah where an independent film she was to be featured. More details to come later. This is Jasmine Fuentes reporting from Channel Five News."

I stared at the television as a Wendy's commercial came onto the screen. I couldn't move, I couldn't think. *Was this really real?*

"Todd, are you there? Todd?" Kai broke my trance.

I shook my head, bringing myself back to reality. "Yeah, I'm here."

I gave the bartender a nod that I was done, and I turned, walking back out of the bar.

"Are you okay?" Kai asked.

I rubbed the back of my neck, felt my throat become dry. "Yeah, yeah...I'm cool."

"Crazy, huh?" Kai continued.

"Yeah, it's um..." I felt myself losing my train of thought as my mind was working overtime to grasp what I just saw, just heard. "Listen, Kai, I will see you in a bit, Ima head home," I said. I hung up the phone before I heard Kai's response.

I walked over to the lounge area in the lobby and sat down on the first chair that I saw. My legs felt a little weak and my mind was numb as well as shocked.

I sat there for another twenty minutes starring at the door, still thinking that any minute Alana would come walking through it, with that signature smile and her sassy walk, ready to deliver an array of sarcastic remarks. I continued to sit there in my chair. Twenty more minutes and still no Alana, twenty more minutes, before it sunk in that Alana was actually dead.

FORTY-SEVEN
TODD

Three weeks later

I was getting ready to take Charlie for her daily walk, when I heard the doorbell ring. I had a million things in my hand and couldn't imagine who might be here so early in the morning. I picked up Charlie and placed her in her playpen and headed to the front of the house. Along the way, I made myself useful and started picking up stray toys, clothes and scraps of food. I was still holding Charlie's sippy cup in my hand when I opened the door to see *Alana* standing in front of me. I froze. My feet felt glued to the floor, and my mouth felt as if it were wired shut.

"Now did you *really* think you could get away from me that easily?"

"Aaaah!"

I jumped up out of a dead sleep. My chest was heaving while beads of sweat covered my forehead.

"Baby, are you okay? You're shaking." I turned, and saw that I had woken up Kai, who was sitting up next to me.

I stared into Kai's face, and felt a stream of steady relief overtaking my emotions. I was slowly realizing that it was a bad fucking dream.

"Yeah, I um, I just had a really disturbing dream."

"What did I tell you about eating those beef burritos before bed?"

I looked at Kai and smiled. "Yeah, I definitely need to X that out of my midnight diet."

We heard Charlie crying from the other room. Kai swung her leg off the bed, and grabbed her robe. "I'll get her before she wakes up Kristopher." Kai headed out of the room, and closed the door behind her.

I shook my head, jumped out of the bed and headed for the bathroom to splash water on my face. I thought to myself that even from the damn grave, Alana still found a way to stalk me. I had to keep reminding myself that Alana was dead.

Suddenly I felt Kai's arms around my waist and I jumped. "Oh God."

"Okay that dream must have been a wild one. What was it about?"

I turned off the water and dried my face. "Nothing I want to talk about. I'm good, really." I picked up my toothbrush and slathered some Crest Pro-Health paste on it.

"You sure? We can sleep with the lights on from now on if that will make you feel safer?"

I stopped brushing my teeth, and looked at Kai with my head slightly tilted. "Oh, you got jokes now, huh?"

"Hey, I'm just saying." Kai grabbed a brush from the drawer and started to brush her hair. "What time are the gardeners coming today?"

I spit and rinsed out the inside of my mouth. "They said ten a.m." I picked up my watch sitting on the bathroom counter and glanced at it to see that it was only 8:15.

"Which gives me just enough time to hit the gym, that is, if you don't mind," I said, wiping my mouth dry with a towel.

"No, go, get your monkey pump on, Kristopher is still sleeping and Charlie is eating and will be sleeping again soon."

"Cool. Monkey pump? You really should leave the comedy to Simone"

I headed out the bathroom to grab my gym gear when I heard the doorbell ring. I turned to look at Kai who gave me a quizzical look.

Now who could that be at eight in the morning, I thought. I headed to the front door and felt my heart starting to pick up the pace as I flashed back to my dream. I saw Alana standing there as I opened the door.

"Alana is dead, Alana is dead," I softly repeated to myself as I headed down my hallway toward the front door. I swung open the door to see not Alana, but Alana's agent, Emanuel, standing in front of me. What the hell was he doing on my doorstep?

"Hey, Todd, I hope it's not too early."

It was way too damn early for a visit, but if he was here on my doorstep then it must've been important. "No, it's cool, what's up?"

"Well, as you know I have been in LA since the funeral, handling all of Alana's affairs. One of those was cleaning out her condo. I have no idea why she didn't just sell it when she left. Anyway, I came across something that..." Emanuel stopped.

"That what?" I said, trying to get him to just spit it out. It was too early for guessing games.

"Well, something that you should see."

"What is it?"

Emanuel held out a jump drive. "It a video and, well, I think you need to look at it."

***

Fifteen minutes later Kai and I sat in front of my computer. We were clueless as to what was on the file Emanuel had given us, but according to the flashy agent, it was a must see.

I took a deep breath and stuck the jump drive into my computer, clicking on the only icon on it titled *Alana Bites Back*.

Alana's face appeared close up on the screen. It appeared to be nighttime and the room she was in was dimly lit.

"Hey, baby, it's me, Alana. It's two a.m. East Coast time and, well, you are pretty knocked out as you can see."

Alana adjusted her camera to show me passed out on the bed. It hit me, this had to be from that night I passed out with her in New York. I felt Kai move uncomfortably on the couch next to me. I cleared my throat, but said nothing.

"We had fun tonight, although I think you had a little bit more fun than I did. So I have a confession to make. I slipped a roofie in your last drink." Alana smiled then laughed. "Don't be mad at me, baby. I had to get you to my room somehow."

Alana waved the camera toward my naked body then up close on her face.

"I could totally take advantage of you. I know exactly what to do to turn you on, but that wouldn't really be fulfilling to me. I want you to want me and I know deep down you actually do. But you know what? I'm gonna play a little game right now, just to prove to myself how much I know that you really want me. When you come to later I'm going to tell you that we made love and you are going to believe it. Why? Because you know that's how you really feel about me, and you know you really want to be with me. That's why. And that is the real reason why you haven't told Kai about me as your newest client, because you don't want her, you secretly crave me."

"Remember in college how you told me you wanted to marry a woman that was safe and stable, but you always loved my adventurous side? Let me enlighten you, Todd Daniels, safe and stable gets old and boring real fast, and that is what Kai is, old and boring. You, my friend, you like a challenge and I am that challenge. You know and I know that is what will eventually bring you back to me. So when you're done pretending you are in love with Kai, I will be waiting and I know you will come for me because actions don't lie."

Alana turned and looked back at me, naked and sleeping. "I guess that roofie did the trick." Alana reached out and stroked my dick, but there was no response, I was out like a light. "Let's stop playing all these games and just be together once and for all, this cat and mouse game is getting tiring."

Alana blew a kiss at the camera and the screen went black.

Kai and I sat in silence while the video played until it finally came to an end. I felt a nauseated feeling in my stomach. I wasn't sure how to take this information or even sure how Kai would react. I couldn't look at her, I was in fucking shock. We didn't move, we didn't speak. Kai finally shifted and slowly looked at me. "If this had been a game of chess I could clearly hear Alana say *checkmate*."

Kai stood, then slowly walked out of the living room, down the hall and into our bedroom and slammed the door behind her.

I took a deep breath. "This is not happening," I said in a low voice. "Alana has managed to fuck with my marriage even from the gotdamn grave."

I stood and walked into the bedroom where Kai sat on the edge bed. She didn't even make eye contact with me.

"Was it true what she said in the video? If she had not died, would you have left me for her?" Kai finally looked up at me with hurt filled tears in her eyes.

"Am I your boring consolation prize, Todd?"

"What? No. We are talking about Alana here. She will say anything to get into your head, you of all people should know that."

Kai looked down, as she shook her head, then back up at me. "Oh my God, is that why you wanted to go see her? To tell her that you wanted her back?"

"Are you serious right now? Kai, I went to finally have closure with her and X her out of my life forever, our lives." I took a big step over towards Kai and dropped down in front of her onto my knees. "Baby, you have to believe me."

"I want to believe you, I really do. But we have been through so much, so much hurt and so many lies." Kai shook her head again while tears fell from her eyes.

"I know we have, but in the end it's us, we are together, me and you forever. Baby, Alana is dead, she will never be able to come between us ever again. Kai, I love you."

Kai's tears continued to stream down her face as she stared at me.

"I want us to spend the rest of our lives together," I continued.

Kai let out a small cry. "Oh God, I want that too. I love you no matter what," Kai said as she dropped down to her knees and we embraced.

I felt a rush of relief flow through my body. I closed my eyes, thought how everything happens for a reason and there was a reason Alana died in that plane crash because in that moment a shocking revelation rang through my entire soul of how *right* Alana was.

THE END

Thank you for your purchase. If you liked what you read, please leave a kind review on Amazon.com.

A special request: If you are so inclined to reveal any part of the story as well as the ending, I would please ask that you preference it with "Spoiler Alert" so each and every reader can have their own experience from beginning to end. Thank you very much!

Look for all my upcoming novels as well as giveaways and release dates at"

www.kellecollier.com

About the Author:

K.Elle Collier started her writing career off by participating in various esteemed writing programs. K. Elle later branched off to other avenues of writing such as screenplays and stage plays, where she adapted the best-selling novel 'Friends and Lovers' by Eric Jerome Dickey for the stage. Here love for writing flowed over to novels in which she currently has two best selling books, "My Man's Best Friend" (Book 1) and "Kai's Aftermath" (Book 2). "Alana Bites Back" (Book 3) is the last book of the series. K. Elle currently lives in Los Angeles, CA.

Made in the USA
Middletown, DE
16 September 2020

Cat Training

in

10

Minutes

Miriam Fields-Babineau

T.F.H. Publications
One TFH Plaza
Third and Union Avenues
Neptune City, NJ 07753

ISBN 0-7938-0530-9

Distributed by T.F.H. Publications, Inc.

The Author wishes to thank the following photographers for their work on this book:
    Tria Thalman p. 113, and Candida M. Tómassini p. 128. All other photos by Evan Cohen.

Book design by Candida Moreira Tómassini

www.tfhpublications.com

Table of Contents

Dedication

To the most awesome cat ever, Davy Crockett

I also want to thank the following people: Thea Verdak and Dolores Claud for all their work with feline rescue and the support they've offered to me in many ways. I've never met anyone with larger hearts.

Introduction

With over 60 million cats in the US, and many more millions as pets and strays in other parts of the world, people are seeking to better understand and live with felines. City dwellers as well as people who work long hours prefer felines for company over canines. For cats do not have to go for walks, can be left home alone for a day or two, and do not need to go outdoors for appropriate exercise. However, cats are looked at as "throw away" pets far more often than dogs are, largely because people do not understand feline behavior. Millions of cats are euthanized each year, because of behavioral problems.

Cat Training in 10 Minutes

Are you one of those people who don't believe a cat can be trained? If so, you must be a new cat owner or never had a cat. Anyone who has ever had a cat is well aware of how well they've been trained by their kitty. Moreover, they are amazed at how easily their cat has learned routines, such as when it's feeding time, or how to obtain attention by sauntering into a room and jumping into someone's lap. This knowledge is not instinctual; the cat has learned your patterns and has responded to them. A cat that comes running at the sound of the can opener has been trained that the sound will bring a food reward. A cat that waits for the door to open and then rushes out faster than anyone can catch him has learned that this leads to freedom and adventure, the likes of which don't happen in the house.

Cat Training in 10 Minutes will instruct you, the busy cat owner, how to overcome behavioral problems, communicate with your cat, and learn about activities you can do with your beloved feline. In just 10 minutes a day, your cat can learn a multitude of positive behaviors both to occupy his time and enhance the relationship with you, his human companion.

Cats can not only learn how to come when called and walk on a leash, they can be used in a multitude of therapies. They help promote a sense of well being for the elderly, infirm, or ill, thus leading to a more positive outlook. Who does not benefit from holding a purring cat? Hearing the purr is as relaxing and as enjoyable as holding the furry beast that cuddles close. Cats can also be useful in helping people with hearing problems, while others can be taught to fetch light objects, aiding people with physical challenges.

Cats are often trained to perform on television and in feature films and advertisements. Who is not amazed at watching a cat perform? In this book, you'll meet some renowned cat trainers who have provided felines for feature films, advertisements, and live shows.

Cat Training in 10 Minutes will teach you how to make your cat a more special part of your life. No longer will your cat be delegated to sleeping all day in the sun or growing fat from lack of exercise; your feline will have something to look forward to, an understanding of his environment, and reliance on your companionship. A trained cat looks forward to his training sessions, often asking for them. Wouldn't it be great to be greeted at the door by your kitty instead of having to look for him to see if he's still napping somewhere?

Learn how to communicate with your cat and have fun together.

All it takes is 10 minutes a day.

Cats Like Training, Too

They roll onto their backs with their feet in the air. They stretch luxuriously in their sunlit spots. They purr in your arms as you caress and cuddle them. They crouch low and slink behind hedges, surprising small wildlife with a rapid pounce. Cats are both comforting and mysterious. Many cat owners claim their cats are very independent. Cats have a strong instinctual prey drive which makes them appear playful, yet superior. But, no, they are far from independent.

Domestic cats are not what they appear to be. Few prefer the solitary life, alone, without human or animal interaction. Often, cats left alone for long periods of time develop neuroses. Many display poor behaviors such as clawing furniture, digging up plants, or roaming on eating surfaces. Your domestic feline is not like a cougar or leopard. He doesn't prefer to remain alone. He doesn't prefer to do nothing all day.

CATS NEED STIMULATION

Did you know that the feline in your life would like to do more than nap in a sunny spot near the window? Cats, like other domestic creatures, are given food, shelter, and medical attention without having to work for it. A wild animal spends every waking minute procuring food and shelter, caring for young, or protecting territory. These instincts are not lost in domestic felines any more than they are lost in tigers and lions. They are very much alive and in need of fulfillment.

> ### Daily Training
>
> *Opening a cat's mind through training may create a "monster" who will harass you until you engage in his daily training session. He will not be satisfied unless you and he have worked together. Use your training time as an opportunity to socialize with your cat.*

Which cat is happiest, the one who has everything given to him, or the one that must work for it? Which cat is more mentally healthy?

The answer is...the cat that works for a living.

Felines are no different from you and I in that regard. We prefer to do something with our lives. Develop a career. Work a steady job. Enjoy a sport. These are all things we prepare for and look forward to.

Cats Need an Occupation

Cats have not evolved into a cultural society. They are still reliant upon the instincts and predatory behaviors that have served them well for millions of years. Watching television is not an option. Playing football or soccer is not on their agenda. They wish to catch small rodents and birds. They mark their territory, search for mates, and maintain their coats and claws for future hunts. Cats need an occupation.

Your cat will enjoy being held. A cuddle makes a good reward.

CATS WANT SOMETHING TO DO

In answer to the question of which cat is healthier, the one who has to work for a living or the one who is given everything, it is very clear that the happier cat is the one who has a job. The cat utilizes more of his brain, body, and instinct. He demonstrates intelligence and the ability to learn that most of us have missed because of our belief that cats are so independent they will not take well to our guidance.

A working cat is a happy, healthy cat. Training your cat gives him a chance to prove that he has a high intellect and the ability to expand both his and your horizons. Your cat's mental development is limited only by your imagination.

What do most house cats do all day? They do not sleep. They are trying to find things to occupy their time. Hunting in the garbage. Terrorizing the hamster. Chasing the dog's tail. Digging in the plants. All of these are natural behaviors based on a cat's instincts. The hunt for food—terrorizing the hamster

Training your cat will improve your relationship.

and sorting the garbage. The territorial control—chasing the dog. The need to cover droppings and mark territory—digging in the plants.

By the time his people come home, the cat is exhausted from all that hard work and can be found lying in a sunny spot by the window. One might think, oh, what a lazy animal.

Keep Your Cat Occupied

Cats that have not learned to control their instincts have not totally adapted to captivity. These cats claw the furniture or show aggression. Many of these felines are disposed of in one way or another. Shelters are filled with them and millions are euthanized each year. This does not have to happen. Even a feral cat can learn to cope with his new environment. This may take much patience and time, but it can be done. Training your kitty will prevent him from becoming a statistic.

Every cat deserves a chance to develop his mind. A cat that has something to look forward to each day, a chance to learn, to cultivate his intelligence, and to communicate with his human companions, is a happy, well-adjusted cat. A trained cat becomes a social, personable feline that is a pleasure to be around. Entertaining and loving, he will greet you when you come home. He will follow you from room to room. He will not exhibit destructive tendencies because he has been taught they are not acceptable in your home.

This cat will be a pleasure and a great companion.

Why not get started? All it takes is 10 minutes a day.

GETTING STARTED

As with other animals, the younger the cat is when you begin training, the more he will be apt to learn in the long run. This is not to say that older cats cannot learn. I have often worked with cats anywhere from two to nine years of age, successfully teaching them numerous behaviors. To prevent behavioral problems, acclimate to a multiple pet household, or to prepare for a future as a therapy cat or animal actor, the cat's training is best started while he is still a kitten. Kittens are far more impervious to changes in their environment than a cat who has become used to only one way of doing things. A kitten will not be as frightened of a new environment or of new people as an older cat.

Cats love to have interaction.

Training becomes part of the cat's life and is something to look forward to. Training is a daily routine that is sorely missed if not performed. Cats need

Some cats prefer a food reward, such as kibble, moist cat food, or tuna.

an occupation as badly as we do. Since you work to provide food and shelter for your family and pet, giving your pet a means of returning the favor makes him far happier and healthier.

The best time to start training is just after the kitten is weaned and has left his litter behind. Cats should initially be taught without the distraction of other animals present. A small, quiet room is best. Make sure you have a 10-minute period of time without distractions. Do the training at the cat's mealtime. This way the cat must work for his food, giving him more incentive to perform. Kittens are rarely finicky and are happy to work for food or a toy.

Motivation

When starting with an older cat, the challenge will be finding what "drives" him. You may have to try a variety of treats. Freeze-dried liver, soft cat food, or any number of commercial treats might work. Barring the lack of interest in commercial cat treats, try cooked chicken or tuna fish. Some cats are so well fed that they will never show any interest in food and you will have to find a toy to use as a reward. Many cats like furry toy mice or a catnip ball. One cat I had loved soft curlers. You never know what will spark Kitty's interest until you try.

There are a small percentage of cats that turn their noses up to everything. Finding a food reward can prove quite a challenge, but it is not impossible. You simply have to have more determination than your feline. This cat needs a strong incentive. He might have to be food deprived for a day or two. Don't worry about doing this. In the wild, cats eat every couple of days, not every day. The daily feeding is merely a placing of our own habits upon our captive felines. A hungry cat will have more drive to work and thus to learn.

Using Food as a Reward

After the cat has been food deprived for a day or so, begin his training using his regular kibble. Offer it from your hand or from a training spoon. When your cat takes the food, use a verbal reward, such as, "Good, Kitty" in a high tone of voice. You can also use a clicker to bridge the behavior. A bridging device (i.e. clicker or praise) is used to reinforce the appropriate response. You give a command and lure the cat to do what you ask. He does it. You bridge and reward him with his kibble. In this case, you are rewarding your cat for eating from your hand. He soon learns to come to you for the food, associating your bridge response with his mealtime. Soon both you and he will enjoy the mealtime training sessions. He'll drool and purr while you smile and praise.

Make Your Own Wand

A training wand, complete with clicker, target stick, and treat dispenser can be made as follows:

Take a half-inch dowel rod, approximately two feet in length, and tape a clicker to one end. (Make certain that you tape down only the edges, leaving the clicking area open.) Take a soft metal spoon and bend it so that the handle is at a 90-degree angle to the scoop. Tape the handle of the spoon to the other end of the dowel rod. Now you have a training wand.

What a great start to a day!

Cats can learn 2 to 3 new behaviors every couple of days, in a period no longer than 10 minutes at a time. However, as your cat progresses with his behavioral repertoire, his attention span will also increase. Some cats can work upwards of 45 minutes at a time. In this situation you must revert to using his regular food or a low calorie treat so that he doesn't become overweight.

Should your time be limited, stick to the 10 minute training sessions, but try to do this several times per day. If you feed your cat twice a day, do his training just before each feeding time. Even if you only feed Kitty one time per day, try training him five minutes in the morning and then again when you get home in the evening.

TRAINING TOOLS

There are specific tools and techniques that you will need prior to training your cat. Being prepared will make the entire process far easier and much more fun.

Bait Pouch—You will need a handy place to put treats. A little bag fastened around your waist works fine. Fanny packs are perfect. Bait pouches can be found at pet shops. These pouches have hooks that can fasten to your belt or on a pocket.

Clicker—Clickers are a popular training tool. Small, plastic clickers are available at pet shops. The clicking sound will attract your cat's attention and get him to focus on you.

Training tools include: treats, a clicker, the target stick, and the bait bag.

Training Wand—The wand can be pointed at an object to show your cat where you want him to focus his attention.

Training Spoon—Some cats become overzealous when going after their treat. You might have your fingers nipped or clawed by a cat that has not learned proper etiquette when taking food from you. In this case, a training spoon will be helpful. A training spoon is also good if you are using a soft cat food or tuna fish as a reward.

You can make your own training spoon by using a teaspoon and a two-foot long slender dowel rod—approximately 1/4 inch thick. (You can also use an old wooden mixing spoon if you can't obtain a dowel rod.) Should you prefer to use a clicker to train your cat, this can be incorporated into the training spoon. Tape the spoon onto one end of the dowel rod and the clicker onto the other end. Be sure that when you hold the end with the clicker that the upper dish of the spoon is facing upward.

Hold your thumb on the clicker with the training spoon pointed toward the cat.

13

A training spoon will allow you to have one hand to offer the reward and bridge while you give visual signals with the other hand. The training spoon can also be used as a target to lure your cat into new behaviors. The cat will smell and/or see the food and follow it.

Vocalization—Cats respond to both our vocal tones and visual signals. They use vocal tones and body language to communicate, just as we do. With consistency, your cat will learn any visual cue when paired with the verbal command. Eventually, your cat can work from either your voice or visual cue. This will not take long as cats are quick studies.

USING A CLICKER

Clickers are devices utilized for operant conditioning. A clicker is a rectangular plastic box with a metal tongue inside. When pressure is applied to the metal tongue it bends. As the pressure is released, it springs back and makes a clicking noise.

The sound of a clicker acts as a bridge between the command and the reward. The bridge is used to let the cat know when he has performed as requested. Since the clicker noise is associated with the cat receiving his reward, he will like to hear the sound of the clicker.

Let's start with basic clicker usage. Begin by having your cat in the vicinity and click the clicker, then offer your cat his reward immediately. Continue doing this until your cat pairs the clicking sound with receiving his reward. As you build on training, you can have your cat Come and Sit, click, and then give him his reward.

Make sure you keep the proper grip on the clicker.

UNDERSTANDING YOUR CAT'S NEEDS

Using cues that already conform to your cat's common language will be most helpful, so I'll take a moment to discuss how to recognize specific emotions. Similar to humans, felines can be moody, so learning how to read your cat is important for a successful training session.

Anger—His ears are back, his tail thumps. The hair may rise along his spine, but mostly this is a tactic cats use to make themselves look larger when confronted with something that frightens them. Some cats will hiss, depending on how angry they are. Other cats will lash out with their front paws and "hit" at the object of their anger.

Fear—The cat's back is arched; the fur is standing on end. Tail is up straight. Eyes are wide and staring. Whiskers are stiff, and the cat will usually hiss and spit. The scared cat will back up or lean against a solid object.

Stress—The cat will crouch and pant, either hiding in a dark closed-in place or actively searching for one. A stressed cat is easily angered and might lash out with a claw or bite.

A calm cat will close his eyes and lie down. What a look of contentment!

Calm—The eyes will squint. The cat might rub against you, flicking his tail around. His fur lies flat. When lying down, some cats will tuck a paw beneath them or lie on their sides. Many cats will roll onto their backs and stretch out their legs, rubbing their heads.

Content—A happy cat behaves in a kittenish manner. He will purr, knead, and rub. Some cats love to cuddle with their people, similar to doing so as kittens with their mother and siblings. A happy, working cat will purr, drool, and rub against you. They will also hold their tails up proudly and watch you with interest. Their eyes will be closed when in a relaxed state, but will be wide open when in training. Many cats enjoy their training so much that they purr and drool throughout.

FELINE VOCALIZATIONS

Cats can be very verbal, especially the oriental breeds, such as the Siamese and Burmese. The Persian-type cats are quieter and tend to be the most placid of the breeds, while the semi-longhair cats, such as the Maine Coons, Ragdolls, Birmans, and Norwegian Forest Cats can exhibit temperaments in the middle of the two former groups.

There are three distinct verbal tones that us non-felines can easily understand. The purr, is of course, usually a happy contented sound, although there are some cats who purr when nervous. The meow is far more difficult to understand, for the oriental breeds can be quite demanding with their meow, while others have a little meow that can mean the same thing, only they aren't as loud. In general, a long meow indicates that the cat is upset, not feeling well, or scared. A short, gentle meow can be contentment. A loud, but short meow means that he wants company or is trying to find someone. A hostile cat will yowl/howl long and loud. He might also spit and hiss. Growling accompanies a major spat.

Understanding how your cat is communicating will help you pick the time to train him. Normally, first thing in the morning he's ready for some food and will be most willing to work. You will see him in an active, relaxed state, which indicates he's ready to perform. You might also see this behavior upon your return home after an extended (normal working hours) absence. He will come to greet you and request his training. Heaven help you if you've begun his training process and you don't give it to him when he has missed you all day. I've often been tackled on the stairs or while walking through the house when my cat wanted his training. At 16 pounds of muscle, this cat was not to be ignored!

Work For Your Food

Your cat will work best when hungry. Do the training sessions just prior to feeding time. This way, your cat will be able to earn his food, much as he would in the wild, making him far happier and fulfilled. If you feed twice a day, take five minutes to work your kitty prior to each feeding.

TRAINING BASICS

Be consistent with your training tactics. Use the same words and visual cues for every command. You will need a word for rewarding your cat as well as separate words for each behavior. This reward word should coincide with the use of a click on the clicker. Some cats prefer the verbal reward to the click. Some even prefer it to receiving food. Your pleasure brings them pleasure. The praise word should be used in a high, happy tone of voice. It does not matter which word you use, provided you use it consistently and in the proper tone. For our purposes, I will use the word "Good." It has a distinctive sound.

The reward word can also be used to encourage the cat to continue behaving in the appropriate manner. For example, use "Good" while the cat remains in a Stay position. You are constantly rewarding him for remaining, yet not telling him that the behavior is complete. The click, as a bridge between the behavior and reward, signals the end of the behavior. Thus, the cat is being verbally praised while he remains. When the behavior is complete, you click and offer the food reward.

Training Tips

The training area should be prepared prior to training. The room should be no bigger than 10 by 12 feet, quiet and uncluttered. Be sure to have plenty of rewards available and easily accessible.

Do all training sessions either when your cat is hungry or well rested. This will give him more drive to perform, which translates into a longer attention span and increased learning capacity.

Cats are creatures of habit. Try to maintain a specific training schedule so that Kitty has a good idea of when to expect his training time. Otherwise, a pushy Kitty asking for training might wake you in the early morning hours. If your cat is aware of a specific schedule then he'll be far more relaxed and allow you to go about your day. After all, you are training your cat to make life easier with him, not to teach him how to rule the roost.

Be consistent and patient when training your cat. Some cats will have an "off" day.

Come to Me, Kitty

Imagine spending an afternoon in the fenced garden with your cat. The two of you take in the sunshine, listen to the birds (your cat far more intently than you), and sip a cool drink now and then. Cats need time outdoors as much as we do. Sunlight is very important for the overall health of all living things. However, it is not safe to allow your cat outside unless he is in a safely enclosed area (or on a leash) and comes when you call him.

Teaching your cat to come when called is the first behavior for him to learn. It gives him the base from which the remainder of his training will be built. Through this process your cat learns to target, follow the target, how to earn a reward, and the meaning of your vocal tones, visual cues, and bridging.

TARGETING

A target is the point at which you want your cat to be attracted. (Sort of like a bull's eye on a dartboard.) When teaching your cat to target, you are guiding him toward your hand or target stick through the use of the bait (a food or toy). Each time your cat puts his nose next to the target (or better yet, on the target), he earns his reward. Within a short time your cat will follow the target everywhere as closely as he would a toy mouse that he wishes to catch.

Target Training

Target training is the easiest means of teaching a cat to do anything. Show the cat a treat or toy, and when the cat shows interest in the reward by touching his nose to it, praise him and give him the reward. As the cat learns that he will receive his reward when he is praised, the reward can be delayed or alternated as the cat works. The praise alone will reinforce his performance. A target can be made of anything—a stick, a ball, a paper towel, or even your hand.

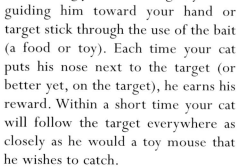

There are several forms of targets. You can use your hand or a stick. Using your hand is easiest, but some cats might bite at your fingers in their excitement, so it would be best to use the target spoon/stick in this case. Eventually, an overzealous feline will learn to control his exuberance and take his reward gently.

Begin by placing the target (spoon/stick or your fingers holding the treat) beneath your cat's nose. When he sniffs the food praise him. Say, "Good, Kitty." When he takes the food into his mouth, click the clicker (if you are using one) and/or say, "Good, Kitty."

Next, move the target a short distance from your cat. Move it just far enough away so he has to stretch his neck a bit to reach it. As he sniffs the target, praise him. When he touches it, click and praise while he takes the bait.

As you establish your praise tone and clicker action with your cat receiving his reward, you can begin to pause a bit between your cat responding to the action of his targeting and his receipt of his reward. Your praise will encourage him on his course. The click will let him know that he attained what you desired and the treat will reward him for his action.

Let Kitty see and have a taste of his reward.

Move the target a short distance and allow the cat to locate and sniff it.

When your cat touches the target, give him his reward.

TEACHING THE COME COMMAND

Now that your cat understands to follow his target, he can learn to come when you call him.

1. Present the target. (Your hand or target stick.)
2. The cat becomes attentive to the target and you praise him.
3. The cat moves to the target and touches it with his nose. You click/praise and give him the treat.
4. You again present the target, first under his nose and then drawing him closer to you by slowly moving the target closer. Say his name and the word, "Come."
5. As the cat moves toward the target, praise.
6. When the cat reaches the target, click and reward.

Each time you present the target and give a command, your cat must cover more ground between each bridge. The first time, ask for him to move only a foot. The next time two feet, and so on. Your cat will be encouraged to continue following your commands to gain his reward. He will soon learn to pair the word "Come" with the action of moving toward his target (your hand or stick).

Reward your cat for doing a good job.

Each time you do the Come exercise, move back further, giving your cat a longer distance to travel in order to receive his reward. This backward motion begins to become part of the recognizable visual cue, along with your targeting hand and/or target stick.

During this initial teaching of the Come command, you'll be using both visual and verbal cues. Eventually, use just one or the other. However, a combination of the two will aid in your cat's learning speed.

Within only 10 minutes your cat should be able to come to you from across the room. After barely a week, he'll come to you from wherever he might be within your house, for he is looking forward to the interaction and rewards of working with you.

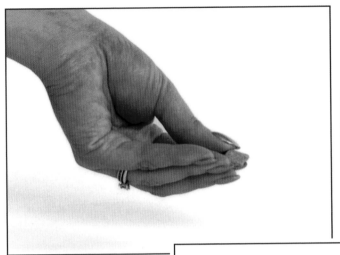

This is the appropriate hold of a target with reward for the Come command.

Praise Kitty as he moves toward the target.

Allow Kitty to sniff the target, and then slowly draw it away from him.

TRAINING TIPS

At this time it would be a good idea to have a word for letting your cat know when training time begins and ends. The word, "Training" said in a high tone of voice is great for starting the sessions and the word, "Finished" is good for ending the session. These are not normal conversational words that you might be apt to use while working with your cat, thus they will have special meaning. Any word can be used, but use the words consistently in the appropriate contexts.

> ### Move It!
>
> *Cats are very visually oriented. Movement really grabs their attention. Use this to your advantage while training. A placement and motion, when used consistently, will translate into a visual cue.*

You will discover that there are a few simple keys to successful training. The first is consistency, and the second is timing. The best animal trainers have conquered these attributes and can quickly train any animal. These abilities are simpler to attain than you might think. With consistency, you simply do the same action or say the same word in the same context. With timing, you praise and reward at the time of the appropriate action, not after or before.

WORKING WITH DISTRACTIONS

Another step of working on the Come command is teaching your cat to come when there are other distractions present. You can invent distractions such as working in a different room other than the training room, or work around other pets or people. Always begin small and gradually increase the distractions as your cat achieves each increment of distraction proofing.

If you find that your cat cannot concentrate, decrease the distractions to the point where he begins to respond again and gradually increase the distractions as he learns to disregard his surroundings while working. Everything must be done in small increments.

Another way to vary this exercise is to set up an obstacle course that your cat must move through as he comes to you. Use a couple of hardcover books set upright, framed photographs, or candlesticks. Get your cat's attention on the target and weave him through the obstacles as he follows the target. If you maintain the same pattern you will soon be able to go to the far end of the obstacle course and call him to come and have him move through the obstacles on the way.

By teaching your cat to come on command you have opened up a whole new world of communication. Your cat will watch you more, remain nearby, and ask for training time. Yes, cats are entertaining while they play, but a cat can be even more entertaining as an interactive companion.

OPERANT CONDITIONING

All animal training is based on operant conditioning. In essence, the animal is taught to respond in a specific way to a stimulus in order to receive a reward. We do this every day. We go to work. We get paid. Cats prefer their payment in the form of food or a toy.

Eventually, you will be able to train your cat outdoors or when there are other distractions present.

The target stick or your hand cue is the cat's stimulus. The praise and click are the bridge between the response to the stimulus and receipt of the reward. Once the behavior has been completed, the click and reward signify that you are satisfied with the cat's response.

Each time you present the target and give a command, your cat must perform more criteria in order to receive his bridge and reward. This builds on the behavioral response. For example, you present the target directly in front of the cat's nose on the first exercise. He touches the target, you bridge and give the reward. The next time, move the target up, then down. When he follows the target with his eyes, praise him. When you have moved the target up and down one time each, bridge and reward. Next, move the target to each side. Again, as your cat follows the target, praise him. When you have completed the requirements, (i.e. moved the target side to side one time) bridge and reward. Finally, move the target a short distance (about six inches). When your cat follows the target, praise, bridge, and reward.

It may take less time for your cat to learn to target than it did for you to read the preceding paragraph. When it comes to filling their tummies, most cats learn quickly. Eventually, many cats will work for the sheer joy of the stimulation, not caring about anything but the praise and/or the sound of the clicker. This is especially true when cats are stressed, such as when working in a strange environment or surrounded by people they don't know. Working is a means of coping and thus being able to relax in the new place.

Sit for a Bit

One of the most common circus tricks for big cats is to stand up on their hind legs and rest on their haunches, their paws raised in the air. While this may be a somewhat complicated behavior for an exotic cat to accomplish, it is very easy for the domestic cat. In fact, it can be the base behavior for many more complicated behaviors, such as a shake, a wave, and jumping onto or through objects.

The parameters of the sitting up exercise encompass first the sit-on-command, then the sitting up on the haunches in the classic "beg" position and then to remain in that position for a period of time. This is far easier for a cat than a dog. Cats have incredible balance and dexterity.

Your feline would most likely learn this behavior in less than five minutes while learning to come and sit. Cats have an inherent inclination to rest on their haunches when something has caught their fancy, leaving their front paws available for grabbing onto the object of their desire.

The Come and Sit commands are the bases for many other tricks your cat can learn.

TEACHING KITTY TO SIT

Most cats will sit whenever they are watching something of interest. However, it's an entirely different circumstance when they learn to sit on command. Yes, they are watching your visual cue (with interest), but they are being lured into position via your visual cue and targeting on their reward. In other words, they are not performing the behavior through their decision, but through yours. However, with teaching a cat to execute anything on command, you have to allow them to think it's entirely their decision to perform.

Once the cat sits, you should not expect him to remain there for any length of time. This will be accomplished by teaching Kitty to Stay (during more advanced work).

1. Once Kitty has come to you, lure his head into looking upward by placing his reward between your middle finger and thumb and putting it between his eyes, a few inches over his head.
2. As his head lifts up and back, his rear end will lower.
3. Point your index finger toward his rear as you move his target in that direction. Be sure to not hold his target too high or he will merely try to jump up to reach it instead of remaining on the floor with all four feet. His nose should almost touch the reward, but not quite reach it.

Begin the exercise by having the cat Come.

The target is lifted a little over his head, which makes him move upward to attain his treat.

Kitty is targeting on the reward as the visual cue is being slowly pushed behind his head. This makes him sit.

4. As soon as Kitty puts his rear end on the floor, click/praise and give him his reward.

You can now use the Sit command either with or without the Come command. Thus, Kitty can Come and Sit, which will be used for any number of future behaviors, or just have him Sit wherever he might be. If your Kitty has trouble coming when called, and yet will sit on command, he will be far easier to catch should the need arise.

Practice this exercise often throughout Kitty's training sessions. It is a base behavior for more advanced training. For example, he'll need to Sit and Stay for learning to Shake, Wave, and Sit-Up. A solid Sit performance will insure Kitty's ease in learning other behaviors.

SITTING UP

The bait you use must be kept mere inches out of reach in order for your cat to follow it upward. Place the bait between your thumb and middle finger, holding your index finger straight up so that you can pair the food lure with the visual cue for the exercise.

Gain your cat's attention by having him come and sit a few times. After two or three successful repetitions, point upward and over his nose as you say, "Kitty (insert his name here), Up." When he looks up, give him the treat. The next time, make him lift his front feet off the floor just slightly before he receives his reward. Gradually, increase the criterion with each Come, Sit, Up combination. Within minutes, Kitty should be going upward and possibly grabbing at your hand with a paw or two.

In order to prevent pattern training, do not do the same combination repeatedly. Sometimes do only the Come and Sit, and others add on the Up.

Always say, "Good, Kitty," when your cat has fully accomplished what you requested. If you say it prior to completion he may think that he has fulfilled your request even if he hasn't. Praise is the bridge between his performing the command and receiving the reward. Be aware of your timing. You must praise (and/or click) the second Kitty has accomplished what you wished.

> ### Training More Than One Cat
>
> Should you have more than one feline companion and both wish to be trained, it would be best to work them individually. Once they learn a few basic behaviors, such as Come and Sit-up, you can work them both in the same room, provided there are other handlers helping you. Do not attempt to work two cats simultaneously unless both are already well versed in training behaviors.

Get your cat's attention and have him sit.

Once he sits, hold the target just out of his reach above his head, giving the Up signal with your fingers.

Allow your cat to balance himself by resting his paws on your hand.

31

Variations on the Up

There are several variations of the Up theme that you can teach your cat. One is to have him balance on his haunches for a few seconds without touching you, another is to grab hold of your hand with his paws, and yet another is for him to rest his paws upon a raised surface.

The easiest variation is for the cat to grab your hand with his paws. This will lead to the next behavior of maintaining the position without touching you. Once the cat understands the command, it can be transferred to his placing his paws upon another surface.

Begin with a Come and Sit. (Always praise your cat as he performs in order to reinforce his behavior.) After his arrival in the Sit, hold his target (your hand or stick with the treat) just above his nose. Pull his attention upward, slowly. For each minor increment, offer praise and his reward. When your cat has reached the full height of holding his upper body off the ground while resting on his haunches, require the other parameters of either touching you or not.

In the beginning, many cats will automatically touch to balance. You can

Blueberry is double-targeting by placing his paws near the target wand and keeping his eyes on the hand holding his tuna fish.

Besides teaching Kitty to rest his paws on the back of a chair, he can also learn to shake and wave while performing this behavior.

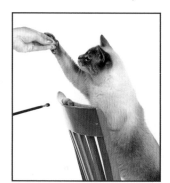

add a command for this by pairing his behavior with the command and the reward. Most likely, the more difficult accomplishment will be teaching your cat to do the Up behavior without touching your hand. If your cat has a habit of using his claws to grip, you definitely want to teach him to not grab your hand to balance. In order to accomplish this, simply pull your hand a short distance away when the cat reaches for you. As soon as he stops reaching, but is still in the Up position, praise and reward him.

Resting Paws on a Surface

To transfer Kitty to resting his paws upon a surface (such as a chair or sofa), lure him to the location with the Come command. When he arrives very close, tell him to Sit. Tap the surface with the target. Kitty will first try to reach his target and treat with his nose. As he sees that both are out of reach he will naturally lift his upper body. Be certain to immediately bridge (praise or click) as he does so and give him his reward.

This cat is performing the Up command, resting his front feet on the back of the chair.

Each time Kitty raises upward, request more and more until he finally rests his front paws upon the surface. Once there, you can teach him to remain in place for longer periods of time prior to bridging and giving him his reward. This will be further reinforced through the use of the Stay exercise (which you will learn in a later chapter).

You can add more criterions to the Up command, by teaching Kitty to "paw the air" like a big cat does in the circus, or to twirl around while standing on his hind legs. First, however, make certain Kitty has a complete understanding of the basic Up behaviors and will perform the three variations without any hesitation.

Get Moving!

The secret to controlling unwanted behaviors is to turn them into desired behaviors. In other words, teach your cat to perform these behaviors on your command in order to reduce his urge to explore them on his own. Cats, as intelligent creatures, will devise ways to entertain themselves. The reward of climbing on the counters or sifting through the garbage is not merely that of getting food, since you already feed him well. Your cat does this because he needs an activity. Searching behavior is something very natural to cats. They are always searching; searching for shelter, searching for a mate, searching for food, or wandering through territories and marking the boundaries. In the wild, your cat would spend his day doing these activities. In your house he has no other outlet than to climb the mountains of tables and counters, or search the hidden valleys of the garbage can. In essence, your cat is bored.

Training your cat gives him an occupation, something to look forward to each day. Why not take natural behaviors and turn them into something spectacular?

Kitty already knows how to Come, Sit, and go Up, with variations on these behaviors. The commands and visual cues are very much the same when asking your cat to move from one surface to another, or to twirl, shake, wave, and even jump through a hoop or over a stick. You'll want your cat to come to a specific point, regardless of the path. Your visual cue for Come will guide him from point A to point B. As you teach these behaviors you will pair them with a word so your cat can become conditioned to the specific sound. Most cats, however, will respond more to your visual cue than to the words you use. Using a verbal command goes further toward keeping the actions straight in our brains than to relate any information to the cat.

JUMPING ONTO A CHAIR

Begin by first choosing two non-slip surfaces, such as wide seat, cloth covered chairs. Place them no further than one foot from each other. Make certain that the chairs are steady on the floor and will not move around easily. Cats do not choose to jump onto unsteady surfaces. They may do it once, but will rarely do it twice. Your cat needs to trust you in order to work for you.

1. Show your cat his treat and slowly guide him to the chair. When he arrives at the chair praise/click and give him his reward.
2. The next time, move the treat halfway up the chair and give your cat his praise/click and treat as he reaches for his target. Gradually increase the distance until your cat has touched the seat of the chair.
3. Place the treat in the middle of the chair and tap near the treat. The tap draws Kitty's attention toward the location of the treat. He will most likely jump onto the chair to obtain his reward. As soon as he jumps, praise/click as he obtains his treat.
4. While Kitty is on the chair, have him do a Sit and an Up.
5. Move a short distance from the chair and call your cat to Come.
6. When he arrives, have him sit and praise/click and give him his treat.
7. The next time you ask him to jump on the chair, simply tap the chair and ask him to Come Up. You should not have to lure him onto the chair as you did originally.

Most cats understand things with less than three repetitions. They are very quick to figure out what to do to receive their rewards. You can use different words for training if you wish, just be certain to remain consistent on which you

Guide Kitty to the chair with the Come command. Place the reward on the chair and tap.

When Kitty jumps onto the chair, allow him to have his reward.

While in the chair, have Kitty perform the Up.

Have your cat perform a Sit while in the chair.

use. However, the words Come and Up signify behaviors the cat already has. Kitty already knows how to come and he knows that when you tap the chair he will get a reward for jumping onto it, so Come Up brings the two behaviors together.

Repeat the Jump-Onto-the-Chair command several times before continuing on to the next step. Your cat should be able to quickly respond to the Come Up (onto the chair) command and then to the Come (off the chair) command before trying the Jump-From-Chair-to-Chair behavior.

JUMPING FROM CHAIR TO CHAIR

Jumping from chair to chair will emulate Kitty's desire to jump onto other surfaces that are off limits, such as the counters and tables. You will be replacing his bad behavior in a positive manner by showing him the appropriate time and place to perform these actions.

1. Have Kitty jump onto the chair.
2. Show your cat his treat and lure him to the edge of the chair. Make certain he sees you lay the treat in the middle of the other chair.
3. Tap the chair next to the treat. (Your cat knows that when you tap, he's sure to receive a treat when he investigates the location of your tap.) He will jump onto the chair. As he does, be sure to praise him as he retrieves his treat.
4. Try the same thing in reverse. Place the treat on the chair he just left, tap the surface and give him a command at the same time, such as "Come over," or "Jump." Praise him as he comes to your tap.
5. Repeat this exercise several times in both directions.
6. Go back to other exercises, such as the Come, Sit, and Up. Then return to having your cat jump up on the chair again.
7. As he's eating his treat, separate the chairs by six inches.
8. Tap the empty chair and tell your cat to "Come over."
9. Repeat this exercise a few times, but do not increase the distance between the chairs again until the next training session.

Your cat will hardly notice the distance increase between the chairs. Cats are very athletic and a jump of a foot and a half is nothing to them.

Show Kitty the treat by tapping.

Your cat will jump from one chair to the other to get the reward.

At each training session, move the chairs a few more inches apart. Do not separate them so much that your cat is at risk of falling or injuring himself. Each cat has individual limitations. A cat that is old or overweight will not be able to jump as far as one that is young and/or in good condition.

Jumping onto Other Surfaces

Once Kitty is confident jumping from chair to chair, add other surfaces to his repertoire. Be sure to refrain from using tables or places that you are trying to teach your cat to remain off of. Be creative. Teach Kitty to jump onto the couch and from there come to you. Or have him jump from a chair to the couch to your lap. Yet another idea is to teach Kitty to jump from the back of a couch or chair onto your shoulder. There are other fun variations, but be warned, you might be turning

Keep reinforcing the training. Make the cat jump back onto the first chair.

Charles taught himself how to jump onto his human companion's shower stall.

Toy Rewards

Because of their predatory instincts, many cats learn equally well if you use a toy instead of food as a reward. This is especially true of well-fed cats who tend to be finicky. Choose a toy that appears most like the cat's natural prey, tease the cat until you get his attention, and then draw him into whichever behavior you wish to teach. When your cat achieves the criterion you set, let him catch his toy.

your cat into a real menace, for once cats begin to open their minds to learning it does not stop. One cat I know, Charles, has learned to peer in on his human companions as they shower. He was taught to jump from the toilet to the towel rack and onto the glass shower surround. Of course, he only does it when he hears the shower running. There's nothing like a cat watching you taking a shower!

RETRIEVING

If you are lucky enough to have a cat who likes to present you with his "catch," then you have a cat who will easily learn how to retrieve. Some cats leave presents for their humans. There have been many mornings when I have gotten out of bed and found pieces of a mouse, neatly arranged, very near where my feet fall onto the floor. Sometimes cats retrieve other items, as well. My Siamese, Ling Ling, loved soft curlers. Every morning she would drop one under my nose and meow in my ear until I threw the curler across the room just to get her to leave me alone. Seconds later the curler was dropped in front of my nose again. This was Ling Ling's lifelong favorite game. As long as she lived in my house I never slept late.

Feline games are based on a cat's nurturing instincts. In the wild they will hunt and return to their dens with food for their young. Apparently, several of my cats felt I needed looking after.

Realistically, these behaviors are merely a means of exercising instincts that are rarely used by a domestic cat. They will find ways to use whatever natural behaviors they have to enhance their lives. Training these cats to retrieve on command offers them a positive means of both using their natural instincts and creating a greater bond with their human companions. A cat that is trained to aid his physically-challenged human companion can also utilize this behavior. Granted, most cats cannot carry heavy objects, but they can retrieve a pen or keys. They can also be taught to push buttons that operate machinery. As therapy cats, the fetching behavior will entertain and brighten the lives of everyone they encounter.

TEACHING THE RETRIEVE

The best means of teaching a cat to fetch or retrieve on command is to use the clicker. This helps to quickly shape a behavior.

Begin by using your cat's most favorite toy. Play with him for a while. You can move the toy side-to-side, play peek-a-boo from behind an object, or dangle the toy in front of your cat; anything to get him involved in playing with the toy. Once you have his complete attention on the toy, throw it a short distance away. If he quickly goes to the toy to fetch it, click and offer his reward directly at the toy. If not, do the following:

1. Touch the toy with the target wand. When he goes for his treat on the wand, click and allow him to take his treat.

2. Repeat this two or three times.

3. Once Kitty goes to the target wand, use it to point at the toy, but do not load a treat in the spoon.

4. When Kitty searches the scoop of the spoon, make certain that he also touches his toy. As he does so, click and give him his treat.

5. Repeat this exercise, requiring more and more contact with the toy. For

Taking the Reward From the Target Wand

It is easy to teach your cat to take his treat from the target wand. Show your cat that his reward is in the spoon of the target wand. Allow him to sniff the wand and as he does so, click and allow him to take his treat. Repeat this at least three times so he learns that his treats come from the target wand.

As your cat learns to retrieve his reward from the wand, transfer some of his already learned behaviors to his targeting on the wand instead of targeting on your hand. For example, have him Come by moving backward as you hold the wand low to the ground. When he arrives, click, and allow him to take his reward. Gradually increase the distance. Use the target stick to tap on the chairs as you work with him jumping from chair to chair. The wand is great for teaching Kitty to move from one point to another and retrieving, but not as useful for specific behaviors such as Sit, Down, Stay, or Wave.

The target wand can be used to draw the cat's attention to any object you wish him to focus on.

The cat will learn to touch the toy without you having to touch it with the target wand.

example, on the first try, the cat may touch the toy by accident. The next time, don't click until he touches it again. Each time thereafter, click as the cat pays more and more attention to the toy, thus targeting on the toy instead of the wand. Your Kitty will learn to target where the wand points instead of on the wand itself.

6. Once Kitty is very reliable on going to the object and touching it, you need to "up the ante" to his having to actually pick up the toy prior to clicking and giving him his reward.

7. Gradually increase your goal to have Kitty pick up the toy and come back toward you prior to bridging the behavior. This may seem as though it will take some time to accomplish, but in actuality, it will most likely take less time for your feline to learn this behavior (especially if he's inclined to fetch anyway), than for you to learn these concepts of building a behavior through small steps.

Chuckie

One of my client's kitties, Chuckie, was taught to jump onto objects as well as Come and Sit up. He is one of four cats and two dogs and is not the most dominant animal in the household, merely the most interactive with others. Chuckie actually chose his own day to learn both the Down and Roll Over. He greeted me by coming to meet me at the door, then lying down, stretching out, and rolling over. He learned to perform these behaviors on command in less than 10 minutes.

He sometimes chose not to perform these behaviors when his human companions would work with him, so I instructed his people to ignore him and begin working with one of their other animals. Chuckie decided to demand their attention by first jumping onto the stairs, then jumping onto the banister and landing on a human's shoulder—a trick he taught himself. Chuckie wanted to return to training. And yes, he did perform the Down and Roll Over for his people for the remainder of his training session. He might've been persnickety but not stupid. Chuckie loved to perform.

Sometimes the best correction for a cat is to be ignored for a little while.

TWIRLING

The twirl trick is very easy to teach and can be done either on the floor or on a chair. It's similar to doing the Come command, only your kitty is following his target in a circle. What's really fun about this behavior is how you can add more and more twists and turns, with Kitty speeding up as he learns what to do.

Begin with Come and Sit. Get Kitty's attention on your target.

Guide his head around by bringing your target toward his rear end.

1. Have Kitty Come and Sit.
2. Show Kitty his target and bring the target from his nose to his tail. Tell your cat to "Twirl." As he brings his head around to touch the target, praise, click, and treat.
3. Each time you have Kitty target, make him turn a little more until he has made a complete circle.
4. After he is adept at twirling one time, add another circle. If Kitty gets confused with more than one twirl, then back up to fewer twirls between his bridge and reward. The last thing you want is for Kitty to lose interest in any of his tricks.

With Kitty knowing how to perform a Twirl, you can advance him to weaving through your legs while standing and then while walking. Again, it's a matter of pointing his target in the direction you wish him to move and rewarding him as he performs each increment correctly. Cats are so eager to perform and learn, that your feline is certain to pick up these behaviors quickly. It's not unheard of for a cat to learn how to Twirl in just a few minutes or to learn how to weave between your legs within one training session.

Each behavior your cat learns can be used as a building block toward a more advanced behavior.

Do not give Kitty his treat yet. Make him turn completely around, keeping the target near his tail.

Be sure to keep his target close to his nose, but don't allow him access, yet.

Once the circle is complete, give Kitty his reward.

45

Stay for Awhile

Do you live in an area where it is not safe for your cat to go outdoors? Maybe you live in a condo or apartment complex, or along a busy road. If you want your cat to remain in one place as you walk in or out of your home, you should teach him the meaning of Stay.

The Stay command is probably the most difficult behavior for a cat to learn. Granted, they often remain in one place for most of the day, but that is on their terms. It is a totally different thing for them to Stay when commanded.

While some cats will learn to remain in place by the mere suggestion of receiving a reward, others will need to be physically returned to the Stay position. This does not mean yanking or dropping the feline back into his spot, but by gently replacing him and rubbing him in a manner as to encourage him to attain the position in which he was told to remain. The moment you become heavy handed or try to force a cat to work is the moment the feline will refuse to perform anything at all. Cats must be coaxed and bribed. The only means of punishing a cat, as a form of negative reinforcement, is to ignore him.

THE SIT/STAY COMMAND

The Sit/Stay is a difficult behavior, and it should be broken down into small goals from a mere second or two to an incremental increase of time and distraction. This is called successive approximation—a gradual increase of the criterion as the cat learns each step of the exercise. Let's break down this behavior as follows:

1. The cat comes and sits.
2. Tell Kitty to stay, holding your hand in front of his face, palm facing him. Praise him the entire time he remains. This will encourage him to continue to stay in anticipation of receiving his reward.
3. Reward Kitty after he remains in place for a few seconds.
4. Repeat, gradually increasing his stay time.

Within a week or two, Kitty should be able to remain in a sit/stay for up to 30 seconds.

What to do if Kitty Will Not Remain in a Sit/Stay

No cat learns how to perform a Sit/Stay without having to be replaced at least a few times. How you do this depends greatly upon Kitty's personality. While some cats could care less about being picked up and replaced, others will become frightened, no matter how gently it's done.

Variations on the Sit/Stay

A fun way to incorporate the Sit/Stay with the other behaviors you have already taught your cat, is to have him perform his Sit/Stay in a chair or on the back of a couch, then call him to Come. Or, have him do a Sit/Stay on the floor and call him to Come to the raised surface. There are many ways you can change the parameters of Kitty's performance and you should never become bored. If you don't become bored, your cat won't either.

Begin with Come and Sit.

Place your palm in front of Kitty's face and tell him to Stay.

Your eager cat may try to grab the treat from you. Be patient and repeat the lesson as necessary.

Lure Kitty back into position, but don't give the treat until you bridge the behavior.

Begin all "returns" by luring Kitty with his reward. When he gets up, put his reward beneath his nose and lure him back into the same position, praising him as he returns. As he sits, again tell him to Stay. Be patient. Kitty may not have been ready to remain in a Sit/Stay for the length of time you requested. Sometimes it's best to regress a bit and build a solid Sit/Stay for a shorter amount of time and then to try to progress for a longer period. Constant correction will quickly turn off your cat's work drive.

The Stay command, combined with the visual signal, will let your cat know what you expect from him.

While teaching Kitty to Sit/Stay, be sure to add other behaviors into the mix. Do a Come and Sit. Practice the surface-to-surface jumping. Teach Kitty to go onto other surfaces. A chair or low table is also a great place to practice the Sit/Stay. Some cats learn how to sit/stay easier if the behavior is taught on an elevated surface. They are less likely to jump off the surface and move than if they are on the floor.

For a cat that does not mind being picked up or is of a dominating personality, you can physically lift and replace the cat where you told him to perform his Stay. Once he's back in place, put the visual cue for the Stay directly in front of his face, bringing it toward his nose as you give the Stay command. Kitty will push his weight onto his haunches as you are giving him the visual cue and will tend to remain in place, for a little while at least. Then, gradually begin increasing the time increments over a two-week period.

Kitty can remain in one place for upwards of 30 seconds it is time to begin distraction and distance proofing. Attaining this level of self-restraint can be

Stay, Salsa

One of the most enjoyable production jobs I have ever worked on was a television commercial for the Maryland Lottery. It starred an Australian Shepherd, Teddy, and featured an orange cat, Salsa. Salsa had to perform a Down/Stay. However, this Down/Stay had to be done outside, in an unfamiliar location with a camera dollying back and forth in front of him and cars going by behind the camera crew. If the director had let me know exactly where the cat would be filmed we might have had some acclimation time, but production personnel rarely think about these things and locations can be chosen at the spur of the moment. Luckily, Salsa is a very easygoing cat and nothing bothers him. Just to be on the safe side, I put him in a harness that was covered by his fur. I shoved the leash under a planter box that he was resting in front of. I placed one trainer to the side of the stair, to catch him if need be. When the camera was ready to roll, I told Salsa to Stay, and backed up to where I would be unseen by the camera but still in Salsa's eyeline. Throughout the filming, I praised him. Salsa was amazing. He had never before worked outdoors, nor in anything near this situation. He remained in place for at least twenty minutes. Moreover, he appeared relaxed. His eyes followed the camera, and his ears twitched around to catch the sounds of the many birds roosting in the trees overhead. This type of cat is one in a thousand.

difficult for most cats. It is best to remain patient and persistent, as well as always willing to regress a bit in order to insure a solid understanding of the behavior.

DISTANCE PROOFING

Let's begin with teaching your cat to remain in one spot as you move around him.

1. Have your cat Come and Sit. Reward him as soon as he sits.
2. Tell him to Stay, using the clear visual cue for the command.

Kitty will soon learn the visual cue for the Stay command. Once Kitty has learned the Sit/Stay, you can increase the time he spends in the position.

3. As Kitty remains sitting, shuffle side to side in front of him. Should he get up, either lure him back into place, or physically pick him up and replace him. Repeat the Stay command and visual cue, and then return to a few shuffles in front of him.
4. The next time you have Kitty perform a Sit/Stay, move around him. Move down both his sides. Never move in just one direction. Kitty must learn to remain where you told him to stay regardless of your motion around him.
5. After several training sessions you should be able to move completely around your cat as he remains in his Sit/Stay.

Once you and your cat have accomplished the movement portion of the Sit/Stay, it will be time to work on distance proofing. This is done gradually, similar to the manner in which you incrementally increased your movement around Kitty as he remained in a Sit/Stay. You must do it in a subtle manner. Don't suddenly move away from your cat and expect him to stay. Walk around him and gradually increase your distance as you move. Spiral out, with Kitty at the center of the spiral. As you near completion of the exercise, spiral back close. Most cats don't like to see someone coming directly at them, especially from a distance.

Begin slowly moving away from your cat as he remains in the Sit/Stay.

Working with your cat is a fun way to strengthen the bond between you. Make training time fun.

Praise your cat throughout the time that he is performing the Sit/Stay. You can never give out too many, "Good Kitties." When you return to your feline, release him from work and give him a treat.

Once Kitty is very reliable on the Sit/Stay, you can begin calling him to Come from that position. Don't always do this, however, or you might disrupt Kitty's ability to remain in a Sit/Stay as you move away. He'll be anticipating a reward upon arrival instead of performing what he was told to do, therefore popping up instead of staying in position. Vary the exercises as much as possible. This will ensure that your cat will wait for a command instead of going through the motions of a learned pattern.

Down and Stay

Now for the most difficult behavior to teach a cat. The Down/Stay. You might ask, "How difficult can this be for a cat that lies around all day, anyway?" Indeed, very difficult. The Down is a submissive position and unless your cat is extremely comfortable with all of his training and surroundings, he will be reticent about attaining a Down position. Either his reward must be really worthwhile, or he should be of the attitude that dominance or control is not important. That attitude is rare in a cat.

TEACHING THE DOWN/STAY COMMAND

There are several ways to lure a cat into a Down position, and I stress lure. Never use force, or your cat will not want to work for you for a while. Each step must be incremental, utilizing the successive approximation you have used with many of the other behaviors. Broken down into smaller parts, Kitty will quickly learn what you desire and be willing to perform.

Break the Down/Stay into the following steps:

1. Head Down
2. Crouching
3. Crouch with Belly Touching
4. Crouching with Legs Moving Forward
5. Lying on the Belly While Crouched
6. Lying in a Relaxed Position

Your cat will become alert and active when it is time for training.

Step #1: Head Down

1. Call your cat to Come and Sit. Have him do a Sit/Stay.
2. Place the treat on the floor, beneath the palm of your hand. Point to the treat with the index finger of your other hand. Tap the floor with that index finger to attain Kitty's attention.
3. As Kitty investigates the location of your tap, lift the hand that was over the reward and praise (click) as he retrieves his reward.
4. Repeat at least two more times, then go on to another behavior for a few minutes.
5. Return to luring Kitty's head toward the treat hidden beneath the palm of your hand. Each time he investigates, click/praise and allow him access to the reward.

You have now taught your cat to lower his head. Now, begin to pair the word Down with this action. Again, mix this behavior in with others so as not to bore your cat. Make certain that he receives lots of reinforcement for performing behaviors in which he is proficient. This encourages him to continue learning and prolongs his attention span.

> ### One Step at a Time
>
> *Successive approximation is the key to developing a behavior pattern, such as a Down or Stay. Each behavior needs to be broken down into small parts and taught incrementally, gradually increasing the criterion with each success of a minor behavior. In this manner, a behavior becomes very solid within a short period of time.*

Your cat will investigate the treat placed on the floor.

Step #2: Crouching

1. Lure Kitty to sniff at the treat hidden beneath your hand. If he does not immediately investigate, tap the floor with the index finger of your other hand, next to the treat.
2. This time, do not lift your hand and allow Kitty access to the reward until he has crouched. As he sniffs at the treat, he'll be trying to reach beneath your hand.
3. Allow him to shove his nose beneath your hand, but do not lift your hand and allow him access to the treat until his entire body has crouched. As he crouches, praise/click and give the reward.
4. Repeat a few times and then mix it into the other behavior patterns.

Step #3: Crouch with Belly Touching

1. Repeat the same steps as the previous exercise.
2. Don't give up the reward until Kitty is not only crouching, but his belly is touching the floor.

As soon as your cat reaches for the treat with either his paw or his nose, reward him by allowing him to retrieve his treat.

Step #4: Crouching with Legs Moving Forward

1. Require Kitty to move his legs toward the hand that is covering his reward. Many cats will do this naturally as a means of obtaining their treat.
2. As soon as your cat reaches for the reward with a paw, lift your hand and give him his reward as he is praised (and clicked).

Once Kitty is lying flat on the floor (on his stomach) give him the reward along with loads of praise.

Step #5: Lying on the Belly While Crouched

1. Hold off on the reward until Kitty settles into a crouched position, even if he's reaching for the treat with his paws.
2. As he lies flat on his belly, relaxing into a Down position, click/praise and give him his reward.

Step #6: Lying in a Relaxed Position

1. Tell Kitty to Down, as you point downward, similar to the gesture you made while tapping the floor next to the hidden treat.
2. As he crouches, praise him, but don't give him a reward.
3. Show him the reward close to his nose and make him turn his head. This will shift his weight to one side.
4. As his weight shifts, one of his hips will move beneath him. As this occurs, click/praise and give the reward.
5. Repeat this several times, only giving Kitty his reward when he is fully in this position. Then continue the training session by asking your cat to perform other behaviors.

Bring the cat's head back by having him target on the reward in your hand as you move your hand toward his shoulder.

DOWN/STAY

Having knowledge of a Sit/Stay will be beneficial in teaching your cat to perform a Down/Stay. The Down/Stay is merely adding another step to a behavior he already knows. Kitty will already know the gist of the word and visual cue, and you can apply the same cues to whatever position you request. The only difference is in how you return him into position.

When Kitty is comfortable in the Down position, you can have him perform the Stay.

As with the Sit/Stay, begin with a very short amount of time in the position. Gradually increase the amount of stay time as your cat becomes comfortable with the position.

In the beginning, keep his reward directly by his nose for the entire duration of the Down/Stay. This will entice Kitty to remain in position. Allow him to sniff at his reward, but do not give it to him until he has remained in the correct position for at least five seconds. This may sound like a short period of time to us, but it is a very long time when working a cat. The entire time your cat remains in position, praise him to encourage the good behavior.

Within a week of daily training sessions (10 minutes each, of course), Kitty should remain in position for upward of 30 seconds, with the reward directly beneath his nose the entire time. There will be times, however, when your cat will not wish to stay for any amount of time. This is where training the Down/Stay can become dicey.

With time and practice, your cat will learn the Down/Stay.

TRAINING TAKES TIME

If Kitty decides that he does not wish to perform, stop working with him. Ignore him for a while. Do something else. Fold the laundry. Do the dishes. Feed or walk another pet. This, in particular, will get Kitty's attention back onto training. Cats are notoriously jealous of other animals receiving attention when they wish to be the center of attention. A trained cat can be even worse about this. Remember when I mentioned that training a cat will not only teach him appropriate behavior and give him something to look forward to each day, but it will also create a monster? A trained cat that desires attention can become very inventive.

As Kitty learns to remain in the Down/Stay for upward of 30 seconds, begin to move side to side while he remains in place. If he should move, lure him back into position with the reward and praise him as he maintains the position. If he should continue moving, go back to remaining in front of him. Regress to progress.

Gradually increase the movement as you did with the Sit/Stay. First move side to side, then move around him, and finally increase your distance as you move around him. Of course, this should be done in small increments over a period of days, not within one 10-minute training session. Each step must be fully accomplished before continuing on to the next step. Otherwise, you are merely setting up yourself and your cat for frustrating, instead of productive, training sessions.

When working with a cat that is persistent about not wanting to remain in a Down/Stay, you can physically place him in a Down and tell him to Stay using your Stay hand signal. As with the Sit/Stay, pushing your visual cue toward his face will make him wish to remain for at least a few seconds. When he realizes that these few seconds were rewarding, he will gradually increase his response time.

Your persistence will pay off.

Let's Go for a Walk

Many cats enjoy being outside. Unfortunately, the outdoors can be dangerous for urban and suburban cats. To give your cat the opportunity to enjoy the outdoors, you must first teach him to acclimate to wearing a harness and walking on a leash. This really is not as difficult or time consuming as it might seem. You need only have this in mind as a goal from the beginning of your training.

THE HARNESS

You should try out several harness types and have your cat decide which one he can live with. There are many different types of cat harnesses. The figure 8 harness is very common, as is the typical step-through and snap harness. There's also a type that straps around the front legs. This type is actually the least likely to slip off your cat as he's putting forth most of his "escapist" effort at his front end. The strap harness is also easy to adjust with a sliding cylinder and is the harness of choice when working with a cat during an outdoor production.

The type of harness you use also depends upon its usage. You can use any type for walking your cat, provided your cat does not have the ability to get out of it and it does not choke him if he pulls hard. You don't want the harness fastened so tight that your feline is not comfortable. Make certain you can fit a finger beneath the strap all the way around.

Salsa

I used the leg strap harness during an outdoor filming of the Maryland Lottery television commercial in which Salsa, an orange tabby, had to perform a Down/Stay on the front step of a house. It was a location in which the cat was unfamiliar and there were squirrels and birds everywhere enticing him to chase them. In addition to this, the camera was mounted on a dolly with an entire film crew moving up and down the sidewalk in front of the house. Talk about distraction! I did not like the thought of leaving Salsa completely off lead in this situation, so we used a leg strap harness with the end hidden beneath a heavy potted plant. With me in front getting Salsa's attention, and one of my assistants beside the step, we managed to get some great footage for the commercial. Salsa appeared to be performing a Down/Stay without any visible restraint. The best part about the outcome was that Salsa did not move anyway, regardless of all the distraction. He remained where he had been told to perform his Down/Stay as the camera and crew dollied up and down the sidewalk.

Allow your cat to become accustomed to the harness before you attach a leash.

HARNESS TRAINING

Begin the acclimation process by allowing your kitty to wear the harness when he is lazing around the house. Allow him to work out the kinks and discomfort of the harness. Be certain to keep a close watch on him. You don't want him to hurt himself by trying to get it off.

When Kitty is comfortable in his harness, put him to work. This will teach him that great things happen while he wears his harness. Many cats will associate training time with wearing the harness. After going for a walk outdoors, your cat will be more than thrilled to put up with the restraints of a harness.

As your feline acclimates to wearing the harness, attach a lightweight leash and allow him to drag it around. At first he might play with it. (After all, it's a built-in chase toy.) Make certain he doesn't entangle himself too much. If you put him directly to work, Kitty will learn to ignore the leash much faster.

Reward your cat for adjusting to the harness and leash.

WALKING ON A LEASH

All leash walking should begin indoors, without distractions. It should also begin without you holding the leash. Allow the leash to drag behind your cat. As with all other behaviors, begin with the increments of only a step or two and gradually increase the amount of movement between stopping and reinforcing, adding turns and change of pace later. Your cat should become used to the weight and feel of the leash in a few training seasons.

1. Begin the training session with behaviors your cat enjoys performing, such as Come and Sit, Sit up, and Jumping from one surface to another.
2. When Kitty has performed several of behaviors successfully, have him Come and Sit.
3. Holding his reward in one of your hands, with that hand along your leg on the same side, (it doesn't matter which hand, provided you are consistent with using the same hand during initial leash training), step forward on that leg and command him to walk with you. I use the command, "Walk, walk." You can make up any word you wish provided you are consistent.
4. Move forward only two or three steps, praising Kitty as he follows along, nose to the reward.
5. Stop and click/praise and give him his reward.
6. Repeat, adding two or three more steps prior to stopping.
7. After your cat understands what is happening, have him sit when you stop walking. This will give him something to do upon stopping and teach him to wait for his next command. In order to maintain Kitty's attention, you need to keep him busy with a command directly after completing one. His attention span will gradually increase if his mind is kept stimulated. A bored cat will go elsewhere.
8. You can also begin to add other behaviors into the Walk. Have Kitty perform a Down along the way, or jump from surface to surface as you walk with him. There are many ways to vary the training, and the more you do so, the more thrilled you cat will be to perform.
9. As Kitty remains with you for a prolonged walk, begin to vary the pace and add turns.

Cats are very intelligent creatures and thrive on stimulation. If you do not offer this outlet your cat will find it elsewhere. Some cats will begin performing their learned behaviors to obtain your attention while you're busy slicing treats, relaxing, or doing housework.

Begin the session by having the cat do simple procedures.

Once Kitty has moved forward a few steps, give him his reward.

Have your cat Sit when you stop walking. It will reinforce his training.

Practice the off-leash walking for about a week, then pick up the leash and do the same exercises. At this point there should not be much difference between the leash dragging and you holding it. Be careful not to pull the leash at all while Kitty is working. The leash is there merely to ensure Kitty's safety while outdoors.

WALKING OUTSIDE

Prior to taking Kitty outdoors, make certain he is current on all vaccines and parasite preventives. Your cat is susceptible to bacteria and other contagions, more so outdoors than indoors. There will also be a higher risk of parasite infestation in a high population community, such as apartment buildings, condos, and town

When your cat has mastered walking on a leash, you can take him outside for walks.

homes, than if you lived in a single family home where you diligently control the parasite population. Inhaling the urine or ingesting the feces of another animal can also cause illness. Another consideration, mostly in the parasite control zones, is the chance of accidental poison ingestion. Your cat could eat grass that has been treated with insecticide or eat a piece of an animal carcass that was killed with poison.

Regardless of where you live and where you will be walking your cat, be responsible about keeping him up-to-date on all vaccinations he needs to remain free of disease and infestation.

Be Aware

Keep a close watch on what your cat is doing while you walk with him. Should he try to eat grass, steer him away from it. Providing cat grass in your home should be sufficient to satisfy his need to eat vegetation. Should he sniff garbage or try to eat a carcass, again steer him away and redirect his attention. As you walk, steer your cat away from low bushes, gutters, and other areas that you cannot easily access. Cats will aim for dark, closed-in areas, where they might feel safer. They will also head for enticing smells, such as rodent lairs or dead birds.

Although you cannot keep your cat in a plastic bubble the entire time you have him outdoors (if that is your desire he should not go outside at all), make certain that you and he are prepared for the experience.

Walking on the leash outdoors will be very different from walking indoors. There are many distractions. The distractions will take Kitty's mind away from everything he's learned. He won't care about his rewards. He won't care about his training. His mind will be on the sights and sounds around him.

> ### Walking Safety
>
> Make sure you keep a close eye on your cat while you're walking. Sudden distractions such as cars, dogs, or birds could startle your cat. Start out slow with short walks in quiet, deserted locations until your cat feels comfortable on his leash.
>
> Turning these walks into a daily routine will give Kitty something to look forward to each day.

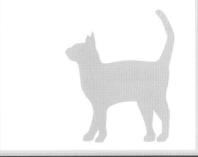

Instead of becoming frustrated with trying to have him listen to your commands, allow him a bit of acclimation time. This can take upward of eight outdoor excursions. Be patient.

Start Out Slow

Try to introduce Kitty to the outdoors by starting in a quiet, fenced-in area. If you live in a community, you might want to get to the tennis court before anyone else, or walk your cat in a fenced back yard. A fenced-in area will be an extra precaution against your cat escaping from the harness and getting into trouble. Once your cat becomes more comfortable with the outdoors and does not try to get free of his harness, you can begin going for walks anywhere. Be certain to gradually increase the distractions, don't suddenly go into a high traffic area.

When Kitty pulls on the leash, you will be tempted to pull back. Don't fall into this trap. Your cat will be able to back out of his harness, regardless of the type. Instead, pick up your cat and place him a few feet away from

Start by taking walks in fenced in, quiet areas, such as the back yard or a park.

where he adamantly wished to go. Coax him to move with you by making kissing noises or by slapping your leg. If he's really hungry, food might regain his attention.

Your cat needs to learn to walk with you instead of you walking with him. As you blaze the direction, he should relax and watch the sights as you walk by. If you must guide him with the leash, use a gentle tug and release. There's really no word to use as a correction, other than "Uh-huh," or "Psst." There is no actual physical correction. A physical correction would only work against your goals, for a cat tends to shut down and not move if physically corrected during training.

Keep in mind that Kitty must enjoy what he is doing or he won't do it. Most felines don't perform to please their human companions. Cats perform because it's something they enjoy. And, yes, they do enjoy your praise and the rewards they receive. This is the true independence of cats. Domestic cats, being lone predators, normally rely only on themselves to obtain food and shelter, not on social activities to maintain a cohesive group for survival as with canines and humans.

Make certain that you have fun on your walks. It should be a happy time for both of you.

> ## Walks Can Be Fun!
>
> *Be patient yet consistent when you walk with your cat. There are lots of distractions outside. Make your walks a fun experience and your cat will enjoy them. Once Kitty acclimates to one place, try another. Each adventure will be a new challenge, fully enjoyed by you and your cat.*

Fun in a Flash

Cats can learn almost anything. The only thing limiting your feline's learning is your imagination. There are many ways to stimulate your cat and you can discover new ones by watching television or a movie that features felines. With your current knowledge of cat training, I bet you can figure out how some of those behaviors were taught. Most cat trainers work the same way—with operant conditioning techniques, using praise, reward, and/or a clicker.

Each final behavior has been broken down into smaller goals, which in turn lead to that behavior. This procedure is used for every "trick" that someone teaches a feline. And, from what you've seen in using the exercises previously mentioned in this book, cats learn faster than most people think, but they must want to learn. Presented in a manner that is both understandable and fun, cats can accomplish any goal their human companions wish—provided, that is, the cat has the propensity for the behavior in the first place.

Were you aware that most of the felines you see gracing the silver screen are doubles for each other? It can take up to eight cats to fulfill every aspect of a specific role. This is because each cat has its own proclivity for specific behaviors. It is indeed a rare cat who can perform everything, in every circumstance. Some cats are couch potatoes. Some love to jump. Others enjoy performing specialized tricks.

Don't be disturbed by your cat not wishing to perform a specific trick. He may not have the interest. However, he's sure to like something else, so don't stop working with him. If he enjoys lazing around, have him do a lot of Stays, Sit/Stays, and Down/Stays. If he enjoys playing, he might like to learn how to retrieve or jump from place to place. A very active cat will like the following tricks: rolling over, weaving through your legs, ringing a bell, or climbing a ladder. He might also enjoy learning how to

Cats can be trained to do almost anything – even work with other "animal actors."

jump onto your lap or shoulder. Your sedate feline would possibly enjoy giving a kiss. Your very friendly and vocal kitty could quickly learn to speak on command.

FUN TRICKS FOR THE ACTIVE CAT

Each of the following tricks are merely extensions of the behaviors Kitty has already mastered. At this point he should know how to Sit, Lie Down, Stay, Come, Sit-up, Jump onto a surface, and how to go to a target on command.

Begin by sitting on a chair and tapping your leg to obtain the cat's attention.

Each of these are foundations to the advanced behaviors described in this chapter. Be sure to reinforce the behaviors your cat has already learned before moving on to more advanced tricks.

Jump Onto Your Lap

Once Kitty has learned to jump onto a chair, this trick is very easy. You simply sit in the chair and use the same cues. Your cat will learn quickly. Make certain you wear something covering your legs when teaching this trick. The last thing you want are scratches on your legs when your cat lands on you. Cats prefer a stable landing zone. Once knocked or tumbled off of you, he may not want to try again. Keep your feet flat on the floor and have a few treats in your hand.

1. Sitting in your chair, tap your leg and tell your cat to "Come, Up."

2. If he hesitates, show him the treat and lure him to you with it.

Since Kitty already knows to Come to wherever you tap, he will soon be on your lap.

3. As you tap, again tell him to "Come, Up."

4. When he arrives on your lap, praise (click) and give him his treat.

5. Repeat this at least four times throughout your training session mixed in with other behaviors.

Jump Onto Your Shoulder

After Kitty is proficient in jumping onto your lap, it is time for him to learn how to jump onto your shoulder.

Dominick

An eccentric, but good cat trainer named Dominick, works at the Sunset Festival in Key West, Florida. He is quite a character and impresses crowds with how well his cats perform. Each of his performances last about twenty minutes and involve three to six cats at a time. The younger, inexperienced cats begin by hanging out in the same area as the performing cats. The key techniques he uses, other than taking the cats into that environment on a daily basis, is food reward, and verbal and visual cues. A person watching can scarcely understand Dominick's words, which are spoken with a thick Creole accent, but the cats understand him clearly. The only words that come through well enough for most onlookers to hear are, "Hurry up, Take Your Time." He says this while the cats are weaving through his legs. His voice lilts upwards as he says, "Hurry up." and is softer as he says, "Take your time." The tone is soothing for the many cats that jump through hoops, hang onto his chest as he runs around in circles, sit on his shoulder for photographs, and catch their treats out of the air. With the numerous stray cats living in Key West, Dominick's source of felines is unlimited. He has taken unwanted cats and given them a job and loving care.

1. Begin with having Kitty "Come, Up" to a high surface, such as the back of the couch or top of a bookcase.
2. Place your shoulder close, so that he can easily step onto it.
3. Put his reward on your shoulder near your neck and tap next to it with your finger.
4. As Kitty reaches for the reward, praise him (and click).
5. Repeat until Kitty is comfortable stepping completely onto your shoulder to retrieve his reward.
6. Next, increase the distance between you and the high surface. To start, go only a few inches away, so your cat can still easily step onto you, but must leave the high surface in order to retrieve his reward.
7. Gradually increase this distance over the period of several days or training sessions, until your shoulder is a foot away. You probably will not want to increase this distance much more than a foot, for Kitty might feel insecure in the leap to use his claws upon landing.

You can, however, practice this trick from several different "high surfaces." Instead of a bookcase, try using the high back of a chair or

Lure Kitty to your shoulder using the food reward.

Once you have Kitty's attention, move the food in front of your shoulder.

Hold very still when Kitty puts his front feet on your shoulder.

couch or the top of the television or a bureau. Each new surface you work with is new stimulation for your precocious feline. Be warned again, though, that teaching your feline tricks like these can turn him into a monster. When he wants attention from you he may jump onto your shoulder or back to demand you work with him.

Begin with a simple Down/Stay command.

Play Dead and Roll-Over

These tricks can only be taught if your cat is very comfortable performing a Down/Stay. He should be at the point where he will lay on his side instead of crouching. You also need to have a cat that is very relaxed when working. This is a great trick for the lazy cat, but slightly more difficult for the hyper cat, especially one that is easily distracted.

Each portion of these tricks needs to be broken down into minute goals. The first goal is for Kitty to lie on his side and look toward his hip. The second, for Kitty to twist his front end around. The third, for Kitty to shift onto his back and Play Dead. To maintain the Play Dead trick, have your Kitty perform a Stay while in that position. Merely, tell him Stay at the right time. To continue with the Roll-over, go on to the fourth step of luring him all the way to his other side. The final step is for Kitty to do

Move Kitty's head around the same way you did as you were relaxing him onto his side, by moving his target toward his shoulder.

the entire movement and end up crouched and ready for his next trick. Let's break it down into steps:

1. Make certain you have a reward that is very good. Use a piece of freeze-dried liver, tuna, chicken, or anything Kitty goes really bonkers over. Moving onto his back into a passive, submissive position will not be easy, especially for a dominant cat. The reward must be worth it.

2. Have Kitty perform a Down/Stay.

3. As soon as he receives his reward for this behavior, bring his treat/target toward his hip. As his head follows the target, praise and reward him.

4. The next time you try this, ask for more head movement before bridging and giving the reward. Make your cat twist his body a bit, or twist and lift a leg. You know your cat better than anyone. If he tends to shy away from performing something if he doesn't receive immediate gratification, go a little slower with your requirements.

Request a little more movement onto his back before giving him his reward.

5. Have Kitty follow the treat all the way around. Keep the treat centered around his hips so that he must reach back with his head. This will help balance him as he rolls over.

6. As soon as he has completed the Roll-Over, bridge (praise/click) and give him his reward.

7. Do this a few times while working on other exercises.

Allow Kitty to grab at your hand. It will help him onto his back.

8. When Kitty is proficient in rolling over from one side to the other, have him roll over and get up again. You need to refrain from bridging and rewarding until you coax him into a Sit position as you give the sit command. However, praise him along the way to encourage the behavior.

9. Another variation is to teach your cat to roll over several times in succession. Begin with one time, and then when he is proficient, move on to two times. He will learn this quickly as he already knows the command.

As soon as he completes his Roll-Over, praise him profusely and give him his treat.

Weave Through Legs

This trick can be done either while you stand still or while you walk. Begin the training process with standing still. Make certain you have very good balance prior to trying it as you walk.

Weaving through your legs is a great trick to impress your family and friends, and to stimulate your cat. Proceed as follows:

1. Show Kitty his target. Praise him when he touches it.
2. Move his target around your legs as you say "Weave."
3. As Kitty follows the target a short distance, stop, praise/click and give him his reward.
4. Gradually increase the movement around your legs, always bridging and giving Kitty his reward for each increment of the overall behavior. Most likely, Kitty will learn this trick quickly for he already knows the basic premise of the entire behavior. He knows how to Come. He knows how to walk with you. He'll easily follow a target around your legs.

You can vary the exercise by having him sit or lay down at certain points.

Your cat will weave and rub up against you.

Guide the cat through your outstretched legs with his target in front of him.

81

Throw in a Roll-Over, or a Sit-up. The more you add to each exercise the more your cat will be stimulated. Cats hate doing the same old thing.

As you add your movement into the training, be sure to begin slowly. Do only one or two steps, and gradually add steps as Kitty becomes proficient. You will need to watch where you walk, because Kitty will be weaving around your feet, and the last thing you want is to frighten or hurt your cat by stepping on him while training.

Once he's through your legs, bring him around one of them.

Ring a Bell

Once your cat knows this trick, be sure to put want him to ring it. He will have the bell away when you don't learned that there is a positive outcome to having the bell move and make noise, making him desire to continue with this behavior. Did you actually think that you were teaching him to ring the bell on command, or teaching him how to ring the bell to obtain your attention? Cats are very intelligent and will easily figure out how to elicit a desired response from their human companions.

Put some tuna oil on the bell and bring the bell to Kitty's nose so that he can discover the great smelling bell.

Urge the cat to interact with the bell by having him do an Up exercise near it.

1. Hang a large jingle bell or medium sized cowbell from a doorknob.
2. Spread some tuna oil upon the bell and tap it with your fingertip. When Kitty goes to investigate the bell, praise/click and allow him to lick the oil off the bell.
3. As the bell makes noise, praise/click and give the cat a piece of tuna or other reward.
4. Once he gets the idea, add the words, "Ring the Bell," as you tap. Within a few training sessions, Kitty will be going to the bell upon your point and command. He will ring the bell when it's time to eat dinner or when he feels it's time to do a training session, or just to get some attention from you.

Reward your cat when he goes to the bell on his own to sniff at it.

Climb a Ladder

This trick is as simple as having your
Kitty come to you. The ladder is
merely a new surface on which he
must become used to. Cats love to
climb, so once Kitty gets the idea of
how to move along
the ladder, climbing
it will be lots of fun.
Most barn cats learn
this very quickly as they hunt
through lofts for rodents and
barn swallows. Being
fond of high perches,
felines search for ways
to tower above their environments, so teaching
Kitty to climb a ladder might help prevent his

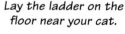

Lay the ladder on the floor near your cat.

climbing the curtains. You'll be inadvertently directing him to climb at an
accepted location.

As with all new behaviors, even one that
changes the process in a minor way, begin with
small increments.

1. Lay the ladder on its side on the floor.
2. Put some treats around the ladder,
   praising/clicking Kitty as he finds each one.

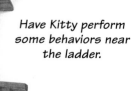

*Have Kitty perform
some behaviors near
the ladder.*

The cat will investigate the obstacle as he receives his reward.

3. Give him a few days to become comfortable with the ladder structure. This is best done by leaving the ladder in an area where Kitty spends a lot of his time.

4. Do a few training sessions near the ladder.
   Some cats will instantly accept the ladder's presence, while others take a few days to acclimate to the new object. Never rush this process, or your cat will never be comfortable working with it.

5. Do some Sit and Down/Stays near the ladder.

6. Have Kitty cross over the ladder as he performs his Come.

Prop the ladder up at an angle and have the cat Come to you.

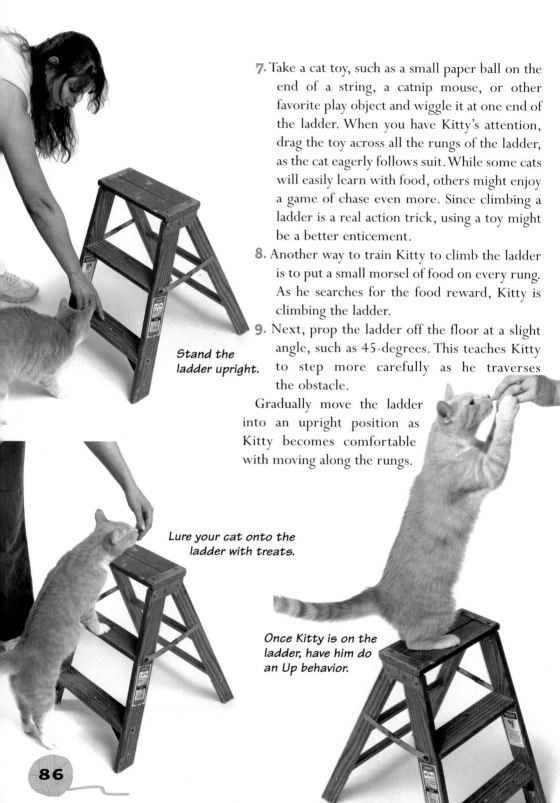

7. Take a cat toy, such as a small paper ball on the end of a string, a catnip mouse, or other favorite play object and wiggle it at one end of the ladder. When you have Kitty's attention, drag the toy across all the rungs of the ladder, as the cat eagerly follows suit. While some cats will easily learn with food, others might enjoy a game of chase even more. Since climbing a ladder is a real action trick, using a toy might be a better enticement.

8. Another way to train Kitty to climb the ladder is to put a small morsel of food on every rung. As he searches for the food reward, Kitty is climbing the ladder.

9. Next, prop the ladder off the floor at a slight angle, such as 45-degrees. This teaches Kitty to step more carefully as he traverses the obstacle.

Gradually move the ladder into an upright position as Kitty becomes comfortable with moving along the rungs.

Stand the ladder upright.

Lure your cat onto the ladder with treats.

Once Kitty is on the ladder, have him do an Up behavior.

TRICKS FOR THE SEDATE, QUIET CAT

Even though the sedate, lazy cat prefers to lie around, he can still learn some very fun tricks. These do not involve any activity other than some head movement, so they should not disrupt his sleep cycle at all. These tricks will also be fun for active kitties. There's no limit to the amount of tricks you can teach your cat. Who knows, what was once a couch potato may turn into an active feline. All he needed was something to do!

Speak on Command

This trick only works on a very verbal cat. Many of the oriental breeds have a tendency to voice their opinions and call out for companionship. However, the average tabby can also discover that being verbal has its rewards. One of my cats, Crockett, a large English Tabby, would always call out to me when I arrived home or when he wished to find me. He would demand attention or verbalize because he was happy or because he wanted some training. If I ignored his rubbing and meowing he would take a paw and hook it around my arm, physically forcing me to touch him.

Every cat has his or her own trademark sound. Crockett had a "meownck;" another cat of mine, Kudzu, had a little "mew," (hence her nickname Little Moo—she was a small, round black cat) while yet another, Bodie, had a soft "meh meh," which is

A sedate cat can learn many tricks.

Some vocal breeds of cat can be taught to speak on command.

very funny considering he was a very large cat. My Siamese, Blueberry, has a very loud meow. He's always calling out to me if we're not in the same room. If your Kitty likes to call out to you to either welcome you home or desire attention, he can learn how to speak on command.

Starting Out

Begin by having Kitty's favorite rewards handy. Whenever he speaks for his own reasons, pair his action with the word "Speak" and give him his reward. As bright as your Kitty is, he will quickly associate the reward with his action. Only be warned, you might incite your feline to become even more talkative. Rewarding any behavior will increase the desire to exhibit that behavior.

You may also want to teach your cat how to be quiet on command. This is not done by removing the reward if your feline speaks when you request him too, but with your redirecting his attention onto something else when you wish him to stop talking. Redirection is always a positive means of curing a bad or unwanted behavior.

Cats are more than couch potatoes. They can get bored easily.

Teaching Toilet Training

This is a cute trick, but think carefully if you'd like to share your commode with your feline, especially if it is the only toilet in your home. If you are bothered by people who leave the seat dirty, don't flush, or worse yet, those who flush too much, you may not want to toilet train your cat. Once a cat learns this trick, it's tough to get him to stop.

Place Kitty's litter box near the commode.

Over a period of several weeks, gradually increase the amount of large books under the box until your cat becomes used to them.

Reward the cat when he uses his box.

Make toilet training fun by adding some training tricks.

However, if you insist you'd rather deal with occasional misdeeds on the toilet than a messy kitty litter box, here goes:

1. Place Kitty's litter box in the washroom next to the commode.
2. Put a toilet seat over his litter box.
3. Over the course of several weeks, gradually increase the height of the litter box until it approximates the same height as the commode. By this time, Kitty may be crossing over to use the actual commode, as it is the same height and shape of his litter box. If not, there are trays specifically manufactured to toilet train cats. They slip under the seat cover and you can put a shallow layer of kitty litter in them to promote their usage, as cats prefer to cover their deposits. Once Kitty learns to flush, however, you may no longer need the tray, for he'll see how easy it can be to cover his deposit with water.
4. As Kitty begins to use the actual commode, take away the litter box entirely.

You will always need to give Kitty access to the washroom and leave the toilet cover up, otherwise you'll be left with a nasty surprise, or a feline that is hopping from foot to foot when you get home, crying to be let into the washroom.

Reward your cat as he explores the commode.

Other cats can watch and learn.

Flushing

Flushing can be taught in several ways.

1. Begin by dangling an attractive toy off the lever.
2. Entice Kitty by swinging the toy from side to side until he grabs hold and pulls, thereby flushing the toilet.
3. When he flushes, he should receive a lot of praise and a special reward.

Teaching Kitty to flush will prevent unwanted surprises in the washroom.

Through observation of Kitty's potty times and following through with enticing him to play with the dangling toy, Kitty will learn to flush on his own.

Another means of teaching Kitty to flush is through target training. You can either teach Kitty to pull on a dangling toy (on command, not at his whim) or to actually step on the lever and press. This is done through the same successive approximation methods used on many of the

Hanging a toy from the lever will attract Kitty into performing the behavior.

behaviors you've already taught your Kitty.

1. Begin by having him touch the lever with his paw by having him target on it.
2. When he moves toward the lever, praise him.
3. If he actually touches the lever, give him lots of praise (a click) and

reward. Each time hold out the bridge (praise) until he moves closer to the lever with his paw.

4. Once he touches the lever with his paw, praise him enthusiastically, click and give a reward.

5. You'll need to teach him to press down on the lever, so you'll need to successively increase the criterion to him putting his body over his paws in order to put weight behind the pressure.

Be forewarned that the sudden flush of the toilet might cause Kitty to race off. Be certain that you have prepared him by having him in the washroom as you've flushed the toilet. Always reward him if he remains nearby when the sound of the flush occurs. The combination of receiving reinforcement when he hears the whoosh, as well as the praise as he pushes the lever, will teach Kitty to clean up after himself.

Teach your cat to give you a kiss.

Give a Kiss

Many cats will eagerly kiss their human companions. Felines are very clean animals and strive to maintain clean coats and a clean environment. This includes making certain those who touch them are also clean. Some cats like to lick their people while being petted. This is their way of getting you in on the grooming game and is similar to their licking a paw and brushing it against their coat. Other cats like to lick the salt or food particles from your skin. Yet others, who remain kittens at heart, will suckle on an ear lobe or chin. Licking is a relaxing behavior, demonstrating affection and togetherness. It will be easy to associate this behavior with a food or petting reward.

1. Place some tuna oil on the area where you would like Kitty to kiss such as your lips and cheeks.
2. Tap the area as you say "Come."
3. When Kitty arrives, continue tapping and say, "Give kisses."
4. As Kitty licks up the oil, praise and reward.

You can change the kiss location at will simply by putting the tuna oil on a different place such as on your arm or cheek.

Oh, Behave!

There is tons of information in bookstores, libraries, and on the Internet that expounds on how to cure common feline behavioral problems. I will not rehash what has already been published ad nauseam. Instead, I will mention that training your cat is the key to overcoming any type of behavior problem that might occur. There are no quick fixes or miracle pills. An animal psychologist may be able to suggest a short-term cure that may or may not work over the long term.

There are many ways of gradually overcoming a problem; going out of your way to change a routine, for example, or adding barriers to prevent access to certain areas. Because you've decided to read a book titled *Cat Training in 10 Minutes,* I'm guessing that you're searching for something that will work quickly both for short- and long-term results. Unfortunately, with most behavior problems, this is not a realistic expectation.

Good Cat?

Regardless of how you go about overcoming bad habits, training your feline is a sure thing. You won't get far doing things halfway. Cats live by the "All or None" rule. They are either allowed to do something all of the time or none of the time. They don't understand the "gray" areas of sometimes, maybe, or "I'm wearing my nice clothes so you can't." Granted, when you're not home anything can happen. The trick will be to condition Kitty to the point where he has more fun being good than bad. He gets more attention when he behaves than when he misbehaves.

The most important rule to live by is to catch your cat doing something right. Cats may have great memories and the ability to reason, but correcting them after the behavior has been enacted will rarely lead to a cure, and may lead to worse behavior. It is more effective to catch the cat in the act and then redirect the behavior into something positive. Cats aren't stupid. They know when a behavior leads to a positive outcome. They will strive for that outcome instead of your negative reaction. A feline only repeats a bad behavior if that is the only time he gets any reaction out of you. Cats are not as independent as most people believe. They think of us humans as interactive toys as well as food dispensers. They can train a person faster than in 10 minutes a day. All it takes is one desired reaction to a specific behavior and they have your number.

CORRECTING IMPROPER BEHAVIOR

And how, do you ask, is the cat corrected when he's doing something bad? First, our human emotions must be held in check. They won't work. Yelling, hitting, charging, and swearing are not in the Kitty lingo. Instead, use feline language. How do cats display displeasure or anger? They hiss and spit. When your Kitty is in the process of relieving himself in your potted plant, or lapping at the uncovered butter on the counter (which shouldn't be left there anyway), try hissing at him while squirting him with a water pistol. There you go. You've hissed and spit!

When you see Kitty relieving himself in his box, or stretching his claws on a scratching post, praise and reward him. If Kitty crosses the room on the floor instead of the counters or tables, praise and reward him. When Kitty plays with you without using his claws or teeth, praise and reward him.

You get the picture.

There are many ways to redirect improper behavior. Conditioning Kitty into appropriate behavior should go hand in hand with making certain he does not have access to the "bad" thing when you are not around. For example, should you work away from home, you might want to confine Kitty in a room where he does not have access to the object of his inappropriate behavior. When you are home, keep an eye on him and, should he try to do the "bad" thing use the Kitty correction and guide him to the appropriate behavior, which results in praise and rewards. Through consistency, praise, and guidance, the correct behaviors will replace the wrong behaviors.

Scratching Furniture

Be certain to always provide an appropriate scratching tool, such as a scratching post, or two. For the very adamant feline furniture redesigner, cover the torn areas with netting, aluminum foil, or sticky tape. Felines hate the feel of these objects on their paws. When Kitty heads for the furniture, presumably to have a nail stretch, ask him to do a Come to the scratching post. When he arrives praise/click and reward. To further his interest, coax his front feet onto the post by luring him with the treat. As soon as his front feet touch the post, praise/click and reward. Each time ask for more action with his front feet before offering him his bridge and reward. Within a short time, Kitty will be scratching at the post, on command, because he gets more out of doing it there than on your furniture. Within a short time, he'll be going to the post for his own sheer pleasure.

Using the Litter Box

There are many reasons why a cat might avoid using a litter box. He might not wish to use his box because it's not clean enough or he may not like the type of litter or box that you made available to him. Kitty might not like sharing his box with other cats, or his food may be too close to the box. If you have tried to correct all these things, still without results, then do the following:

A sturdy scratching post can also be a fun toy.

97

Regardless of the reason, be aware of where Kitty is at all times. When you're not home, he needs to be confined in a small area with his box, food, and water. While you are home, keep an eye on him. Should he start to relieve himself in the wrong area, hiss and spit.

Throughout this process, be sure to show him that his litter box is the right place to be by making it positive. Lure him there by doing the Come command. Have your cat remain in the litter box by requesting him to Sit/Stay or Down/Stay. (Yes, he can do tricks while in the box.)

Watch him while he is in his small enclosure. When you see him relieving himself in his box, praise/click and reward. This positive reaction to his going to the proper potty area will encourage him to continue to do so. Always praise and reward him any time he does the correct behavior. This will strengthen Kitty's desire to perform.

When he has become reliable with going to his box both when you are away (in his enclosure) and when you are home, then gradually increase his free time while you are gone. Begin with a short trip to the store and gradually increase the time, within a period of several weeks to a month, to include your workday. (Also, see Toilet Training, pages 88-92.)

This entire process should not take much time out of your day. The only things you'll need to concern yourself with are making certain Kitty is confined when you are not home and keeping an eye on him when you are home. What can be more entertaining than playing with and observing your cat?

Walking on Counters and Tables

Cats love to laze around in high places. Searching for food on counters is extra fun, too. Not only does Kitty get to be somewhere high off the floor, but he is being rewarded for doing so. Did you leave the butter out again? How about that turkey dinner cooling on the counter? Nothing on the counter is safe from a cat that counter surfs.

Cat ownership does not mean having to constantly deal with cat hair and paw prints on eating surfaces. Your climber can easily learn to avoid these areas by your providing appropriate high resting areas. A window bed, for example, can be very comfortable for Kitty. Not only will he be up high, but will be able to watch the outdoors as well. Some kitty condos are built high enough to reach a ceiling. These, too, will provide a means of peering at the world below.

Having taught Kitty to jump from one spot to another, you have also given him an outlet for his desire to leap from place to place. He now does this behavior on command. You can easily acclimate him to a window bed or kitty condo in the same manner that you taught him to jump. Again, you will be redirecting him away from the inappropriate behavior to something both stimulating and rewarding.

And what to do if you catch him on the counter? Hiss and spit! Always follow through by coaxing him to the correct place for his activities and rewarding him when he does so. Be careful not to fall into a pattern, however. Some cats become very wise to a pattern of obtaining your attention by doing something inappropriate, only to be rewarded when redirected. Felines aren't stupid. Far from it. That is why you need to break up the pattern and not fall into Kitty's trap. Do different things at different times of the day.

Catch Kitty doing something right and reward him for that. Whatever it is.

Train your cats to stay off the counter. Training your cat to obey a simple command will end this unwanted behavior.

Cats in Our Lives

In historical times, cats were revered by the Egyptians and throughout the Old World they functioned as controllers of rodent populations, companions, and bodyguards. Cats have been mummified to accompany their former human companions into the afterlife and presented in paintings as family members. Not much has changed since those times. Cats still perform these tasks and more.

Although most felines aren't much more than home adornments, they can be useful members of our society. They not only rid farms, ships, and homes of pests, but also aid the physically and emotionally challenged. From their use in nursing homes to lift the spirits of the residents, to alerting a hearing impaired person of a ringing telephone or doorbell, cats live up to the challenge.

In the latter part of the 20th century, cats were larger than life in theaters and on television. Their antics grab our attention. From those runaway Siamese of the *Homeward Bound* movies to the world-dominating cats of *Dogs and Cats,* these wondrous creatures play upon our emotions.

WORKING CATS

One doesn't have to belong to the Delta Society or any other animal therapy club in order to bring happiness to others. You need only check with the institutions in your area. And, if allowed, arrange a time to share your Kitty. You'll make the day of the elderly or ill when they see your well-trained feline. (I guarantee they'll be talking about your cat long after you've left.) Having made the day brighter for so many, you and cat are sure to be welcomed back with open arms. Not only will you feel good for helping these people, but Kitty will adore all the special attention.

Cats are also making their place in the pet assistance world. Although most people don't realize it, cats are just as capable as dogs of helping the physically

Farm Cats

Do you feel sorry for cats that live outdoors on farms? Don't. They're probably the happiest cats in the universe. They have freedom of movement to hunt or play. Most receive loving care from their owners, including all the necessary vaccines, flea prevention, and attention. Who wouldn't adore a cat that kept their facility free of rodents? This is the core of the feline purpose; why they have been part of human society for thousands of years. Yes, it's true there are people who don't give appropriate care to their barn cats. If this is the case, the cats need to be relocated to homes where they will be given better care. It is wrong to allow feral cat colonies to breed and infect others in the farm environment or nearby homes solely because of the lack of interest or ignorance on the part of the owner. However, I have seen some very happy barn cats living, and working on farms all over the world.

Farm cats receive lots of love and care from their owners.

challenged. They may not be able to pull a wheelchair or steady someone on their feet, but they can alert someone to a ringing doorbell or telephone. They can also fetch lightweight objects such as pencils, keys and utensils. Just like dogs, felines thrive on having a purpose.

FELINE ADOPTION

If you already have one cat living in your home, you may want to adopt a friend for your feline companion. Consider adopting a cat from a rescue organization or animal shelter. Many animal shelters have purebred as well as mixed breeds of cats and kittens awaiting a good home. You can choose the breed, sex, and age of the cat you wish to adopt, and most cats in shelters have already been spayed or neutered. Moreover, you will be instrumental in saving a feline life or two, for you not only save the life of

Adoption

Cat breeders will always be able to sell their kittens, but you'll find just as much love from an adopted kitty and have the satisfaction of knowing you saved a life. Keep in mind that some of the best feline actors and company representatives such as 9 Live's Morris the Cat, were adopted strays.

All cats that live in rescue/foster residences must learn to get along with each other, especially during mealtimes.

Blueberry

I recently took in a beautiful stray. He's a Blue Point Siamese I named Blueberry. Blueberry had been a stray for several months, and was hanging out in one of my client's neighborhood. My client was telling me that a stray cat distracted her dog whenever she walked him. As I'm always looking to find homes for homeless animals, I asked about the cat. As she described the stray, my eyes lit up. I grew up with Siamese cats. I hadn't had a Siamese for most of my adult life and desired one for production work. Blueberry turned out to be a purebred Siamese, neutered, friendly, and extremely intelligent. He learned more behaviors in five days than most animals learn in five years.

The moral of this anecdote is that you, too, can find the cat of your dreams by adopting a homeless kitty. Every cat has the potential for greatness.

the cat you adopt, but you open up a space in that rescue organization's foster home for another cat.

Most feline rescue organizations and shelter are very careful about where their cats will live when adopted. Volunteers will do home checks. After all the time, money and care they've given a cat, they want to be certain the cat will be going to a good and permanent home. When filling out an adoption application, don't be surprised if they ask about your financial situation or family activities. The people who have cared for the cat know much about his personality and have a good idea if the cat will adjust to a specific situation. For example, if the cat tends to use his claws when playing, he should not be placed in a home with young children. Or, if the cat dislikes other cats, he should not go to a home with existing cats. Once you become attached to your new friend, you don't want to go through the heartache of giving him up because your new pet will not acclimate into your household. You and your new cat should have a long and happy future together.

CAT SHOWS

Purebred cats are often taken to cat shows. These are similar to dog breed shows in that the cats are judged on their conformation and desirability as representatives of their breed. They are also judged on behavioral attributes, as a judge would not look favorably upon a cat that scratched

While acclimating Kitty to a car, he can also learn some new behaviors, such as driving.

and bit. A show cat must easily acclimate to new places and people as much as a feline used as a therapy cat or in the media world.

Most cat shows are organized by the Cat Fancier's Association (CFA), of Manasquan, New Jersey.

The CFA recognizes 37 breeds including three miscellaneous breeds–American Bobtail, LaPerm, and Siberian. The following purebred felines are recognized:

Abyssinian, American Curl, American Shorthair, Balinese, Burman, Bombay, British Shorthair, Chartreux, Colorpoint Shorthair, Cornish Rex, Devon Rex, Egyptian Mau, European Burmese, Exotic, Havana Brown, Japanese Bobtail, Javanese, Korat, Maine Coon, Manx, Norwegian Forest Cat, Ocicat, Oriental Persian, Ragdoll, Scottish Fold, Selkirk Rex, Siamese, Siberian, Singapura, Somali, Sphynx, Tonkinese, Turkish Angora, and Turkish Van.

The Cat Fancier's Association

To obtain more information about showing your feline, go to the CFA website at: www.cfa.org, or contact them at Cat Fancier's Association, P.O. Box 1005, Manasquan, NJ, 08736-0805, (732) 528-9797. Their website features lots of information about cat breeds, showing, judging and stewarding and much more.

Cat Training in 10 Minutes

Daily training will let you spend quality time with your feline companion.

A cat show normally takes place in a large hall, where several concurrently running individual shows are presided over by single judges for specific breeds. Each judge presents awards to the best representative feline of its class. When all judging has been completed for all the divisions, all the winners are brought together for the championship judging, where the top ten cats of the show are chosen. The only cats not judged according to the CFA standard are household cats. Yes, you read that correctly. Any cat can take part in the show and each is judged as an individual work of art.

Cat Show Titles

There are many titles cats can attain and they don't have to be breeding animals to receive celebrity. Even cats that have been neutered or spayed can achieve a distinguishment. The levels begin with a Champion (CH) title. This goes to an adult cat that has competed at CFA shows and received six winning ribbons. The Premier title is similar to the CH title but is awarded to an altered cat. The Grand Champion (GC) title is awarded to a cat that has accumulated 200 points in its category. The Grand Premier (GP) title is awarded to an altered cat that has accumulated 200 points in its category. The National Winner (NW) is the highest and most prestigious title to be achieved. This denotes a cat that ranks at the top in the country. The Breed Winner (BW) title is similar to the NW, but for cats that have achieved a best of breed win, not just second or third. The Regional Winner (RW) is for a cat that has ranked top in the region and the Divisional Winner (DW) is for a cat that ranks top in the specific division, such as fur type or color. The Distinguished Merit award is given to the cat that has produced the required number of GC, GP or DM cats. This is five for a female and fifteen for a male.

As you can see, cats are more than window-dressing and cuddle bundles. They strive to have fulfilling lives just as we do. It was not their choice to have nothing to do all day, every day. For those who obtain a cat simply to have a companion to sit around with, think again. Try a stuffed toy, it's just as furry, easy to care for, and never messes in the house or spews on the carpet. Cats are living, breathing, thinking creatures. They have emotions and the ability to reason. Felines need purpose in their life.

Be a good human companion and offer your cat a chance to shine. Give him a job.

The Delta Society

In recent years, organizations such as Delta Society have brought cats and other animals into nursing homes, hospitals, and prisons. The presence of these animals helps the residents of these institutions. The ailing, infirm, or depressed are instantly brightened in the presence of a cat. Many pet owners have had to leave their beloved pets behind when moving into a full-care facility or institution. The presence of a well-behaved kitty brings back good memories and induces good attitudes, in turn aiding the healing process. It is a proven fact that cat ownership lowers blood pressure and increases the cat owner's lifespan.

Cat "Stars" & Their Trainers

I have been training animals from the time I was a child. I began working with horses, then domestic felines, exotics, and finally dogs. Of all the animals I've worked with, cats seem to have a distinct rise in personality attributes as their training progresses. Dogs enjoy working and do thrive when they learn how to please. Horses acquiesce to their rider's guidance. But with cats, it's as though a new window of opportunity has opened up in their minds and they strive to reach higher and higher levels of intelligence. Their abilities are unlimited.

Throughout this book I've mentioned how one can turn a couch potato into a "monster." That "monster" being a cat that adores his training so much that he wants it all the time. I've met many such felines who now drive their human companions crazy with their desire to work. I've introduced several of them to you. There's only one place for such cats…in the movies!

The author, Miriam Fields, checks out her list of photo shots while a feline actor waits his turn in front of the camera.

MEDIA CATS

A media cat has to have many special qualities. Besides being well trained, he must also be very social, both with other animals and people. He must be fearless, adventurous, in good physical condition, and photogenic.

However, it's not just the cats that make themselves stars, but the people who work with them. There must be good communication, enthusiasm for the job, and a bond unlike any other. With all the distractions of a production, a cat must keep his eyes on his trainer. Kitty has to trust his human companion to not put him in jeopardy. And how is this done? Through time, patience and reward.

No feline star is formed overnight. It can take anywhere from months to years to make a perfect production cat. Only through experience, travel, and exposure to new things, can the cat learn how to quickly acclimate to any situation.

MY SHOW BIZ CATS

My very first production job was for the Smithsonian Institute in Washington, D.C. One of my mentors, Kayce Cover, who taught me how to train seals and sea lions at the National Zoo, recommended my cat to the producer of a show about cats. It was a pilot show, trying to garner the interest of potential investors. Although the show was not contracted into a series and my part in it was very small, it changed my life. From that point on, I knew I wanted to pursue a career in training cats for TV and film. I've trained many cats but a few special felines stand out.

A quick tap on the wrist and Bodie is waving.

Most cats love to roll in the grass. Doing so on command is a great accomplishment.

A cat that is comfortable outdoors will be able to perform under most production conditions. Bodie, a ginger Tabby, is performing a Down. Notice how "tuned in" he is on the visual cue.

Bodie is demonstrating how a cat can perform both in a high distraction environment, such as outdoors, and do several behaviors at once – the Up and Wave.

Ling Ling

My cat, Ling Ling, was a Lilac Point Siamese. I had trained her to perform basic commands, jump through hoops, jump onto my shoulder, and fetch. I had worked with her merely for the love of it, and the fact that she enjoyed it so much. The producer of the show wanted a cat to sit on someone's lap during an interview. The actor Robert Guillome, who was currently portraying a butler on the television program, "Soap," would be the one to hold her. I was offered $100 to supply the cat.

We had many hours in the green room (waiting area). Ling Ling was so stressed that she spent most of the day meowing loudly. By the time we got on stage, about five hours later, Ling Ling was so tired she fell asleep on Robert's lap. I think there was only one take where her eyes were open. The producers loved her. They could do the interview over and over without the cat moving. I was hooked.

So, in 1983 I started another branch of work—Animal Actors.

In 1985 Ling Ling passed on. It was merely a month later that Davy Crockett entered my life. He was most adventurous, outgoing, and intelligent cat I have ever met.

Davy Crockett

Davy Crockett was a stray. I was walking out of a hair salon at a busy strip mall. Along came a kitten, running through people, dodging legs, and running directly toward me. When he arrived at my feet, without hesitation, he climbed up my pants and shirt and came to rest on my shoulder, purring and licking my ear. The little kitten was a gray/brown tabby with big green eyes, a white chin, and amber fur on his belly. I was still grieving for Ling Ling. I brought him home.

Crockett was outgoing from the start. I shared my home with two Springer

Davy Crockett

One of my top performing cats, Davy Crockett, would hide his head when he became stressed. He felt that if he could not see what was happening, then no one could see him. During a photo shoot for Rowe Furniture, we had no preparation time. (Unless cats go to new places on a daily basis, they often need at least an hour to acclimate to new environments.) We were rushed into the studio and put to work immediately. Crockett had to perform a Down/Stay at the base of a couch, while a Jack Russell Terrier, Ike, was to sit on the couch. Ike had been performing in productions almost as long as Crockett. He knew to remain where he was told to stay regardless of what occurred. Crockett decided that the floor was no place for a cat, especially if the dog was allowed on the couch. He jumped onto the couch and buried his head under Ike. Ike sat there with Crockett's rear end and tail sticking out from beneath him. Eventually, Crockett calmed down enough to work and performed his Down/Stay as instructed. He just needed a chance to get used to the idea of being below a dog, which is not a desirable position for a cat.

Spaniels at the time, but as soon as Crockett stepped into my home, he ruled. The dogs never phased him. New people were merely new high perches. No one was exempt. New places were adventures waiting to happen. This was a production cat!

Crockett was extremely photogenic and throughout his 17 years he appeared in numerous productions, including several National Geographic specials, including one in which he had to dress up in three different outfits. Crockett and my Old English Sheepdog, Thumblina, are still seen on Oreck Vacuum Cleaner mailings across the country.

Although many cat trainers provide doubles for their cats in order to keep a production going smoothly, I never had to do this when working with Crockett. During one particular filming with National Geographic (for the Alison Argo Production of "The Secret Life of Cats"), he worked for 11 hours. Between scenes he rested in a room or visited with the crew. When it was time to work, he was all business. That's how much he enjoyed being a star.

There are many feline trainers in the world. I've had the pleasure of interviewing a few of them for this book so that you can learn the ways that cats are trained and handled on production sets. Regardless of how they work their cats before, during, or after a production, there's one thing they all have in common: They love living with and training felines.

Davy Crockett wearing his sailor costume for National Geographic's "Secret Life of Cats."

Huckleberry, an American Tabby, has been working with Miriam Fields since he was 4 months old. Here they rest together between takes on a Claritin photo session, as the photographer instructs the human models.

GLORIA WINSHIP–SWEET SUNSHINE ANIMAL ACTORS

Gloria Winship has been an animal trainer most of her life. It was only since 1997 that she began providing animals for production work as her full-time vocation. All it took was one movie, with fifteen cats and a very tight space. *The Gingerbread Man* might've been the toughest production she has ever done, but it also hooked her for life.

Living by two main rules, The Six P's (Prior Planning Prevents Piss-Poor Performance) and the credo, "You Never Get a Second Chance to Make a Good First Impression" Gloria provides any species of animal for any type of production, not only satisfying and highly impressing her clients, but making new friends everywhere she goes. Hence, the name of her company, Sweet Sunshine Animal Actors.

Gloria has gathered a network of trainers throughout the US upon whom she can call to provide animals and assistance wherever she works. This includes the work she performs with felines. For the feature film, *Jeepers Creepers,* she provided 30 cats, 15 of which were her own pets; the other 15 were obtained through a local humane society. Her personal cats have spent their lives on movie sets and traveling. They are familiar with every type of distraction and nothing deters them from performing. The cats she obtains through humane societies are taught to come to their food dishes and to

The target wand is a common training tool.

ground tie, which means learning to remain in a specific spot, via a collar around their waist and a leash. The collar and leash are the color of the cat(s) and do not show up on film.

Gloria's Style

Gloria loves her cats. They are always with her and always in training, loving every minute of it. She believes the more socializing the better. Hence, she never keeps anybody on the set from saying hello to her feline stars. Her cats know the difference between social time and work time. They thoroughly enjoy both and rarely are her cats crated. They either freely roam her recreational vehicle, where she lives while on a movie set, or her farm in Georgia, where they all accompany her, with numerous other animals, on evening walks.

The basic behaviors each cat learns are, Come, Stay, and Ground Tie. Distraction proofing comes with exposure and experience, but once a cat can perform these basic behaviors, other tricks can easily be added. This allows for abrupt changes in the scenes, which is more the norm than not when working on a production. A cat that focuses, regardless of surroundings, is a great performer.

All of Gloria's cat training is done with food (especially tuna), praise, and sometimes a clicker. The feline's normal diet is kibble, making the on-set diet more exciting. Gloria will begin a performance with either steak or turkey breast. Turkey breast is used if they want the cat to look sleepy, for the enzymes in turkey are suspected to cause mammals to become drowsy. When the cat begins to lose interest, the stakes are raised to tuna fish, and then to salmon. Due to their familiarity in the production environment, Gloria's cats are relaxed enough to eat while working, although they are not being fed constantly. She makes them perform several takes before receiving a food reward. Between food rewards, she uses verbal praise.

Gloria has obtained most of her personal cats by rescuing them. Three in particular can claim a stray-to-star story: Daisy, Tux and Ike. These cats were

Training Tip

One of Gloria's on-set training secrets is to never allow her cats to wander around the set between takes. She holds them or puts them in their "green room," waiting area. She wants the cat to know that the only thing they are to do at the set is to work, not look for a place to hide, or someone to greet. This causes the cat to focus on work instead of other things. Another trick is to use an air gun if the cat appears to be falling asleep. Air guns are used by film grips to clear the camera lens, or to clean dust off electronic equipment. The sudden burst of air quickly gets a cat's attention.

slated for destruction at the animal shelter. Being over three years of age, they were not easily adoptable. Through a friend, Gloria heard about them and quickly saved them from euthanasia. They have since appeared in the feature film *Gingerbread Man*, "TV Funhouse" on the Comedy Central Channel, and in the feature film, *Jeepers Creepers.*

Working in Film

One of Gloria's most memorable auditions was for the producer Robert Altman in 1997, for the feature film, *The Gingerbread Man.* She was competing with Birds and Animals Unlimited, one of the busiest animal actor companies in the world. While waiting for her chance to speak with Mr. Altman, she placed her cats on high perches in the waiting room. Gloria and Mr. Altman had to leave the room to discuss storyboards and script details. When they returned several hours later, the cats were still waiting in the same spots. Gloria got the job then and there.

During the filming, the only time her cats became alarmed was when a gas-powered wind machine was suddenly turned on. Prior to that, a quieter, electric wind machine had been used. However, after the gas-powered machine had been turned on and off three times her cats were acclimated enough to return to work.

> ### Stress?
>
> *Often, cats become stressed when placed directly in front of a camera or in any new situation. If you are on a production set and this occurs, remain calm. Allow the cat to touch you, cuddle, and rub against you. Be patient with your cat. Felines will not be forced into anything in which they are unwilling to participate. Prove to your cat that the situation is not frightening and he will adjust within a short period of time.*

Some of Gloria's other training tips include getting all feline action shots in the morning, (as cats are more active during this time), and to get a cat to weave through a set, appearing to search for something, strategically place tuna in the hidden spots to condition the feline to search those areas. As for appropriate preplanning of a lengthy production job, she provides identical cats. For a twelve-hour filming day, the cats can double for each other, allowing one to rest without disrupting the filming schedule. If the day is a six-hour day, she will bring two distinctive cats and allow the client to choose the "look" they want, although she will often make suggestions, which most directors or producers will easily accede.

ROB BLOCH–CRITTERS OF THE CINEMA

Rob Bloch's company, Critters of the Cinema, has been providing felines for media productions since 1981. From his early work with other theatrical animal trainers, to earning his degree in Animal Training and Management from Moorpark College in California, Rob has become a major supplier of feline actors throughout the country. Critters of the Cinema maintains memberships in SAG, AFTRA, Teamster's Local #399, and the California Animal Owner's Association.

As a child, Rob had not fostered any ideas of earning his living as an animal trainer. Raised in Brooklyn, New York, Rob had aspirations of becoming a sports broadcaster. He rarely took part in the care of his family pets and wasn't even interested in working with animals until he met a woman who was having problems with her Doberman. She asked his advice. He based his answer on his own common sense and it worked. She suggested that he follow a career in animal training. Since he was undecided on where he was going at the time, he did just that. Rob spent many years working for other animal talent agencies, such as Frank Inn (the trainer of Benji), Karl Miller and Steve Martin's Working Wildlife. Not wishing to be second fiddle, he opened his own animal talent agency, Critters of the Cinema, featuring mainly domestic animals.

His credits include the Friskies and Fancy Feast advertisements, for which he has had an account since 1996, a "Got Milk?" commercial with an elderly woman and her cats, many television shows including "Star Trek: The Next Generation" (four cats played Data's orange tabby, Spot), "Hill Street Blues", "CSI", "General Hospital", "Sabrina", "90210", and "Felicity" (among others). His feature films include, *Poetic Justice, Gepetto, Three of Hearts, Stuart Little, Coyote Ugly* and many more.

Rob did a very interesting commercial for a store in Oklahoma, where cats appear to be pulling a dog sled, harnesses and all. The commercial required only six cats but he brought fifteen, so those that tired could be replaced. The filming required some difficult behaviors and long working hours. Rob was happy he had brought extra cats, because his lead cat, Boo, decided that he did not feel like working that day and had to be replaced by Rover and Bud, who took turns in the lead musher position. Although it looked like all the cats were really pulling the sled, there were only five of the six pulling, (actually Coming) while the other was simply walking. Rob says that if they had just a few more cats pulling, that they would've actually moved the sled on cat power.

117

Cat Training in 10 Minutes

The Training Team

Rob and his trainers travel throughout the country putting on over twenty 30-minute stage shows annually with the Friskies Cat Team, in which noted feline trainer, Karen Thomas, participates. When working on a production, there are at least two trainers always present with one cat, but other than that the amount varies depending on the project. If numerous cats have to work at a time, Rob will have a one to one trainer to cat ratio with one extra person. If several of the cats are backups or not being used simultaneously, then he'll have as much as a five cat per trainer ratio.

Critters of the Cinema

The Critters of the Cinema website (www.crittersofthecinema.com) features photographs and descriptions of all of Rob's animal actors. Fifty of his cats are featured, sometimes with their doubles, triples, and so on.

The feline members of Rob's team are procured through cat breeders, animal shelters, and kitten ads in local Los Angeles newspapers, depending on the type of cat they are looking for. He has over 86 trained cats, many of which are teamed with doubles or triples to handle long filming schedules or behaviors in which one might excel over the other.

When looking for a feline actor he will assess the personality as much as the appearance. A theatrical cat must be outgoing, confident, and photogenic. With his look-a-likes one can be a couch potato while the others are good at motion behaviors. He has as many as seven black cats that double for each other (on the "Sabrina" set) as well as seven orange tabbies. He also has a threesome of all white cats with yellow eyes.

All of Rob Bloch's cats are trained using food rewards and taught to perform all the basic behaviors such as Come, Sit, Down, and Stay. The cats are not worked with daily, except for those that are always on the stage, such as the Friskies cats. The average training time is once per week when not working, and two to three times a day when preparing for a production. The cat is given extra training time when a specific behavior is required. As each project is different, both the felines and trainers remain motivated. Rob Bloch confesses to being easily bored and prefers to do different jobs in different places on a daily basis.

On the Set with Rob

Between film takes and even after the crew has wrapped for the day, Rob will take advantage of the crew down time by exposing his animals to the ambiance of the set. He feels that the more exposure they receive the better they will perform in the future. Thus, he sometimes brings animals that are not going to be performing on that particular production just to give them the experience of working in a situation with a myriad of distractions.

Rob is always prepared to accommodate his clients in whatever manner realistically possible. However, as with most production situations, there are last minute changes that will require additional training or a change of filming angles. One of Rob's pet peeves (and that of many other trainers of animal actors) is that producers rarely understand the importance of the trainer being told every nuance of a scene, often leaving out information that can make a huge difference in a cat's performance. What had been a simple point A to B performance, turns into something far more difficult due to lack of important

Media Stress

One of the most difficult cat productions I have ever worked on was for a political commercial. Five days before the filming I received a call requesting 11 cats and a dog. The producer said it was a simple shot—the cats merely have to sit in chairs around a conference table with the dog on a chair at the head of the table. I knew it would not be simple. I had no preparation time. When training cats, one needs weeks to months to prepare for something like this, and getting that many cats to sit still for even ten seconds was near impossible. It turned out to be almost as big a disaster as I had expected. The dog performed beautifully, of course. The cats were fighting with each other, trying to hide, or simply laying around panting from stress. Several of the cats rose above the situation and did perform according to plan. They saved the production. They remained on the table and interacted with the actor as he said his lines. I think I was more stressed than the cats.

detail. Something as rudimentary as adding running people, traffic, or a wet surface can totally offset a feline's performance if the cat is not used to these distractions. To correct these misunderstandings the scene might have to be changed or eliminated. Lately, however, production companies are becoming more and more aware of an animal's physical and emotional limitations and are more amenable to working around them.

Rob's most important training tip is to make certain that the cat is totally prepared for anything, even things that don't normally occur on an everyday basis. One never knows what will happen on the set.

Stunt Doubles

In the movie, Stuart Little, *Karen Thomas, Snowbell's trainer, used the talents of six cats for the role. Some were good at performing stays, others were better at motion behaviors, such as jumping from place to place or running through the house. With the long filming hours and the need to exchange cats in order for them to receive appropriate rest, cats were chosen and worked with on the behaviors they performed best. This is similar to how people tend to specialize in specific vocations. Not everybody has the desire or inclination to do anything and everything. We make our living doing the jobs in which we excel, or have received an education to perform.*

KAREN THOMAS

Karen Thomas has worked with Critters of the Cinema for 12 years. She has lived and worked with the Friskies Cat Team since 1996. She and her assistants travel around the country performing at cat shows so that people can see how much fun cats have when they're trained and performing. Some of her other activities with the kitties include the movies *Stuart Little, Ed TV* and the television shows, "Star Trek: The Next Generation" and "Felicity."

Karen earned a degree in Zoology and started working with animals as a volunteer zookeeper. Although she had initially desired to work with big cats, she seemed to really click with the domestic cats. And clicking is what she does. She mainly uses clicker training with her kitty teams. Karen feels that animals learn new behaviors and respond faster when she uses a clicker to bridge the commands.

Talent and Training

As with most kitty actors, she chooses her talent by selecting outgoing personalities that are photogenic and have a common appearance, such as a tabby or specific breed. She prefers to have cats of different energy levels, for portraying one who might be jumping and then another for a lazy cat, or even cats of similar energy levels in order to exchange a tired kitty for a fresh kitty.

Karen works with a cat for upwards of a year to prepare it for show business. The cat has to learn to accept traveling and to stay in strange places and to accept all types of environments. This takes time and none of her cats are pushed beyond their limits. Karen wants the cat to enjoy itself. This is only done through positive reinforcement, understanding the individual feline, and loads of patience.

CAPTAIN ARTHUR HAGGERTY– HAGGERTY'S THEATRICAL ANIMALS

> ### Bonding is Beneficial
>
> *Training your cat is a means of bonding. Karen Thomas believes that everyone should spend at least 10 minutes a day working with his or her cat. This should be a special time together. Not only will this make your cat happier, but will also ease your own troubles. People need to develop their feline pet's minds so that they live longer and healthier lives.*

Captain Arthur Haggerty has been in the animal training business for longer than he can remember. Starting with an interest in showing dogs, through taking charge of the 25th Infantry Scout Dog Platoon, to forming his own dog training and animal actors company in New York, Captain Haggerty has been an influence in the lives of many animal trainers. Although the mainstay of his business is the teaching of dogs and their owners, he has also worked with felines both to solve behavioral problems and to direct them on a production set.

Captain Haggerty enjoys working with cats because most people don't believe that cats can be trained. He was involved in the first Morris, The Cat television commercials for 9-Lives Cat Food. Prior to appearing in this commercial, the former stray orange tabby appeared in the Burt Reynolds film, *Shamus*. He strolled onto the pool table as Burt Reynolds lay upon it. Captain Haggerty and his assistant, Bob Martwick, handled the cat for these productions. Bob Martwick now spends his time handling Morris look-a-likes for the 9-Lives company.

Most of the cats obtained by Captain Haggerty for use in productions are procured through associates who own trained cats. These cats are primarily pets and are kept in the best of health. On occasion, he obtains cats from the shelters and then, after their work is completed, he finds them permanent homes.

Training Tips

Feline stars are taught how to perform some basic behaviors such as Stay in a Sit, Down, or Stand as well as how to go to their crates both on command or

A well-trained cat can remain in position despite outdoor distractions.

when frightened. Live mice are often used to entice or distract a cat. As cats tire easily on a set, a live mouse will quickly brighten their eyes and perk those ears forward. (The mice are kept in cages and not endangered by their proximity to the feline stars.)

Stressing appropriate handling techniques over intense training, Captain Haggerty has learned how to "get in the tempo" with a photographer as well as assess camera angles and production direction in order to obtain the specific behavior requested by the director. He believes that this knowledge goes beyond mere training, for there are many ways to obtain a desired response on film without spending hours, days, or months of preparation.

For example, to have a cat speak on the set he will use squalene (shark liver) to have the cat licking his lips or moving his jaw. More often than not, a behavior will be requested at the time of a production that was not requested when the feline was booked for the production. Thus, being inventive with handling techniques will further ingratiate the feline trainer in the eyes of all involved with the production.

Training Tip

Captain Haggerty prefers to use natural training devices (namely, his voice and touch to shape a cat's behavior). He also uses warmth to his advantage. Cats love to lie in the sun and soak in the heat. A warm carrier can be very enticing for a cat to go to when upset or seeking privacy. He does not believe in the use of clickers, buzzers, or squeakers for, in his experience, they can be an inconvenient crutch.

There are several rules Captain Haggerty follows when working with cats in a production. The first is to have a two-to-one ratio of two handlers per one animal. If working outdoors, he prefers to have four extra handlers. One never knows when a cat may decide to go after a bird or run into a road and there must be enough people on watch to insure the feline's safety. He also carefully questions the director and cinematographer regarding camera angles and weighs these facts in with the behaviors the cat must perform. If he believes that the cat might not be able to perform the behavior requested while using that particular camera angle or within the parameters of the scene, he will discuss this with the director and suggest another way to obtain the scene.

One of the most familiar disruptions on a production is to be told that the cat has to perform a specific behavior and then to arrive and have that behavior altered or totally changed. For many feline trainers this can cause much upset, for they have spent a lot of time preparing for the production and have conditioned the cat to perform a specific way. Captain Haggerty can always find a way to make it work, either by changing a camera angle or breaking a long scene into several shorter ones. He will also use enticements, such as a mouse or a cat toy. Most of his cats are trained to go to their carrier, so to obtain a scene where the cat must walk from point A to point B, he will have one of his assistants hold the cat in a Stand/Stay, place the carrier at the target location and then have the handler let the cat go upon the director's call of "Action."

SAMANTHA MARTIN– AMAZING ANIMALS BY SAMANTHA

Samantha Martin knew she wanted to work with animals from a very young age. She graduated from a two-year college with a degree in Animal Husbandry. Then she worked at every job she could that involved animals such as veterinary clinics, pet shops, zoos, and other animal actor companies. While working at Animal Kingdom in Chicago, she performed weekend cat shows for the astonished crowds. By then she was hooked on cat training and cat performances for both live audiences and media productions.

Amazing Animals by Samantha actually began as a specialized niche in the animal actor world. She provided trained rodents for productions. As her company grew, she began working with the most popular animal actors, canines. Then, she also began collecting felines, offering their services approximately five years ago. She currently has 13 trained cats at her facility. They all live in her house.

All of Samantha's felines know basic behaviors such as Sit, Sit-up, Come and Go to their mark. Many also know more difficult behaviors such as; roll-over, play the piano, jump from point A to point B, jump through a hoop, and more. She believes that all of her animals need to have complete knowledge of everything commonly requested by producers and directors so that her cats are prepared for anything.

Samantha's training methods include the use of click and treat, a beeper, and lots of praise. When a job calls for more felines than she maintains or for one of a type other than she has available, she networks with local cat owners who have felines that she has worked with.

Training Tip

Samantha's tip for those who wish to offer their felines as animal actors is to not only make sure the cat is well trained, but also well socialized. The cat should experience a variety of new places, people, and other animals, prior to performing on any set.

Although she prefers to work with male cats, for they tend to be more laid back and less apt to be emotional when confronted with new situations, her best performing cat is Tara, a Russian Blue female. Tara has shown a propensity for performance unlike any other cat Samantha has worked with.

Although most of Samantha's credits include photo sessions for clients such as Nutro Max, Iams, Hammacher Schlemmer Catalog, Montgomery Ward and Miracoat (vitamin supplement), she has had the opportunity to work her felines in several television commercials as well. These include Old Bay Furniture company and IBM. Because she lives in the Midwest, the opportunity to offer animal actors for feature films is very limited.

On the set, Samantha prefers a two-to-one ratio of trainers to cats. She believes that having two people keep an eye on one cat offers a better safety zone than just one handler. Also, she will allow only the actor who is performing with the cat to interact with the feline. In this manner, the cat maintains its attention on her direction when so many distractions abound.

ANN GORDON–ANNE'S ANIMALS FOR FILM

Ann Gordon has been providing animal actors for film for over 17 years. In that time she has trained a huge variety of species to perform in more than 55 feature films, 28 television movies, 41 television series and hundreds of television commercials and print ads. Although she offers the services of wolves, horses, domestic farm and exotic animals, most of her work entails the training and handling of dogs and cats. Being in Hollywood, California has been a huge asset in the growth of her company, Anne's Animals for Film.

Ann began her career as a zookeeper at Woodland Park Zoo in Seattle. Her initial work was with the hoofed animals in the African Savanna area. When promoted, she began caring for and training the big cats. The zoo had an ongoing breeding program where the offspring were sold to other institutions. After raising lion cubs, which were sold to an organization in California, Ann went with them and was exposed to the animal film world. Intrigued with the challenge of providing animal actors, Ann returned to her home in the Pacific Northwest and started her own company providing animals for educational seminars—a Zoomobile. As with many film animal trainers, she prefers to do different things on different days, and not repeat the same tedious job.

Feline Fame

Although Ann provided many exotic animals for movies before doing one with domestic cats, she states how much she enjoys the reactions she receives on the set when having her felines perform. The first movie in which she provided a cat was a feature titled, *In Your Face.* The cat was in one scene where it had to jump onto a desk. Her next film with a feline was *Singles.* A cat had to sit in a window. While these behaviors may outwardly appear easy and natural, they are rarely such while on a movie set. There are many parameters, such as the distractions of the people, equipment and outdoor environments.

Unless a producer requests a specific breed of cat, she prefers to choose a cat for temperament in preference to appearance. Most of her kitties come from shelters or rescue groups. Ann will choose a very outgoing kitten or cat, although she prefers to obtain her felines as kittens. If obtaining a kitten from a litter, she'll perform temperament and aptitude tests. These tests include bringing a toy and seeing which kitten is first to investigate it, offering some canned tuna to observe food drive, and making loud noises to assure a kitten is not frightened easily. A kitten must pass all of these tests successfully in order to be considered a good candidate as a feline performer.

Ann's Advice

Ann suggests checking with your local film commission offices to locate film animal trainers that might have an interest in holding some photographs or a video of your pet and giving you a call if the pet is chosen for a production job. Keep in mind that the cat owner is rarely allowed on the set unless well versed in the training techniques because many animals are distracted by their human companions. If the production requires a difficult behavior, the trainer might request the cat remain with him or her for a period of time prior to the filming and you would have to tolerate this, trusting the trainer with your beloved feline.

Praise your cat as he watches the target and follows your commands. Training your cat is something you can be proud of.

Ann has noticed that specific behavioral tendencies are related to the breed and color of the cat. Other than the laid back behavior of a Ragdoll or a Persian, there are specific colored tabbies that might be more or less apt to respond to a specific training tool or learning experience. Ann says that the orange and red tabbies as well as the tuxedo colored (black and white) cats tend to work best for about anything, while the calicos and tortoiseshell cats tend to have attitudes. Old style Siamese (with the apple heads, not the elongated faces) are also brilliant as are Abyssinians.

Training Tips

Each cat is trained through the use of voice and visual cues, a target stick, clicker, and food reward. The cats are also heavily socialized with film crews and taken to many different locals throughout the training process. The basic behaviors each cat is taught are: Sit, Down, Stay, Stand, and Go to mark. The clicker is used for anything from basic to advanced behaviors, while a beeper is used to signal a Come command. Ann says that using a clicker is invaluable, as cats don't respond as well to a human voice. She also uses a laser pointer to get a kitty to go to a specific point on a wall or door. A waist tie-down is also used on a cat that must remain in one place for a long period of time among a lot of commotion.

Ann, like many other cat trainers, works her felines in pairs so that when one kitty becomes tired, another can take its place. Or, if several difficult behaviors are requested, one may have the aptitude to perform a specific behavior while the other cat will be more likely to perform another behavior. Ann says that every cat has his or her own aptitude for specific behaviors and that a good trainer will work within these parameters to provide a good performance. This insures that the director and producers are always satisfied with her work.

Ann's Special Cats

When working on the movie *Homeward Bound,* she had eight cats performing as "Sassy." Ann recalls the first day of filming when she placed "Sassy" on a windowsill and told him to Stay. The director, Jodie Foster, was intrigued, not realizing that cats are trainable. She learned that this is possible as she completed the movie with the ease of the eight fully trained cats.

One of Ann's special cats is Velvet, a silver tabby. This particular cat had been found in a neighbor's barn while a kitten and groomed for stardom by Ann Gordon. Velvet had the thrill of working with Arnold Schwarzenegger in the feature film, *The Sixth Day.* In her scene she had to remain on some stairs and Arnold was to pet her on his way up. Instead, Velvet kept jumping onto his shoulder, since that was her favorite trick. After several takes, Velvet and Arnold were making a game out of the behavior and having a great time. Eventually, Velvet settled down and allowed Arnold to continue up the stairs without her.

Another of Ann's special cats was Indy. She was nicknamed Clay Cat, for she would allow Ann to position any part of her and would remain in that position until released. Producers began asking for the cat by name, for the filming would be completed in half the time allotted due to this incredible kitty, saving a lot of production costs.

Her latest film work with felines is the feature, *Air Bud V.* The cat work in this film is only in the background, since the golden retriever is the star.

After a hard day at work, your cat will have earned his cat nap.

This does not make it any easier, however, for the cats have a lot of distractions. Ann employs three full time assistants and three to four part-time assistants.

Getting Started

Ann writes a column for the website HollywoodPaws.com, which is geared toward garnering the attention of animal film trainers to pets that are made available for production work. Some of the most common questions are how to prepare a cat for production work and how to obtain an agent.

Her main answer for the preparation of cats is intense training and socialization. The cat must be friendly, outgoing, and able to focus when many distractions are present. He must listen to commands on the first request. Obtaining an agent is very difficult, for there are few agents for animals. Most animal film trainers have a stable of their own animals, fully trained and prepped for any production. Occasionally, they will need to seek animals outside their facility, but if they do, they will network with other production animal trainers.

Ann occasionally subcontracts other assistants if the need arises and she procures them through other training agencies. While on the set with a domestic feline, she prefers to have a two trainer to one cat ratio, unless the kitty is doing a simple Stay, indoors with little distraction.

Ann does not allow crewmembers or cast, other than those interacting with the feline in the scene, to pet or talk to her kitties. She feels that the act of petting the cat is not always the cat's choice and doesn't wish to overly stress the animal. She also believes that she'll obtain a better performance if the kitty is focused solely on her. New friends might distract from that.

For Ann Gordon, the best part of providing cats for a production work is taking an untrained and unsocialized feline and developing him into a confident performer. The second best part is the awe on the faces of directors, actors, and film crews when they see what a cat is capable of doing.

Regardless of the difficulty of turning your beloved cat into a film star, the training preparation is never wasted. The process is more rewarding than the possible income. You and your cat will form a stronger bond and result in a relationship unlike any other.

So, what's keeping you? It only takes 10 minutes a day.

Appendix A

SIGN LANGUAGE FOR YOUR CAT

When training any animal using visual cues, the trainer must be consistent. Below are some suggestions for visual hand cues to use when training your cat. These cues work well because they target the cat's attention in the appropriate direction to accomplish a given behavior or skill. Many of the signals can be combined or moved in a specific way for more advanced behaviors. You can use whatever visual cues feel comfortable, however, just use them in the same manner for the same meaning.

This is the visual cue for the Come command.

This is the visual cue for Stay.

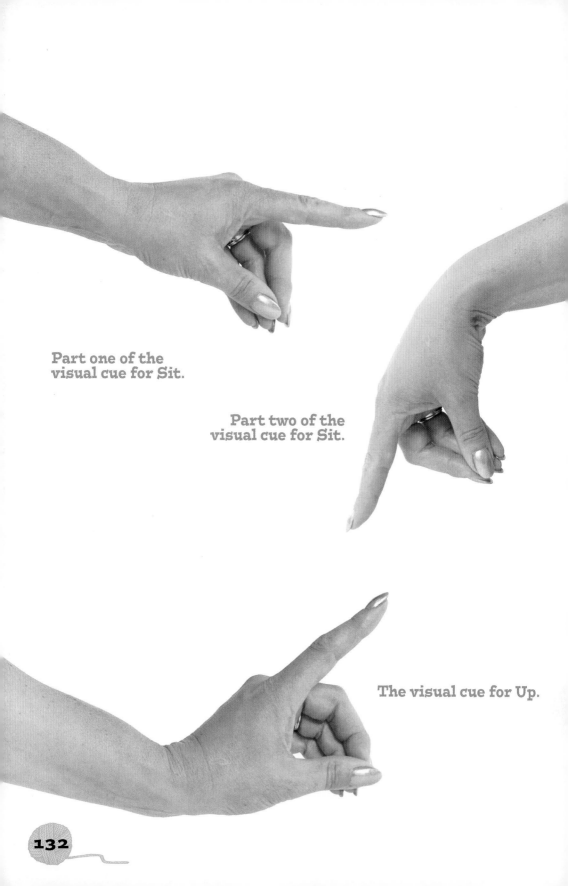

Part one of the
visual cue for Sit.

Part two of the
visual cue for Sit.

The visual cue for Up.

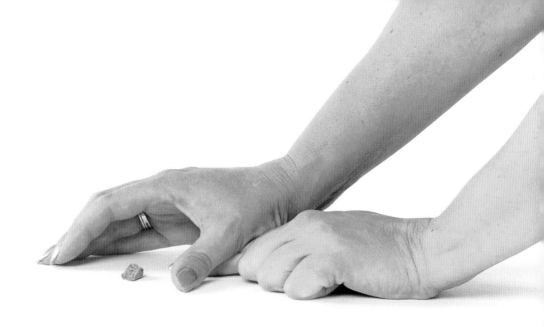

Part one of the
visual cue for Down.

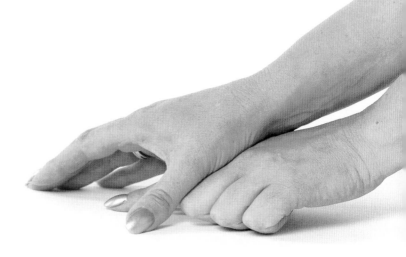

Part two of the
visual cue for Down.

Part three of the
visual cue for Down.

Appendix B

CONTACT INFORMATION FOR ANIMAL ACTOR AGENCIES

Ann's Animals for Film
Ann Gordon
Monroe, WA 98272
Phone: (604) 929-1333
Website: www.Hollywoodpaws.com

Birds and Animals Unlimited
25191 Rivendell Drive
Lake Forest, CA 92630
Email: contact@hollywood-animals.com
Website: www.hollywood-animals.com

Critters of the Cinema
Rob Bloch and Karen Thomas
P.O. Box 378
Lake Hughes, CA 93532
Phone: (661) 724-1929
Fax: (661) 724-1868
Email: info@crittersofthecinema.com
Website: www.crittersofthecinema.com

Exotic Animal Training and Management Program
Moorpark College
7075 Campus Road
Moorpark, CA 93021
Phone: (805) 378-1441
Website: www.moorparkcollege.com

Haggerty's Theatrical Animals
Captain Arthur Haggerty
P.O. Box 3462
Beverly Hills, CA 90212
Toll-Free (888) 796-6991
Phone: (310) 398-4676
Email: Captain@HaggertyDog.com
Website: www.haggertydog.com

Haggerty's Theatrical Animals
Palm Beach County office
P.O. Box 30423
Palm Beach Gardens, FL 33420
Phone: (561) 747-8181
Fax: (561) 746-8590
Email: Babette@HaggertyDog.com
Website: www.haggertydog.com

Hollywood Animals' Animal Actors Agency
4103 Holly Knoll Drive
Los Angeles, CA 90027
Phone: (323) 665-9500
Fax: (323) 665-9200
Email: info@animalactorsagency.com
Website: www.animalactorsagency.com

Samantha's Amazing Animals

Samantha Martin
3555 N. Milwaukee Avenue
Chicago, IL 60641
Phone: (773) 549-3357 or
800-903-3357
Email: contact@amazinganimals.biz
Website: www.amazinganimals.biz

Sweet Sunshine Animal Actors

Gloria Winship
Epworth, GA 30541
Phone: (706) 632-6246 or
(404) 312-6472 or
(800) 803-9606
Fax: (706) 632-6242
Email: gloship@tds.net
Website: www.animal-actors.com

T.I.G.E.R.S.

1818 Highway 17 North, Suite 316
Surfside Beach, SC 29575
Phone: (843) 361-4552
Website: www.tigers-animal-actors.com

Training Unlimited Animal Actors, Inc.

Miriam Fields-Babineau
Stafford, VA 22554
Phone: (540) 659-8858
Fax: (540) 657-5676
Email: totalpetz1@aol.com
Website: www.miriamfields.com

Working Wildlife

Steve Martin
14466 Boyscout Camp Road
Frazier Park, CA 93225
Phone: (661) 245-2406
Fax: (661) 245-3617
Email: smartins@frazmtn.com
Website: www.workingwildlife.com

Appendix C

RESOURCES FOR FINDING/ADOPTING A CAT

These are just a few of the humane societies and rescue organizations that have kittens and cats waiting for loving homes. Check your phone book for animal shelters in your local area.

Alley Cat Allies
1801 Belmont Road
Suite 201
Washington DC 20009
Phone: (202) 667-3630
Fax: (202) 667-3640
Website: www.alleycat.org

Alley Cat Rescue
39120 Argonaut Way
#561
Freemont, CA 94538
Phone: (510) 713-8674
Email: info@alleycatrescue.com
Website: www.alleycatrescue.com

ASPCA
424 92nd Street
New York, NY 10128
Phone: (212) 876-7700
Email: information@aspca.org
Website: www.aspca.org

Best Friends Animal Sanctuary
5001 Angel Canyon Road
Kanab, Utah 84741
Phone: (435) 644-2001
Email: info@bestfriends.org
Website: www.bestfriends.org

Cat Rescue of Maryland, Inc.
6400 Baltimore National Park
Box 305
Baltimore, MD 21228
Phone: (410) 747-6595
Fax: (410) 747-1233
Email: catrescueofmd@mindspring.com
Website: www.catrescueofmd.org

Feral Cat Coalition
9528 Miramar Road
PMB 160
San Diego, CA 92126
Phone: (619) 497-1599
Email: rsavage@feralcat.com
Website: www.feralcat.com

Feral Cat Coalition of Oregon
P.O. Box 82734
Portland, OR 97282
Phone: (503) 979-2606
Email: feralcats_oregon@yahoo.com
Website: www.feralcats.com

Feral Cat Foundation
P.O. Box 1173
Alamo, CA 94507
Email: info@feralcatfoundation.org
Website: www.feralcatfoundation.org

Feral Friends
13410 Preston Road #1237
Dallas, TX 75240
Phone: (972) 671-0429
Email: onecatsluv@attbi.com
Website: www.attbi.com

For the Love of Cats
P.O. Box 130944
Ann Arbor, MI 48113
Phone: (734) 663-8000
Email: kzimmer@tlconline.org
Website: www.tlconline.org

Forgotten Felines of Sonoma Country
P.O. Box 6672
Santa Rosa, CA 95406
Phone: (707) 576-7999
Email: domino@sonic.net
Website: www.forgottenfelines.com

Hawaii Cat Foundation
P.O. Box 10696
Honolulu, HI 96818
Email: hcf@hicat.org
Website: www.hicat.org

Humane Society of the United States
2100 L Street, NW
Washington DC 20037
Phone: (202) 452-1100
Website: www.hsus.org

Kittico Cat Rescue
P.O. Box 600447
Dallas, TX 75360
Email: exec_director@kittico.org
Website: www.kittico.org

Kitty Angels, Inc.
P.O. Box 638
Tyngsboro, MA 01879
Phone: (978) 649-4681
Email: info@kittyangels.org
Website: www.kittyangels.org

Meower Power Feral Cat Coalition
P.O. Box 9696
Chesapeake, VA 23321
Phone: (757) 399-0001
Email: meowerpower@hotmail.com

Metro Ferals, Inc.
P.O. Box 7138
Arlington, VA 22207
Phone: (703) 528-7782
Email: info@metroferals.org
Website: www.metroferals.org

Safe Haven for Cats
270 Redwood Shores Parkway
PMB #139
Redwood City, CA 94065-1173
Phone: (650) 802-9686
Email:jmd@safehavenforcats.com
Website: www.safehavenforcats.com

Safe Haven for Cats
8411-133 Garvey Drive
Raleigh, NC 27606
Phone: (919) 872-1128
Email: info@safehavenforcats.org
Website: www.safehavenforcats.org

FELINE RESCUE LINKS

There are many useful websites and weblinks you can use to find information about adopting a cat, or to gather information on basic cat care. The following websites and links contain lots of useful information for all cat owners.

www.fabcats.com is one of the most informational web sites available for those who wish to rescue cats or learn about their behavior.

www.Petfinder.org is the largest database of feline rescue organizations and lists cats that are available for adoption.

Other useful websites are:
www.Felinerescue.net
www.safercats.org
www.mygem.net
www.saveacat.org
www.siameserescue.org
www.fancycats.org
www.sabrecats.org

www.angelfire.com/ct/forgotten felines
www.ffgw.org/rescuegroups.html
www.houseofmews.com
www.Forgottenfelines.com
www.Felinesandfriends.org
www.Scottishfoldrescue.org
www.Fanciers.com
www.detours.net/spca
www.homelsscatnetwork.org
www.animalallies.net
www.felinerescue.org
www.Kittenrescue.org
www.Folsomfelines.org
www.Azfelines.org
www.Towncats.org
www.Whiskersnwags.org

Index

(continued on following page)